SUBURB OF HELL

''We'd better backtrack,'' Hayes said when the path dead-ended in an open spot where a tall heap of rubbish smoldered. It was a primitive courtyard, bounded on all sides by shacks jammed wall to wall, but with no signs of teeming life. There was only the oppressive silence that seemed like a threat, and the heavy stench.

Barrabas opened his mouth to ~~speak~~ but the words died on his ~~lips~~. Footsteps. Behind th~~em~~. Stealthy.

He turned. Vague s~~hapes~~ fringes of the ruddy p~~~~ ~~li~~ghts cast by the refuse fire. ~~glinted~~ off the blades of many ~~knives.~~

They were surrounded.

JACK HILD

THE BARRABAS STING

A GOLD EAGLE BOOK FROM

WORLDWIDE ®

TORONTO • NEW YORK • LONDON • PARIS
AMSTERDAM • STOCKHOLM • HAMBURG
ATHENS • MILAN • TOKYO • SYDNEY

First edition August 1988

ISBN 0-373-60102-6

Special thanks and acknowledgment to
Alan Philipson for his contribution to this work.

THE BARRABAS STING

1

Juan Carlos Nochenegra descended the palace steps amid a throng of well-dressed supplicants. The mirror lenses of his aviator sunglasses reflected a jostling mass of honey-brown faces, of outstretched hands frantically waving sheafs of paper—business contracts, requests for official indulgences and reprieves—like so many white flags. Urgent pleas for attention came from all sides at once: *"Presidente... Presidente... Presidente..."* What little was visible of his own face beneath the mirror mask and the gold-filigree-encrusted visor of his white officer's hat remained impassive, distant.

Nochenegra's khaki-uniformed bodyguards kept the pack at bay with their grip batons, clearing a path, allowing the short, stocky man to reach the open door of his limousine. Ducking his head quite low to keep the high peak of his hat from bumping the top of the door-frame, he slipped into the glove-leather-upholstered interior, as to his back, behind the barrier of raised batons, full-blown panic set in. The petitioners had each paid dearly, greasing a legion of open palms, to get this close to the self-appointed "president-for-life." Seeing their chance to curry favor about to vanish, they abandoned any jot of dignity left to them. They surged down the steps, trying to break through the line of guardsmen. Juan Carlos slammed the limo's heavy door, cutting off their shrill, desperate cries and the authoritative thud of clubs cracking middle-class skulls.

These were unpleasant and highly disturbing sounds.

Sounds unheard of in a country where the bourgeoisie always played by the rules, no matter how unfairly written or perversely enforced, preferring to pay for privilege in coin rather than with blood, taking the long view of things. The president-for-life gritted his teeth. Even the dog-loyal middle class had begun to lose faith in a future that was Juan Carlos Nochenegra. He leaned forward and slapped a hand against the glass barrier that separated him from the driver.

At once the Mercedes shot away from the palace's motor entrance, down the wide, palm-lined drive, past tiered, splashing fountains, past arbors ablaze with blooming bougainvillea. The limo's tires crunched over fallen, fan-shaped branches, and its whirlwind wake stirred curbside drifts of fiery petals.

Two hours before, a tropical rainstorm had swept across the island, ripping down palm fronds, flooding the inadequate drains and antiquated sewers. The storm was a daily occurrence, a midafternoon fact of life. In the low-lying sections of the city it created ponds of contaminated water where excrement floated, where feral pigs wallowed and naked children frolicked. For thirty minutes after the storm the island became a haven of coolness, the smothering humidity a memory; in the words of Mandelo, the island's universally revered folk poet and philosopher, the rain was "our singular blessing: our daily glimpse of heaven."

Heaven was gone for today. Despite the limo's heavy-duty air-conditioning, Nochenegra's white uniform shirt stuck wetly to his shoulders. It clung to the seat as he turned to look back for his security team—four armed guardsmen closely following in a camouflage-painted jeep.

The little entourage pulled up beside the helicopter pad at the far end of the palace grounds. On the concrete slab a jet-black Sikorsky corporate chopper idled, rotor blades thrashing the heavy air. Painted on its side amidships was a yellow oval; inside the oval was a stylized two-headed, fire-breathing dragon, the insignia of the Democratic Republic of Mantuego and the Nochenegra regime. The Sikorsky was the Mantuegan equivalent of Air Force One.

The Mantuegan equivalent of the Secretary of Defense, a man clad in a khaki dress uniform resplendent with medals and decorations, an officer's hat and gleaming oxblood shoes, hurried over to the limo as it came to a stop beside the pad. On his heels was a lieutenant in jungle boots and camouflage fatigues. The junior officer opened the near rear door, then stood at attention and crisply saluted as Nochenegra exited the vehicle.

"*Presidente*, is this wise?" were the first words out of General Bonifacio's mouth.

Juan Carlos bristled. He was not accustomed to having his decisions publicly questioned by senior staff. For a long moment—a punishing moment of silence—he searched the much taller man's sweating face. Bonifacio had aged ten years in the past few months: deep lines etched his forehead and cut the corners of his mouth below a ruler-straight pencil mustache. The job was eating him alive.

"You have some further news from El Infierno, I take it?" Nochenegra said.

The general's frown lines deepened. "We expect disturbances again tonight, *Presidente*," he said. "There is every reason to believe the outbreaks will be more violent and more widespread than last night's. Our concern is that they could even spill over into the city. Under the circumstances, *Presidente*, perhaps you should reconsider leaving the palace."

"Are you telling me your internal security force can't handle the situation?"

"No, sir. Of course not. It's a question of image. Your image. In a time of national crisis, the leader—"

Nochenegra cut him off with a wave of his hand. He was sick to death of hearing about the "national crisis." In his opinion it was wishful thinking on the part of his enemies, a bare-faced fabrication gleefully spread by international media, clearly intended to panic the Mantuegan people and weaken the external support of his government by the United States. He had an answer for the general and the whining prophets of doom. "If, in my absence, things get out of control," he said matter-of-factly, "I give you full authorization to blow both of the dams."

Bonifacio's face went simultaneously slack and gray. "But, *Presidente*..."

"Come on, Lieutenant," Nochenegra said, striding past the general, across the concrete apron to the helicopter's lowered stairs. His bodyguards had to run to catch up.

The inside of the Sikorsky was laid out like a cozy lecture hall. In the rear two-thirds of the main cabin, separated by a central aisle, were two banks of empty seats facing forward. In the front of the cabin, its back to the bulkhead and door leading to the cockpit, was a single, much larger, much more sumptuously padded chair. Set upon a low dais, it faced aft and overlooked the main cabin. Juan Carlos ignored his usual seat and took a place in the back by a window. The interchange with Bonifacio had put him in a singularly foul temper. As he buckled up his safety belt, he addressed the lieutenant, who was supervising the security team raising the stairs and sealing the door. "Ortega!" he barked. "What are we waiting for? Get us out of here!"

"At once, *Presidente*," the officer said. He opened the cockpit door a crack and spoke brusquely to the pilot.

In seconds the Sikorsky lifted off the pad, rising above the thirty-foot-tall, five-foot-thick masonry walls of the palace. As the copter cleared the top of the barrier, the whole sprawling panorama of Mantuego City was brought suddenly into view. The presidential palace stood on a high, solitary limestone bluff overlooking verdant suburban foothills, where the whitewashed mansions of the Mantuegan elite clung to steep slopes. Thousands of feet below, the broad, almost treeless urban plain spread out to the edge of a placid bay.

The helicopter banked and descended, cutting a diagonal path across the capital city, passing beyond its northwestern limits, flying directly over El Infierno. From a height of one thousand feet, Juan Carlos stared down at a vast shantytown. The El Infierno slum had been a Mantuegan institution for as long as anyone could remember. It had sprung up on a stretch of marshy ground between the island's two main rivers, the Sueño and the Letargo, just beyond their convergence point. Until the mid 1950s, when the rivers had been dammed by Nochenegra's predecessor to provide the capital with a reliable water supply, floods had washed away the accumulation of squatter's huts every few years. Without the regular natural cleansing of the watershed, El Infierno spread like a cancer northward, onto even softer ground, where it became a jumble of clustered shacks on stilts and pilings, connected to one another by elevated narrow plywood paths—the whole claptrap assemblage perched above acres of reeking, pestilential muck. The most conservative estimates put the current population at 100,000.

As far as the president-for-life was concerned, El Infierno was a source of contagion, both biological and political. It was from the slum's desperate poor that opposition to Nochenegra's regime took much of its strength: the Social Democrats of Dr. Emilio Soarez wallowed in middle-class guilt over their plight; the Communist terrorists of the Party for a Free Mantuego—PFM as they became known internationally—recruited them as guerrilla fighters.

As Juan Carlos considered the effect blowing the dams would have, a lazy smile twisted his lips. It would be like flushing a toilet of geologic proportions. He visualized hundred-foot-high walls of water cascading from the foothill reservoirs, scouring away the human filth, washing it into the sea. It was pure fantasy, of course. He knew that Bonifacio would never give the demolition order he had so offhandedly authorized; that, on the contrary, the general would do everything in his power to forestall such callous and indiscriminate mass murder—even if it meant an unprecedented, and potentially suicidal, door-to-door sweep of the slum by shock troops of his Fuerza Seguridad Interna—FSI.

The authorization was in reality more of a personal threat against the general than against the denizens of El Infierno, a bit of calculated arm-twisting to force him into taking direct and unpopular action against his president's most visible, most vocal and, to American eyes, most ideologically acceptable successor: Dr. Emilio Soarez. Nochenegra had Bonifacio right where he wanted him. If the general refused to clamp down hard on the Social Democrats, he would be made to carry out the demolition—and be forever branded the Mantuegan Adolf Eichmann. If he refused to carry out the demolition, he would be executed as a mutinous traitor. In point of fact, the blowing of the dams was an empty threat on the president's part. If El Infierno was the island's center of political contagion, it was also the main source of cheap, exploitable labor. No way could Nochenegra obliterate it and retain the all-important backing of Mantuegan big-business interests.

Still, cataclysm was a solution that very much appealed to Nochenegra's sense of scale and history. He had always considered himself a leader with visionary powers. And like the dead philosopher Mandelo, he felt he truly understood the soul, the unexpressed desires and longings of the Mantuegan people.

Nochenegra knew he could not hope to match the great Mandelo in words and ideas; since his death in 1899, the native philosopher had been twice proposed for sainthood. Juan Carlos was a man for the tangible; he brought powerful ideas to life, made unexpressed longings into reality. He considered himself a builder, not so much after the fashion of Franklin Roosevelt—erecting grim, functional edifices to a faceless federal will—but rather, after the more adventurous and personal styles of Amenhotep and Ramses. It was to the lasting monument of his quarter-century of rule that he now traveled, on his weekly pilgrimage.

The Sikorsky continued northwest, flying over large plantations where bananas, sugarcane and cocoa grew, climbing gradually to clear the lowest of Mantuego's steep-sided, jungle-draped mountains. The ridge of peaks curved in a line that paralleled the island's boomerang shape, forming a jagged spine that ran almost from tip to tip. The summits of the tallest mountains at the island's midpoint were lost in fleecy puffs of clouds.

As the helicopter descended the far side of the mountain, the rugged north coast of Mantuego came into view. It was the weather side of the island. There were no broad sandy beaches, no reef-protected bays. The foothills, foreshortened by erosion, plunged straight into the roiling sea; above and tightly behind them, the mountains jutted up almost vertically. A thin ribbon of road wound around the coastline's promontories of land, skirting precipitous drops. Along the shore at irregular intervals pinnacles of rock stuck out of the sea. Carved by the elements into fantastic shapes, these enormous spires had been named by the superstitious: Satan's Dagger, the Three Witches, the Dragon.

El Dragón was Nochenegra's destination.

The monolithic beast's huge, hulking body tapered to a thick neck that ended with the heavy horizontal block of its head: Tyrannosaurus rex, forever squinting into the wind.

On the mainland, directly across from the wave-washed flanks of El Dragón, was a broad, man-made mesa, a promontory whose top had been lopped off. On this table of land stood a monster even larger than the bedrock dinosaur. Its stout gray cooling tower rose hundreds of feet in the air; at its base were a pair of broad concrete hemispheres, the twin humps of its reactor domes.

Until the dictator muzzled it, the opposition press had had a field day with the blatant phallic shape of the President Juan Carlos Nochenegra Nuclear Power Facility, the consensus being that form followed function: there was no question as to what it was, what it was intended to do and to whom. The islanders, despite official pronouncements, universally rejected the lengthy name and used *El Dragón* to refer both to the power plant and to the pinnacle . . . and, in the privacy of their own homes, to their president-for-life.

From a distance of about a mile, the plant looked as though it might be operational, but as the Sikorsky closed on the site, it quickly became apparent that that was not the case. Scaffolding encircled the cooling tower and reactor domes. The latter were only half completed; like cracked concrete eggs they sat in muddy craters, their unfinished edges bristling with rusting reinforcement rods.

Juan Carlos muttered an oath as the helicopter circled and swung in for a landing inside the site's fortified perimeter fence. The scaffolds and catwalks were deserted. There were no construction workers to be seen, and the only people in evidence stood near the helicopter pad. A double row of fatigue-uniformed soldiers armed with FN FAL assault rifles held back a crowd of men in sport shirts and shorts armed with video cameras and microphones. It looked like the entire foreign press corps awaited him.

"Ortega!" Nochenegra snarled as the helicopter set down on its skids. He pointed at the civilians on the other side of his window. "What are those newsmen doing here? I gave strict orders that they not be admitted to the site!"

"I do not know, sir."

"Bring me the garrison commander at once! And have the troops move those reporters back. *Way* back."

"Yes, *Presidente*," the lieutenant said. He made a quick exit.

Nochenegra watched Ortega through the window. He trotted over to the officer in charge, a captain of the

Army Corps of Engineers, and spoke to him briefly. The captain shouted orders at his men, then followed Ortega back to the helicopter.

Responding to the command, the soldiers rudely backed the protesting newsmen off the pad, herding them with rifle butts to the very edge of the cliff. The implication was unmistakable, even to journalists.

Pleased, Juan Carlos got up, walked to the front of the cabin and took a seat in his elevated chair. His bodyguards, their Heckler & Koch MP5A submachine guns at the ready, paired off and flanked him. When the captain and Ortega entered the Sikorsky, the president-for-life pointed a finger at the power plant's commanding officer, then to a seat in the first row. The captain removed his fatigue cap, saluted and sat.

"Where are the workers?" Nochenegra demanded.

"Gone, during the night, *Presidente*," the man confessed, his gaze fixed on the carpet. Sweat beaded his forehead, then poured down his face. "The PFM frightened them off."

"Your job, Captain Elisar, was to keep precisely that from happening."

"It was the snipers, *Presidente*. Shooting from the jungle above us. Our daily patrols could do nothing to stop them. To climb the scaffolds was to die."

"Climbing the scaffolds has always been a risky business," Nochenegra replied with venom. He despised lame excuses. Since the start of the nuclear project, marksmen of the PFM had made even the job of ditchdigger hazardous. It was to be expected: the PFM controlled the slopes overlooking the site. Because of the dense jungle canopy and steep terrain, high-tech surveillance gear was useless against them, as were attempts to sweep clean their operating areas. Day or night, from strongholds in the mountain passes, the guerrillas moved at will down a rat's maze of trails. Though they had rockets and mortars in their arsenal, the Communists had yet to use them against the plant; instead, they directed small-arms fire against random single targets. They didn't want to destroy the facility. They wanted to keep the regime's public embarrassment ongoing, the media regularly reporting the numbers of construction workers killed and wounded, the cost of expensive equipment sabotaged.

"But, *Presidente*," Elisar continued, "for the past few days the accuracy of the sniper fire has been absolutely awesome. The PFM must be using some new kind of sighting equipment. They are scoring multiple hits every time." He gestured toward the cooling tower. "Going up there has been like stepping in front of a firing squad. It completely demoralized the construction crew."

"Then you should have anticipated a mass desertion and done something to head it off."

"Yes, sir," the captain said, staring at his boots.

Juan Carlos watched the man strangle the brim of his fatigue cap. It was refreshing to see him acting so contrite for once. Elisar came from an old Mantuegan family with powerful connections in the armed services. Because of those connections, the young captain had come to expect special consideration. In this case, however, he could not be sure that his relatives in high places would be able to protect him from the wrath of the president-for-life. Nochenegra did nothing to alleviate the man's concern, but continued to study him in silence from behind the mirror shades, letting Elisar stew in his own salty sauce.

As far as Juan Carlos was concerned, there was both an up and a down side to the continual harassment of the site workers by the PFM, and even to their mass exodus.

The down side was obvious: it showed the outside world
that he could not control a vital section of his own territory. On the up side, it provided legitimate excuses for
construction delays that had already put the facility
eighteen months behind schedule. In point of fact, Nochenegra and his business cronies had never intended the
power plant to go on-line. From its inception, it was
meant to be an international scam, intended to bilk foreign investors and governments out of hundreds of millions of dollars. The United States was by far the biggest
loser. It was so desperate to export nuclear technology
that it had underwritten fully one-third of the total cost.

The President Juan Carlos Nochenegra Nuclear Power
Facility was a domestic flimflam as well. Not because the
Mantuegan treasury had been looted to pay for it, but
because it diverted funds and attention from more practical concerns. The earthen dams on the Sueño and Letargo were in desperate need of rebuilding. They were in
such bad shape that a minor earthquake could crack and
dislodge them—with catastrophic results. The necessary
repairs could easily have included installations that would
have provided hydroelectric power at a fraction of the
cost of nuclear. But the idea wasn't to save money or to
spend it wisely; it was to spend as much as possible. The
higher the price tag, the more could be safely skimmed
off the top.

Just when Elisar had started to think the worst was
over, Nochenegra broke the silence. "And the press,
Captain? How did they get in here?"

Elisar grimaced. "The workers who deserted during
the night must have gotten word to them, *Presidente*.
They were here at daybreak, climbing the fence to get in."

"Why didn't you order your men to shoot?"

"The newsmen were filming, *Presidente*."

"And you decided *that* made a difference?"

The captain swallowed hard. He opened his mouth, then thought better of it and shut it.

"Because of your spinelessness, Elisar," Nochenegra said, "I am forced to answer questions about the missing workers before I have had a chance to prepare a statement. If you think you can do so without bringing another disaster upon us, go out and tell the reporters I will give them a brief news conference shortly."

The captain rose, saluted and beat a hasty retreat.

"Lieutenant," Juan Carlos said, "bring me my weapon."

Ortega opened an overhead locker and removed a white leather shoulder holster of extraordinary length. He passed it and the heavy weapon it held to the dictator.

Juan Carlos took hold of the inlaid mother-of-pearl grips and unsheathed a great hog leg of a stainless-steel wheel gun. A gift from a former American president, the .44 Magnum Smith & Wesson Model 629 had a barrel almost 8½ inches long. Nochenegra considered it part of his public persona, a symbol of his power; he never allowed himself to be photographed without it.

Ortega cleared his throat to get the president's attention. Like a valet, he held out an oddly cut white vest with Velcro closures at the back. Juan Carlos put aside the gun and unbuttoned his shirt. The lieutenant helped him off with it, then on with the Kevlar vest. After the steel trauma plates had been inserted, the shirt went back on and over it the soft leather straps of the shoulder holster harness. Nochenegra shoved the 629 into the holster's formfitting clips. The butt of the pistol hung just below his left armpit; the muzzle tapped him at midthigh. Despite the rig's cross-bracing, the handgun's weight made his burdened shoulder sag noticeably.

Thumbing his sunglasses back up to the bridge of his squat toad of a nose, the president-for-life followed his security team down the stairs and onto the concrete pad. From their precarious position vis-à-vis the drop-off, the reporters immediately began shouting questions at him. Because of the distance that separated president from press, their words were unintelligible. Ignoring the clamor, Juan Carlos paused halfway across the pad, stopping to look up, to admire the gray sepulcher of the cooling tower.

So much more impressive, he thought, than any hydro dam or four-lane highway, because it was never intended to perform a mundane public function. Because it was strictly ornamental, it was a true and fitting measure of, and monument to, his power. It was his pyramid; it would cast a monstrous shadow over the landscape for thousands of years, reminding all who looked upon it of his glory. He could not stand beneath its majesty without feeling a vague, pleasurable stirring in his loins.

It was the pronounced pain in his neck from craning his head back so far, however, that broke the spell. Nochenegra continued across the pad, stopping some twenty-five feet from the line of soldiers that held the highly agitated newsmen in check.

The bastards were all shouting questions at once. Nochenegra held up his hands for quiet, but the reporters, smelling blood, would not cooperate. If anything, the chaos got worse.

Captain Elisar unsnapped the flap of the canvas holster at his hip, an action that amused Juan Carlos. Did the captain anticipate serious trouble from network correspondents? A barrage of paper clips or perhaps pencil lead?

"Now!" Elisar bellowed at his men as he drew his service .45. Five of the dozen soldiers responded, turning away from the newsmen, swinging assault rifles up to their shoulders. As the captain pivoted to take aim at an astonished president-for-life, he shouted to the others, "The head! Aim for the head!"

The .45 auto blazed. And suddenly Nochenegra was hatless, a giant finger having flicked it off his head. Lieutenant Ortega shouldered him out of the line of fire and shoved him down into a squatting position as the soldiers and his bodyguards exchanged sustained full-auto bursts at close range.

Screams pierced the clattering din as, behind the swirling, acrid curtain of cordite smoke, men dropped on both sides, bowled over by the barrage of bullets.

Juan Carlos, though no longer swift of foot, still had fast hands. As he dropped into the squatting position, he grabbed for the pistol butt under his left armpit. The nickel-plated Smith & Wesson seemed to jump into his hand. In front of him, Captain Elisar advanced through the smoke, miraculously untouched by the meat grinder that churned around him; the Colt automatic in his raised fist blinked orange as it bucked. Freight trains of jacketed lead alloy thundered past Nochenegra's ears. He fired once, double action, a snap shot.

And got lucky.

The 240-grain slug caught Elisar midchest, lifting him clear of the ground by two feet and sending him crashing spread-eagled onto his back.

The shooting stopped as suddenly as it had begun. For a moment there was complete silence, then the moans of the mortally wounded could be heard, faint and scattered. It only took the steady onshore breeze a few seconds to blow away the shroud of gun smoke. No one was standing. Two of the president's bodyguards were dead; all of the would-be assassins had been killed. The non-participating soldiers and the newsmen were prostrate on the ground.

Juan Carlos straightened up and hurried over to where Captain Elisar lay sprawled. The man's body quivered violently, arms and legs jittering in the dance of death. Beside himself with rage, Nochenegra raised his pistol in both hands and fired five more rounds, each time riding the Magnum's prodigious recoil wave back onto his target. The bullets' impact kicked the corpse along the ground like a bundle of rags.

When the hammer fell on a spent shell Nochenegra lowered the Smith & Wesson and looked over at the international press, who lay belly-down not fifteen feet away. A couple of the cameramen were gamely filming the grim doings. Not one to miss a prime photo opportunity, with a flourish Nochenegra dumped the spent casings into the dirt, then scowled menacingly for the cameras.

Lieutenant Ortega, meanwhile, was bullying the loyal soldiers to their feet. They moved slowly, tentatively, truly stunned by the turn of events.

One of the more seasoned wire-service boys called out from his place of safety on the ground, "*Presidente*, was this part of a larger coup attempt?"

"It's a little soon to speculate on that," Nochenegra replied in a voice thick with emotion.

"Do you suspect anyone else was involved?" a second reporter followed up.

Juan Carlos knew others were involved. Elisar had never been a master of strategy—as evidenced by his failed assassination attempt. He had simply drawn the short straw. How far up the chain of command the conspiracy went was anyone's guess, but it most certainly included Elisar's high-ranking relatives. "I suspect everyone," the president-for-life said grimly. Then he turned to Ortega. "I want these newsmen detained here until I reach the capitol. If any of them try to escape, shoot to kill."

That set off a chorus of protest from the journalists and brought them all to their feet. They were citizens of the world. They had inalienable rights. They had deadlines to meet.

One of the cameramen tried to convince Nochenegra that letting them fulfill their professional duties was in his best interests. "*¡Presidente!*" he yelled. "We've got some great footage of you in action. Guaranteed you'll make the network tease on every station in the States."

"It will have to wait," he snarled back. "This is a matter of Mantuegan national security. I want my enemies to think they succeeded. For this I require your cooperation." He nodded at Ortega, who growled an order to the soldiers to fix bayonets and advance.

The journalists' cries of foul play quickly dwindled, falling off in direct relation to the proximity of their heels to the sheer drop to the sea.

Juan Carlos walked up and down behind the line of troops, finally stopping behind a short, stoutly built private. He clapped a paternal arm around the young man's shoulders and said, "How would you like to do your country and your president a very special service? Yes, I thought you would."

LUISA NOCHENEGRA TAPPED the sharp points of her long, carmine-painted nails against the dazzling white of her perfect front teeth. The Mantuegan first lady was in what was for her a familiar quandary: she was trying to make up her mind what to wear. It was not an easy decision in a palace that boasted more than two hundred closets, some the size of small ballrooms, all of them packed with a wardrobe so extensive, so elaborate and so expensive that to be maintained properly it had to be computer cataloged, inventoried and mapped like the National Archives. She stood in a subsection of her "Pump Room," a secret closet hidden at the back of what could only be described as a high-heel warehouse. In the privacy of her inner sanctum, Luisa was wearing what she considered her "minimum": black garter belt and nylons, and black six-inch spike heels. The minimum accentuated her charms to the maximum, particularly the length and shape of her legs. Mrs. Nochenegra was not ashamed of any part of her body. And why should she have been? Every silky inch of it was certifiably gorgeous.

Hanging on the rack before her were paired outfits, female mated with its male counterpart. On this occasion she was choosing attire not only for herself, but for a significant other, and in order to create the desired mood. Selection was a problem not of taste or style, but of titillation.

As she wasn't feeling particularly energetic or bizarre, she had already eliminated as possibilities the Space Queen and the Mutant Astronaut, the Animal Tamer and the Bear, and the Mermaid and the Scuba Diver. It wasn't the sweatiness those costumes caused that bothered her— Luisa believed that there was a good deal to be said for perspiration in lovemaking—it was the oppressive weight that she did not feel up to.

After a good deal of thought, she had pared her choices down to three: the Penitent and the Priest, the

Village Girl and the Guerrilla, and the Schoolteacher and the Pupil.

Of those three, her personal favorite was the first, primarily because there was a stage set to go along with it. The palace had its own chapel complete with confessional. At the first lady's request, certain modifications had been made in the internal structure of the confessional, modifications that allowed more than hushed conversation to pass back and forth between compartments. She slipped the penitent's gray silk dress off its hanger. It was cut like a knee-length robe, open down the front from throat to hem. Luisa shrugged into the garment, overlapping the lapels, then pinning the outermost to her hip with a matching sash belt that wrapped twice around her slender waist. Easy on, easy off—it was ideal for doing the kind of "penance" her current "father confessor" routinely meted out.

As she smoothed the fabric over the curves of her hips, there was a discreet knock on the door. "Yes?" she said, without taking her eyes off her reflection in the triptych of floor-to-ceiling mirrors.

"Madam," said the male voice on the other side of the door, "you have a visitor."

"I am not receiving," was her terse reply.

"Madam, it is the senator."

Luisa's amorous thoughts instantly evaporated. "The senator?" she said. She jerked open the door and assailed the uniformed servant with questions. "What is he doing here? He never comes for a visit without first warning us. What does he want with me? Did you tell him the president is out?"

"I most definitely told him, madam. But he insists upon speaking privately with you. He said that it is most urgent. More than that he would not say."

"Where is he now?"

"He is waiting on the terrace, madam."

It irked the first lady that the American legislator could barge into the palace without an appointment and demand an immediate audience with her; it irked her even more that she had no choice but to grant it to him. "Very well," Luisa said tightly. "Take me to him."

With the servant in the lead, she exited the Pump Room and turned down a long pink marble corridor. The corridor walls, above the marble wainscoting, were lined with tall, elegant mirrors; facing each other across the hall, they reflected their gilded frames and gilded sconces back and forth, back and forth, into infinity.

The manservant opened the double French doors at the end of the hall and Luisa stepped past him onto the terrace. It was built on the cliff side of the palace: a broad, landscaped balcony that overlooked the city, the aquamarine bay and the dark blue sea beyond. The sun was starting to set, the clouds on the horizon shot with vivid color.

The senator sat in his electric wheelchair, staring out at the view with his back to her. His bald head was tinged with the sunset's rosy glow. At the sound of her high heels clicking on the tiles, he pushed the control lever at his right hand. The chair whirred and did an abrupt 180.

"Luisa, my dear," the senator said through an unctuous grin. "How marvelous you look."

"Wonderful to see you again, Senator," she said, giving him a dazzling smile, her eyes sparkling with an artificial delight that was most convincing. In his black three-piece suit, starched white shirt and black string tie, the man looked to her like an undertaker. A decrepit mortician on wheels.

The senator jammed his control lever forward and the chair lurched toward her, engine whining shrilly. She squelched the urge to back away, to retreat to safety behind one of the wicker settees. When he stopped, just short of running over her foot, he reached out for her hand with both of his. It was part of the official protocol; she had to permit the liberty. She allowed him to take her hand and kiss it. The sensation shocked and revolted her. The lawmaker's aged lips looked so dry and thin, yet his mouth was hot. And wet. It left a glistening mark on the back of her hand.

"Such lovely skin," he murmured.

"You are too kind," Luisa said, repressing a shudder. She loathed the senator for any number of reasons. Because he was a disgusting old cripple. Because even though crippled he still had incredible power—enough power to sway her husband, enough to make Juan Carlos dance a jig at high noon in front of the Mandelo Arch. She hated the senator because of the way he looked at her—as if she was nothing more than an expensive bit of stuff, a high-class whore. And she had heard stories about what the senator liked to do with that hot, slobbering mouth of his. He was a man who could make beautiful women do exactly what he wanted; because of that she feared him, too.

"Juan Carlos is a lucky man," the lawmaker said, caressing her fingers.

Juan Carlos, Luisa thought, is an impotent fool—just like you. She firmly drew back her hand. Beaming down at the senator, she said, "To what do we owe the pleasure of a rare visit from you?"

"A sad mission, I am sorry to say. One of the saddest it has ever been my duty to perform. Come with me, my dear, I want to show you something." He again pivoted his chair, then steered it back toward the terrace railing.

Luisa followed. Though alarmed by his words, she did not allow it to show. She walked over to the railing and looked out, sighing audibly at the beautiful panorama before her. Evening was falling. Far below, the lights of the city were starting to blink on, feebly twinkling against the splendor of the sunset.

"Take a look at El Infierno," the senator said.

The first lady turned her gaze to the island of squalor between the two rivers. She looked without seeing. Not so long ago, as the senator well knew, it had been her island. She had been born in the shantytown, one of its *condenados*, its damned. Only her remarkable beauty had saved her from a life of poverty and despair. At the age of fifteen she had gotten her first modeling job and from there she moved quickly into film work for a local production company. As "Luisa D'Amor," she starred in *The Vampire's Brain*, a low-budget, low-tech venture whose success in the Spanish-speaking world inspired a half-dozen sequels. During her brief acting career, Luisa was invariably typecast as a dark and fiery seductress...in other words, she always played herself. One did not climb out of the sewer of El Infierno standing up: the men who left made their exits on their bellies, the women who managed it did so on their backs.

"Don't you see?" the senator prompted.

"I'm sorry," she said, shaking her head.

"The fires, my dear. Half your precious slum is burning."

Tendrils of smoke from scores of scattered blazes rose and commingled in the liquid tropical dusk. Luisa could make out the crackle of distant small-arms fire. She turned to the American. "I see nothing new," she said.

"There have been disturbances every night for the past week. The stupid *condenados* think that if they burn down the slum the government will be forced to rebuild it for them. They want us to put in riverside condominiums and give them all free rent. Senator, I have been assured that the FSI will soon have the matter under control, the guilty parties under arrest."

"It has gone well beyond that stage," he said. "Look at the commercial district."

Luisa was stunned to see fires quickly spreading in the city, too. Fires at the bases of downtown high rises, along the elite shops of Market Street, sending vast plumes of smoke spiraling up into the darkening sky. The crackle of gunfire from below had become almost continuous.

"What's happening?" she cried.

"My dear, I'm afraid it's all over."

"What do you mean? What is over?"

"The ride. The fun and games. You and Juan Carlos have a bona fide revolution on your hands."

"This sort of thing has happened many times before," Luisa countered. "The army is completely loyal to my husband. It will crush the Communists in a few days."

The senator shook his head. "If only that were the case..."

"I don't believe you. Juan Carlos will not believe you."

"Please, let's not make this any more unpleasant than it already is. My government is satisfied that the PFM Communists and their sympathizers aren't the only ones out there setting fires. Juan Carlos has lost his power base. He has no solid support from any segment of the island's population. His regime faces a coalition of determined enemies from business, the military, the bureaucracy. With the backing of the United States, he could probably suppress this revolt, but that support will not be forthcoming.''

"What!''

"Not only has he lost the confidence of the Mantuegan people, but the gross human-rights violations his FSI troops have committed in the name of keeping the peace have been very embarrassing to the United States administration. They were the proverbial last straw, I'm afraid. As much as it grieves me to say this, the United States is assuming a neutral position on the outcome of the conflict here. We are cutting Juan Carlos adrift.''

"You can't do this to us!''

"Believe me, my dear, I fought tooth and nail against the decision. I was both outnumbered and outvoted. All I could do was buy you and Juan Carlos a little time. And for that, I had to call in every favor owed me.''

"And that's the only reason you are here? To warn us?''

"No, of course not. How could I desert my old friend Juan Carlos? I have come to help you both escape. The administration won't go public with the final decision for a day or two, I have been assured of that. When the news gets out it will be too late for you to flee. The Nochenegra government will fall, the airport will be closed, a bloodbath will follow. I have arranged for your evacuation out of the country. An American Air Force transport plane will land tomorrow morning at the main Army base. It will take you and your possessions to American soil and safety.''

"You are doing all this in the name of friendship?'' she said. "Putting your own life at risk?''

"I have deep feelings for you both, my dear.''

Luisa scowled at him. The man was an abominable hypocrite. "What would happen if evidence of your illicit financial dealings with Juan Carlos fell into the hands of the opposition?" she demanded. "What if the opposition passed it on to the press? Everything you've worked for would be taken from you, your wealth, your power. You might even spend your final years behind bars."

The senator smiled unpleasantly. "There are some loose ends I intend to tie up before I leave."

Flashes of hard white light blossomed in the heart of the City, then winked out. Two seconds later the string of rocking explosions reached them.

"Mortars," the senator said. "The PFM is firing from the foothills."

"Where is the air force?" Luisa exclaimed. "Where are the helicopter gunships?"

"Grounded for the duration. Sides have already been taken."

"Wrong!" Luisa shouted, pointing a finger at the dim horizon to the north. "There is our air force!"

The running lights of a single helicopter streaked toward them, its path crossing directly over the City.

The first lady was undaunted. "It will make them pay," she announced.

Floodlights from every corner of the City shot up into the night sky; crisscrossing beams of white locked onto and illuminated the speeding craft.

Luisa's heart stopped.

It was not a gunship. It was Air Force One.

"Juan Carlos!" she cried.

Even as she spoke, from the black perimeter of El Infierno a thing sparked to life. It arced into the sky, a meteor returning to space. The rocket followed what seemed to be a lazy, looping track. For a second she thought it would miss its target completely. She prayed that it would miss. Then at the last instant, it abruptly changed course. It could not miss. It was a heat seeker.

Luisa screamed as the Sikorsky exploded in a ball of flame, as burning wreckage pinwheeled to earth.

2

On a heavily treed knoll on the northern outskirts of Mantuego City, an American-made M113 armored personnel carrier idled, its lights off, its rear gate open. The APC's crew and passengers stood nearby in the shadows along the edge of the slope, peering down at the capital through a break in the tree line. Though they were all seasoned soldiers, what they saw below struck them speechless: fires raged out of control not only in El Infierno, but all along the main boulevard leading to the Mandelo Arch; mortar rounds whistled high over their heads, falling inside the city center with maddening precision. And the chaos of incessant small-arms fire, exploding shells, people screaming, sirens wailing, made their hearts thump triple time, their fingers sticky with sweat as they clutched the stocks of their assault rifles.

Then the Sikorsky appeared from the north, flying low and fast, and the men on the knoll momentarily put aside thoughts about their burning capital, fear for their own safety.

"Come on, Little Jorge!" one of the soldiers cheered, thrusting his FN FAL in the air.

"You can do it, boy!" said another.

When klieg lights pinned the helicopter, skewering it in space and time, a shudder passed through the little group. Then they all began to yell and stamp their boots, urging the valiant ship onward.

"Go, Little Jorge, go!"

"Yee-hah, Jorge!"

They were at the wrong angle to see the rocket's launch, to see it homing in on the Sikorsky. One second the helicopter was scooting along through the gauntlet of spotlights, the next it was a ball of flames, dropping out of the sky.

The cheers stopped abruptly.

Little Jorge was no more.

On the wooded knoll the short, stout man wearing the dead private's uniform cleared his throat and solemnly addressed the entire crew: "Your friend, Jorge, was a true hero, a martyr to the cause of Mantuegan freedom. The cowardly traitors will pay for his murder, I promise you all that. The streets will run red with their blood."

"Yes, *Presidente*," Lieutenant Ortega said without force.

Juan Carlos looked from face to face. Some of the men were actually glaring at him. Nochenegra felt a sudden chill. It had been a mistake to bring up the dead man's name. When push had come to shove, Private Jorge had not exactly been a willing "martyr to the cause of freedom." Several of the men present had had to hold him down, while the rest stripped, then dressed him in their president's white uniform. Tied and gagged, the white officer's hat jammed down over his head, Little Jorge had been strapped into a window seat—president-for-an-hour.

The APC crewmen had much more to chew on than the loss of their comrade. They lost comrades all the time. They had come under PFM fire twice on the way back from El Dragón. Ambushes on the coast road were to be expected. But to see a revolution in progress, one's seat of government in flames, was something entirely different; it made one reconsider things like duty, honor, loyalty. Juan Carlos sensed that this was not the time for a presidential pep talk. It occurred to him that the men who had just risked their lives to return him to the capital might well switch sides if they thought he was weakening. To save their own skins, they would become his executioners.

"We must return to the palace at once," Nochenegra said.

The troopers did not respond. They looked warily at one another.

"Now!"

The steel in his voice snapped them out of it. Like guilty children they hurried back to the APC.

Juan Carlos took a seat beside Ortega near the vehicle's rear door. The closed compartment reeked of fear; it was so intense it made his eyes water. He grabbed hold of an overhead strap to brace himself as the APC lurched off. All things considered, he was very pleased with his own performance so far. He had analyzed the situation at the power plant and correctly deduced that without confirmation of his death at the hand of Captain Elisar or some other member of the hit squad, the attempts against his life would certainly continue. He had arranged to make the next try appear successful. He had also arranged to be there for the show, delaying the takeoff of the helicopter until he was within striking distance of the city in the APC.

Over the roar of its engine and the clank of its steel tracks on pavement, the personnel carrier's radio crackled with static, shouts, gunfire. The situation looked worse than it actually was. According to the radio reports, the insurgents had moved quickly through the capital, setting fires, throwing grenades, creating as much havoc as they could. Then they had melted back into the slum, making no attempt to take or hold new territory.

They were waiting for the mortar bombardment to soften up the army's hard sites. Because large sections of the capital were still under government control, it was relatively easy for the APC to return to the palace, albeit by a circuitous route.

Despite the two attempts on his life and the all-out attack on Mantuego City, Juan Carlos was confident that he would come out on top. He had survived several coup attempts over the years. He knew how to pull his forces together, to throw confusion and suspicion into the enemy camp, dividing allies. More important, he had the money to buy off some of the key generals, if necessary. He had done it before. The important thing was not to concede anything to the Communists or their sympathizers. To do so was to weaken one's moral authority. One did not bargain with the devil. The situation, that of open warfare, offered possibilities otherwise available only if he were to risk his image abroad. It was an opportunity to kill PFM and its supporters indiscriminately. To impose martial law and lay waste to the Social Democrats, too.

There was always a silver lining if you took the time to look for it.

According to radio reports there had been no large-scale defections from the army. The military leadership was holding things together, despite the fact that probably two-thirds of the island's population had seen the Sikorsky go down in flames.

The APC stopped at three fortified checkpoints that had been set up along the palace road. Each time it was challenged, searched and, when the president made his presence known, allowed to pass on. The main gate of the palace had been sealed and heavily sandbagged, so they were forced to clank along the outside of the south wall, passing under the guns of the fortress, entering the grounds via the side gate. Juan Carlos exited the vehicle and made for the palace stairs.

The palace guards stationed at the doorway stepped forward to block the path of the very determined-looking private.

"¿Presidente?" one of them exclaimed in astonishment. "Is it you?"

"No, stupid, I am a ghost," Nochenegra said, pushing the soldiers aside and hurrying past.

Behind him the guards laughed aloud. Not at his joke, but in relief that their leader was still among them.

As Juan Carlos rushed down the hallway, he spoke to Ortega, who was following tightly behind and to his right. "Get me a proper uniform at once. I'll be in the communications room."

The lieutenant nodded and turned off down a side corridor.

Juan Carlos took the elevator to the third floor. He had already planned the initial stages of his counterattack. The first thing he had to do was get his air force into the fray. A few rocket and strafing runs against the PFM hillside mortar positions would keep them out of the fight. Then he would put the screws to Bonifacio. What was called for was a no-holds-barred FSI interdiction into El Infierno, a clean sweep with armor and artillery that would put the fear of God into the insurgents and their supporters.

The third-floor communications center was occupied by a trio of harried radio officers and an old man in a wheelchair.

The senator gawked at the dictator and vice versa, their surprise complete and mutual. The American seemed genuinely pleased to see Juan Carlos. Juan Carlos was anything but pleased. The lawmaker's presence at this time did not bode well.

"Demoted yourself, eh?" the senator said, beaming as he sized up the uniform. "I knew you'd find a way to survive."

Nochenegra gestured at the technicians. "Leave us," he said. After they had scurried out, he took a seat on the edge of a desk and searched the American's flinty eyes. "So, tell me. How is your government going to play it?"

"Hands off," the senator said. "All the way."

Even though he had guessed what was coming, Juan Carlos stiffened as if he had been slapped. "After so many years of unquestioning loyalty, this is what I get," he said bitterly. "When times are hard, you find out who your friends really are."

"My government sees the situation as no-win."

"To hell with your government! I don't need its help. I have my own resources. I have Bonifacio and the army. I can handle this by myself."

"No, you can't."

Nochenegra's heart thudded in his throat, his hands clenched into fists. "Explain yourself," he demanded.

The senator spoke in a flat, cold voice. "Your regime is going to fall in the next twenty-four hours."

"You mean the United States is going to back Soarez against me? That's hardly what I'd call hands off."

The senator paused before he replied, not to wait for Juan Carlos to calm down—there was no hope of that— but to give weight to his words. "Dr. Emilio Soarez is the only logical alternative."

"I should have killed the four-eyed bastard myself years ago, when he was nothing but a loud-mouthed, overeducated nobody."

"Juan Carlos, everything comes to an end. You've had a good, long run here. It's time to pack it in. You can still go out a winner, but you've got to accept the situation. If you try and fight the tide of history, it will destroy you and everything you've worked so hard to build."

The dictator scowled. Mandelo had once said that he found foreigners fascinating because they saw only what suited their interests. He called them "our poor, self-blinded brethren." What had this American senator learned of Mantuegan history in twenty odd years? A few worthless facts? He understood nothing of the drive, the human spirit behind it.

Juan Carlos suppressed his fury. Now was not the time to let emotion rule him. "Your government sent you here to tell me this?" he said. "Using an old, trusted friend to soften the killing blow?"

"I wasn't sent. I came because we have had a long and mutually profitable association. I came because I want that association to continue. I have arranged for your transport to California tomorrow morning."

"In return for . . . ?"

The senator's mask of concern flickered for an instant, exposing the hint of a smile behind his eyes. "The records of our transactions must be destroyed," he said. "For both our sakes."

"Of course," Nochenegra agreed. "I will order it done at once."

"I would prefer to be present."

"As you wish," Juan Carlos said.

Someone knocked on the communications-room door. Nochenegra opened it to Lieutenant Ortega. He had brought the fresh uniform.

"And how is my wife taking the news?" Juan Carlos asked the American as he changed clothes.

"Not well, I'm afraid," the senator replied. "She was already pretty shaken up by the bad news I brought, then she witnessed the destruction of your helicopter. The palace physician has sedated her."

Juan Carlos looked at Ortega for confirmation. The lieutenant nodded.

"Poor thing," Juan Carlos said. "She will have another shock when she wakes up. There isn't going to be enough time to pack all her clothes. By tomorrow night the rabble of El Infierno will be fighting over her Paris gowns and designer hats. I want her sedated until we are in the air. We have enough to deal with without her hysterics."

"The records?" the senator prompted.

"Yes, the records," Juan Carlos agreed. The three men returned the communications room to the radio operators and took the elevator down to the subbasement of the palace. They followed purple-on-yellow signs on the walls, which pointed in the direction of the building's fallout shelter. It had been cut deep in the side of the limestone mountain, built to withstand a nuclear direct hit. The shrill, whining sound of the senator's wheelchair echoed down the long empty corridor. Along the walls were electric lights in cages.

Before they reached the end of the hallway, Nochenegra stopped at a heavy steel door set in the left-hand wall. Its hinges were on the inside. He reached up to the light beside the door and clicked a hidden switch at its base.

"Burglar alarm?" the lawmaker said.

"Not quite," Juan Carlos replied. He punched a code into the electronic door lock. The door clacked and popped open an inch or so. Ortega pulled it all the way back, exposing a small room hewed out of the native rock. The pale walls were lined with metal shelves on which cardboard cartons were stacked to the ceiling. Each carton was dated and labeled.

The senator motored into the room and peeked into one of the more recent boxes. Inside were floppy disks, legal documents—the memorabilia of fraud and deceit, of the Nochenegran piracy that had kept Mantuego in the socioeconomic Dark Ages for a quarter of a century.

"How are we ever going to get rid of all this?" the senator asked as he let the lid drop. "You don't even have a shredder."

Juan Carlos pointed at a wooden crate on the floor to one side. Its lid was askew; wires led out from under it, along the base of the wall, then up the wall beside the door where they disappeared into a hole the size of a nickel.

On the side of the box was printed THERMITE.

"Senator, please," Juan Carlos said, indicating with a wave of his arm that it was time to return to the hallway. Once they had done so, he told Ortega to shut the door.

It clacked when pushed home, bolts automatically locking. The dictator rearmed the detonator by tripping the hidden switch in the hall light.

"Touch the door lock," he told the senator. "Try any five digit sequence."

The American reached out and punched in random numbers. When he hit the fifth, simultaneously the hallway rocked and a roar burst from the sealed chamber. Then a heat wave so intense, so clobbering, that it made all three raise shielding arms to their faces. The stench of chemical fire and cooking steel flooded the corridor.

"So much more efficient than a shredder, don't you think?" Juan Carlos said.

The lawmaker dabbed at his sweating face with a handkerchief. "We should have one in every government office."

As they returned to the elevator, Juan Carlos said to the lieutenant, "I'm putting you in charge of the transfer of valuables. Have the paintings crated. Get some forklifts and move the bullion into the parking level. We will need some armored transport; arrange for that, too. I will join you as soon as I complete my last official act— an address to the Mantuegan people on television and radio."

The senator smirked. "And what exactly are you going to tell them?"

"That rumors of my death have been greatly exaggerated, that the Communists are in full retreat, that everything is under control."

"Which should keep your enemies guessing for a few more hours at best."

Juan Carlos shrugged. *"Après moi le déluge."*

COLONEL RIBAN ENRIQUEZ crossed the palace's underground parking garage at a pace that gave his jowls and belly a life of their own. The underarms and back of his sky-blue FSI uniform were dark, soaked through with sweat. In one hand he carried a briefcase, in the other a small kit bag. He stopped, out of breath, before two regular army noncoms, who were loading gold bars into an armored van. "The president?" he said, puffing. "Where is he?"

The noncoms looked at the colonel with contempt and continued loading.

"I asked you a question, dammit!"

One of the soldiers paused, and through a wicked smile said, "Wow, I think *el presidente* left for the airport already, Colonel Enriquez."

The small, wide-set eyes of the FSI intelligence-operations director blinked rapidly. His nose began to run, dripping into the top of his mustache, but he made no move to wipe it. Terror was nothing new to Enriquez; being terrified himself was. From his HQ in the basement of the Hall of Justice, he ruled a fiefdom of fear. To be brought in for "questioning" by the FSI was not simply a death sentence, it was a promise of torture. Those few who had been released from custody, their freedom purchased by relatives and loved ones, refused to talk about their ordeals, but their bodies bore the marks of electrodes, barbed wire whips, blowtorches.

"Over here, Colonel," said a voice behind him.

The president-for-life stood on the rear bumper of a second armored vehicle, supervising the loading of his treasure. In his right hand he held a leather attaché case, which was handcuffed to his wrist. The colonel hurried over to him.

"I've been trying to reach you for hours," Enriquez said, wiping his nose on his cuff. "The rumors about your leaving are true?"

"Did you bring the material I requested?"

"Yes, of course, *Presidente*," he said, holding up a gray Samsonite briefcase. "It's all here. The dossiers you requested."

Nochenegra took the case from him and set it flat on the van's bumper. Then he opened the lid and looked inside. It was packed with rolls of boxed microfilm, unlabeled as he had instructed. He closed the case and tucked it under his arm. "Thank you, Riban," he said, turning to walk in the direction of the limousine.

"*Presidente*, wait! You aren't going to leave me behind. Please! You know what they will do to me."

Nochenegra stopped and looked back. "Exactly how much do you weigh?"

"*¿Presidente?*"

"How *much*?"

"Three hundred pounds."

"Are you worth your weight in gold to me?"

"*Presidente*, I do not understand," Riban said desperately.

"Then I will explain it to you. There is limited space on the transport plane. For you to get on, gold must come off." He paused to calculate in his head. "If you are to ride with me, about one million seven in bullion must remain behind. A lot of money for one fat sweating pig."

"I will pay! I will pay!" He frantically zipped open the kit bag and thrust it out, an offering to his leader. Inside the bag, loose diamonds sparkled—payment for freedom granted, lives spared.

Nochenegra smiled. "Yes, Riban, you most certainly will."

Lieutenant Ortega rode up to them on a forklift. "That is the last of it, *Presidente*," he said. "The escort is assembled outside the main gate."

"Good work," Juan Carlos said. As he started off once more for his limousine, the colonel fell into step beside him. "No, Riban," he said, "You will ride in the van. Let Ortega help you with your luggage."

"Yes, *Presidente*," the colonel said, meekly surrendering his booty to the lieutenant.

Nochenegra got into the rear of the limo. Luisa lay slumped against the far door, fast asleep. He winced, visualizing the tirade that would ensue when she was finally allowed to wake up, when she realized that he had left her wardrobe behind and that all she had were the clothes on her back. Women could never see the big picture. He set the two briefcases carefully on his lap.

Ortega climbed into the front passenger seat of the Mercedes. He carried the kit bag with him. The privacy window between the driver and passenger compartments was down; the radio crackled with details of the fighting.

The limousine pulled out ahead of the two treasure vans. Armed soldiers opened the parking level's steel doors, and the vehicles shot up the steep ramp and out into the daylight. The air had a rosy tinge, from the fires still smoldering in the city below.

Waiting at the main gate were three APCs. Two of them immediately pulled out in front to take the point, the third bringing up the rear. Single file they rolled down the center of the road, down the hill.

Ortega monitored the communications between the lead APCs and the army checkpoints along their chosen route. The anticipated Communist push into Mantuego City had never materialized. The shelling had stopped around midnight. It was thought that the fires the PFM had set had worked against them, cutting off units that were supposed to regroup for a big assault.

After the convoy passed the last palace-road guard post, it turned onto a winding lane. One side of the road was a sheer drop, the other side a high bank. Perched on the sheer side were the mansions of the Mantuegan well-to-do, people rich enough to have their own security teams. Men with shoulder-slung automatic weapons and guard dogs on chains patrolled back and forth in front of the barricaded gates.

Without incident, the six vehicles moved quickly through the foothills. Descending the bluff from the palace was like traveling down through the layers of Mantuegan society. The closer to sea level one got, the lower the status of the people.

Luisa stirred in her sleep. Juan Carlos watched as she raised her right hand to her mouth, inserted her thumb between perfect lips and began to quietly suck—as vulnerable as a child. It was a sight that warmed his heart; it made him feel both protective and strong.

Reports of skirmishes between the army and the Communists made the convoy change its intended route several times. PFM fighters were filtering into burned-out areas of the city, trying to outflank the military's positions.

The vehicles picked up speed when they reached the flat. The middle-class neighborhood on the other side of the window from Juan Carlos was a blur of one-story, stucco homes in pastel colors—some had front yards of sand, some had yards of concrete painted a gaudy green. There was no one about; all the shades were drawn. The road itself was a cratered travesty, a testament to the sham of Nochenegra's public works. The driver slalomed around the worst of the potholes.

As the convoy barreled down on an intersection with a much larger street things happened fast. Bad things. Without warning, a rapid series of explosions enveloped the cavalcade.

The limo driver hit his brakes to avoid crashing into the APC in front of him, swerving hard to the left as he came to a stop, giving the presidential party a view of the lead APC tipped over onto its side and engulfed in flames in the center of the intersection. The felled APC's guard unit struggled to get out of the rear door. They blundered from certain death by fire to certain death by gunshot, stepping into a withering cross fire from concealed positions up and down the larger street.

"Go!" Ortega shouted into his radio mike.

The APC in front of them backed up a few feet, then accelerated around the burning hulk. The armored vehicle made it almost completely across the intersection before being hit by a half dozen rocket-propelled grenades at once. The impact sent the personnel carrier skidding sideways, then it veered diagonally, out of control. It jumped an open sewage ditch and crashed through the side of a corner house, burying itself in peach-colored stucco rubble.

The limo driver, who had started to follow, took his foot off the gas.

"Don't stop!" Ortega growled, shoving the muzzle of his service automatic into the man's right ear. "Go for it."

The driver stomped the accelerator. Auto-rifle slugs whacked the bullet-proof glass windows and thumped the armored doors as the Mercedes rocketed into the intersection. The PFM guerrillas were converging from both sides of the cross street, running to cut off the president's escape. They stood in the middle of the road, trying to get their RPGs ready.

"Get 'em! Get the bastards!" Juan Carlos cried.

The driver slashed the wheel hard over, veering right for the half-dozen PFM who could not escape. He annihilated them. Some were ground under; some were knocked into the air. The heavy car bounced over the former even as limp bodies flew up onto the long hood, splattering the windshield with blood, then sliding off as the limo gained speed.

The lieutenant reached over and turned on the windshield wipers, smearing red to pink. He hit the washer switch and the pink swished away.

With two-thirds of their escort gone, it was white-knuckle time until they reached the gates of the main army base. The limo drove straight onto the airfield, stopping beside the United States Air Force transport being refueled by Mantuegan ground crews.

Partly because of the tension of the trip from the palace, partly because of the frenzied activity that had preceded it, Juan Carlos had not fully prepared himself for this awful moment. He was leaving his beloved island, forced from it by lesser men, by circumstance. Tears rolled out from under his mirror sunglasses. It was a sad morning, indeed—the saddest of his life.

In times of pain and doubt, Juan Carlos always found strength in the words of the great Mandelo. "Even the worst of times has an end," the philosopher had said. "Look beyond what is, and take comfort in what will be."

Nochenegra patted the briefcase on his lap, a warm glow filtering up through the crushing weight of his sorrow. What they contained was worth more to him than the van-loads of booty, more than the sum of his secret Swiss bank accounts. They assured him of his revenge. Of his rightful place in history.

They were his ticket back.

The senator wished to God he had never heard the name Juan Carlos Nochenegra.

His motorized wheelchair sat parked in front of a gunmetal-gray desk in a small corner office in the basement of the White House. Looming over him was one of the President's national security advisers, a pink-cheeked boy of no more than thirty with a crew cut that started two inches above his eyebrows.

"I assure you," the adviser said, "the administration is sympathetic with your concerns about the stability of the Soarez government, but in point of fact we are not convinced that the situation in Mantuego is nearly as grave as you make out."

The senator protested, his face suffusing with hot blood. "Goddammit, the reports I've been getting—"

The adviser cut him off. "Are the same ones we've been getting. It's a matter of interpretation."

"Or gutlessness."

"Senator, the bottom line is that the administration is doing a high-wire act on Mantuego. We're trying to balance public relations and democratic ideals with a genuine desire to avoid the creation of another Communist beachhead. Frankly, you aren't helping matters."

That was putting it mildly.

The veteran lawmaker had been engaged in an all-out misinformation blitz for nearly six months, spreading blatant falsehoods about the island's duly elected government, claiming that it was "soft on communism" and susceptible to pressure to form a coalition with the PFM.

The baby-faced bureaucrat then tossed off his bombshell. "We know about the plans for a countercoup."

"What countercoup?" the senator said, glaring up at the smiling man.

The adviser laughed, then crossed his arms in front of his chest, hugging himself. He was *that* pleased. "Come off it, Senator, the intelligence community has been predicting a move by Nochenegra to retake power for months. The only thing holding him back has been his financial situation."

It was true, of course. A few days after the dictator's departure from the island, the Swiss banks, in response to injunctions filed by the new government—which claimed the money had been looted from the national treasury—had been forced to freeze all of his numbered cash accounts. The Soarez people had a weak case. Juan Carlos was not stupid; he had covered his tracks well.

The adviser went on. "Once he gets control of his funds, we won't be able to stop him from trying to overthrow Soarez by force of arms. Successful or not, such an attempt would make the United States look bad. We support him through thick and thin for a couple of decades; then we get him out of the country when the crap hits the fan and harbor him while he plots a return to power. To the whole world it will look like our public backing of the democratic regime was a sham; like we were behind the coup from the start."

"So, *get* behind it."

"You know that's politically impossible. Nochenegra has been an albatross around our necks for too long. It's not just the human-rights stuff, either. He's burned us one too many times. Like that nuclear-power thing. Jesus! We'll be taking flak for that fiasco for years to come."

"What does the administration intend to do about it?"

"Officially, the administration intends to do nothing. Unofficially, after lengthy consultations with the CIA and NSC, a decision has been made. If he can't be stopped from pursuing his present course, arrangements will be made to terminate Mr. Nochenegra before he becomes a further embarrassment."

A cold fist squeezed the old man's heart. "Why are you telling me this?" he demanded. "Juan Carlos is an old and valued friend of mine."

"Precisely. You have a long-standing and cordial relationship with him. He trusts you. The administration wants you to talk him out of attempting the coup. Tell him anything, short of warning him about the death sentence hanging over his head, but get him to back off."

"He won't listen to me. I know because I've tried to reason with him. He's obsessed, goddammit."

"Senator, like it or not, keeping him out of Mantuego is the only way to save his life. If you really are his friend, you'll try again. You're his last hope. If you refuse to cooperate, we have no choice but to order his immediate termination."

The old man shifted on his seat. And a very hot seat it was. Hot enough to make his withered buns sizzle like bacon in a smoking skillet. All the years of double-dealing had finally caught up with him. With an ass-frying vengeance. At that moment there was nothing the senator would have liked better than to see the dictator put to a slow and painful death. But he could not allow it. Juan Carlos, ever the crafty son of a bitch, had him fast by the short and curlies.

"How much time have I got?" he asked.

"Not much. Twenty-four hours, give or take a few."

"If I can't convince him, but I can come up with an alternative to his immediate execution, will you consider it?"

"Of course we'll look at any reasonable alternative. Senator, believe me, this isn't a course of action we want to take—not that Mr. Nochenegra doesn't deserve it. You and I both know that the termination of a head of state, even a deposed head of state, is always risky; it could backfire with devastating results if word leaks that this administration was behind it."

"Certainly."

"Don't try to pull a stall on this," the adviser warned. "It won't work. And you'll make some new enemies upstairs." He jabbed a thumb toward the ceiling.

"I'll get back to you first thing tomorrow morning," the senator said, shifting his chair into reverse, then forward, motoring to the office door.

"Good luck," the adviser said, opening the door for him.

The senator didn't respond, didn't look up; he could feel that huge infuriatingly unwrinkled face beaming down at him. He jammed the chair in gear and whirred away down the hall. What a fucking mess! On the way to his waiting car, he racked his brain, trying to think of an edge, an angle to use. He came up with nothing. It was no surprise. He had been beating his head against the same brick wall for six months without success.

His driver helped him out of the chair and into the back of a dark blue Lincoln Continental where his new private secretary waited, her long, slender, nylon-clad legs very much in evidence below the hem of her black leather miniskirt.

"Senator, what's wrong?" Ms Hartel said with concern, leaning across the seat toward him.

That the dazzling redhead's proffered décolletage, the cleavage between perfect breast-moons so delectably exposed by the plunging V-neck of her cashmere sweater, did not bring an immediate smile to his thin lips or return the color to his sunken cheeks gave proof of his disturbed state of mind. Ms Hartel was the latest in a long string of his extramarital romantic conquests, a string that went all the way back to the late fifties when he had first taken the solemn oath of office. Washington had always drawn lovely young women, much in the same way as Hollywood and New York had. And much the same type: women attracted by power, moths to the flame—eminently exploitable. Once the senator had such a woman in his sphere of influence, escape was next to impossible. He knew how to use his position, his clout on the Hill, to alter theirs—from the upstandingly vertical to the pliantly horizontal. He made offers women like Ms Hartel could not refuse. And if they did refuse, he threatened, he badgered, he pursued until he found a way to get what he wanted. Though the senator was a man of diverse interests, the seduction of beautiful women was his one true hobby.

"The Hilton," he ordered his driver.

"Senator?" Ms Hartel said.

"Quiet," he told her. "I need a moment of quiet."

He shut his eyes and saw his own downfall. He saw himself subpoenaed to the hilt, sitting before countless congressional investigating committees, his humiliation and disgrace televised in prime time, paraded in banner headlines. And the bitterest pill of all, he had the certain knowledge that the lower he sank in the public eye, the higher his self-righteous inquisitors would rise in the opinion polls. Seated behind a table with a bouquet of microphones in his face, he would be essentially defenseless, his most powerful media weapon, his wheelchair, nullified.

Without a doubt getting his spine snapped in Central America was the best thing that had ever happened to his political career. It had breathed new life into a very tired public image. As the only survivor of "Jonestown II," he had become an overnight hero; conveniently, because he was the sole survivor, his complicity in the unsavory events surrounding the massacre would forever remain his little secret. The senator used his "weakness," his obvious physical disability, like a blunt instrument, to hammer sympathy and support from voters, to blindside his political foes. Without that weakness to wield, he was useless.

In the matter at hand, his old friend Juan Carlos had snookered him but good. The thermite bomb in the documents vault had been pure theater. Nochenegra had had the foresight to have microfilm copies of everything made long before the collapse, and had smuggled the highly incriminating negatives out on the plane with him. Upon his arrival in Southern California, the dictator had turned the material over to a trusted attorney with instructions that if he should die before his glorious return to Mantuego, the evidence against the senator was to be handed over to the Justice Department and the press. Accordingly, the senator had no choice but to help Nochenegra until the moment he set foot on the beach of Mantuego. That included spreading elaborate lies about Soarez, producing patently false but voluminous "white papers" to support his position, groveling behind closed doors to try to obtain funding for the return to power and, in general, wasting hard-earned political favors and making a perfect ass of himself. He hadn't had any success going through official channels. Everyone inside the Beltway, it seemed, was more than ready to dump on good old Juan Carlos.

The Lincoln stopped under the hotel's front awning. The driver immediately got out and proceeded to wrestle the wheelchair out of the trunk. Concerned over her boss's sullen silence, Ms Hartel turned to him and asked, "Is there anything I can do to help?"

The lawmaker's sour expression softened momentarily. He put a proprietary paw on her leg. "Maybe later, sweetheart," he said, giving her thigh a squeeze.

The driver then helped the senator into his chair. When he offered to steer the chair into the building, the old man waved him off impatiently. The power chair rolled up the sidewalk ramp into the lobby, proceeding directly to the elevator. He rode up to the top floor, the penthouse.

The elevator doors opened onto a reception area. Two men in dark blue private security-guard uniforms greeted him, then escorted him into a spacious and airy suite. The outer walls were huge floor-to-ceiling panes of amber-tinted glass. On sofas and armchairs a dozen or so men of roughly the senator's age lounged and sipped whiskey. Though some of the men were high-ranking active military, none was in uniform. Heads nodded to him as he motored into the middle of the room.

This was his last hope.

His best hope.

It was "the committee," a venue unspoiled by the fads and fashions of national politics. The committee was an informal group of very wealthy and powerful private citizens. They came from varied walks of life—business, science, academe, the military—but they shared a common vision of justice.

The committee was a star chamber, the dispenser of long overdue punishment, the kicker of deserving asses. Independent of constitutional checks and balances, of the restraints of international treaties and law, of the budgetary restrictions of Congress, it applied surgical military solutions to long-standing global problems. Solutions too dirty or too dangerous for the CIA or its surrogates to touch.

In a world hobbled by second-guessing diplomats, by spineless national leaders always looking over their shoulders at opinion polls, the committee was a refreshing change. It had no public image to protect—it had no public image, period; it was a secret organization. It didn't care squat about moral issues, human-rights abuses, graft and corruption. Its only concern was the maintaining of the status quo and its decisions were arbitrary and unequivocal.

"Gentlemen," the senator said, "I need an answer. I need it now."

The members exchanged looks that ranged from irritation to mild amusement.

"I know this isn't customary," the lawmaker continued, "but the circumstances are unusual and the window of action on this project is closing fast."

"Perhaps you'd better explain," said the CEO of a multinational conglomerate.

"I've just received word that the administration intends to assassinate Nochenegra. If we are to influence the final outcome in Mantuego, we must make a decision today. We must make it now."

One of the military men spoke up. "I've got no problem with that. We've all had ample time to study the documentation you've worked up. In my opinion, the Soarez experiment in democracy is too fragile to withstand the assaults of the kind of determined guerrilla movement you describe."

"It's the supply lines that really worry me," said another old soldier. "If the Soviets are providing weapons and matériel to the insurgents in the quantities you report, Senator, we can count on a major escalation of conflict in a matter of weeks. I'm talking full-scale war. Which means the administration will have to step in to avert a Communist takeover, maybe even send in U.S. troops."

"I think what we really have to face," an oil baron said, "is the fact that the government of Dr. Soarez could be just as bad for international business as the Communist PFM. His reforms to date haven't amounted to much, but under pressure from the left he could be forced into taking a harder line, more in his national self-interest."

"We need a strong leader in Mantuego," the senator said. "That leader is Juan Carlos Nochenegra, a man of proven loyalties. I'd like to call for a vote on the matter."

Heads nodded in agreement.

"All those in favor of facilitating Nochenegra's return to power..."

The vote was unanimous.

"Gentlemen, I am very gratified," the senator said.

"May we assume that you have a plan in mind to save Nochenegra from the hit and return him to Mantuego?" another member asked.

The room grew very still.

The senator plucked at his string tie as his prominent Adam's apple bobbed up and down. Until that moment, he had nothing, not a clue as to which course to take. Fear about what Juan Carlos held over his head and frustration over his failure to sway government policy had paralyzed what he considered his most formidable talent—the ability to manipulate people and events to serve his own secret agenda—a talent so potent, so uncanny that it had made him unique among the legions of puppet masters in D.C. Now that he had the backing he needed, he could see a way out. The puzzle that had for months seemed so complex and so unfathomable suddenly clicked into place like the brightly colored bits of glass in a kaleidoscope. It was child's play.

The senator smiled broadly. "Yes, I think I do...."

THE NSC ADVISER FLICKED the steel-tipped dart across the breadth of his small office. With a thunk it stuck in the bull's-eye, where a cluster of similar feathered missiles were embedded.

"So," he said, crossing to the circular target in two giant strides, seizing his darts and plucking them out en masse, "you couldn't make Nochenegra come around." He didn't sound very broken up about it.

"I spent practically all night on the phone with him," the senator lied. "He wouldn't budge. He still sees the odds in his favor. He thinks he can win back his country."

"I'm sure you did your best," the adviser said, returning to the far side of the room, once again facing the target. "You fulfilled your duty as a friend. You've got nothing to kick yourself in the butt over." He hurled a dart. It was a blur of red and green, a blur that abruptly stopped in the tiny center ring, where it became a dart again. Thunk. "Now I think even you'll agree, we have no choice but to proceed with the extreme measures I outlined yesterday."

"Yesterday you said you'd listen if I came up with a viable alternative."

"Yeah," the adviser agreed, lowering the dart poised in his hand. "I'm listening."

"The primary concern of everyone," the senator began, "is to safeguard the interests of the U.S., to keep the government from being embarrassed by the ill-considered schemes of a former ally. I put it to you that killing Nochenegra now jeopardizes those interests."

The adviser looked doubtful.

"Obviously," the senator continued, "the best possible scenario is one that produces no risk. Ideally for everyone, Juan Carlos's big plans for a return to power fall apart and he fades away into obscurity."

"Which means?"

"Which means if we go to the final solution now, while there are still other courses of action open, we are taking an unnecessary risk."

"What other courses are you talking about?"

"Between now and invasion day on Mantuego a million things can go wrong. I propose that a million things *do* go wrong. I propose that we arrange for Juan Carlos to hire some professional military coordinators/advisers to help him with his campaign. It will be easy to make him think that they're his choice and not ours. These men will closely observe, hinder, sabotage, do everything in their power to stop the planned invasion. And if all else fails they will kill the man before he sets foot on the island."

The adviser tossed the darts onto his desk. "You mean a dirty-tricks squad inside the bastard's command structure?" A grin spread over his boyish face. "I fucking love it! Have you already got a team picked out?"

"No," the senator lied once more, "but there's a man we're both familiar with who can set up the whole thing."

"Who's that?"

"Walker Jessup."

"The Fixer? Yeah, he could do it. Why don't you give me a couple of hours to run this by my superiors? I think you've come up with a winner."

The senator nodded. He only backed winners, even if he had to fix the game.

4

In the fifteen years that Walker Jessup had been a fixture on Capitol Hill, he had earned two reputations among the heavy-duty movers and shakers. First, he was a facilitator, a shadowy man behind the scenes who, for the right price, could make things happen anywhere in the world. He had his own private intelligence network. He did subcontract spooking for his government and others. He arranged for men and weapons to be at certain places at certain times, and guaranteed certain results. If it was too dirty to touch, Jessup got a call. He was "the Fixer."

Second, he was a hall-of-fame glutton in a town where standards of gustatory excess were purely Olympian. Not surprisingly, Walker Jessup, in terms of body type, was a tugboat. Though always blessed with an enthusiastic appetite, in his younger years, being a big man and physically active, he had been able to get away with it. After his Vietnam service with the CIA, however, his metabolic rate had taken a nosedive. Now he was nearly as wide as he was tall. His weight was in the neighborhood of 380 pounds, and climbing. When it came to food, he had no willpower whatsoever.

It was against this second reputation that he currently sported a mouth full of bright stainless steel, a subject the senator brought up first thing.

"Had the old trap wired shut, eh?" the lawmaker commented as he motored up to the restaurant table.

"Yush," Jessup said with difficulty through teeth artificially clenched, clenched so tightly that nothing more than a thin broth could pass through them

The senator was highly amused. "I suppose it's preferable to having one of those stomach staple jobs. How long have you had it on?"

Jessup looked at his watch. "Wenty minush."

The senator opened the red leather-bound menu and smacked his meager lips. "I am absolutely ravenous," he announced. "What are you having?"

The fat man held up his glass. It was full of water and ice cubes and garnished with a lemon slice.

When the liveried waiter stepped up, the senator ordered with gusto. "I'll have the Oysters Rockefeller with a split of the Heidseck, the escarole salad and the Steak Oscar with a bottle of the '62 Lafitte."

The waiter wrote it all down, then smiled at Jessup expectantly, pencil poised. When he got no response, he prompted. "For you, sir?"

Jessup shook his head. His stomach growled ominously, the demon within wanting out. He felt a touch of panic but he was sure he had done the right thing. There was only one way to cure a "Jones," he told himself, and that was cold turkey. The unfortunate metaphor made him wince. When the waiter departed, he got down to business immediately. "Whash the deal?"

The senator attacked a basket of hot French bread, slathering a thick chunk with butter from an iced silver server. "I have a job that needs doing. It's right up your alley."

"Details?" Jessup asked, trying not to watch the man chew the crusty bread.

"Mmm," the senator said, a glint of malice in his eyes, "this is really good. Fresh-baked. What were you saying? Oh, yes, the mission. It has to do with a personal friend of mine, a foreign national currently residing in Southern California. A former head of state. Do you know who I mean?''

Jessup nodded. He knew, all right. He had no particular fondness for the likes of Juan Carlos Nochenegra. He couldn't stand the senator, either. The man was slime, a political opportunist of the first water. In Jessup's line of work, having a warm relationship with one's employer was not required. In his line of work, it was usually out of the question: as often as not, you couldn't tell the assholes apart without a scorecard.

"This friend of mine is very homesick," the senator went on. "He's making plans to go back."

The fat man had heard whispers to that effect. He said nothing.

"I've been working on his travel arrangements at the request of mutual friends. We all agree that it's time he went home."

"Whish friendsh?"

"Highly placed friends."

"Offisshal friendsh?"

"Official friends expressing unofficial policy."

Jessup leaned back in his chair. It creaked in protest. He had worked through the senator many times before, and almost always the old man had been fronting for the mysterious, faceless "committee." If Jessup had really wanted to, he could have used his contacts in the intelligence community in order to find out who the anonymous members were. But he had decided from the word *go* that it was better to maintain a solid position of deniability than to satisfy his curiosity. The services he had provided in the past included setting up secret, White House–unauthorized incursions into Soviet, Iranian and

Afghan territories to accomplish limited military objectives. This operation apparently was not a "committee" job, but he wanted to make sure before they proceeded further. "I need shome clarificashion on who the prinshipalsh are."

"Jessup, this one is as squeaky-clean as they come. Straight from the basement of the big white house on the Hill."

"Undershtood."

"My friend needs some travel advisers. Experienced men who can coordinate his transportation, baggage, and make the appropriate connections at the other end."

"At what shtage are theshe travel plansh?"

"My friend has bought his tickets; his luggage is packed. He has already arranged for a welcoming committee and a place to stay when he arrives. He needs some troubleshooters to guarantee a successful and enjoyable trip. Some outside professionals with no conflict-of-interest problems."

"You have a shanction for thish?"

"I have a goddamn blank check."

A disclosure that made Jessup's heart go pit-a-pat. "We are talking logishtic shupport only, then?"

"Given the nature of the trip and the current climate at the destination, there may be the odd occasion when the travel advisers will be called upon to provide some personal-safety assistance."

"How many shhaperonesh are we looking at?"

"I think four will suffice. I had someone in mind to lead the mission."

"Yush?"

"Nile Barrabas."

"Good choish," Jessup said. Barrabas would have been his first choice, as well. The fat man had known and worked with the ex-Army colonel for a long time. Their relationship went all the way back to Nam.

Barrabas was a hard-bitten mercenary of the old school—a man who got things done, no matter what. He pushed and inspired the men under him not by threats and intimidation, but by his own unstinting bravery. Barrabas had paid his dues, rising through the ranks from buck private to full colonel in a span of seventeen years. He had left the service of his country shortly after the fall of Saigon for "personal reasons." He took it personally when the Army tried to court-martial him, taking the word of a CIA renegade over his, listening to his enemies at MACV, the incompetent, featherbedding bastards who, because he got things accomplished, had been clamoring for his head on a pike for years. And when the charges had fallen through, as a buy-off to keep him from countersuing, the Army awarded him the Congressional Medal of Honor—which, as far as Jessup knew, Barrabas had never bothered to collect. Nile Barrabas was a strange man, a man not of his time. He did not bend. Ever.

"Is he available?" the senator asked.

"Ash far ash I know he ish. What short of retainer ish involved?"

"I've been authorized to go seven figures. Half up front, the rest upon my friend's safe return home. What do you think? Is it doable?"

Jessup smiled broadly and nodded. His mouth looked like the grillwork of a '59 Buick.

The waiter stepped up to their table bearing a covered silver tray. Under his arm was a half bottle of champagne wrapped in a towel. He put the tray down in front of the senator and removed the cover with a flourish.

Steam rolled out and up.

Fragrant steam.

"Don't they look marvelous?" the senator said of the half-dozen oysters on the half shell.

Jessup moaned softly, like a lovesick hound.

The waiter popped the cork on the mini-Heidseck and poured the senator a tulip glass full. "Enjoy your food, sir," he said as he backed away.

Unable to avert his gaze, unable to breathe, Jessup watched the old man tie into the oysters. His jaws ached from the strain as he tried to open his sealed mouth, as he attempted to chew along.

"Fantastic," the senator said, washing down the shellfish with a bit of the bubbly. He regarded Jessup's tortured expression with undisguised amusement as he speared a second oyster. "Maybe you should have waited until after lunch to get your mouth zipped up?"

For a terrible instant Jessup visualized himself lunging across the table, shoving the legislator back and snatching the dish away from him. That wasn't the worst part. He saw himself trying to gobble down the pirated Oysters Rockefeller. He imagined himself grabbing at the shellfish with his bare hands, mashing the succulent meat, the delicious topping against the front of his teeth, mashing it to gruel with the heel of his hand so he could suck it through the gaps.

It was more than a possibility.

He knew if he didn't get the hell out of there at once, he damn well was going to do it.

"Eshcuse me," Jessup said, shoving his chair back from the table, lumbering to his feet. "Got to go. I've another appointment."

"What with?" the senator said, laughing at his retreating back. "A pair of side cutters?"

5

Nile Barrabas lowered the copy of the *International Herald-Tribune* just enough to see over its top edge. Across the boulevard from him was the main entrance to Amsterdam's Vondel Park, an oasis of lawns and open space in a city of tightly packed buildings, narrow cobblestone streets and murky canals. Typical for a warm Sunday afternoon in May, the oasis was crowded, the park entrance clogged with humanity. Families wandered in and out, losing one another in the throng, finding one another after much shouting and waving; groups of school children traveled in double file under the watchful eyes of their teachers; lovers walked hand in hand, oblivious both to the chaos around them and to the green serenity beyond. Dampening the flow through the main gate were the assembled street people—musicians, jugglers, fire-eaters and vendors of assorted, purportedly handmade rubbish.

Barrabas had his eye on two of the latter: a huge blond man in a tie-dyed string vest, matching headband and round sunglasses, and his companion, a statuesque blond woman in jeans and a bolero top.

From a cross-legged yoga position on a small rug on the ground Gunther Dykstra hawked his wares to passersby, a shit-eating grin plastered on his mug. Spread out on the rug before him were crudely finished brass peace symbols and animal totems of dolphins, whales and seals, all strung on leather thongs. He had bought the junk jewelry from a bona fide counterculture vendor. He had also bought the getup.

No doubt about it, the Dutchman was in heaven, Barrabas thought as he viewed his old friend. Hippie heaven. Born too late to be a flower child, Gunther had spent a good deal of the past fifteen years steeping himself in the culture of the era he had missed. He was more than a collector of sixties memorabilia; he was a connoisseur of things and ideas "sixties-ish." Especially rock and roll.

In this case the disguise wasn't just a bit of role-playing fun. It was intended to facilitate the transfer of smuggled goods. Smuggling was the foundation of Dykstra's real business. The family company, Netherlands Imports Management, had been providing the same sort of friendly, personal service for more than one hundred years. It specialized in moving high-ticket items in a tax-free, duty-free environment, back and forth from the entrepreneurial free fire zones of the Third World to the population centers of the West. The objects shuttled included gold, art, precious gems and sometimes men and weapons.

The stunning blonde in the bolero was Gunther's sister, Erika. She carried a voluminous straw bag slung over her right shoulder. Her right arm was concealed to the elbow inside it. Her right hand held a 9 mm Beretta autopistol. She stood behind her brother, leaning against the iron rails of the border fence, watching the crowd intently.

Ordinarily the transfer of property was not such a complicated affair, requiring costumes, stage sets, lookouts. But this was not ordinary property. The item in question was an uncut diamond of exceptional size and quality. It hung in the suede pouch around Gunther's thick neck. He and his sister hadn't stolen the gem and they were not acting as middlemen, marking it up and reselling it for a profit; what they were selling was their confidential air-freight services. They had moved the stone for its current owner, from the Far East to Holland. Barrabas had tried his damnedest to talk them out of doing business with the expatriate South Vietnamese mafioso, but the paycheck had been too tempting. Gunther and Erika had decided it was well worth the risk. Not that they trusted their employer. That was why they had arranged for the exchange to take place in a public place in broad daylight.

Barrabas shifted his spine against the stout tree he was using as a backrest. He was getting that itchy-twitchy feeling from too much standing around, waiting for something to happen. Under his light windbreaker the straps of his shoulder holster were digging into his trapezoids. He reached inside the open jacket and adjusted the ballistic nylon webbing. A little more than a kilo of Browning Hi-Power autopistol and its complement of thirteen Silvertip hollowpoints hung in a cross-draw rig under his left armpit. When he had lost the argument about taking the diamond job, he had insisted on being the mission backstop. He checked his watch again. The party in question was fourteen minutes late.

He returned to his paper. On the front page was an article on Juan Carlos Nochenegra. Since he was deposed three months before, the dictator had been trying to get his funds released from Swiss bank accounts. He was on the verge of pulling it off, despite the efforts of the Soarez government, which claimed that the money had all been stolen from the Mantuegan people. The accompanying photo showed Nochenegra and his beautiful young wife getting out of a limo in Zurich. According to the article the contested amount was in the hundreds of millions. A

sidebar to the money story told of the difficulties the
Soarez government was having in trying to institute democracy on the island. It was getting pulled from both
sides. The right-wing military faction wanted to slow
down Soarez's reforms; the Communist insurgents were
demanding immediate radical change. The new government was teetering on the brink.

Barrabas looked up again and saw a pair of young
Asian men moving through the crowd. They had on sunglasses and untucked short-sleeved sport shirts, the kind
that barbers and Spaniards wear—square across the
bottom, two pockets high, two low. Their hands were
empty. Barrabas watched as they approached the Dykstras and struck up a conversation. These were definitely
the guys. It was difficult for Barrabas to get a clear view
of what was going on because of the volume of passing
foot traffic. Gunther stood up, towering over the Vietnamese duo. Erika remained against the iron rails of the
park fence, her right hand hidden and presumably on her
gun.

Then, surprisingly, she was handing her shoulder bag
over to the Asians. She stepped aside a little and Barrabas got a glimpse of a man standing behind her, on the
other side of the fence. Evidently, he had sneaked up
from the rear and gotten the drop on her.

"Shit!" Barrabas growled, ditching the paper, running out into the street. As he ran, he held up his hand for
the cars to stop. They did, with much screeching of
brakes and sounding of horns.

He had four busy lanes to cross. Before he managed it,
Gunther and Erika had been escorted to a waiting gray
minivan, two Asians in front, two following behind.
Barrabas realized he couldn't run fast enough to cut them
off. And he couldn't open fire, either. There were too

many bystanders for him to start blazing away with the 9 mm. Even assuming that he could hit his targets every time, he couldn't guarantee that innocent people wouldn't be struck by the parabellums, which had a nasty tendency to go through and through.

He turned away from the kidnap-in-progress and sprinted in the opposite direction. As he reached the driver door, he had the keys to Erika's Porsche in his hand. He jumped in and hit the ignition. The turbocharged engine howled. Then, tires spinning, he shot away from the curb, into the flow of cars.

He couldn't see the minivan so he cut into the far left lane. He still couldn't see it. His view of the road ahead was blocked by traffic, and it was so tightly packed, there was no way to weave through it. Barrabas knew the lives of his friends were on the line, that if he didn't make contact in a hurry he was going to lose whatever chance he had to rescue them. "Fuck it," he said, cutting the steering wheel hard over to the left, slashing across the white warning bumps that separated the opposing lanes of travel. He stomped the gas and got an instantaneous response. The Porsche rocketed forward with a sickening lurch; the rear wheels broke free of the pavement, sending the car into a crazy fishtail skid. As Barrabas powered out of the slide, oncoming cars slammed on their brakes, swerving to avoid a head-on collision. He slipped through the first wave of cars, the Porsche's engine redlined in second, then he cut back across onto the right side of the road before the next wave arrived. Now ahead of the traffic pack, he could see the gray van. It was turning left at the next corner.

At a much more sedate pace, Barrabas followed the van down a tree-lined street, keeping two cars back. He had been in tight spots with Gunther and Erika many times before. His relationship with them had started in Vietnam, when they were ferrying CIA recon missions into Laos and Cambodia. He knew how they would react under the circumstances. They would wait until the last possible second for him to come to their aid, then regardless of the odds against them, they'd go down fighting. Barrabas had to be there for them when the numbers ran out.

The van crossed the Amstel Canal at Waterlooplein and continued on to the wharfs at Oosterdok. Without signaling, the driver turned hard left, crossing in the middle of the street and pulling in front of a partially demolished warehouse. The building's lower floor windows were crisscrossed with two-by-fours, the front door boarded over with a sheet of plywood. Barrabas drove past, watching in his rearview mirror. The van's side door slid back and its passengers began to get out. End of the line. He turned at the next corner and parked up on the curb.

When Barrabas ran back to the corner and looked around it, the van was still there, but no one was in sight. He crossed the street and walked along in front of the unbroken line of warehouses; because land everywhere in Amsterdam was at a premium, all of the buildings shared side walls. There was no way he could make a rear approach to the building they had entered. Unless he swam all the way around. The rear thirds of the warehouses extended on pilings over the body of seawater behind. He was going to have to go in the same way they had.

Barrabas unsheathed his Hi-Power and swung open the edge of the sheet of plywood over the doorway. It had no nails at the bottom and sides, so it was possible to squeeze through. He stepped into a short foyer that led to small offices on the left and right. The glass was broken out of the office doors and the rooms were littered with debris, chunks of plaster, newspapers, rags; they smelled strongly of urine. The door at the end of the foyer was open. He heard angry echoing voices coming from the other side of it. Stepping carefully over the shards of glass, he moved to the door.

It opened onto a cavernous warehouse. Puddles of water and grease blotched the concrete floor, and chunks of rusted metal, beams and sheet roofing were heaped in the center of the open space. The end of the hangarlike structure had been fenced off at one time. The fence had been breached and Barrabas could see water beyond. He looked up and saw blue sky. About half the roof had fallen in.

Gunther and Erika stood near the fence, surrounded by five armed Asian men, about 150 feet from Barrabas. Three other Orientals were walking away from the larger group, toward the gash in the hurricane wire and the water.

"If there was a problem with the price we could have worked it out," Gunther called out to their backs.

The three men stopped and turned. The oldest of the three, a man in his late fifties with slicked-back jet-black hair, spoke. "We have worked it out. You did the job for nothing."

"Okay, fine," Gunther replied. "You burned us. We can accept that. Why kill us?"

"So you can't find a way to get even," the Vietnamese stated flatly.

"You're a scumball, Tran," Gunther said. "But you're not as stupid as you look."

Tran turned to the gunmen. "Kill them both slowly," he said. "And kill her first. Make him watch."

The trio exited via the slit in the wire, then disappeared down some stairs at the end of the dock. After a few seconds, Barrabas heard a marine engine starting up, then a boat roared off.

"We can still make a deal," Erika said, taking a step toward the nearest man. "How is your boss going to know you killed us? If you let us live we will give you money."

The man didn't seem impressed.

She put a hand on her hip. "Or anything else you might fancy."

The Asians muttered to one another, obviously intrigued by the come-on.

Barrabas knew she wasn't really offering herself to five men. It was endgame. She was trying to get close enough to make her move. "Want a peek?" she said, untying the sash that held her bolero top together. She held the garment open.

It was certainly a major distraction.

Barrabas braced against the doorframe and took a two-handed grip on the Hi-Power as the Asian stepped forward and reached for Erika's exposed breasts. Two of the gunmen had SMGs; they had to die first. He picked the target farthest away from his friends and tightened down on the trigger. At the same instant, Gunther lunged, bellowing, at the man in front of him. The Browning barked in Barrabas's fist, its action cycling in a blur. Before the spent brass plinked on the floor, its Silvertip warhead whacked meat. A man at the rear of the group suddenly spun and dropped, his knees buckling, half his face blown away by the explosive expansion of the soft alloy hollowpoint.

Even as the gunshot roared, Erika deflected the man's groping hand with her forearm, using his momentum to turn him, his elbow to guide him around. Even without the distraction of the gunshot, the man was a goner. Before the second round went off, she had him from behind in a neckbreaker. She gave his chin a vicious twist to the left, something cracked, and his legs began to shiver and kick.

Gunther meanwhile had hoisted his man up over his head. He had the guy by the shirtfront and trouser waistband. Like some kind of maniacal wrestling superstar, he drove the hit man nose down onto the concrete, putting all of his 260 pounds behind the slam. The man's skull shattered like a coconut, cratering all the way down to the eyebrows. Steaming brains splattered in a wide circle over the floor.

Barrabas tracked and fired three more quick shots. The other guy holding an SMG never got his weapon around. He staggered sideways, firing a reflexive burst into the floor as he was drilled by the 115-grain hollowpoints. The mushrooming slugs tore through his lungs, exited from his back and slapped jagged holes in the sheet metal of the side wall. The man collapsed onto his butt, then flopped onto his back, clutching at his chest and writhing in pain.

The remaining gunman opened fire on Barrabas with a snub-nosed wheel gun. It was a futile act: he was too far away for accurate shooting. The doorframe above Barrabas's head disintegrated in a shower of splinters. The former Army colonel dropped to one knee and unleashed furious return volley. Slugs stitched up the man's torso, plucking open his barber's shirt from belly to throat, each impact sending him jerking backward. He crashed onto his back and was still.

Barrabas bolted from cover, dumping the spent mag as he ran, pulling a fresh clip from his jacket and slapping it home with his palm.

Gunther had scooped up one of the dropped weapons. He held an el cheapo SMG, everything but the barrel made of stamped steel, and aimed it at the head of the body nearest him while he gingerly prodded it in the ribs with the toe of his size-thirteen Air Jordans. The corpse rocked limply back and forth. "That was damned fine shooting, Nile," he said, looking up. He grinned broadly. "You put every round in the ten ring."

"This one's still kicking," Erika said, reknotting her bolero as she stepped around the lung-shot Asian. She picked up his Star Z-70/B submachine gun, checked the chamber for a live round, then took a closer look at the downed man. "He isn't going to last long," she told her brother and Barrabas. "What now?"

Gunther walked over to her. "It's get-even time." He knelt and grabbed a handful of bloody shirt, then he jerked the dying Vietnamese up off the concrete. The man's eyes were unfocused. Pink blood bubbles boiled out of the holes in his chest. Gunther put the ball of his thumb on the man's right eyeball...and pressed. The man awoke with a scream. "Where's Tran headed?" Gunther demanded. "To the cutter?"

The man nodded his head weakly. "Doc-tor..." he gasped. "Doc-tor..."

"Sure, buddy, coming right up," Gunther told him. "Just tell me which cutter."

The eyes started to fade once more. Gunther gouged the dying man again, and again he came to with a shriek.

"The cutter's name?"

"Roektner."

Gunther let the man down gently. As he did a huge blood bubble formed in the gory rent in his chest. When it popped, there were no more. The Asian was no longer breathing.

"We're not going to try and intercept Tran at the diamond-cutter's place, are we?" Erika said.

Barrabas looked at Gunther. Then all of them looked at the bodies curled up on the greasy floor. They were in a dicey situation. Every mercenary has to have a home ground, a sanctuary, somewhere he or she isn't "wanted." The rule was you didn't discard an established sanctuary on a whim, and certainly not until you had a new one lined up. For Barrabas and the Dykstras to take matters a step farther, for them to pursue Tran into the diamond district with intent to do murder, would have been self-defeating.

"No," Gunther said, obviously galled by the circumstances, "I guess not. We don't want to answer the questions the police are going to ask about what happened here. We want Mr. Tran to answer them. I think it's time for a discreet phone tip to Amsterdam's finest."

"He'll lose his damned diamond and go to jail," Erika said. "It isn't the punishment he deserves but..."

Barrabas smiled and reached into his pants pocket. "Here's some change," he said, handing it to Gunther. "Tell the cops he's just killed five guys. Give 'em this address. Dutch police don't get the chance to see stuff like this very often; they get to dish out lethal force once in a blue moon. With any luck, they'll get so pumped up they'll blow him away the second they lay eyes on him."

THE PARIMA LAY NESTLED like an old, fat spider in the coiled heart of Walletjes, Amsterdam's notorious red-light district—a place of ancient, narrow, winding cob-

blestone streets lined with sex shops, erotic theaters and
ground-floor houses of prostitution where, after dark,
girls in negligees sat on stools behind picture windows,
posing, beckoning. The Parima's four stories of smog-
blackened stone were advertised by an incongruously
bright and cheery plastic beacon sign as a "Three Star
Student Hotel." It was meant to lure, to beckon the un-
wary, like the breasts swaying beneath filmy black ted-
dies, like the long bare legs.

Beacons only worked in the dead of night, or during
blinding storms. It was not night; the sun was out and
daylight was unkind to Walletjes and its denizens. Without the cover of darkness or driving rain, without the
frenzy of flashing marquees and blaring rock music, it
had no glamour, no style. It was small, cramped, and the
pleasures it offered seemed stale and purely mechanical.

Day or night, Barrabas liked the Parima. It appealed
to his admittedly bleak sense of humor. The bottom floor
of the hotel was given over to a shabby bar. The walls and
ceiling were decorated in a nautical theme: rotten fish-
nets and cork floats hung like drapes. The jukebox played
nonstop heavy-metal hits. Upstairs, where the bar
stopped and the "student hotel" began, was a place of
cesspit nightmares.

Imagine an exhausted first-time European traveler,
Japanese or American, fresh off the plane and suffering
from terminal jet lag. Imagine such a person cut adrift in
a strange city that speaks an unintelligible language.
Imagine this person blindly, desperately following the
advice of some supposedly experienced travel writer, the
author of *Europe on Two Bits an Hour*, crawling through
the hellhole of Walletjes with his or her baggage to reach
the advertised low-budget comforts of the Parima.
Imagine the shock when said exhausted traveler sees what

low budget really means. On the lockless doors of the Parima's upstairs rooms the names of popular travel writers are scrawled like subway obscenities. The rooms are dorm style: tiers of metal bunks, walls kicked in, peeling paint hanging from the ceiling, bare light bulbs, cold linoleum floors. Hammered rooms for hammered people, rooms where a person might conceivably be murdered in his sleep for his shoes. Assuming sleep was possible. Outside the windows an ancient clock tower rings the hours and all night long street hookers ply their trade, amid honking car horns and loud haggling over acts and prices.

Why did Barrabas like the Parima?

Because it asked nothing of him. It had no expectations of behavior or appearance. It was the hangout of social lepers, of the vestigially human. When he got nostalgic for the Third World sewers where he plied his trade, he returned here. For him it was home away from home.

The black bartender set down a full bottle of Johnnie Walker and two glasses. He had a small monkey clinging to his shoulder. It hid behind its master's neck and blinked enormous eyes at Barrabas.

The front door opened and a fat man lumbered in. He walked straight over to the booth where Barrabas sat and slipped in opposite him.

"When are you going to lose that fucking monkey?" Jessup asked the bartender. "This place smells like a zoo."

The bartender gave him a sour look and turned away.

"You should've smelled it before he got the monkey," Barrabas said, sloshing some Scotch in the glasses. He pushed one toward Jessup. "If you had you wouldn't complain."

The Texan took the glass and sipped from it. He winced as the fiery liquid washed over his tender gums, freed by an astonished orthodontist two hours after he'd done his lovely chrome-and-wire deterrent. "Is this what you usually have for breakfast?"

"No, I usually dump a couple of raw eggs in it. A health drink."

"There's only one way I can handle booze before 9:00 a.m." Jessup reached inside his suit jacket and took out a small plastic bottle. He opened the twist top and poured three tablespoons of lime-green goo into the whiskey. Then he stirred it with his pinkie.

"Maalox and Scotch," Barrabas said. "Jessup, you are one tough bastard."

"Up yours," the fat man said, raising the glass in salute, then slamming back the concoction. He pushed the empty glass aside. "I got something you might be interested in."

The white-haired mercenary sipped his drink. "So, let's hear it."

"Do you know who Juan Carlos Nochenegra is?"

"An island dictator out of a job."

"If you've been following the Mantuegan situation at all you know that things are pretty shaky there. We've had word that the Communist PFM is on the verge of mounting a major offensive against the Soarez government. To put it bluntly, no way can Soarez win. He doesn't have the balls to beat them back. Juan Carlos is planning to exploit the crisis to stage a comeback."

Barrabas stared at his drink. He had worked with and for Jessup for many years, and in that time he had learned the hard way that the fat man, like all "sneaky petes"—intelligence personnel—could only be trusted within the parameters of how far they could be shot-putted. In Jessup's case that wasn't very far.

As Jessup opened his mouth to continue, Barrabas held up his hand. "No, wait a minute," he said, "let me guess. Either you're going to ask me to kill the son of a bitch or you want me to help him return to power. Given the long-standing relationship between Mr. Nochenegra and the United States, I'd say you want him back in the saddle."

"I've been authorized to pay one million U.S. for a seasoned team of advisers to help him get back to Mantuego. Half the money up front, half when you finish."

"He needs outside advisers? That doesn't say much for the people around him."

"You know what kind of sycophants a guy like that attracts."

"Flies to shit."

"None of them can be trusted not to sell him out. We want him to get there alive. To restore order."

"How many men are you looking for?"

"No more than four. You'll mostly be doing liaison work between Nochenegra's supporters in California and troops loyal to him on the island. Once you arrive on the beach in Mantuego City you'll be helping him to plan battle strategy. Given those requirements, you can see there's no need for a presence of any real size."

Barrabas thought for a moment. "Some of my regulars are unavailable," he said. "Beck is in Mexico and hard to reach on short notice. Dr. Hatton is at a medical seminar in Florida. I don't have a clue where O'Toole is. That leaves Nanos, Starfoot and Hayes."

Jessup frowned. "Hayes is a good man, straight arrow, but those other two! I don't think they've got half a brain between them."

"They're only loose cannons in civilian life. In a fire-fight they're about the best."

"There is one more thing."

"Yeah?" Barrabas was not the least bit surprised. He had been waiting for just such an addendum. The drop of the other shoe, as it were.

"Your job will also include protecting Nochenegra from his enemies."

"Bodyguards and nursemaids," Barrabas said. "Our stock in trade." He downed his Scotch, then asked the big one. "What are the odds?"

Jessup smiled. "Nobody's giving any."

"If they were," Barrabas said, "you wouldn't be talking to me, right? What I really want to know is who's going to back him up if things go sour? Will the U.S. step in? Or will it let him take it in the shorts?"

"I can't say. It depends on the scenario. This government isn't going to let the PFM take over. If Juan Carlos pulls his people together and makes a fight of it against the Communists, he'll get all our backing. If he can't handle it, the power will shift to the generals."

"A military junta. How refreshing."

"Do you want the job or not?"

Barrabas poured himself another drink, sipped at it and thought. As it always did sooner or later, Amsterdam was beginning to bore the living hell out of him. He was boozing it up more and more, and things were becoming strained between Erika and him. They had been lovers a long time. They had been through a lot together. Separation was an inevitability, given the kind of profession he was in, given the kind of man he was. Erika could always sense him drawing away from her; she could sense that she was losing him to the pull of distant places, of other people's wars. He knew from experience that it was better to go now, before things got worse.

Barrabas reached into his shirt pocket and took out a cigar case. He opened it and offered a hand-rolled Havana to Jessup. Both men bit off the ends and spit them out, then the mercenary lit up the stogies. He puffed a plume of blue smoke up at the ceiling nets and floats. "I've never been to Mantuego," he said, grinning.

"I know you're going to like it," Jessup told him, massaging his heartburn.

6

William Starfoot II, known to his friends as Billy Two, sat precariously tilted back in his office chair, his cowboy boots propped up on the desk in front of him. The six-foot-six-inch, half-Osage, half-Navajo had his aquiline nose buried in the current free catalog of the Fun University, a nonaccredited, nonacademic, noninstitution that was open to everyone with cash, check or credit card. Fun U. offered classes in a wide variety of vital subjects, from Meeting Mr./Ms Right to Tofu Cookery and Dog Psychology. The full-color cover displayed a gorgeous female model in a radically French-cut swimsuit and carrying a denim book bag. Your typical Fun U. student, dedicated to self-improvement and spiritual growth. Billy lowered the catalog and addressed the bronzed and muscular man sprawled on the office couch. "Hey, Alex, here's a course that sounds good," he said. "'Bare Bones Accounting for Home and Business. Previous study of bookkeeping not required.'"

Alex "the Greek" Nanos grunted noncommittally without looking up from his own reading material. He had heard it all before. His longtime paramilitary sidekick, fellow hell-raiser, and, more recently, business partner in the San Diego-based Nanostar Securities Specialties was chin deep in human-potential-and-horizon-expansion mode. A cyclical frenzy that coincided with negative cash flow.

The Indian turned the page. "Here's a course we can really use. Basic Advertising. Taught by a former ad exec. It includes production, layout and creative technique."

Nanos said, "Hmm." He continued to flip through the glossy magazine with one hand, while with the other he rhythmically squashed a hard rubber ball. The tendons in his leg-of-lamb forearm twitched and jerked as he worked up a good burn. Nanos was a power lifter, not a bodybuilder. He lifted weights because he couldn't stand to see them sitting on the floor, doing nothing, not because he wanted perfect pecs and delts. Oh, he liked to look at himself in the mirror as much as the next guy, but what he saw glaring back at him wasn't Mr. Universe-cute. His was a body built to raise iron plate—big legs and buns, powerful back and neck.

"Are you listening to me?" Starfoot asked.

"Yeah, I'm listening," Nanos said, intently studying the magazine photograph under his nose. "Billy, we don't need courses. We need clients."

"You get clients through advertising. We've got to have a slogan, an ad campaign to get public recognition."

"What about those matches I had printed up?"

Billy reached over to the desktop and picked a book of paper matches from the full box. On the cover, the name of the company and its phone number were printed in modest type. He flipped open the book. Inside was a cartoon of a man in a fatigue suit holding a .45 automatic. In place of his head, and grossly oversized for the body, were a pair of eight balls. The white circles and number eights stared off in opposite directions, one up, one down, giving the character a decidedly whacko ambience. The catchphrase beneath was simple and to the point: Balls for Brains.

Billy flipped his matchbook at him. "Yeah," he said, "these ought to bring us a lot of classy high-paying work."

"Hey, lighten up," Nanos said, ducking the missile. "The matches were just a joke. A printer friend of mine owed me a favor so I had him make them up. Business is in a slump now, but it'll turn around. It always does."

The Indian shook his head. "In case you haven't noticed, business has been going steadily from bad to worse. All we do is throw mission money into it. And there isn't much left of that. This is our third office in a year. Each one has had a worse address. If you've got the stones to come down to this part of town, you don't need security." He gestured in disgust at the furnishings. "This place is a fucking dump."

Nanos looked around. The lone office desk looked like the victim of an interior decorator inquisition: cigarette burns marred its plastic veneer top, its modesty panel had been kicked in, its drawer handles ripped off. The chairs, like the private investigators, were ex-military. They were painted olive drab, the seat cushions torn, exposing the crumbling yellow foam pads. The venetian-blind slats over the two small gun-emplacement windows were half-missing. The blue shag rug had a life of its own. "I've seen better," Nanos admitted, returning to his magazine.

"It's our rep, Alex. We've got a funky rep. We've got to change our image in this town."

"You mean change our names and get plastic surgery."

Billy rose from behind the desk. "I'm serious. Let's go down to Chuey's and think it through over a few *cervezas*."

That *was* serious.

"Yeah, why not?" Nanos said, getting up from the couch. He waved the magazine at his friend. "Have you ever heard of this? *The Journal of the M.B.O.A.*?"

"The what?"

"The Mexican Bordello Owners Association." Nanos passed him the magazine. Billy leafed through it quickly, passing photo essays on "The Courtesans of Yucatan," "Bordertown Delights," "Donkey Love."

"In the back they offer package tours," Nanos said. "Five days, six nights, ten whorehouses."

"This has got to be a put-on, man." Billy shoved the magazine back.

Before the Greek could reply there was a knock on the door. Billy moved back behind the desk. Alex stuffed the magazine under the couch cushions. Then he opened the door.

A tall, painfully thin old man shuffled into the room.

"Hey, Mr. Lovecchio, what's shakin'?" Alex asked.

It was a silly question. Mr. Lovecchio was oscillating slowly from head to foot. He had some kind of nervous disorder. It didn't interfere with his hobby, though. He puffed on his Lucky Strike. His fingertips were stained ocher, as were his front teeth.

"Good afternoon," the old man said.

"Have a seat, Mr. L.," Billy Two told him, handing him an ashtray, which he balanced on his knobby knees.

The two "securities specialists" exchanged happy looks. On several occasions they had approached Mr. Lovecchio about doing some free-lance work for him. The old guy was a middle-level bail bondsman. Heretofore, he had given them a polite brush-off, preferring to use family for "collection problems." His nephews did all his muscle work.

"What can we do for you?" Alex asked.

"I might have a small job for you boys," Lovecchio said. He sized up the room and grimaced. He had crevasses in his face, not lines. "If," he added politely, "you have the time for me."

The Indian smiled. "We have a couple of irons in the fire, but we can always squeeze you in. What's up?"

"I've got a 'skip' I want back for trial," Mr. L. said, lighting a fresh cigarette from the quarter-inch-long stub of his last.

"What's wrong with your own crew?" Billy asked. "Why can't they handle the job?"

"They've tried—and more than once, I might add—without success."

"And the cops?" Alex said.

"They aren't interested. It's a minor-assault beef. Old news."

"If your boys can't find him," Billy said, "what makes you think we can?"

"You don't have to find him. He's in a trailer over in El Cabron. The Sunny Hills Trailer Court, space 23."

Billy and Nanos looked puzzled.

"The turkey's bond was $1,500. Which means I'll lose fifteen grand if he's not brought back. I'll give you each $1,500 if you bring him in."

"What's the deal, Mr. L.?" Nanos said. "You drop fifteen grand on a Chargers game and think nothing of it. And why is this guy so hard to bring in?"

Mr. Lovecchio slowly rose from his seat. They could hear his knees popping and creaking. "The big deal here is the precedent. I don't want people to think they can get cute with me." He shuffled toward the door. "The trial is tomorrow morning at 10:00 a.m. I want him in the hallway outside the courtroom at 9:45. As for why he's so hard to bring in, well, I'll let you find that out for yourselves. But don't worry, he's not armed. His name is Wally Duchamp."

"We'll have him there on time, don't worry," Alex promised.

"We really appreciate the business," Billy added.

Mr. L. nodded and left.

The owners/operators of Nanostar Securities slumped back into their respective seats.

"Who is this Duchamp guy, anyway?" Nanos asked. "Chuck Norris? You've seen Mr. L.'s nephews. Christ, that one Kenny, he's built like a Patton tank."

"Do we really care? We could sorely use three grand about now."

"At least it's legal, right?" Nanos said. "Right?"

Billy shrugged. "No use in putting it off."

They exited the office and made a beeline for Billy's truck. Because of the neighborhood, he kept it parked in back of a local service station under the owner's constant watch. It was his "machismo mobile." A metallic-red, full-size Chevy pickup, with four-wheel drive, a 454 V-8, and humongous off-road wheels and tires. The wheels, tires and suspension had the cab jacked so far off the ground that even Billy had to use the handhold to pull himself up and in.

Billy drove to the nearest freeway on ramp and they headed for Interstate 8 East and El Cabron.

El Cabron was a changing city. At one time, it had been a kind of hayseed adjunct to the sleepy metropolis of San Diego; instead of a bedroom community, it had been a barnyard community, peopled by folks right out of *Deliverance*. What had once been called by animal-rights advocates "the duck-fucking capital of the Southwest" now comprised genteel, five-acre horse farms and suburban shopping malls. Gradually the junked-car and broken-refrigerator lawn ornaments, the chicken coops and pigsties were fading into the serenity of the split-level, the ranch style. The sounds of banjo picking and ducks screaming had given way to programmable car horns playing Barry Manilow and the smug hum of backyard satellite dishes tracking, tracking, tracking.

The Sunny Hills Trailer Court was part of old El Cabron.

In the hierarchy of mobile-home parks it was one step above parking your trailer in a field and pissing out the side door. Most of the vehicles in the court either were up on blocks or had flat tires. All of them had been there a long time. None of them was leaving. Scattered around almost everywhere, two or three to a trailer space, were shopping carts stolen from nearby supermarkets.

"God, this is a cheery place," Nanos remarked.

The jacked-up Chevy bounced over the speed bumps as they cruised through the park looking for space 23. It was way in the back. Once the trailer had been two-tone turquoise and cream—back when Ike was in office. The intervening thirty years of rain and sun had bleached out the green until it was one tone—ugly. The trailer was small, not more than eighteen feet long. Scorch marks from an ancient fire had blackened and blistered the paint above one of the louvered windows in the side. The sole door, also in the side, was sprung and dangled ajar by its hinges.

"Now what?" Billy said as he shut down the Chevy's big mill.

Nanos reached under the front seat and pulled out a .45 Colt Service automatic. He stuck it in the front waistband of his pants. "I don't give a damn what Mr. L. said. I'm not going into that dump unarmed."

"When in El Cabron . . ." Billy said, digging a matching pistol out from under his seat. He checked the clip. "I repeat, now what?"

"We could march up there, kick our way in, pull our guns and demand this Duchamp character comes with us or else," the Greek suggested.

"I have a feeling that's already been tried," Billy said. "Check out the door."

It definitely had a kicked look.

As they pondered the situation, a middle-aged woman came out of the trailer next to Duchamp's. She walked over to Billy's truck, and shouted up at him, "If you've come for Wally, you're never going to get him out of there."

The Indian smiled down at her. She was wearing a plastic shower cap with daisies on it, a blue chenille bathrobe and pink fuzzy slippers. Under the shower cap her hideously red hair was in curlers. "Now why do you say that, ma'am?"

"You're the third bunch that's been here this week," she told him, grinning. "None of the others could do it. You won't be able to, either."

Nanos leaned across the cab and said, "What's he got in there, lady, attack dogs or something?"

She laughed. "No, nothing like that. He's too big. You won't be able to get him through the door."

"Huh?" Billy said.

"He's too fat. He won't fit through the door anymore."

Starfoot and Nanos looked at the sprung door.

"If you don't believe me, why don't you go have a look for yourselves."

The securities specialists hopped down from the four-by-four's cab.

"Wally used to be a pro football player," the woman said to their backs as they headed for the concrete-block steps. "But he got too heavy, so he switched to wrestling. He was on TV. After a year or two, he got too big for that, too. Sort of took the heart out of him. He's been here at Sunny Hills for three years. Just eating. Getting bigger. For the past two months he hasn't been able to get out of that door. Has his groceries trucked in once a day."

Billy and Nanos climbed the steps. Nanos slapped a hand on the outside skin of the trailer and shouted into the open door, "Hey, Duchamp! Rise and shine! You got visitors."

There was no answer. From the front end of the mobile home came the sounds of a TV game show. Then footsteps, heavy footsteps approached, and as they did, the trailer shifted and creaked on its foundation.

A vast body appeared on the other side of the door.

"Holy shit!" Nanos groaned.

Wally Duchamp, man mountain, was naked except for a bedsheet, which he wore drawn up between his legs and around his enormous waist like a Sumo wrestler's diaper. In one hand he held a half-gallon of butter brickle ice cream—it looked almost dainty in his fist—and an ice cream scoop.

"Who're you?" he asked, gouging a scoopful out of the container. His hand was covered to the wrist with melted ice cream. He plopped the serving-size gob straight into his mouth. Beneath pendulous layers of fat, his jaws worked; after a few seconds, he swallowed.

"It's about your court date, Wally," Nanos said. "We want you to make it."

"I'll tell you what I told the others," Duchamp said, gouging another scoop for himself. "Fuck off."

"We understand there's a problem with the exit, here," Billy said, patting the ruined doorframe, "and we'd like to come in and discuss some solutions with you."

While Duchamp was formulating a reply, Nanos tried to slip into the trailer. He figured that once inside he'd be free to wave his gun around in a threatening manner without having the neighbors call the El Cabron P.D. He got halfway in when Duchamp realized what was happening and took a momentous step forward. Suddenly Nanos found himself pinned between Duchamp and the doorframe. The air whooshed out of his lungs.

"Help!" he moaned, trying to wriggle free.

"How do you like it?" Wally said, leaning over farther. The trailer groaned. Nanos groaned.

"Do something!" he gasped.

Billy responded, stomping on Duchamp's bare toes with his cowboy boots. The huge man let out a piercing shriek and pulled back. Billy grabbed Nanos and jerked him out of the trailer. He yanked so hard that he knocked them both off balance and they tumbled down the steps backward, landing in a heap at the bottom.

Much to the amusement of the woman in the shower cap—she was nearly hysterical. "Hee, hee," she shrieked, pawing the air. "Oh, Lordy, I think I'm going to wet myself. Hee, hee."

The two men struggled up and dusted themselves off.

Nanos was livid. "You are going to trial, man," he promised, pointing a finger up at Duchamp, who stood staring at them from inside the doorway.

Duchamp spit a mouthful of butter brickle at him, then turned back into the trailer. As he lumbered through it, it creaked and shifted again. The sound of the TV got suddenly louder. He had cranked up the volume on his game show.

"Got any bright ideas?" Billy asked.

"You're goddamn right." Nanos walked over to the plywood skirting around the bottom of the trailer and ripped it off, exposing a double set of wheels and tires. The whole rig was on concrete blocks; the wheels raised an inch or two from the ground. He kicked the tires. They were hard. With Billy's help, Nanos tore off the rest of the skirting, then they moved to the trailer tongue. The hitch was fastened to a heavy steel pipe set in concrete. Nanos unfastened it.

Billy beamed at him. "Alex, my man, you are a fucking genius. Now, we'll just drive him away."

"Not without unhooking the utilities from that rig first," the shower-capped woman said. "He's got gas and electrical and water lines. You rip 'em out and you'll black out the whole park."

"Show me how to unhook them," the Greek said.

"How much are you willing to pay?"

"Pay? Oh, hell!" Nanos reached for his wallet and pulled out a twenty.

"For twenty more, I'll go you one better," she offered. "I'll unhook it for you myself."

He gave her the money. She pulled a foot of chromed crescent wrench out of her bathrobe pocket—a handy deterrent to would-be rapists, she told them—and set to work.

Billy Two backed the Chevy around next to the hitch. When he got out to look, he said, "We got problems." There was a world of difference between the elevation of the truck's rear bumper and the trailer's hitch.

"I'll have to lift it up and drop it on the ball."

"Can you do that? I mean, Baby Huey is sitting at this end of the rig."

"I can damn well try."

Nanos flexed his knees and took hold of the tongue of the trailer. With a grunt, he started to lift, straining against the bar. His eyes shut tight, cheeks puffed out, veins in his neck bulging, he put everything he had into breaking the thing's inertia. The muscles in his thighs and buttocks burned, then trembled, then locked as he exerted maximum force. The tongue wouldn't budge an inch. From years of weight lifting he knew when he was outclassed. Nanos could squat nearly five hundred pounds, but the weight on the trailer tongue was more. A whole lot more.

With a moan he released the bar and staggered back. "Shit!" he grumbled, shaking his head and pounding his fist on his seized-up quads. "Shit! Shit! Shit!"

"We've got to get him into the other end of the trailer," Billy said. "Lady, is there a market nearby?"

"There's a Munch-A-Bunch just around the corner."

"You rest, Alex, I'll be back in a minute." Billy jumped in the truck and roared off. He returned a few minutes later with a couple of full shopping bags. Grease had soaked through the paper.

"What have you got in there?" Nanos asked.

Billy showed him. Inside the bags were assorted glazed pastries, cherry cheese coffee rolls, nut logs, cinnamon buns, jelly doughnuts. "Get back on the hitch," he said. "And be ready to act quick."

The Indian walked up the steps and took out a Danish. He chucked it around the door, into the front end of the trailer. "Hey, Duchamp, chow time!"

He threw a couple more small tidbits in that direction, then heaved the rest of the stuff into the rear of the trailer.

After a few seconds, the trailer started to creak under the weight of heavy footsteps, and as Duchamp passed the fulcrum point of the rig, the tongue of the trailer as if by magic began to rise.

"I need some help!" Nanos cried, hoisted bodily into the air as he tried to swing the hitch over onto the truck bumper.

The two of them wrestled the hitch on and looped the safety chain around the frame.

"We got your ass!" Billy shouted at the trailer as he climbed into the Chevy's cab. He shifted into four-wheel drive and then compound low.

Tractor-pulling low.

Stump-pulling low.

He goosed the big V-8 a few times, making the truck twitch and jerk, then he mashed the pedal to the metal and let her rip. The truck engine bellowed blue thunder, all four wheels spinning madly on the dirt, grinding in, taking hold. The truck bucked and slewed amid the dust cloud it raised. Then with a crunch and a shower of sparks, the trailer's undercarriage broke free of the blocks, and truck and trailer bounded onto the tarmac.

Everything in the front of the rig shifted suddenly to the rear. Wally, who was already in the rear, was buried by his belongings.

Nanos opened the truck's passenger door and piled in, all smiles.

As they hit the first speed bump, Duchamp hollered, "No!" His voice sounded distant and desperate.

Nanos leaned out the window and shouted back to him, "Fasten your seat belt, Wally."

Billy was merciless. He pounded the Chevy and the trailer over the rest of the speed bumps. They traveled to the sounds of crashing furniture and dishes. The shower-cap lady waved goodbye to them with the two twenties.

"We can park him downtown for tonight," Billy said after they got back on the freeway headed west.

"You know we still have a major problem," Nanos said. "We've brought the mountain to Mohammed, but we can't tow his trailer into the courtroom."

"Let me sleep on it."

THE NEXT MORNING at 9:25 Billy and Nanos hauled the turquoise-and-cream trailer up to the Superior Court's side entrance.

Duchamp was sulking inside. "You'll never get me out!" he taunted them.

Nanos replied, "Don't bet on it."

Starfoot took a small electric generator from the bed of his truck, pull-started it and let it warm up. Meanwhile Nanos got out the other stuff they had rented. He hooked up the heavy-duty power cords to the generator, then stretched them around on either side of the trailer. That done, he set up a pair of extension ladders, one on each side of the mobile home, that reached the roof.

A small crowd of the curious had gathered to watch— off-duty cops, court workers and lawyers on their way in.

"Please stand back, ladies and gentlemen," Nanos said, brandishing a savage-looking saber saw. "The fellow inside has a date with the judge."

"Never!" shouted Duchamp.

Billy Two picked up his saw, and the two securities specialists mounted their respective ladders and climbed on top of the trailer. The saber saws whined as they sliced through the sheet metal, sending sprays of golden sparks. Billy and Alex worked quickly, starting at the middle of the roof and cutting away from each other. When they got to the edge of the roof, they sliced down opposing side walls; when they reached the floor, they crawled under the trailer and met in the middle. In less than ten minutes the back end of the rig and its assorted debris crashed to the pavement, leaving a gaping hole.

"No way!" Duchamp hollered, clinging to the jagged edges of the trailer wall. "I'm not going!"

Nanos jumped up into the trailer, swinging his whirring saw back and forth menacingly. "We never promised to get you out in one piece," he said.

Billy hopped up beside him. "Yeah, we're gonna take you out in steaks."

Duchamp surrendered without further struggle. Gathering his bedsheet around him, Wally meekly let himself be led into the building.

"Piece of cake," Nanos told the surprised Mr. Lovecchio, who was flanked by his equally astonished nephews—a pair of 280-pounders in silk suits.

"Kenny, Louis," the old man said, "help Duchamp in."

Nanos and Billy watched Duchamp and the nephews squeeze three abreast through the courtroom's double doors while Mr. L. counted out their fee from a bulging wad of greenbacks. "You boys do quality work," he said, handing them the cash. "You've got initiative and you've got style. I'll remember that."

"You need something else done, you give us a call," Nanos said as they turned away.

Outside, they were confronted with a minor problem. A nagging eighteen-foot detail.

"What the hell are we going to do with the trailer?" Billy said.

"Unhitch it and split," Nanos answered. "It's his problem, not ours."

As they began to do just that, a man spoke to their backs. He sounded like a cop with a bad case of hemorrhoids. "Hey, you airheads can't just leave that shit here."

They looked up into the smiling face of Nile Barrabas.

7

A raw, northern wind ripped across the frozen cemetery grounds. Claude Hayes squinted into the gusts, his eyes tearing. The full-length leather topcoat he wore did nothing to cut the chill factor. He stamped his feet to keep the circulation going in his toes. "It feels like it's going to snow," he said to the tall, slender black woman standing next to him before the ice-crusted grave.

"It could" was her terse reply.

He felt he had to keep talking, to keep trying, so he did. "But it's spring," he said.

"You haven't been in Detroit for twenty years," the woman said in a voice as cold as the breeze, a voice full of accusation and bitterness. "For every balmy sunny spring we have, there are three just like this. With ice storms or freezing rain or late snow."

Hayes looked at his sister, Janine. The last time he had seen her, she was a long, skinny, junior high schoolkid with a bedroom full of stuffed animals. While he had been away fighting other people's wars, without any help from him she had matured into a beautiful, intelligent woman. She had earned herself a doctorate in urban studies, and had married a fellow professor and had two children with him.

"Are you ready to go?" she asked with impatience, glancing meaningfully at her wristwatch.

More than two decades of separation was proving to be an impenetrable wall between them.

Hayes stared down at the polished marble headstone one last time. Carved into the stone were the names of his parents, their dates of birth and death.

Their surname was not his.

He had given it up, years ago. As he had given up the family and the love that bound it. Not by choice. Never by choice. That was something that Janine either couldn't or wouldn't understand.

Claude's mother and father had died two years apart. On both occasions he had been out of the country on a mercenary mission with Colonel Barrabas. He had missed both funerals. Truth be told, he probably wouldn't have attended them anyway. After all, what was the point? Long before, he had disappointed his middle-class parents, who had expected him to become a lawyer or a teacher, by dropping out of college. That had been in the sixties. He had left school to fight for civil rights in the South. When Dr. Martin Luther King was assassinated, Claude lost control. His rage at the inequities and cruelties of the system exploded...in the wrong place, at the wrong time. He got sentenced to hard time on a Tennessee chain gang. He was too strong and too resourceful to stay there for long. After he escaped, he changed his name, enlisted in the Navy, became a Seal and served with distinction in Vietnam. From the moment he was arrested, he had severed all ties with his family, having decided that he had brought enough shame and hurt to them. Even though subsequent to his arrest he had built a new life for himself, he had continued to keep his distance, unsure how his parents would feel about a son who was a mercenary.

In the months since he had learned of his mother's death, the barriers he had put up to keep out memories of his childhood had started to crumble. He remem-

bered the happy times: his dad driving him to David-
son's Ice Cream Parlor in Highland Park on the way
home from a Tiger game at Briggs Stadium, the whole
family going down to the Greyhound station to meet his
grandparents' bus from Jackson, Mississippi. He remembered wearing his dad's old Army hat and pretending to be a fighter pilot.

He talked about the memories and the feelings they
stirred in him with one of the elder brothers at the con-
templative order in Northern California where he sometimes decompressed after a mission. The brother had told
him flat out that he ought to return to his boyhood home,
to visit his parents' grave and make his peace with the
past. Hayes had resisted the advice. He thought it was too
late, what with his mother and father both dead. But the
memories wouldn't let him be. They dogged him day and
night. In the end he had called the only other person
whose opinion he trusted in matters personal, another
member of Barrabas's mercenary squad, Dr. Leona
Hatton.

She had agreed immediately with the brother's coun-
sel. "You never got to say goodbye," she had told him.
"You never buried your past in a healthy way. Go back.
Walk by the house you grew up in. Go to the cemetery.
And, for God's sake, look up your sister."

He had taken that advice, and despite the chilly reception from his sister, he was glad that he had. His only re-
gret was that he hadn't been able to come here while his
parents were alive.

Janine shattered the reverie.

"Claude?" she said, the made-up name spoken with
evident distaste. "Are you ready? I've got to pick up
some papers in my office before they lock up the building."

He nodded. They walked in silence to her car. The lowering sky promised an early dusk and another bitterly cold night.

"I wonder why they didn't retire someplace warmer?" he asked.

"Like Mississippi? They liked the north."

In the past two days he had seen his sister in a number of different settings, and in each of them she had shown a quick intelligence, an empathy for other people, great warmth—to everyone but him. "I don't blame you for being angry with me," he commented as they pulled out of the cemetery parking lot. "I know I haven't been much of a brother to you, but..."

"We went over all that last night," she returned. "Frankly, I don't see the point in rehashing it."

They traveled several blocks on a residential side street. It was an old part of Highland Park, not far from where he had grown up. The houses were carefully maintained, as were the tiny lawns and hedges.

"What happened to the old house?" he asked.

"They sold it when they moved to the lake."

"Somehow I can't picture them living on a lake in the country. I remember them as urban. Didn't Dad miss going to the Tiger games?"

"He watched them on TV."

"What did they do all day?"

"They gardened and fished."

"Mom fished?"

"Yes. She loved it."

For the first time Claude sensed a slight thaw in his sister. Not much. "When did they start doing that?"

"Dad bought a boat right after he retired. They fished practically every day from April to October. It never mattered to them if they came back with a full stringer or an empty one. They were really..." Janine caught herself. She had responded more openly than she wanted to. "They were happy," she concluded in a voice without animation.

To signal that she didn't want to talk anymore, she inserted a cassette into her tape player. He recognized it immediately, it was a recording of "Bye, Bye, Blackbird" by the classic Miles Davis quintet, with Coltrane on tenor, Red Garland on piano, Paul Chambers on bass and Philly Joe Jones on drums.

Brother and sister listened to the music without talking as they drove toward her office on the campus of Wayne State University.

"Do you like Miles's new stuff?" he asked when the side was finished.

"No," she said without taking her eyes off the road.

"I don't, either. He's playing for people who pretend they like it because the man is supposed to be so hip. Posers. I don't think he gives a fuck anymore."

She glanced at him. "I didn't imagine that you'd like Miles at all."

"What kind of music did you think I'd like?"

She shrugged. "I don't know. What kind of music appeals to a mercenary?" She spit out the word like a curse. "John Philip Sousa? Guy Lombardo? Motorhead?"

Instead of being insulted or angry, Claude began to laugh. He stopped when he saw the fire in her eyes. "Who or what do you think I am, sister?" he said.

"What," she said. "You are definitely a *what*."

"And what's that?"

Janine glared at him. "A right-wing mercenary soldier of fortune, a freebooting bastard who will kill, who will do anything those senile, racist cocksuckers in Washington tell you to."

Claude had known it was coming—the gulf between them, his desertion of her and their family symbolized, compartmentalized, sanitized by political arguments. And he still didn't know what to say to her. He had been a stubborn, even defiant man all his adult life. He had never taken crap from anyone. And he wasn't the kind of person who wasted time trying to explain himself to others. During the past few years, however, he had begun to change. He had looked into his future and seen a dead end. And he had gradually realized that his work with the oppressed and unfortunate in the far-flung corners of the world mattered more to him than the adrenaline rush of his missions with Barrabas. Was he losing his edge? he often wondered of late. Was he, God forbid, mellowing out?

He didn't know.

The person sitting next to him was the closest thing he would probably ever have to a family, now. She was the only one in the world whom he could talk to about his parents and his childhood. And he knew he had to try to connect with her somehow.

"Look, Janine," he said. "Will you please pull off the road and listen to me for a minute?"

"Why?"

"Because I want to talk to you, and I want you to listen to what I have to say without thinking about driving. Then if you still despise me, I'll get out of the car and I promise I won't bother you again."

"The school is just a couple more blocks," she said. "I'll park there."

They rode in silence. She parked in a faculty lot behind an old brick building.

"I don't know what you could possibly say to change my mind," she said, "but go ahead."

"First of all, I want you to know that I'm not ashamed of being a mercenary. I'm a member of an elite team that works for the U.S. government from time to time. I'm not ashamed of that, either. We operate on a case-by-case basis. If the team leader takes on an assignment I am opposed to, I walk."

"It's that simple."

"That simple. More important, I don't do anything just because some politician tells me to. I live by my own code. So do the other members of the team."

"I'm sure that you've all found interesting ways to rationalize covert warfare, the overthrow of governments and murder for hire."

"Sis, the world can be a very nasty place, and sometimes you have to take a side. Sometimes that means backing the lesser of two evils."

"But you kill people for money."

"What bothers you the most? The killing? Or that I do it for money?"

"The killing."

"Sometimes there isn't any other way."

"There's always another way."

"No, Sis, not always."

"I don't agree with you. I never will."

"I'm not asking you to. I just want you to understand where I'm coming from."

"If what you are doing is so noble why do you take money at all?"

"I don't always," he replied. "I've fought for nothing. In fact at times I've paid to fight. Bought my own ticket, my food, my gear."

"Where?"

"In Mozambique."

"Which side were you on?"

"FRELIMO."

Janine stared at him. She knew about FRELIMO. It was the Communist guerrilla organization that ousted the white-dominated Portuguese colonial system, one of the most brutal and exploitative regimes ever seen in Africa.

There were many more things he could have said in his own defense. He could have told her that most of the money he made as a paramilitary soldier went to relief organizations for the downtrodden and those without hope, people suffering and dying in the wake of corrupt politics, border disputes, economic disaster. He could have told her of his work with Dr. Hatton during the Ethiopian famine. He could have, but it wouldn't have changed anything; he could see it in her face. To his sister, he was a coward, a deserter and worse. As intelligent and educated as she was she could not see beyond the stereotypes, and her own long-standing hurt.

He reached for the door handle. "I want to thank you for seeing me," he said, opening the car door. "I mean that sincerely. I love you, Sis."

He got out and shut the door. Without looking back he crossed the slick parking lot. He walked the campus for a while, trying to come to grips with his failure, his sense of loss. Before making contact he had at least had the fantasy of being the prodigal son. That was gone, now. What was behind him was truly done. Buried. Sealed forever.

He stopped at a pay phone and called his hotel. He asked if there were any messages for him. There was one—from Nile Barrabas.

8

Barrabas, Hayes, Billy Two and Nanos were met at Los Angeles International Airport by a white limousine. The uniformed driver helped them load their bags into the trunk, then ushered them into the posh comfort of the vehicle's rear compartment.

"There's nothing like riding in style," Nanos said through a broad grin as the long Cadillac pulled away from the passenger-loading-only zone and headed for the nearest freeway on ramp.

Nothing, indeed. Soon, however, they were going nowhere in style.

The traffic on Interstate 405 was gridlocked, bumper to bumper for as far as they could see. When the limo did move, it crept up a few yards, then stopped. Nobody honked. Honking was like pissing in the wind. Around them was a city tinged with sulfurous gloom—the by-product of its citizens' gainful employment. Factories barfed a particulate stew into the air; workers driving to factories sweetened the pot with car exhaust. L.A. is an unlovely city, with or without smog. A city of concrete and asphalt and crisscrossing overhead power lines. A city with water that tastes like formaldehyde.

Cancer town.

Coronaryville.

Juan Carlos Nochenegra's estate was in the exclusive sub-suburb of Bel-Air Heights, high in the hills above Los Angeles. A place with genuine deciduous trees, instead of scabrous-looking palms. It took them 2½ hours to get there. Not surprisingly Nochenegra had chosen to surround himself with neighbors of similar socioeconomic station. Oil sheikhs. Movie moguls. Princes. Other forcibly retired dictators.

To enter Bel-Air Heights, the white limo had to pass through a security checkpoint that was even more heavy-duty than the Tijuana–San Ysidro international border crossing. It had guards armed with Heckler & Koch SMGs. The gate house was steel-reinforced concrete, and in front of it were staggered concrete slabs four feet high and ten feet long, barriers that would force potential suicide car bombers to swerve and slow down before hitting the gate proper. Set in the pavement on the estate side of the gate house were pop-up, bulldozer-blade barriers made of heavy steel; they could stop a Kenworth doing ninety. Nobody got into Bel-Air Heights without an invitation.

The limo was stopped by the guards outside the gate and everyone was ordered out.

"What is this shit?" Starfoot asked as he was forced to "assume the position" against the side of the limo.

"It's okay, Billy," Barrabas told him.

The guards patted them down and then double-checked their work by running metal detectors over them.

"We've got armaments in the trunk," the colonel said.

While one of the men stood guard, the other ordered the driver to open the trunk, exposing their luggage. He unzipped the ballistic nylon kit bags, which were packed with 9 mm autopistols, mini-Uzis, flash grenades and body armor.

"Son of a bitch!" the guard exclaimed.

"We're special-security consultants to President Juan Carlos Nochenegra," Barrabas said. "We're expected."

"Keep them covered, Bob," the guard said. "I'm going to get Bruno." He trotted into the gate house and returned in a minute with a German shepherd on a lead. The bomb-sniffing dog gave the limo the once-over, inside and out; it even crawled underneath. Except for the kit bags they were clean. The pooch passed its sign of approval by hiking its leg on one of the rear tires.

Only after obtaining clearance from the Nochenegra estate were the SOBs admitted to the grounds.

Starfoot turned and looked back at the gate as they continued up the curving, tree-lined drive. "I don't know about you guys but I thought any minute those dudes were going to pull on rubber gloves and ask us to touch our toes."

"Definitely creepy," Nanos agreed.

"The people who live here have a lot to be afraid of," Hayes said. "They didn't get here by being nice."

The second security gate was just outside the grounds of Nochenegra's estate, which was bordered by a high solid wall topped with iron spikes. The guards were Mantuegan nationals in sand-colored uniforms. They were cross because their guardhouse card game had been interrupted. To everyone's surprise they waved the limo through without checking anything.

The mansion loomed ahead, a Spanish-style monstrosity—seven thousand square feet of flamingo-pink stucco. On the front balconies and windows there was ornate ironwork; there was a splashing fountain, and a row of life-size statues on pedestals. Arched over the main entrance was a bas-relief sculpture of a dragon in flight.

The limo stopped at the foot of the wide entry staircase where they were met by a young lieutenant.

"Good afternoon, Colonel," the officer said, extending his hand. "I'm Ortega. I hope you had a pleasant trip. *El presidente* wishes to see you at once. Your luggage will be attended to. If you will all please follow me..."

They trailed him up the stairs to the main doors and into the mansion. Everything inside was on a truly grand scale. The ceilings were thirty feet high; the floors a giant's checkerboard of black and white marble squares. Featured in the decor were antique furniture, medieval armor, trophy animal heads, Greek and Roman sculpture and full-size trees in great marble pots.

Ortega led them through to the oak-paneled library, where more stuffed animal heads dotted the walls. Behind a huge desk stood a short, stout man in a snow-white uniform shirt with gold shoulder accents. His mirrored aviator sunglasses covered most of his face.

The lieutenant made the introductions, then left the room as Nochenegra bade the Americans to sit down. They took places on the leather-upholstered sofa and armchairs in front of the lifeboat-size desk. Juan Carlos stood, his hands locked in the small of his back.

"I have heard much about you and your private army," the dictator told Barrabas.

"Some of it's probably true."

Nochenegra smiled. "The part about your being immune to bullets?"

"Not that, I'm afraid," Barrabas replied. "And I've got the scars to prove it."

"That's a pity. I was hoping to get a demonstration." Juan Carlos smiled again. "At any rate, I want to explain the current situation to you, both here and in my country. A sort of prebriefing briefing to get you acclimatized, if you don't mind, Colonel."

"Not at all," the white-haired man said. "The sooner we get up to speed the better."

"Excellent." Juan Carlos leaned against the front of his desk. He removed his sunglasses. His eyes were small, brown and wide-set, the whites shot with yellow. There were pinch marks from the sunglasses on the sides of his nose. "As you can no doubt imagine, I have surrounded myself here in Los Angeles with Mantuegans who have served me well in the past—people willing to give their money and their blood to save Mantuego from the Communist threat, people willing to go to the wall for me. I have also maintained close links with my many supporters on the island. Through them, I've been in contact with the three top-ranking generals of the Mantuegan armed forces, who share my concerns over the fate of my country's freedom. All of my sources tell me that the time is ripe, that the people are clamoring for my triumphant return, for an end to the Soarez experiment. It is clear that the reforms of Dr. Soarez aren't working; the economy is in chaos—the price of a bag of rice has gone up five hundred percent since I left. And worse, the PFM is gaining strength by the day. I have irrefutable proof that they are being armed by the Soviets and the Cubans, and that their leaders have been trained by them in guerrilla warfare and tactics."

The dictator began to strut back and forth before his desk, his eyes suddenly unfocused, distant; his expression distinctly pleased. "I am a man of history, like Mandelo there." He gestured toward the large oil painting hanging on the wall behind him. It was of a man in a tropical peasant costume—cutoff baggy cotton slacks held up with a rope belt, open sandals and a frayed straw hat, which he clutched in both hands. He was gaunt but bright-eyed, his head shaved clean as a cue ball. "Do you know of him?"

There were shrugs all around.

Nochenegra picked up a slim leather-bound volume from his desk and handed it to Barrabas. "Read that and it will change your life."

Barrabas accepted the book with reserved thanks. He had done some research of his own on the dictator before coming to L.A., using his connections in the CIA and NSA, and Jessup's private intelligence organization. He had learned that the "man of history" bit was a fiction created solely by the United States intelligence services, a fiction Nochenegra had expanded on and used for his own personal and financial advancement. After the Second World War, the PFM had begun to make its presence known on the island, staging bold daylight bank robberies and bombing military barracks. Nochenegra's predecessor had been an old man, unable to cope. So, to forestall a Marxist takeover, the CIA and NSA created a hero for the people to rally round, a fearless and deadly fighter of communism.

Actually, at the time, Juan Carlos had been little more than a backwoods gangster. He headed a group of roving, apolitical brigands who terrorized farmers, big and small, demanding protection money against pillaging and burning. The CIA "discovered" Juan Carlos and arranged for him to take credit for a series of devastating military victories over the then fledgling PFM. In fact, the CIA had engineered the attacks using mercenary forces recruited from Belgium. It had also engineered an international media blitz, which showed the much younger Nochenegra standing among Communist corpses heaped like cordwood with his stainless-steel Smith & Wesson. The hog leg had been the gift of an American president, all right, but the Disneyland boys had picked it out. They figured it would be a great image builder, and it was. This was the era of the TV cowboy and the off-beat signature weapon—how the hell else could you tell them apart? Shows like *The Rifleman*, *The Rebel*, *Wanted Dead or Alive*, among others, all had trademark guns. Rifles, shotguns and handguns hacked off, stretched out, hoked up; the viewing public ate it up—as they did the little brown cowpoke with the huge shiny pistols.

If Nochenegra was nothing but a fraud and a crook, the PFM threat was real. And that was the bottom line. That was why Barrabas had signed on.

"How many troops on the island are loyal to you?" Barrabas asked Juan Carlos. "What sort of resistance force can we reasonably expect?"

Nochenegra smiled. "By my estimates, ninety percent of the common soldiers will back my return. You see, the good Dr. Soarez is rabidly antimilitary. He wants to cut the equipment budget in half, reduce the standing army by a third and pour the money saved into programs for the poor. He thinks he can buy the loyalty of the masses with free medicine and housing."

Claude Hayes almost said something. He would have if Barrabas hadn't caught his eye and signaled with a look. This was not the time or place for debate.

The dictator walked over to an easel and pulled down a map of the island. He used a wooden pointer to indicate the capital city. "This is the key to victory. Once I have control of Mantuego City, the island is mine."

"Are we talking about a major invasion force?" Barrabas asked.

"No. A few hundred shock troops. My real power will come from the army, from men already there."

"What is the scenario?"

"The generals will order the seizing of the TV and radio stations, and a blockade of the palace. Meanwhile, troops not loyal to me will be isolated and locked in their barracks, put under house arrest. The city will be placed under strict martial law."

"That's when you'll hit the beach?" Barrabas asked. "Then the landing force you're talking about is nonfunctional."

"On the contrary, it is highly functional. It is theater. And the Mantuegan people like nothing better than a good show—with fireworks and a little blood. My goal is to unite and mobilize the armed forces in an all-out push against the PFM. As you can imagine, they'll be trying to do the same against me, to take advantage of the chaos."

"And you're sure of the generals?"

"They want me back in a bad way. They know I'm the only one who can unify the country. They know I'm committed to destroying the PFM. I think it's important to the success of the mission that you meet them face-to-face. I've arranged for you to go to Mantuego in two days' time to meet secretly with the cadre of generals and my other supporters there. You will work out the details of the preliminary operation and set up the timetable for my return to power. Is that agreeable to you?"

"Yes, of course."

"Until then I would like to offer you the hospitality of my house. Tonight there will be a party in honor of my seventh wedding anniversary. You're all invited."

Lieutenant Ortega had waited for them outside the library. Now he escorted them out a side entrance to their quarters in a converted carriage house on the far side of the formal gardens, which were already decked out for the party. Japanese paper lanterns hung in chains from tree to tree. There was a bandstand and, under brightly colored awnings, long buffet tables had been set up. In the garden pools pale blossoms floated, releasing a heady, heavy perfume. Mantuegan and American flags sprouted atop the three strategically placed bar kiosks.

"If there is anything else you need," Ortega told the SOBs, "just use the phone in the kitchen. My office number is listed in the directory."

Nanos waited until the lieutenant left before he spoke. "What do you think, Colonel? Is this whole thing for real?"

Barrabas shook his head and pointed at the door. "I need some air."

They had to assume that the place was bugged.

Outside, in the garden, the four mercenaries walked slowly and talked softly.

"Discounting the fact that the man is a total swine, that what he stands for is corruption and oppression," Hayes said, "from a purely tactical standpoint this operation is full of shit. We have only Nochenegra's word that he has overwhelming support on the island. If he isn't in control of the military, he isn't in control of anything. He's got nothing to back him up. A few hundred guys are going to get used up in the first five minutes of landing."

"Oh, ye of little faith," Billy said, clucking his tongue.

"No, Claude's right," Barrabas said. "This could be a very sticky deal for everybody. And we could be caught square in the middle. We've got to make some decisions, but not until after we see the generals and get a read on them."

"So, we may want to take a walk on this one, Colonel?" Billy asked.

Nanos frowned. "El prezo ain't gonna like that."

"We'll worry about that when the time comes," Barrabas said. "Meanwhile, we're going to do what the man said. We're going to enjoy ourselves."

The Greek, a wicked gleam in his eye, nudged Starfoot with an elbow. "Party hearty."

NANOS AND BILLY TWO STOOD next to one of the long buffet tables, frosty glasses in hand, people-watching. Or to be more exact, female-people-watching. They had given up on the enormous piles of food after a bite or two. The delicacies were all of Mantuegan origin. It was a cuisine that prided itself in the use of the fringes of the edible, things embryonic, cartilaginous, scaled, clawed, overripe to the point of putrefaction. Even the imported salad greens seemed hostile, made as they were of coarse leaves, fuzzy stems, spiny fruits.

There were a lot of women to look at, stunningly beautiful women. Most had escorts.

"And we thought we'd feel out of place here," Billy said. He swept an arm around at the crowd. "Hey, these are our kind of folks."

Nanos nodded. It looked like a goddamn Soldier of Fortune convention, what with all the fatigue pants, camou fabric, webbed belts and jungle boots. About half the guests at the party were Rambos and Rambolinas. His own Army-issue olive drab athletic T-shirt and matching pants fit right in.

Except these folks weren't soldiers. They were accountants and tax consultants. Computer-software CEOs. Young actresses. Fashion models. There were older people, too, guys who looked as if they had retired from heading up some giant corporation, their blue-haired wives in khaki walking shorts and ballistic nylon utility belts. Some of them were obviously Mantuegan. Most of them were not. Juan Carlos had invited American big spenders, people whose business interests would be served and protected by his return to power.

"No doubt about it," Nanos said with a grin, "we're chic as shit."

A curvy blonde in an olive-drab string bikini stepped in front of them to reach the food. "What looks good, guys?" she asked, eyeing Nanos's bulging biceps and pecs with more than casual interest.

"You do," he said, beaming at her creamy flesh.

"I mean the food."

"Well, I thought those round things in red sauce were okay," he said, "until the waiter told me they were sliced sheep nuggets in salsa."

She jabbed a red-painted fingernail at the steaming silver tray. "You mean the *testículos al moho*? Hey, those are great. Classic Mantuegan cooking." She helped herself to a large portion.

Nanos winced as he watched her gobble and chew.

"Say, where did you get those threads?" she asked between mouthfuls. "They're so authentic they're unreal. At Ramon's of Pico?"

"Uh, no."

"Show me the label." She reached for the back of his shirt.

"Uh, I . . ." Nanos muttered.

The blonde looked at the maker's tag and laughed. It was a shocked little laugh, which she instantly stifled. "Oh, my. Oh, you must excuse me..." she murmured as she quickly backed away and melted into the crowd.

"I think we've got a problem, man," Nanos said dejectedly.

"We're too friggin' authentic," Billy said.

In fact, they were major-league rough trade compared to the dinky pseudomercs swaggering around the garden. People gave them a wide berth; the food at their end of the buffet table remained barely touched.

Then Nanos locked eyes with a sinuous and exotic creature, a raven-haired woman of remarkable beauty and grace. She smiled and walked straight for him. Her gait was like a female panther's. She had a wide mouth, huge eyes, high cheekbones, and wore an olive-drab long-tailed officer's dress shirt, belted at the waist with a matching strap. The shirt had only two buttons done up; the two in the middle. The top and bottom of the shirt gaped open as she moved. Nanos could see silky cleavage and belly. And silky upper thighs.

"Are you two enjoying yourselves?" she asked, gazing rapturously up into his face.

"Yeah, it's great," Billy replied.

She ignored the Indian. "God, you're a beautiful beast," she said huskily to Nanos. She put her hand flat against the rock-hard ridges of his stomach. "Umm," she whispered. "I like the feel of that."

Behind them, the band began warming up. It was a Mantuegan group, made up of the customary drum set, congas, accordion, clarinet and violin.

"Oh, I must go now," she said, giving his belly a very friendly pat. "I have to mingle before the music starts. Perhaps later?" She winked at him and left.

"I'm in love," Nanos groaned.

"I don't want to hear this," Billy said.

"No, I mean it, I'm really in love this time."

"Don't you know who that was?"

"Yeah, the girl of my dreams."

"You are the dumbshit of dumbshits," Billy said. "That was el prezo's first lady."

BARRABAS AND HAYES WALKED away from the bar with
drinks in their hands. The colonel sipped his Scotch, the
black man a diet cola.

The party had quickly filled up. There was standing
room only around the bandstand, where guests gyrated
to the insistent beat of the Mantuegan power quintet. It
was an interesting mixture of people and costume. Men
in their sixties in formal attire boogied with svelte star-
lets a third their age clad in the briefest of paramilitary
swimwear. Middle-aged women in evening gowns pogo-
danced alongside crew-cut Schwarzenegger clones in
battle fatigues. All sectors of the world of the movers and
shakers were represented: the diplomatic corps, the military, the multinational conglomerates. And all of them
were hell-bent on having a good time at the dictator's
expense. Barrabas recognized a few of the faces, having
seen their pictures in the media.

"Looks like the dynamic duo is striking out for once,"
Claude said, indicating Billy and Alex with a nod of his
head.

"It's just as well. I need them clearheaded tomorrow."

"Good evening, Colonel," said a voice behind them.

Barrabas turned and looked down at an old man in a
motorized wheelchair—an old man wearing a black string
tie, starched white shirt and black three-piece suit.

"You don't look surprised to see me," the senator remarked, inching his chair forward.

"I figured you'd turn up sooner or later," Barrabas
told him. "After all, Juan Carlos is your boy."

"And from what I gather," the senator said, his eyes
gleaming, "for the foreseeable future you are Juan Carlos's boy. Doesn't that mean you're working for me?"

Barrabas felt a flush of anger creep up his neck. The bad feeling between the two men went back years. As far as Barrabas was concerned the senator stood for everything negative in American political life. He was a lying, scheming, double-dealing son of a bitch who made a mockery out of a supposedly representative form of government. In his quarter century of office, the only thing the senator had ever represented was himself, his own interests. He had sold out everyone he had ever worked with, the liberals, the conservatives, the military, the welfare advocates, and had always come out of the dung heap smelling like designer cologne. It was a funny world—if you liked black comedy. Sometimes the senator's personal interests—those of lining his own pockets and expanding his power base—coincided with the interests of freedom and democracy. As much as he loathed the legislator and what he stood for, Barrabas was enough of a realist to understand that playing the man's game was sometimes the only way to get important things done.

"I was only joking," the senator went on through a smug expression that said just the opposite. Having scored a hit, he immediately withdrew. "We're all working together for the same end."

Barrabas sipped at his drink.

"Nobody wants a Communist government in Mantuego," the lawmaker went on. "I understand that you're going to pay a visit there in a few days. You'll see for yourself how important this mission of ours is. The people of Mantuego deserve better than the yoke of Marxist tyranny."

The mercenary leader turned out the set speech. He looked over the old man's head, watching the couples dance. The native music had a certain lilt to it, melodies set in minor keys and accompanied by a jerky beat. The slow songs, like the one the band was playing now, brought tears gushing from the eyes of expatriate Mantuegans.

When the song ended, a short man in mirror sunglasses climbed onto the bandstand and took the microphone out of its stand. It squealed in protest until the sound technician adjusted the volume. "Welcome, welcome, everyone," Juan Carlos said. "I hope you're all having a wonderful time."

The guests responded with cheers and wild applause; the drummer played along with rim shots and snare-drum rolls.

"As you know," Nochenegra continued, shouting over the tumult, "this party is being given to celebrate the seventh anniversary of my marriage to Luisa. In honor of the occasion she and I are going to sing a special song for you." He gestured at the side of the stage. "Come, Luisa," he said, waving her up. "Come."

"HOLY SHIT," Nanos groaned. "Is this for real?"

"Dueling dictators," Billy said as they watched Luisa join her husband on the stage. She flashed a brilliant smile to the audience as she, too, took a mike from a stand.

Juan Carlos snapped his fingers in the manner of a brown-eyed Sinatra giving the band the tempo. The musicians came in together, and with gusto; Luisa started dancing to the beat. The sway of her hips, the shimmy of her shoulders drew everyone's immediate and complete attention. She was a knockout when standing still; in motion she was nothing short of phenomenal.

"I know that tune...." Nanos frowned as he tried to recall the name.

"Oh, Luisa..." Juan Carlos sang, crooning to his wife of seven years.

"Yes, Juan?" responded Luisa over her shoulder, hips provocatively tilted.

"How do you call your lover boy?"

"Come here, lover boy."

"And if he won't come?"

"Oh, lover boy..."

"And if he still won't come?"

"Bay-baby, ooooooh, bay-bay..."

It was gross. It was disgusting. But of course the crowd loved it. Juan Carlos and Luisa played the lovey-dovey duet broad as a barn, mugging and hamming it up as they traded lines back and forth.

"I think I'm going to puke," Nanos said.

"I told you she was his wife," Billy said. "I didn't say she could carry a tune."

"Would you look at those legs?" the Greek moaned. "Look at what she's *doing* with them."

"Yeah, yeah," Billy muttered.

The tribute to Mickey and Sylvia went through two false endings and two encores. The dictator and his beautiful wife descended from the stage to riotous applause. The band picked up right where it had left off, playing Mantuegan torch songs.

Nanos watched Luisa as she hurried through the crowd, making a beeline for the mansion. "I'm gone, man," he told the Indian as he pushed into the throng.

Billy caught up with him and clapped a hand on his arm. "Hey, where are you going?"

"She wants me, I know it."

"You don't know diddly squat. She was just being friendly. A proper jet-set hostess."

Nanos deflated momentarily. Even he had his doubts. "Well, I've got to find out, one way or another, or it's going to drive me nuts."

"You're already nuts. And you're going to get us both in big trouble."

"Look, Starfoot, I'm not asking you to stick your neck out for me on this. I don't need a chaperon. You don't have to tag along."

"Yeah, right," Billy said, "I'll just stand around choking my gopher while you get yourself diced and sliced and made into some kind of spicy side dish a dog wouldn't eat. Someone's got to watch your back."

"Come on, then."

They followed her into the mansion, through a ground floor packed with celebrating people. She headed up the main staircase to the second floor. Starfoot and Nanos discreetly pursued, pausing at the top of the landing to peer down the hallway. They were just in time to see her enter a room on the right and shut the door after her.

"What now?" Billy asked.

"Wait here."

"Alex . . ."

The Greek hurried down the hall to the door she had entered. He turned the handle and it gave. He opened the door quietly. Before slipping in, he gave Billy a thumbs-up sign. The Indian rolled his eyes in exasperation and made hurry-up gestures with both hands.

You got no romance, Redman, Alex thought as he pushed into a small guest suite. His intent was to throw himself at Luisa's lovely feet, profess his undying lust for her and pray to God she took mercy on him. His intent was sandbagged at once. Sandbagged by sounds coming from the other side of the suite's only visible door. Most disturbing sounds, they were. Luisa the luscious was not alone. He tiptoed to the door, which stood slightly ajar, and peeked in.

What he saw poleaxed him.

Like a kicked dog with his tail between his legs, he retreated to the hallway and carefully shut the door after him.

"Well?" Billy demanded as he approached. "What the hell happened? You were only in there a second."

"She already had company."

"Huh?"

"The first lady is in there getting it on with some other guy. And Billy, it was just like that song."

"What song?"

"The one she and el prezo sang."

"You mean, 'Love is Strange'?"

A crooked grin twisted the Greek's lips. "Man, what was going on in there was strange-and-a-half."

9

"So glad you could join us on this special night," Nochenegra said to the senator as he motored his chair into the mansion library.

"My pleasure, Juan Carlos," the old man replied. "My distinct pleasure."

The dictator shut the library door and walked around to his desk.

"I must admit that I get a vicarious charge out of successful marriages like yours," the lawmaker went on expansively. "It reaffirms my faith in the abiding rightness of the institution. I have always believed that it is the bedrock of our—"

Nochenegra cut him off. "The real reason I asked you here was to request that you do me another small favor."

The senator's face tightened for an instant, then relaxed into an overly broad smile.

Nochenegra purely loved it. For years he had shifted in the breeze blown by Washington, in the hot air gusting from the lips of men like the senator; it was the wind of power. Oh, he had steered his own course, right enough, and the course of his country, too, alternately tacking, running full out, but his movement was dependent on the wind's velocity, its direction, its constancy.

Now, the dictator was the hot wind.

And they both knew it.

"Of course, Juan Carlos," the legislator said, the picture of genial affability. "You know I'm ready to back you to the limit."

"I'm gratified to hear you say that, because it is time to execute phase two of my plan."

"Phase two?" the senator repeated, his brows furrowing. "Since when is there a phase two?"

"There has always been a phase two," Nochenegra told him. "You just didn't need to know about it until now."

"I'm listening."

"I'm sure you recall the many reports I passed to you on the weaponry being supplied to the PFM by the Soviets and their client states."

"Reports that I used to great advantage in swinging support to your cause."

Juan Carlos smiled. "Would it surprise you to learn that those reports were only partially true?"

"You gave me photographic evidence of PFM arms caches uncovered by Mantuegan government troops. The weapons were all of Soviet design, if not Soviet manufacture: AK-47 assault rifles, RPK light machine guns, RPG-7 rocket-propelled grenades. Now you're saying the photos were faked?"

"No, I am not. The weapons caches were real enough and the matériel involved was ComBloc."

The senator's face took on a rosy glow, not the glow of good health but the flush of rapidly building irritation. He didn't like being toyed with. "I don't have a clue what you're getting at."

"It's simple," Juan Carlos said. "Since my departure from the island, the PFM has been supplied with Soviet arms, but the Soviets did not do the supplying."

The lawmaker's face turned a darker shade of red as he pondered the puzzle. Then, as it suddenly all became clear to him, his jaw dropped.

Juan Carlos found the senator's shock most satisfying.

"You?" the old man exclaimed. "You have been delivering weapons to the guerrillas?"

Nochenegra shrugged. "An inspiration? Or perhaps a touch of genius? Think about it. How could I let the PFM wither and die? They are the enemy that my supporters are the most fearful of. That fear is what makes them unite behind me, what ultimately gives me my strength."

"So, the repeated Communist attacks against the Soarez government have been your doing."

"The last thing I want is for Dr. Soarez to defeat the PFM or make peace with them. I need the guerrillas to remain a potent force. I need them to keep the pressure on Soarez, to appear to be gaining purchase despite his best efforts. Given the nature of the PFM, its leaders and its followers, I am much more concerned about their running out of bullets than about their coming to terms with the Social Democrats."

"But how? Do the guerrillas know who's sending them the guns? I thought these people were rabid Marxist-Leninist ideologues."

"Oh, they are. No doubt about it." Nochenegra let the old man simmer a few seconds, then he continued, "When I left the country I took with me the entire FSI file on the PFM. I had names, backgrounds and physical descriptions, if not photographs of all the leaders. Through an intermediary, I made contact with El Ticón and Major Zed."

"This is astounding. They didn't have any idea who they were dealing with?"

"*Are* dealing with, Senator. And they do have an idea—it's just a mistaken one. My intermediary happens to be a Cuban, who knows some Angolans whom the PFM had approached in the past, seeking military assistance. The PFM thinks it is being supplied by Castro."

"They are that stupid?"

"Put it this way, when they see ten crates of brand-new Kalashnikovs, their IQs drop seventy points. And they forget all the questions they had made up their minds to ask."

"If you've been supplying them all along, what's this phase two?"

"I have been supplying them limited quantities of matériel. Fairly precise amounts, actually. Precise and purposefully imbalanced. Thanks to me they have quite a few guns, but their ammunition stockpile is very low. Roughly fifteen rounds, one-half magazine per man. I have been maintaining it at that level for months now. I keep them frustrated, conservative, but able to stage skirmishes, small raids, to snipe, to harass and infuriate. I am providing them with weapons, but I have absolutely no interest in seeing them win."

"Of course."

"Phase two will open the arms and munitions flow and, accordingly, allow the guerrillas to widen the scope of the conflict. I still don't want the PFM to win, but I do want them to appear to be a real threat, able to seize power. I want the Soarez government to think its back is to the wall. While it's battling the Communists I have armed, I will move in and take control of the country. When I am done with Soarez and his liberal cronies, I will deal with the PFM. I will kill enough of them to reduce the threat they represent, but I will certainly leave enough of them alive to act as a nucleus and a springboard for the group's future resurrection."

The senator shifted uneasily in his chair. "And just what is this small favor?" he said.

"I want you to arrange for the delivery of the phase-two weapons shipment."

For a moment the senator was speechless. Then he exploded. "Me? You want me to send guns to Communists? Are you completely insane? Do you have any idea what would happen to my political career if word ever leaked out? If complicity was ever even hinted at? The White House, Congress, the intelligence community, they'd all think I was a traitor. A goddamn Soviet double agent, a deep mole. Everything I've ever done on the Hill would be sifted through, analyzed; facts and figures would have to match up. And they wouldn't. I'd be dead meat in forty-eight hours."

Nochenegra nodded. He knew, all right. "That's why you're just the right man for the job. You're highly motivated. And I know you'll be very, very careful."

The senator fumed. He sputtered. His Adam's apple bobbed. But gradually, with a great deal of effort, he regained control of himself.

"You've got me, we both know that," he admitted. "As long as you hold the evidence against me I must do as you say. But I want a guarantee right now that in terms of my personal risk, this is the end of it. There won't be any more nasty surprises before you land in Mantuego City."

"You have my word," Nochenegra promised. "This is the last favor I will ask of you."

"And the incriminating documents about our dealings in Mantuego, all copies of same, will be turned over to me the moment you set foot on the island?"

"I have so instructed my attorney here in Los Angeles. If you care to call him to verify those instructions, I will give you his name."

"Yes, under the circumstances, I think I will call him."

Juan Carlos scribbled a name and number on a pad, then tore off the page and handed it to the legislator. "You and I have had a long and mutually profitable relationship, Senator," he said in a conciliatory tone. "I trust that what I have been forced by fate to do, for the sake of my country, will not stand in the way of our continued friendship after I have regained the presidency."

The senator glanced at the name and number, then folded the paper once and tucked it in the watch pocket of his black vest. He looked up at the dictator and held him in a steady gaze. "I'm not a man to hold a grudge, Juan Carlos."

The dictator had to turn away to keep from laughing in the lawmaker's face. Not a man to hold a grudge! What a rich joke that was! Once Juan Carlos was back in power, the senator would come crawling to him on his belly, his useless spindly legs dragging behind, begging to be allowed to renew their long association.

Not that Nochenegra would turn him away. The senator had important contacts. He had the goods on people in the right places. He could swing votes, arrange for last-minute amendments. In short, he held the key to a whole galaxy of possibilities.

But the terms of the partnership, the terms would be much, much different.

WHEN LUISA ENTERED the mansion's guest suite she had no idea what slavering horror lay in wait for her. Therein was the thrill, the lure—the unexpected, the monstrous hunkered somewhere just out of sight. She could sense its presence; it gave off waves of heat that throbbed against her skin and set her pulse pounding at her temples, made her breath come in short, quick gasps.

She took a look behind the door she had entered through.

Nothing. A blank wall.

Cautiously but quickly she advanced into the room. She angled herself so she could peer around the back of the sofa from a secure distance. Her every nerve, every sinew on edge, she was ready to scream and flee in panic.

The unkillable, ravening beast was not behind the sofa. She wanted to turn back, to leave while she was still safe, to leave without knowing what it was, but she could not. Something drove her on.

The former actress was lost in a role of her own making. A part that, while not particularly original, was very juicy, indeed. She had first played it as a girl of twelve in the cardboard shacks of El Infierno. Not by choice, then. Her uncle had done the script. Her awful drunken uncle. After she had fully come of age, blossomed as a young woman, her experience had stood her in good stead. It had helped her in her career in more ways than one. She knew how to perform—both in front of the cameras and on the casting couch.

Acting was an escape for her. The escape she needed from her life, from herself, from her husband of seven years.

It was her balm and solace.

As she moved away from the sofa, she didn't think once about her lost wardrobe. She didn't call up once the

stomach-wrenching image of slum-dwelling sluts split-
ting her Paris gowns as they hauled them down over their
pendulous breasts and mushy bellies, over hips yards
across. And best of all, she didn't have to visualize the
looting bitches trying on her shoes. Seeing their coarse,
rank, unwashed feet, toenails ingrown, blackened, long
and thick like talons—stout, clublike feet jamming into
her slender and artfully turned slippers, stretching them
into unrecognizable, ruptured things.

It was a tragedy that existed only inside her mind. Her
wardrobe was eminently replaceable. There was plenty of
money now to rebuild it. What she couldn't get over was
that her clothes, her shoes, her accessories had been left
behind and vandalized. They were more than fabric and
tanned animal hide. They were part of her, reflecting her
good taste, her personality, her wit. She felt the loss as
strongly as she might have the death of a close sibling, a
twin.

Luisa considered calling out to break the tension. *Is
anyone there? Darling, is that you?* Dialogue from her
films popped into her head unbidden. No, she mustn't.
She must prolong the delicious tension.

Her hands trembling, she pulled aside a Chinese
screen.

Nothing.

She did a complete turn. The room was empty.

Surely, then, the bedroom was the hiding place. Her
knees gone suddenly soft, ankles wobbling as her high
heels caught in the pile of the carpet, she moved to the
door. She put her hand on the doorknob—and jerked
back with a moan. An electric shock, static from the rug,
had zapped her. She stared at her hand, her shaking
hand, and felt a quick stab of fear, which changed, even

as she recognized it, into something warm and tingling that took her breath away.

She caught the knob again and turned it, pushing open the door. As she did so, she raised her right hand in front of her face, a reflexive gesture to ward off the anticipated attack.

None came.

She moistened her lips. Soon, now, surely. Soon it had to happen. As she stepped forward, she felt the tingle again, only stronger, deeper.

The bedroom had a king-size bed with a pink satin comforter. There was no one on it or under it.

She found herself facing two doors. One led to the bathroom. The other was a sliding door that covered the room's walk-in closet.

The bathroom, she told herself. It had to be the bathroom.

She threw herself at the door, entering in a sudden blind rush, daring it to happen. Panting, she swept back the shower curtain, exposing dry white tile, translucent pink soap in the soap dish, a back scrubber.

Then it was the closet, after all. Heart thudding in her throat, she turned back—and came face-to-face with terror.

Looming over her was a huge brown bear with yellow pig eyes, lolling red tongue and dripping fangs.

"Uhhh!" she cried, recoiling, stepping back, fluttering her slender arms.

The bear snarled and advanced, driving her back into the bathroom.

Luisa retreated until she could go no more, then she jumped atop the toilet seat and pleaded for mercy. "No, no, please," she gasped, leaning helplessly against the wall.

It moved closer, shaggy bear arms encircling her, and she could smell the beast, its dense and matted fur. Bear stink, raw, primal, enfolded her.

With a low growl, the bear thrust its broad muzzle against her belly. She felt the points of its teeth through the fabric of her shift, against her flesh.

The muzzle dropped lower.

"Oh, God!" she cried.

The bear was sniffing her, then nuzzling, driving at her.

She tried to push the heavy, coarse-haired head away, but she couldn't. The beast was too strong. The sensation of complete helplessness made her feel faint.

While she was struggling with its head, the bear somehow got her belt loose. Her shirtdress fell open. The animal's great paws were inside, fur against the silk of her skin, the long curved claws teasing over her naked body.

She wanted to fight but she couldn't. It was too strong, too determined. A paw slipped down between her legs. She cried out. Not from pain, but from delight.

"Oh, please, stop. Please," she moaned. "Don't do this to me."

Of course what she meant was just the opposite. Luisa was a very complicated lady. As for the bear, it was not stupid. It knew exactly what was required. With a roar, it scooped her off her perch and bore her into the bedroom.

Luisa shrieked at the feel of all that dank fur against her bare skin. She shrieked and hung on to it for dear life.

The bear put her down on the bed on her stomach, then quite gently lifted her up onto knees and elbows and paused to fumble with its zipper.

"Hurry!" she groaned, burying her face in the satin coverlet, then chewing it.

The bear hurried. It took her after the fashion of a bear, from behind, with savage thrusts.

Luisa, for her part, knelt under the hairy, befanged, beclawed onslaught, caught in the power of the bear embrace, surrendering utterly to ursine passion.

It was wonderful.

She told the bear so in no uncertain terms.

She told him she loved what he was doing, that she didn't ever want him to stop.

Hearing this, the bear, being only human, came to the end of its tether in short order. The mad squirming on the satin coverlet doubled and redoubled, peaking, then it slowed and gradually stopped altogether. The bear slipped off the bed and rolled to its hind feet.

Luisa lay on her side, panting, peering at the glassy-eyed creature. "No, don't take it off yet," she said as the paws reached up to the head. "Another minute..."

The bear groaned.

And Luisa relented. "Oh, all right."

The bear removed its head, exposing a beet-red human face drenched with sweat, and black, short-cropped hair plastered to its skull. The man quickly unzipped the front of his costume and stepped out of it, his naked body gleaming.

"That damned suit!" Lieutenant Ortega gasped, bending over and grasping his knees. "It's like an oven inside. I can hardly breathe."

"Poor baby."

"You can laugh, Luisa, but that damned thing is going to kill me one of these days."

10

At eleven the next morning, a cleanup crew was busy in the garden, clearing away the aftermath of the party, taking down the Japanese lanterns, fishing glassware from the ornamental ponds, raking cocktail napkins and swizzle sticks from the flower beds. Barrabas sat on a garden bench, watching the activity without actually seeing it, his mind focused on other, more important things.

In every dangerous mission there was a fail-safe point, a point after which there could be no turning back. Since his very first command, he had always made a habit of identifying that crucial point, nailing it down tight, before he led his people into action. That was one of the reasons that he had survived so long in what was primarily a young man's game. It was also one of the reasons why he had managed to gather such a good team around him. They knew that, as much as was humanly possible, Nile Barrabas left nothing to chance. Every mercenary, every foot soldier for that matter, knows that luck, good or bad, can affect the outcome of any mission. The trick was to avoid giving chance more than its due.

Of course, the trouble was sometimes that the damned fail-safe point changed after the ball got rolling. Sometimes it came and went before you could do anything about it. Or before you even knew it. Nile Barrabas was not a man troubled by nightmares. When he was disturbed, he flat out couldn't sleep. Fear of miscalculating or missing the fail-safe, of getting his men in a fix he

couldn't get them out of, of being ultimately responsible
for their deaths, had kept him staring at the ceiling all of
the preceding night.

This mission was turning into one of the spooky ones.
There were too many unanswered questions. Too many
players. Too many possibilities. It was conceivable that
they were already too far in to back out without a fire-
fight—assuming that Nochenegra wanted to keep his
plans for a countercoup secret, and that he would kill
them to do it. And there was also the possibility that the
generals in Mantuego had their own plans for succession
and that Juan Carlos didn't fit in with them. By going to
Mantuego as the former dictator's emissaries, Barrabas
and his men were putting their butts on the line.

"So deep in thought," Juan Carlos said, stepping up
quietly behind him. "Has the writing of the great Mandelo already stimulated your mind?"

"To be honest," Barrabas said, "I haven't had a
chance to more than glance at the book. I was planning
to read it tomorrow during the flight to Mantuego."

"Very appropriate. It will prepare you to understand
what you are about to see. I suggest that you pay particular attention to his 'Ode to Servitude.' It is most in-
sightful."

"Thanks, I'll remember that."

"And now, if you and your men are not busy, I
thought perhaps you'd like to accompany my little entourage down into town. We have a duty call to make on
one of my newest franchise operations."

Barrabas nodded. "Sounds great. I'll get my people."

"Meet us in front of the mansion." The dictator smiled
and walked on.

Barrabas returned to the carriage house where the
others waited. They looked bored and restless. The run

would do them good. "Get your gear together, men," the colonel said. "We're going to take a ride with Juan Carlos."

"As what?" Billy said. "Security?"

"More like backup, the way I read it. Who knows? Take your handguns and get into your body armor. You're going to have to start getting used to wearing it. From now on, I expect you guys to sleep in it."

Hayes frowned at him. "Do you know something you aren't telling us, Colonel?"

"I've got a feeling, that's all."

The others looked at one another. They knew all about the colonel's "feelings." His sixth sense had saved their behinds more than a few times.

Hayes, Nanos and Starfoot joined their leader in pulling off their shirts, putting on the Kevlar, then pulling their shirts back on.

"I want you guys to stay tight, understand?" Barrabas told them. "Full-time tight."

"Sure. You got it," Nanos said, shrugging into his shoulder holster. He pulled his Beretta 92 SB from its sheath and dropped the magazine into his palm. With his thumbnail he counted fifteen 9 mm hollowpoints. Satisfied that the clip was fully loaded, he returned the mag to the pistol butt and slid the automatic back into the holster. He then checked the two spare magazines that hung as a counterbalance from the opposite shoulder strap.

They all finished gearing up within seconds of one another.

"Let's roll," Barrabas said.

They walked around to the front of the mansion and, at Lieutenant Ortega's instruction, got into the second of two white Caddy limousines. Ahead of the matching limos was a big gray Mercedes sedan, the point vehicle, which carried the armed security team.

Already in the back of their limo was a rotund Mantuegan with a mustache. He introduced himself as Colonel Riban Enriquez. He wasn't wearing a military uniform; instead he had on an expensive silk suit. He had egg on his tie.

"Do you know exactly where we're headed?" Hayes asked the stranger as the convoy pulled away from the mansion.

"Certainly. We're going to attend the grand opening of Juan Carlos's one-hundredth franchise restaurant. It's quite a milestone for him."

"Franchise restaurant?" Alex repeated incredulously. "I didn't know he was into things like that. I heard all about his real-estate holdings, the shopping malls, the apartment blocks, the time-share-condo business on Maui, interests in South African goldfields, things like that. I'm surprised that he would mess around with something as rinky-dink as fast food."

"You would be surprised, I think, to learn just how profitable *el presidente*'s franchises have become. I don't have the figures on the tip of my tongue, but I know it must be in the tens of millions of dollars. Annually."

"Nothing to sneeze at, for sure," Billy agreed.

"What branch of the armed forces are you in?" Hayes asked the Mantuegan.

"The FSI," Enriquez replied. "The Internal Security Force. It's a very important job, what with the Communist threat my country faces. Infiltration and subversion, as well as overt acts of violence. The enemy can be quite subtle when it suits his needs."

Hayes kept prodding. "Didn't the new president, Soarez, disband your unit as his first official act?"

Enriquez's expression changed. Under his golden skin, there was a flush of red. "Dr. Soarez has made a public show of trying to break us up. To please the PFM, no doubt. But my men are still one hundred percent loyal to me—" he paused to correct himself "—to President Nochenegra. When he returns to Mantuego, they will rise up and rally to the cause. You see, we are the military elite of my country. We wear special uniforms. We have special, separate barracks. It is a testimony to our importance to the security of the nation."

"I read something about human rights abuses," Hayes continued, playing dumb, much to the amusement of Nanos and Starfoot.

"So much to-do over nothing," Enriquez scoffed. "The so-called exposés about our treatment of prisoners and the disappearance of students and opposition leaders were Communist fabrications. The FSI is the most potent weapon we have against the spread of the PFM. Dr. Emilio Soarez is not at all interested in stopping the PFM, so he did away with the FSI."

Barrabas knew enough about the tactics and procedures of the FSI to be able to make comparisons—with SAVAK under the Shah or the Ton Ton Macoute under Papa Doc. A bunch of illiterate bullyboys with guns and clubs, sadists turned loose on a defenseless populace, the purpose being to keep everybody afraid, cowed, under control.

Conversation, such as it was, petered out; Hayes had tired of the game. The group rode in silence down to Westwood, then turned onto Santa Monica Boulevard and headed for the beach. The convoy drew little or no attention from fellow motorists. In a town where Rolls-Royces and Ferraris were a common sight, a couple of one-way-windowed limos were no big deal. A sight not even worth a second look from the drivers and passengers who pulled up alongside them at stoplights.

In Santa Monica proper, the convoy turned into a shopping-mall parking lot, one quarter of which had been cordoned off, surrounding a fast-food restaurant that occupied a corner of the block. The limos pulled up to the sawhorse barricade and stopped so that men in flame-orange vests could move the barriers out of the way, allowing the cars to enter the secure area.

Alex leaned forward to fully take in the restaurant's prominent sign. "Mr. Cheesy?" he said.

"Mr. Cheesy's Restaurant," Enriquez corrected him.

"Cute," Billy said, wincing.

The restaurant sign was itself rather remarkable. A twenty-foot-tall, cuddly-wuddly, jauntily whiskered gray mouse clung to a barber-striped pole. From his back, extended like a cape blowing in the breeze, was the place's name and its slogan: Mr. Cheesy's Restaurant. Where The Fondue Never Stops. Also cute was the big banner across the front entrance proclaiming the place to be the one hundredth in the Mr. Cheesy chain.

The building below the sign and banner was modern, stark, utilitarian. Its outside was paneled in gray-stained wood; it had floor-to-ceiling barber-striped poles in the service area.

Barrabas and the others got out and joined the Nochenegra party under the banner. Immediately they were surrounded by members of the Los Angeles press corps. All of them seemed wildly excited, as though they were experiencing the biggest event to hit L.A. in twenty years.

Juan Carlos's security team, which was made up of stocky, alert ex-military types, put themselves between the dictator and the press. The reporters clamored for attention, jumping up and down, shouting questions to Juan Carlos, questions that wouldn't wait.

A female correspondent for *Entertainment Tonight* shrieked the loudest and got the former president-for-life's attention. "How do you feel, Mr. Nochenegra?" she bleated.

The other journalists were disgusted. It was the one question they all were dying to ask.

Juan Carlos smiled for the cameras. He waved. "I feel wonderful," he said. "This is a great day for everyone connected with Mr. Cheesy."

From the back of the media crowd, a reporter from the Public Broadcasting Station shouted, "How true are the rumors about the collapse of Dr. Soarez's government?"

Nochenegra answered by saying, "Everyone, please, let's go inside. Today lunch is on me."

The TV news teams and print journalists did lockstep quick turns and herded en masse into the restaurant. Barrabas and his men brought up the rear.

Inside the place everything was white enamel and stainless steel. At the counter one ordered one's choice of fondue—four kinds of cheeses, two kinds of chocolate and a mixed tropical fruit sauce—which was served up in a white plastic bowl, piping hot, fresh from the microwave. Prices for the fondues ranged between $3.00 and $5.00. Something to dip was also offered. A plate of bread crusts—sourdough, pumpernickel, or whole wheat—cost $2.50. Fresh raw-vegetable medley was $3.25. Fresh thawed fruit was $4.00.

So, for around six bucks and change the customer could have a hell of a light snack.

"Sure smells cheesy in here," Nanos observed, wrinkling his nose.

"Smells like money," Hayes said. "Do you have any idea the kind of profit these people are making? The ingredients plus labor on this junk must be under fifty cents a pop."

It was definitely not Barrabas's idea of a fun place. Cloying was more like it. The background music was predictably light and cute. A Muzak, all-strings version of "The Teddy Bear's Picnic."

Juan Carlos and Luisa bellied up to the service counter to take ceremonial first bites of chocolate-dipped strawberries, feeding each other for the cameras.

"Delicious!" the dictator pronounced. "Now, everyone, please help yourselves."

The journalists crushed forward, chowing down to beat the band, raving as they did so about the "quality of the food," the "integrity of the decor."

Barrabas tried some of the Swiss-cheese fondue when it was pressed upon him. The bread was stale and the fondue pasty and lukewarm.

Mrs. Nochenegra, her public duty done, worked her way through the crowd to the door, smiling stunningly. She was followed by Lieutenant Ortega. They headed across the asphalt to the first limo. Ortega saw to it that she was comfortably ensconced inside, then he started back for the restaurant.

The Greek frowned into his plate.

"Still nursing a little thing for her, Alex?" Billy inquired.

Nanos shook his head. "No, I'm off her. Definitely. Completely. A relationship with a woman like her would be way too much work."

"Nice work if you can get it."

"A strain..."

"On the body?"

"No, I could handle that. A strain on the imagination."

Barrabas smiled. After a thirty-year childhood, Alex Nanos appeared to be growing up finally. He turned to drop his plate in the trash receptacle and something slammed him.

Something tremendous.

It knocked him over the can and drove him shoulder first into the wall.

The explosion was so loud and so close he didn't even recognize it as sound. It was impact. Collision. It short-circuited his ears, his nerves. He had an instant of crystal clarity before everything went black. He saw the plate-glass windows whooshing out onto the parking lot, followed by flying shadows—bodies and parts thereof.

As he bounced off the wall, landing on his feet, a heavy weight hit him behind the knees and he fell. That was when he blacked out. He came to almost at once, coughing and choking. Dense black smoke poured over him and rushed out the open window frames.

He shook off the dazedness, trying to focus. The wall in front of him was so splattered with blood it looked pink. He twisted up to a crouch. Between him and the counter, behind which the explosion had taken place, there was nothing but carnage. The journalists who had been tightly packed in front of the counter had been blown apart, practically vaporized by the blast. On the floor was a tangle of bloodied bodies, a maze of legs, arms, all beginning to stir. Beginning to scream.

Hayes had collapsed. Barrabas could see the black man rousing from semiconsciousness, groaning. He appeared to be unhurt, though it was hard to say for sure, what with all the gore that had drenched him. Likewise, Nanos and Starfoot seemed to be all right. They struggled up out of the mass of bodies, fisting the blood from their eyes.

The security-team survivors started shouting, *"¡Presidente! ¡Presidente!"* They blundered about, turning over the dead and the wounded with little regard for decorum or comfort, searching for their missing leader.

At last they found him, and saw that Juan Carlos was soaked with blood. But not his own.

"Out of the way!" the security-team leader bellowed, bulldozing a path over and through the fallen people, leading his men and his president to the door.

"Wait!" Barrabas reached out for the security chief with one hand while he yanked his Browning clear of shoulder leather with the other, but the team leader had darted past him to dash through the doorway and out onto the parking lot.

Autofire rattled from across the lot. A tight, controlled burst. The security man crashed to earth, his face hanging down over the curb, blood surging from multiple torso through-and-throughs.

"Everybody down!" Barrabas shouted.

More automatic-weapon fire grazed through the ruined restaurant.

Hayes, Nanos and Starfoot moved up beside the colonel, their guns in their fists.

"Do you see them?" Hayes asked.

"No," Barrabas told him, "I've got no clear targets. The fire is coming from the parked cars on the other side of the barricade."

Bullets whined overhead, clanging into the stainless-steel cookware.

"We're pinned down but good," Billy said.

"Get me out of here!" Juan Carlos shouted at their backs.

Across the lot, Lieutenant Ortega was down, wounded by flying glass from the explosion or a slug from the hit men. There was only one limo in the cleared area; the one Luisa had gotten into was gone, its driver having pulled away the instant after the explosion. The remaining limo was between the lieutenant and the source of the auto-fire, shielding him from it. As they watched, Ortega pushed himself up to his knees.

"Get the limo over here!" Barrabas shouted to him, but the lieutenant seemed dazed.

Another barrage forced everyone in the restaurant back down to their bellies. The bullets were coming from two directions now; the survivors of the explosion were caught in a cross fire.

"What's he waiting for?" Nochenegra cried. "Ortega, get the car! Ortega, damn you!"

Time was a-wasting. Any second the shooters were certain to advance on Mr. Cheesy and mop up on the survivors.

Barrabas couldn't wait any longer. "Put up some covering fire," he said, pausing for a couple of seconds while the other three mercenaries got into position. Then he inhaled sharply and jumped out of the doorway, running in a low crouch, his weapon out in front.

Machine-gun slugs thwacked and skipped off the pavement at his heels as he sprinted for Ortega. Behind him, Hayes, Nanos and Starfoot returned fire. They were all excellent marksmen, and for a second the SMG barrage stopped. The pause was long enough for Barrabas to reach the lieutenant.

"You okay?" Barrabas asked, putting an arm around him and hurrying him to the side of the limo.

"Uhh, yeah. I think so."

But Barrabas saw that the man's eyes were unfocused. He had been going to suggest that Ortega drive, but it was out of the question in the condition he was in. He opened the limo's passenger door, slid across the seat, then pulled the stunned lieutenant in after him.

Slugs pounded the driver's side of the Caddy, shaking the heavy vehicle on its springs, spiderwebbing the armored glass. But it held.

Barrabas found the ignition and started the engine. Jerking it into gear, he stomped on the gas and swerved the long car around to block the line of fire into the restaurant's entrance.

Hayes rushed out and opened the near rear door. Nanos and Starfoot hauled Juan Carlos between them like a bag of laundry and shoved him into the back of the limo. Colonel Enriquez, his right arm badly lacerated, his face ashen with shock, followed.

The instant he was safely inside the car, Nochenegra started shouting at Barrabas. "Drive! Go!" He pounded on the privacy window with his fists. He was hysterical.

Barrabas did not drive, did not pull away. He waited for his men to clamber to safety in the back of the Cadillac.

It proved to be a few seconds too long.

A hail of bullets slapped the limo broadside. Then the tires on that side fore and aft both blew out, and the limo slumped to the right.

"Shit!" Barrabas stomped on the gas again and the car veered crazily. The limo wouldn't steer straight. It slewed insistently to the right.

Across the lot, he could see five men in flame-orange vests advancing—the parking lot crew—automatic weapons blinking in their hands.

"What are you doing?" the dictator cried as Barrabas brought the car to a sudden halt.

"They're gonna overrun us," Nanos said.

"Bail out, let's take 'em!" Barrabas growled, slamming the transmission into park and throwing open his door.

He stood to face the oncoming killers, using the car's bullet-proof door as a shield. The other mercenaries did likewise. All the doors popped open, and above each door was a head and a handgun.

Barrabas squinted into the sizzling wind of death, rested his Browning against the top of the door and fired. He kept firing at a running man, aiming low, leading the rapidly advancing target until it finally went down.

Bullets skipped off the windshield and rattled the door against his knees. Barrabas ignored the danger and swung his sights on another of the advancing men. Something seared his cheek, a red-hot blade, and suddenly his neck was wet. The wetness was sliding down inside his shirt. Barrabas bore down, squeezing the trigger with precision, punching out round after round.

The second man stumbled and, arms outstretched, fell onto his face.

Hayes, Nanos and Starfoot, firing from the other side of the car, had cut down two others.

That left the last attacker sort of high and dry, running full tilt into oblivion. He came under fire from all their guns at once. Bullets hit him four at a time, driving him back and down. Down for the count.

The frenzy of the moment evaporated. It was as though a hypnotist had snapped his fingers, rousing the survivors from a trance. They were back in the real world, in real time. Spent shells littered the asphalt at their feet, and the air was heavy with the stink of cordite. In the distance they could hear car horns, airplanes. From much closer came the cries of the wounded and dying.

"This place is too damned hot," Barrabas said, moving to the limo's rear and pulling Nochenegra out. "Let's take the Mercedes."

"I'll get it," Billy said. He ran over to the other car, got in and drove it up beside the wounded Caddy.

Barrabas aimed the dictator at the Mercedes's back seat. He didn't have to coax. Nochenegra piled in and got down on the floor behind the front seat. In half a minute they were roaring out of the mall's parking lot.

As they shot past the restaurant, Barrabas looked back and up. Mr. Cheesy had been blown off his barber pole perch. He lay belly up on the crushed red cinder of the roof.

11

Walker Jessup slowly trudged up the long flight of stairs to the main entrance of the Capitol Building. The stone steps were architecture—meant to be seen from a great distance. Their broad, majestic sweep called for being appreciated in concert with the lines of the building above. Up close, and one at a time, they were a royal pain. Especially to Jessup.

He had to stop several times to catch his breath, while geriatric cases in monogrammed sweats and two-hundred-dollar jogging shoes zipped past him. A couple of them, twice. Showing off.

Dotted with perspiration, he lumbered into the building, passed under the rotunda, then made his way to the senator's office.

The lawmaker's secretary, Ms Hartel, looked up from her desk and stared at him as he entered. A ravishing creature, indeed. She did not hold the same opinion of him. The look on her face was one of total disgust. She didn't even deign to speak to him without prompting.

He got not a "Hello," not a "Good morning," and not even a "Huh?"

"I'm Jessup," he said, shutting the door behind him. "The senator asked me to drop by."

With obvious irritation Ms Hartel put aside her Neiman-Marcus mail order catalog and pulled out a desk appointment book. She opened it to the red ribbon marker, then looked up at him again, a question on her lips—but out of her ripe red mouth came nothing.

"Jessup," he said, anticipating her query and ending the weighty silence. "Walker Jessup."

She ran a long carmine fingernail down the page, then finally found her voice. "Yes, I have it," she said. "If you'll take a seat, I'll tell the senator that you're here."

Jessup regarded the outer office's pair of armchairs with grave doubt. He could get into one, but he'd need the jaws of life and a fire-department rescue team to get out. "I'll stand if you don't mind."

Ms Hartel didn't care if he dropped stone dead as long as he didn't land on her size-five Gucci pumps. She rose from her steno chair and walked to the senator's door.

A remarkable backside, no doubt about it, Jessup thought. And a pair of legs that wouldn't quit. He wasn't surprised. The senator's taste in secretaries was legend. As was his taste for them. He went through front-office help at a prodigious rate. The luscious redhead had a wondrous tush but that didn't mean job security.

She disappeared into the adjoining office for a moment, then returned. "Go right in," she said, walking past him without making eye contact, as if he didn't exist.

Given his bulk, she had to have a powerful imagination.

As Jessup ambled into the senator's office, he made the floor creak and shudder.

"Shut the door, Jessup," the old man said, motoring out from behind his desk.

When Jessup did so, the legislator pointed at a tufted leather love seat against the wall. "Sit."

Jessup sat with confidence in the double-wide chair.

"Got rid of the wire, I see," the senator said, squinting up at his face.

"Damned uncomfortable."

"And inconvenient."

Jessup grunted.

"I've got another job for you," the senator said.

"Always glad to help in any way I can."

"It's a touchy one, I'll warn you of that right up front. It must be handled with absolute confidentiality. If anything goes wrong, heads will roll all over D.C."

"Sounds interesting. What's the locale?"

"Same as last time. Mantuego."

"What sort of deal is it?"

The senator's eyes sparkled. "A resupply mission. It's part of Nochenegra's plan to retake power. As you undoubtedly know, certain extreme factions loyal to him were driven underground by the Soarez government."

"You mean the FSI? His tropical Gestapo?"

"Exactly. They've regrouped on a plantation north of the capital. Once rearmed, they will play a major role in securing Juan Carlos a victory."

"You want me to supply the guns?"

"No, that's already been taken care of. What I need is for you to pick up the weapons and transfer them through enough cutouts and paperwork dead ends to thoroughly confuse anyone trying to backtrack their source. And I want you to deliver them to the plantation."

Jessup tried not to show it but he was disappointed. If he had been the one supplying the guns, his profit margin would have been astronomical. "Who's paying for the guns?" he asked with a smirk. "Or is that a state secret?"

"You have no need to know."

"If it's as you describe, it doesn't sound like too taxing a job."

"You'll need three or four others to help you with it."

"Others? To help *me* with it?"

"Yes, I want you to personally see to this job."

Jessup waved him off. "That's not what I do, Senator. I just arrange for things to happen while sitting at my cozy desk. My field days are over." He winced, then leaned forward as if to speak confidentially. "The weight, you know."

The lawmaker shook his head. "If you don't want the work, I can go to my second choice. I just thought I'd give you the opportunity."

Jessup said, "Sorry."

"I figured you'd jump at the chance to pick up this kind of money so easily."

"What kind of money?"

"Two million in laundered bills. You hire the crew you need. You negotiate their salaries. Less expenses, the difference you get to keep. We're talking a couple of days' work at most. A pleasant plane ride and a quick trip home."

Jessup pulled at his lowermost chin. It sounded too frigging easy. "Why is all the secrecy necessary? I mean, after the coup is a fait accompli who will give a damn who supplied the FSI with guns?"

The senator shrugged. "There's always the possibility that the countercoup might fail. In which case a lot of people are going to be looking for someone to blame. I want to make sure that no one points the finger at me."

It made sense. "I can guarantee that won't happen," Jessup told him. "I'll leave a paper trail so twisted that anyone trying to follow it will end up turned inside out. You know it's too bad that you didn't fill me in on this before I sent Barrabas off to join Nochenegra in California. I could have made it a joint operation, using the rest of his people."

"Can't you still use them?" the senator asked with an innocent smile.

"I always work through Barrabas. He's the go-between. I've never had that kind of contact with the people under him. I doubt that they would sign on with me without him."

"But you can get hold of them, can't you? I would actually prefer to have them on this mission. I've used them in the past and I know how professional and discreet they are."

"I suppose I could contact them. I could certainly try to convince them."

"Good. Then do it at once."

"I'll need half the money in advance to finance the necessary transportation and paperwork, and to convince the mercenaries that this deal is on the up-and-up."

"No problem. Why don't you stop by my home this evening and I'll give you the money and documents pertaining to the arms shipment."

"Where is it now?"

"On a well-guarded dock in Taipei."

Jessup pushed up to his feet. "That makes it even easier," he said. "Taiwan is my kind of place. Wide-open free enterprise."

"I'll expect you later, then," the senator said.

Jessup said goodbye and backed out of the room. Ms Hartel didn't look up from her catalog as he passed through the outer office. The 380-pound shadow slipped out into the hall. As he did so, he had a sudden pang of anxiety. He wondered if he was being crafty smart or major-league dumb. The senator was not a man to be trusted even in the most straightforward operations. There was always the possibility that he was playing both ends against the middle, that there might be unwelcome surprises somewhere down the line.

"What the hell," Jessup said aloud. He was looking at a million bucks in profit. And a million bucks was a million bucks.

THE SENATOR WAITED until he heard the outer door close, then he let out a croaking whoop of triumph. Had he been able to jump for joy, he would have. Instead he had to content himself with jamming his steering/throttle control hard left and sending his chair into a series of wild, tight revolutions.

A carnival ride.

After a few seconds he got dizzy and stopped the chair. His mind, however, was still reeling.

When you had the courage to sit out the tight spots, he thought, and the intelligence to see through the maze of action and reaction, to pick a path that set adversary against adversary and cleared the way for your own advancement, you knew you were at the top of your political form.

In effect the lawmaker had sold out everyone connected with the deal.

No one he had dealt with had the straight skinny.

They were all getting gored. All but him.

There was, of course, a downside.

If one small part fell out of place, if one lie was uncovered, if the opposing parties ever got their heads together, the whole thing would collapse.

He refused to consider that possibility. He knew he was already in too deep. There was no way out for him. Any one of the groups he had double-crossed was perfectly capable of having him killed at the drop of a hat.

He had to roll along with the flow, thinking positively, staying alert.

What tickled him most about the way things had worked out was that he had arranged to supply Nochenegra's guns to the PFM and get rid of Jessup and the rest of the Barrabas mercenary team all in one shot. The latter was absolutely necessary. He could not leave any of them alive. He had to eliminate the possibility of their seeking vengeance on him after he pulled the plug on their noble leader.

All his enemies were going to die.

That included Juan Carlos, of course. As a payback for blackmailing him and running him through the wringer for months on end.

The senator felt as if he was about to burst with joy. About to was not close enough. He motored over to his desk and pressed the intercom button.

"Ms Hartel?" he said.

"Yes, Senator?" she replied through the machine.

"I need you."

12

"Look, John," Leona Hatton said to the tall, tanned California orthopedic surgeon, "if I can spare the time from my patients who are recovering, and if there's enough medicine to go around, I do it...."

"But don't you agree," John Barksdale interrupted, "that when you treat patients who have been diagnosed by triage teams as having no chance for survival, you risk draining your own energy enough to significantly affect your performance on patients who do have a chance for survival?"

The two doctors had carried the discussion from the third-floor conference room—and a symposium entitled "Disaster Triage: Ethics in Chaos"—down the elevator, and into the lobby of the University of Miami Hospital.

Barksdale continued without waiting for her reply. "And, more subtly," he said, "don't you think that constant exposure to the hopelessly ill has an erosive effect on a doctor's attitude? And isn't the attitude we bring to our patients in a holocaust scenario just as important as our skill and our medicine?"

"Of course, it is erosive," Hatton told him. "And every physician has his or her limits in that regard. A mind and body trained, dedicated to healing can only take so much...failure." As they had so many times in the past week-and-a-half, memories of the Ethiopian refugee camp at Borem flooded her mind. Once again, she smelled the acrid smoke from the dung fires and heard the lamentations of the mourners; she looked into the hollow eyes of the dying, saw their skeletal hands reaching out to her, begging for help that was beyond her power to give. A familiar pain rose in the back of her throat, a dagger of defeat slowly, inexorably twisting.

Dr. Hatton swallowed the burning pain and drove the images from her mind. Borem was over. Done. Making sense of it from a medical point of view, making future Borems easier for other professionals to deal with, was the concern she focused on. "The trouble is, John, we are talking about horrors that defy the imagination. Face it, you can't sit in a Palm Beach bar over a few piña coladas and figure out how much defeat your psyche can handle in one day. Until you're there, in the middle of it, juggling life and death on a battlefield scale, you don't know what you can take. You don't even know who you are."

"I envy you your military surgical experience," Barksdale said as they crossed the lobby and headed for the front doors. "It must've made what you went through in Ethiopia easier to take."

"Easier only in the sense that I knew what was coming and how I was going to react. Believe me, knowledge doesn't make it any less painful. For me it's become a tape loop—a series of self-rediscoveries, stages that the disaster experience forces me through every time. Even knowing what I know, as a physician going in, I can't help wanting to save everyone. Very soon the impossibility of that hope sinks in. And from that moment on, seeing, hearing and ministering to the multitudes that you know you must watch die, is a soul-crushing experience. You see just how frail your skills are. You either crack under the strain or you get on with it."

The Californian shook his head. "For the short term maybe," he conceded. "But can you honestly tell me that dealing with death hundreds of times a day, week after week, doesn't have a long-term destructive effect on you?''

Lee searched his face with her large, dark eyes. "No, I can't," she said.

They walked out of the building into the humid South Florida evening.

"God, it's dark already," Barksdale said. "The sun was barely up when we got here this morning."

On the other side of the parking lot, cabbage palms rustled in a soft breeze. Scudding clouds off the ocean cast dark shadows across a full moon. In the distance, the wailing of an ambulance cut the stillness of the spring night.

"Let's go get a drink," Barksdale said. "I could use an outrageously dry vodka martini."

"Sorry, John," Lee said, "I've made other plans for tonight. I'll join you some other time."

Barksdale looked devastated. "You sure?"

She nodded. She was sure that she wanted to keep their relationship strictly professional. A stunningly beautiful woman, Dr. Leona Hatton had had plenty of experience with the downside of good looks. They muddled up friendships, personal accomplishments; they complicated the simplest situations. To Dr. Hatton, what she had made of herself inside was infinitely more important than the external structure she had inherited. Accordingly, as a matter of habit, she did as much as she could to diminish the charms of that structure. She never used makeup and she wore her raven-black hair cut so close to her head it could have almost passed for Marine style. Her success in reducing her attractiveness was mixed, however. The short haircut only served to emphasize the size and depth of her black eyes, her generous mouth and the fine bone structure of her face.

Leona liked Barksdale. He was a good man, a skilled physician committed to his profession and to the service of humanity. She smiled warmly at him and patted his arm. "I'll see you in the morning, bright and early."

He groaned, put his palm to his forehead and said, "Don't remind me, please."

As she walked away, he called out to her back, "Hey, Lee! Have some fun, whatever you're up to tonight."

She turned and waved. "You, too, John."

LEE WEARILY SHIFTED the grocery bag from one arm to the other as she crossed the Biscayne Bay Mini-Mall's parking lot. Since the Institute of Tropical Medicine's Disaster Management conference had begun, she had put in twelve consecutive eighteen-hour days. The seminars, lectures and assigned reading were fascinating, but she had been getting by on four or five hours of sleep a night, and she had been subsisting almost entirely on food from the hospital cafeteria and convenience stores.

Tonight she had decided to forgo her reading, to cook herself a decent meal and to go to bed early. She had bought fresh fish and vegetables and the makings of a green salad and wanted to top it all off by buying a bottle of white wine from Manny's Short Stop.

"Ahh, the lovely Dr. Hatton," Manny said as she entered the tiny, cluttered bottle shop. "Why is it that a hardworking man like me doesn't have a beautiful young woman doctor? Old Jacob Roth, my G.P., is a good man. But he looks like a prune with a hairpiece and his hands are as cold as George Steinbrenner's heart."

Lee laughed. She had stopped in at Manny's a couple of times before—for something to wash down a TV din-

ner or Chinese takeout. The first time she walked in he
had read her name off her hospital ID tag and had immediately struck up a conversation. In his late fifties,
Manny was robust, outgoing and thoroughly obsessed
with the sport he loved so much and had been forced to
give up. On the wall behind the service counter hung
framed pictures of Manny in a Baltimore Orioles uniform, framed newspaper clippings with his name in
headlines and an ancient but perfectly maintained short-
stop's glove; on little shelves sat baseball trophies and
trophy baseballs. A wild pitch had ended his playing career right at its peak. Lee liked Manny because he wasn't
bitter about the hand fate had dealt him and because he
told some of the funniest baseball stories she had ever
heard.

"What can I get you tonight?" he asked her.

"I'm too tired to think," Lee said as she put the bag on
the counter. "You pick something. I'm going to grill a
fillet of pompano."

"For pompano you're going to want something white
and dry and very cold." He thought for a minute, then
nodded sagely. "I've got just the thing for you in the
cooler. It's an Alsatian Riesling. Light and crisp. It'll be
perfect."

"I'll take it."

He stepped into a walk-in cooler behind the counter. In
a moment, he returned with a tall, green bottle and a big
smile on his face. The shop door opened behind Lee, and
the smile on Manny's face winked out.

Three toughs in their early twenties walked into the
shop. Looking nervous and at the same time angry, they
filtered up to the counter.

"What can I get you fellas?" Manny asked.

"Everything, old man," the tallest of the trio snarled back. He reached under his sleeveless Levi's jacket and produced a .38-caliber snub-nosed revolver, which he shoved into the store owner's face. It was an ugly little piece—a Taiwanese knockoff of a Brazilian knockoff of a Smith & Wesson Model 36—and it had seen some hard service: the blueing was practically nonexistent and its checkered plastic grips were held on with electrician's tape.

Before Lee could react, a meaty forearm locked around the front of her neck. She didn't resist.

"And don't try nothing," the shortest of the three warned Manny, "or the lady with the crew cut gets a nose job." He stepped up to Lee and waved the point of a Filipino butterfly knife under her nose. Its six-inch blade was nicked and stained with rust; it would leave a nasty wound. Inside the knife-waving man's arm, running from elbow to wrist, Lee could see a peppering of tiny scabs and scars. Some of the more recent junk tracks looked like little bee stings.

"Give us your money," the one with the gun told Manny.

"All right, I'll do what you want," Manny said, holding up his empty hands, "just don't hurt anybody." He opened the cash-register drawer and stepped back.

"You take it out," the gunman ordered. "Hand it to me."

The arm tightened around Lee's neck, and its owner twisted her around so he could keep an eye on the parking lot. He outweighed her by sixty pounds and he was eight inches taller. Each time the lights of a car passed by the shop, he flinched.

Lee took a deep slow breath to calm and prepare her-self. As she did so, she watched the junkie with the gun. He was the only one who counted.

As Manny removed the money from the till, the punk with the knife yelled at him, "Hurry up, asshole!"

"I'm doing it as fast as I can," Manny snapped back.

Lee didn't like the edge to his voice or the flush of color rising in his cheeks. Manny was getting ticked off, and he was taking too long. Meanwhile sweat was sliding down the sides of the junkie gunman's face and his gun hand was starting to shake. Lee could smell the fear and hate all around her; she could feel it crackling against her skin, generating the static of evil. Something bad was going to happen.

Manny slapped the short stack of used bills on the counter.

The one with the knife scooped up the wad and fanned it. "Who you tryin' to fool, sucker? There ain't even a hundred bucks here. You got more than this. Give it!"

Glaring at the robber, Manny reached into his hip pocket, removed his wallet and slammed it down. "That's all there is," he said, "unless you want me to bag up the coins in the register."

"Don't hand us that shit," the one holding Lee said.

"It isn't shit," Manny told him.

"Neither is this!" The man with the knife lunged across the counter, slashing left to right in a broad arc.

Manny jumped back, but too late. The blade sliced across his upraised right palm. Blood spurted from the gash, splattering the countertop with bright red drop-lets. Manny cradled his wrist, staring at the wound in disbelief. As shock faded, a grimace of pain twisted his face.

"You want some more?" the junkie screamed at him, wildly hacking the air with his blade.

Manny shook his head.

"Then give us all the money," the gunman said through clenched teeth.

"Okay, okay," Manny said. He turned his back to them and faced the cash register.

Lee's scalp crawled, her heart thudded from the adrenaline blast coursing through her body. She knew Manny wasn't going to give them what they wanted. The expression on his face said he wasn't going to take any more; he was going to fight back. She wanted to shout "No!" to him, but it was already too late. Manny spoke as he began to turn back.

"This is all I got," he said.

Even as she recognized his stance—feet squared, shoulders tense—Manny's arm uncoiled in a blur of savage power. Lee didn't actually see the bat, a blue aluminum job, until it stopped, connecting solidly with the side of the knife-wielding junkie's skull.

It made an almost musical sound, a short, muted, bell-like tone.

Snot exploded from the man's nose as his head snapped hard right. As his head sprang back, his face contorted, then went slack; the whites of his eyes suddenly became pink as they were shot with blood. He stood swaying for a second, then his knees softened and he slumped to the floor.

The robber holding Lee shouted at the astonished gunman, "Shoot him! Kill the fucking son of a bitch!" As he spoke, he slightly relaxed his grip around her neck. Lee bent her knees, letting her weight settle into the soles of her feet, rooting herself to earth.

Before she could move to free herself, the tall one fired. In the small room, the short-barreled .38's report was deafening, a thunderclap that rattled bottles on the shelves. Lee watched Manny, his face gray with pain as he staggered back against the cash register. He still held the bat. There was a small black hole in the right shoulder of his sport shirt, a hole instantly filled with crimson, sliding, spreading quickly out and down.

"Shoot him again!" Lee's captor hollered. And as he cried out, he relaxed his grip on her neck even more. He no longer had control. She moved into the vacuum, stomping down on his instep, feeling the bones crack under her heel. As he shrieked, she ducked, twisted her head and lifted his arm up and off. It was all one motion, fluid, precise. She turned all her weight into him, driving with her shoulder, knocking him off balance, sending him crashing to his back on the floor.

Lee pivoted and charged the man with the gun. As he spun toward her, bringing his sights up he brought the target she sought into view. Her mind blank but for the bull's-eye, the ten ring, Leona launched the flying kick to end all. Pure, focused power exploded from the center of her being, surging up through her right leg to the ball of her foot, which drove deep into the gunman's solar plexus. Lee felt an instant of resistance, her force meeting the inertia of the man's body, then it yielded. With a grunt the gunman went flying backward, ten feet backward into a pyramid of champagne bottles. The pyramid collapsed under him, bottles shattering, corks popping. The gun clattered to the floor at her feet. Lee bent down and picked it up.

"You fucking bitch!" a voice snarled at her back.

Lee turned. The junkie she'd pushed over was scrambling to his feet.

"You're dead!" he bellowed, lunging for her.

"Stop or I'll shoot," she told him, raising the weapon.
He didn't even slow down.

When he was three feet away, she pulled the trigger.
The shot got him in the face, the muzzle-flash crisping his
eyebrows and dusting his sweaty face with dull cordite
soot. Those were the least of his worries. The bullet entered just below his left eye. It blew away the back of his
skull as a spray of brains and blood splattered the ceiling, walls and floor. Lee turned aside, covering her nose
and mouth with her free hand, letting the man's momentum carry him past her, onto his face on the floor.

Gradually, the ringing in her ears faded and she realized that someone was shouting at her. It was Manny. He
was sitting slumped on the floor behind the counter.

"Did you see the stroke I gave that punk, Doc? It
would've been a four-bagger in any ballpark in the
country!" His voice was shrill, manic. He tried to get to
his feet.

"Stay right where you are," Lee told him.

She made him sit down, then she tore open his shirt
and checked his gunshot wound. The bullet didn't appear to have broken any bones or nicked any major vessels. She found a clean towel under the counter, pressed
it against the wound and told him to hold it there as
tightly as he could.

Then she picked up the phone and dialed the emergency number. "This is Dr. Leona Hatton," she told the
dispatcher. "There's been an attempted robbery at
Manny's Short Stop on Collins Avenue near the JFK
Causeway. There are multiple critical injuries. We need
at least three ambulances. Three of the men down are intravenous drug users and blood is everywhere. Advise

emergency personnel to be prepared to take precautions against AIDS.''

''Oh, hell!'' Manny exclaimed, his eyes widening. From where he sat he could see contaminated gore dripping from the overhead light fixtures.

She knelt beside him again and took his pulse. It was rapid, but steady, and his color was improving.

''Am I going to be okay?'' he asked her.

Lee smiled as she checked his wound. The flow of blood had slowed to a trickle. ''Keep the pressure on and you're going to be fine,'' she assured him.

Then she got up and walked around the front of the counter. The guy Manny had whacked was a goner, the whole left side of his skull caved in. She moved carefully across the blood- and champagne-slick floor to the gunman who lay sprawled in a heap of broken glass. She could see he was still breathing. When she moved closer, she saw a bright stream of arterial blood pulsing from a deep gash wound in his arm.

''Shit!'' she said.

''What's wrong?'' Manny asked, pulling himself to his feet so he could see.

''This one's going to bleed to death before the ambulance gets here,'' she said.

''Who cares!'' Manny said.

Lee stepped quickly to the counter and upended her sack of groceries, then dumped green spears of asparagus and red new potatoes out of the clear plastic bags she had packed them in.

''What are you doing?'' Manny asked.

''Making gloves,'' she replied as she pulled the bags over her hands.

She found another clean towel and walked back to the bleeding junkie. Squatting over him, she covered his wound with the compress and applied two-handed pressure.

"Why are you trying to save him?" Manny demanded. "That scumbag was going to shoot you."

"Because I'm a doctor," she said.

THREE MORE HOURS had elapsed by the time Lee trudged up the walk to her rented bungalow. It was in a little court of similar houses. As she started up the concrete steps, something moved out of the shadows. Something huge. Her heart triple-timed, adrenaline roaring through her veins. Not again, she thought. But she was ready to fight, ready to chuck her bag of groceries in the mugger's face, then pull his arms off at the sockets.

"Dr. Hatton?" a familiar voice drawled, then the fat man stepped out into the light.

"Jessup! What are you doing here? What do you want?"

"I've got to talk to you about something important," he said. "It has to do with Barrabas."

"Come on in," she told him.

Sitting on the couch in the cramped combination living room and kitchen, Jessup made his case to her. He told her that Barrabas was on a very risky job with half the mercenary team. If the mission was going to be successful, if Barrabas and the others were going to have a chance of coming out of it alive, a second group had to go into action on another front. He told her what that action was.

"All we have to do is deliver some arms to the anti-Communist forces?"

"That's right. A simple little job. And for doing it you earn yourself a quick hundred grand."

Lee glared at him. "I don't give a damn about the money. If it was just for the money, I'd tell you to go to hell. I've got better things to do with my time. It's Barrabas and Hayes and Nanos and Starfoot that I care about."

Jessup smiled and nodded. "The goods are already in transit. We'll rendezvous at the trans-shipment point at 6:00 p.m. tomorrow. Delivery is scheduled for around midnight." He reached into his pocket and took out an envelope. "Here's your plane ticket. You'll be flying alone on the first leg. I've got to make one quick stop before I join you."

13

Nate Beck knew he had no business back in his old apartment in Manhattan. And for the life of him he couldn't figure out what he was doing there.

The apartment on the West Side had gone to Beverly as part of their settlement at the time of their divorce. She had divorced him on the grounds that he was a "wanted man." Which was true. At one point he was number nine on the FBI hit parade. It was also true that being "wanted" made it difficult for him to appear in court and give his side of things; namely, that his beloved wife had been the one who had turned him in to the Feds over the trifling matter of a few million dollars he had switched from one bank to another, using his office mainframe. Nate Beck was a bona fide computer genius, a self-made millionaire at the age of thirty-three, and as a contradiction in terms, bored mindless. That was why he had stolen the money. For a kick. To put some oomph back in his life.

After so much water under the marital bridge, Beck was understandably alarmed at his location. He was standing just outside what had been their bedroom door. He put the flat of his hand against it and pushed. It swung inward.

"Hi, Beverly," he said to the woman sitting on the edge of the bed.

It was Beverly and it wasn't. At least not the Beverly he had gotten used to in the past.

Beverly's idea of a negligee was a flannel nightie that buttoned all the way up to the chin. And she kept it buttoned up. Minimal access. The lady sitting before him had on a black lace teddy that covered very little, and she was making no effort to keep her legs together.

Beck stared at her flanks and felt a pang of desire. He had always been a sucker for a well-toned sartorius or a tensed adductor longus.

She crooked a finger at him.

Nate jerked forward on stiff legs, legs suddenly without knees. He wanted her so badly that his soul cried out.

He knelt on the bed and kissed her. She kissed him back with passion, her mouth hot and wet. As she did so, she pulled at his clothing, loosening his pants.

In his short and dismal married life Nate Beck had never been able to quite figure out his wife. She was nothing like a computer. She was totally unpredictable. If, miracle of miracles, he happened to stumble upon an amorous technique that aroused her, it rarely worked a second time. His attempts to repeat his hard-earned successes were met with disdain and often disgust. The reason he had stuck with her so long was that he couldn't abide a puzzle that he couldn't solve. She certainly kept him guessing... and, of course, miserable.

But it was his lucky night. The gods had smiled on him, and it seemed he could do no wrong. Wherever he touched her he drove her crazy, and the more he touched her the crazier she got. She scratched his back, bit the tip of his tongue, arched herself against him and made strange noises. High-pitched, excited whimperings she had never made before, not even in what had passed for her throes of ecstasy.

As he was anticipating final fulfillment, he caught a whiff of a strong and unpleasant odor. A familiar odor, but one he did not connect with sex. And certainly not sex with Beverly, to whom personal hygiene was a religion.

It grew stronger, and in fact so strong that he stumbled back from her pliant, eager body, coughing.

Nate awoke with a start, sitting bolt upright in bed. The room swam for a long moment and he couldn't be sure where he was. He blinked and shook his head. Then he remembered. He was in Mexico. He was in his little seaside hideaway on the Baja California coast. His tangled bed was empty. But the rancid odor that had awakened him hung over the room like a pall, and the high-pitched whining continued.

He also became aware of an ongoing scratching sound from over by the bedroom door.

"Fifi," Beck said, addressing his 110-pound rottweiler bitch, "what the hell are you doing?"

Fifi unleashed a baleful "Wooof" and resumed her frantic scrabbling.

"Jesus!" he groaned, throwing back the sheets. "What *is* that smell?"

There were no clocks in the bedroom. Beck had given up on clocks and calendars. He could tell by the grainy gray light filtering through the windows that it was not long after dawn. He stuck his hand under the mattress, fumbling for the Colt .45 Gold Cup he kept tucked away there.

He didn't pull it out. The way Fifi was wriggling her back end and wagging her stump of a tail did not presage danger or lurking trespassers. Fifi was definitely not in her guard-dog mode.

"What is it, girl?" he said, standing up. He felt for his pants on the end of the bed. Whatever the rank odor was, it was damned nasty. Ordinarily Beck savored waking up each morning, inhaling the salty tang of the Pacific. Now he had to breathe through his mouth or puke.

He stepped into his sandals and crossed to the double French doors leading to his little stone patio overlooking the beach, some 150 feet below. As he pushed out onto the patio, he noticed that the gulls screeched louder than usual and with a new, frenzied quality.

Beck looked down over the railing and saw the reason for the stench and the keening gulls.

A dead California gray whale.

It had washed up on the beach with the high tide of the previous night. The animal was nearly forty feet long. It rested on its side, high and dry, a good ten yards from the waterline. It had been dead for a while, too. The bloat of decomposition had already distorted the whale's graceful lines. Great chunks of blubber and flesh had been ripped from its flanks and underside, probably by the hammerheads and brown sharks that patrolled the ocean off the coast. Hundreds of gray and white gulls wheeled and dived over the carcass, fighting to get at the exposed meat. The easy pickings.

Beck was revolted and at the same time fascinated by the sight. He wanted to get closer, to have a proper look.

Having spent most of his life in Manhattan, he hadn't had much of an opportunity to study nonhuman creatures. The odd poodle or the cockroach that escaped his mother's lightning broom, maybe, but nothing really wild and free. He had lived most of his life inside his own head, developing computer programs, dreaming dreams of swashbuckling action, of high adventure. Beverly had been interested in animals, but only those whose skins looked good on her back.

Since Beck's fall from grace, he had embarked on a high-paying part-time career as a mercenary. It gave him a lot of free time. After moving into the stone-and-timber bungalow beside the Pacific, he had devoted considerable time and energy to the study of local marine life and seabirds. Beck's mind was vigorous and far-reaching. In a matter of a few months, his knowledge of the creatures of the Mexican littoral had become almost encyclopedic.

None of the animals captured his imagination more than the gray whales that appeared seasonally off the Baja coast. Weighing up to thirty-three tons, they passed by twice each year on their six-thousand-mile migration from calving grounds in the Sea of Cortez to their summer feeding grounds off Alaska. For Beck, there was something soothing and reassuring about the predictability of their return, and the tranquillity of their lives.

As he backtracked through the house to the bedroom door, Fifi started barking wildly and spinning in circles, aching to sink her teeth—and perhaps wallow—in whatever was responsible for that wonderful and putrid stink. As he had no interest in scrubbing dead whale goo off his pooch, he commanded her to sit, then locked her in the bedroom. He cut down along the side of the house and half ran, half slid down the steep path to the beach.

As he neared the whale, the stench of rotting flesh grew even heavier. It was hard for him to believe that it could get worse, but it had. Tiers of gulls rose from the whale corpse, screaming at him. Things were moving on the body, in the body. Rats and land crabs were having a field day. As were flies and maggots. Beck's eyes began to water. As he knuckled the tears away, he inadvertently breathed through his nose.

And abruptly puked.

One second he was looking over the dirty white line of barnacles and yellow-orange patches of whale lice, and the next he was on his knees in the sand, barfing his brains out. The reek of that mass of rotting flesh had been more than his stomach could handle.

Choking, coughing and spitting, he pushed back up and backed away from the corpse. He wiped his mouth with the back of his hand. And suddenly he saw the whale in an entirely different light. Not as an interesting specimen for study, a believe-it-or-not exhibit, but as an incredible nuisance.

Something he was going to have to deal with.

He walked down to the water and checked the whale's position relative to the high-water mark and tide. The tide was still more than halfway out; it wouldn't flood again for several hours. Nevertheless, he could tell from the whale's location in relation to the preceding night's high-water mark that it would take an even higher tide to re-float the carcass.

He scrambled back up the hillside. A tide just a foot or so higher should be enough, he thought as he reentered his house. Then I can hire a few local fishermen to pull the thing off the beach with their boats. Pull it off and tow it someplace else.

Anyplace else.

He walked quickly to his cramped little office. It was crammed with computers, bookshelves, file cabinets. He found his tide book and flipped through the pages until he found the correct month and day. "Shit!" he said. According to the table, the previous night's tide would not be bested for nine more days.

He sniffed tentatively and groaned. No way, he thought. I've got to do something before then. After a couple more days of tropical sun, that whale will stink so bad I'll have to pack up and leave.

The taste in his mouth was awful. He went into the kitchen and poured himself a large glass of orange juice and splashed a sizable shot of tequila on top, to clear his palate. He took a long drink, then walked into the living room and stood before the large picture window that offered him a panoramic view of the beach and ocean. Already the number of wheeling gulls had almost doubled. And two turkey vultures, having vectored in on the aroma of death, rode the thermals above the whale.

Beck sipped the drink and let his keen analytical mind range over the problem. He knew that it would be pointless to call in the Mexican government. Not only would they refuse to do anything, but they would probably find a way to blame the situation on him. He also knew that it would take weeks to locate the backhoes and road graders necessary to drag the carcass down the beach and bury it. The only practical solution was to render the whale into pieces small enough to be carted away. The only way to do that would be to get a crew of people on it with chain saws, machetes and whatever else was handy. It would have to be done quickly, before the whale decomposed into blubber Jell-O.

Beck left the house and jumped into his Land Cruiser. He bounced down the rutted dirt track that was the only road into his hideaway, then covered the five miles of gravel one-lane to the nearest village in a little less than six minutes. He skidded the jeep to a stop in front of the dilapidated combination general store and gas station that was the nerve center of the tiny fishing village.

Beck stepped under the corrugated tin awning, walked across the wooden floor of the porch, then through the doorless doorway. It took several seconds for his eyes to adjust from the harsh glare of the Baja sunshine to the murky light inside the store. Music blared tinnily from a transistor radio. The air smelled of tobacco and beer.

"Buenos días, Señor Beck," said Paco, the owner of the store. "What can I do for you today?" In a greasy apron, he stood behind the bar, which consisted of a sheet of three-quarter-inch plywood laid across two sawhorses. Four young fishermen sat on beer crates before him, nursing bottles of Tecate. They looked at the gringo with great anticipation.

"I have a little problem, Paco," Beck said. *"Uno poco problema."*

That made the fishermen break into peals of laughter. They slapped one another on the back, slapped their own thighs, laughing until tears ran down their cheeks.

"¡No, no, señor, es uno problema grande!"

"¡Muy, muy grande!"

Beck grimaced. "I see news about the whale has gotten around."

Paco wiped his hands on the front of his apron. He was actually biting his lip, trying to keep from laughing along. He didn't want to offend such an important customer. "One of the fishermen saw it this morning on his way back from the Rockpile." The store owner closed his nose with his thumb and index finger. "It is most unfortunate for you."

The fisherman cracked up again.

"I'm going to need some help getting the whale off my beach," Beck said. He looked at the young men. "I'll pay twenty-five dollars a day for anyone who helps."

"How do you intend on doing this thing?" Paco asked.

"We'll have to cut it up and . . ."

Even Paco laughed at that.

Beck had to join in. Who the hell was he kidding? Nobody in his right mind would spend a couple of days under a broiling sun dicing a putrescent whale into bite-size chunks. Not for all the *cerveza* in Baja. *"Muchas gracias,"* he said, walking out of the cantina.

He got halfway to the Land Cruiser when it hit him like the proverbial ton of bricks. Of course. It was so fucking simple. He did an about-face and returned to the cantina.

"¿Sí, señor?" Paco said warily.

"I want to send a telegram," Beck told him.

"Bueno," the proprietor said. With great dignity he walked around to the ancient cash register, reached under the counter and produced a yellow pad and a pencil, which he handed to Beck.

Nate thought for a moment, then composed a brief note, scribbled the address and handed the paper back to the Mexican with a ten-dollar bill. "See that it gets out today, Paco. *¿Hoy, comprende?"*

"Sí, sí, señor."

Beck left the cantina with a broad grin on his face.

LIAM O'TOOLE CLUTCHED the handhold on the dash for all he was worth, wedging his stout, powerful legs against the fire wall. Pushing down as hard as he could, he still couldn't keep his behind planted on the seat. All the way back from the Loreto airport, Beck had kept the pedal right against the floorboard. He hadn't slowed when he hit the dirt road. He was rampaging down it as though it was the last twenty miles of the Baja 1000. The Land Cruiser's redlined engine was howling so loud that conversation below a bellow was impossible.

Twice since he landed, O'Toole had asked Beck why he had been summoned. Once, right off the bat, when he stepped off the plane, and again as they were loading his gear into the jeep. Beck's answer both times had been, "Just be patient, Liam, you'll see."

From the telegram Nate had sent, O'Toole had been prepared to face a horde of PCP-crazed, Uzi-toting bandits at the very least. "Situation desperate," the note had said. "Come at once."

Yeah, sure, the red-haired Irishman thought, hurry up so you can get your kidneys rattled loose. Ouch! There wasn't even any interesting scenery. Or if there was, it might as well have not been there. Road dust the color of malted-milk powder coated the windshield and the side windows. Beck had to use the wiper spray to clear a dim arc of visibility.

Not that O'Toole had been doing anything important. Except drinking Bushmill's—something he could do almost anywhere, but here. And writing poetry that he couldn't stand. He had broken through the barrier of writer's block that had paralyzed him for so long, only to realize that he had reached a plateau in his work. He could see that what he had done in the past was pure derivative crap. A combination of Charles Bukowski and Rod McKuen. Obscene greeting-card verse. Sentimental smut. But he had no idea how or where to go from there. The harder he tried to figure it out, the farther away the solution seemed to slip. He had begun to wonder if he would ever enjoy his calling again.

And then there was the matter of Fung-Qua, the originator and sole master of the drunken parrot style of t'ai chi ch'uan—a besotted genius who had introduced Liam to his *chi* machine, for the nominal cost of two hundred dollars an hour. It was, in Liam's terminology, a "psychic tanning booth." After a single treatment O'Toole fulfilled the master's promise: he flew. *Flew.*

Slipped like a well-buttered oyster between the warp and weave of time and space.

The trouble was, between the time Liam had been first psychically energized and had gone on a mercenary mission with Barrabas and the time he returned, the old man had disappeared, *chi* machine and all. The treatment that had worked such wonders gradually wore off, leaving Liam worse off, because he had glimpsed the astounding possibilities. How to reach them again by himself? The alternative, according to Fung-Qua, would be to spend decades practicing the soft martial arts, working with the breath, the root to earth. Even then, the heights offered by the *chi* machine might not be attained.

Given those rather depressing circumstances, O'Toole had been more than ready for some excitement when the telegram had arrived. He had dropped everything—the bottle was empty anyway—and dashed to JFK, catching the very next plane to Baja.

For what? He had yet to discover.

Beck turned off the main road onto a two-rut track that roller-coasted over scrub and sand. Liam looked behind them and saw the plume of tan dust they were raising. It looked like a goddamn tornado.

"Not long now!" Beck shouted.

O'Toole nodded gratefully. He needed something cold and wet to wash the grit from between his teeth. Like the Land Cruiser, he was dusted liberally inside and out with a very abrasive substance.

Beck pulled up in front of a sorry-looking cabana. They waited until the dust cloud swept over them, then got out.

"What do you think?" Nate asked.

Liam started to reply when it hit him.

The stink.

"Sweet Jesus!" he groaned, clamping his hand over his nose and mouth.

"I told you it was urgent," Beck said.

"What have you got around here, another Jonestown?"

"Close, but no cigar...which reminds me," Nate said, reaching back in the glove compartment and pulling out a pair of monumental Mexican stogies. "These help a lot."

"Gimme," Liam said, stuffing the cigar into his mouth.

They both lit up and puffed energetically for a few minutes.

"See? It helps, doesn't it?"

"Yeah," Liam replied, "I much prefer the smell of burning rope to abandoned tropical slaughterhouse."

"Come on, let's go in and get a beer, and I'll fill you in on the grim details."

As Beck opened the door, he said, "Don't let Fifi get out, whatever you do. The little tart got loose yesterday and it took me practically all night and four gallons of tomato juice to clean her up."

Fifi knew and loved O'Toole. She jumped and pirouetted with joy, licking his face, squirming, throwing herself onto her back and showing him her silky belly and groaning with ecstasy as he tickled her.

"She kind of smells like a Bloody Mary," the Irishman mused.

Nate grabbed a six-pack of Tecate from his refrigerator, tossed one to Liam, then led the way out onto the patio, waving his cigar back and forth like a censer.

O'Toole looked down. Whatever he had been expecting, what he saw was not it. "Oh, Lordy," he said, pulling the cigar out of his mouth and chugging back the brew in one long gulp. He crumbled the empty can, and puffed hard on the stogie.

Standing downwind of the whale was like being caught in a sandstorm naked. The stench was so acrid, so intense, it abraded the senses.

"I only got one question, Beck," O'Toole said, accepting another Tecate. "Why the fuck did you call *me*?"

Nate beamed at him. "Because you're the one person I know who can get that mess off my hands."

Liam gave him a doubtful look.

"You're a demolitions expert."

"You are out of your tiny mind."

"No, it's the only way."

"That thing must weigh twenty tons!"

"Closer to thirty, actually."

"Hey, I've blown up lots of things in my time—people, cars, bridges, buildings—but..."

"Think of it as the greatest challenge of your career. Your magnum-fucking opus."

Liam drained the second beer in a swallow, burped demurely behind his hairy, dirt-streaked hand, then said, "What the hell, I guess it won't hurt to have a closer look. You got another seegar?"

Armed with a fresh pair of pungently smoldering El Misteriosos and another practically frozen six-pack, they descended to the beach.

"What I want," Beck told him as they crossed the sand, "is for it to disappear." The buzz of carrion flies was tremendous; it made them both shiver. The squadrons of gulls didn't try to fly off as the men got closer. Most of them couldn't; they had eaten too much. They looked like bowling bags with wings. "I don't want anything left," Nate continued. "Blowing it into chunks the size of Virginia hams is not the answer."

"You're talking bite-size, then."

"You got it. And the other thing is, I want it all to get blasted out to sea. I don't want my house coated with liquefied whale guts."

"That's understandable. Do you think we could get upwind for a minute?"

They walked around the corpse and faced the stiff onshore breeze.

"Well?" Nate said.

"Okay," Liam told him, chewing at the butt of his cigar, "you got a couple of interesting problems here. The bite-size bit is going to be tricky, because el whalo isn't the same density all the way through. There are heavy bones and other skeletal junk to deal with. We're talking precision work, here. It's a matter of placing the charges in the right spots and synchronizing detonation so they all go up at once."

"I've already got all the dynamite we're going to need," Beck told him. "A full case, with blasting caps, wire, detonator, the works."

"Where the hell did you get it? That stuff is hard to come by in Mexico."

"A friend works at an oil-exploration company up the coast. He misplaced the stuff for a price. What about the other problem you mentioned?"

"Actually two problems in one, having to do with the dispersal of the whale tidbits. You want every speck of it to go out to sea. That means we're going to have to aim that dude before we set him off."

"Aim?"

"Give the charges something to push against, an angle, so he goes out and away, not up and all over. After we set the dynamite, we're going to have to break out the shovels and build a berm of sand against and over his back."

"A berm? You mean a goddamn mountain. Our friend is fifteen feet thick."

"I was trying to break it to you gently. The other thing is, even with a berm, if we've got the kind of onshore breeze that's running now, your house is still going to get coated. We've got to wait until the wind turns offshore and pop him then."

"Sounds like a plan to me," Beck said.

"There's just one thing, Nate. How the hell are we going to plant the charges in that thing? I don't feature digging tunnels ten feet deep in rotten whale meat with a hand trowel."

"No sweat," Nate said. "I've already got that end of it covered." He waved Liam over to a tarp stretched out on the sand nearby. When he pulled back the covering, he exposed two sets of foul-weather bib fronts, two pairs of hip waders, an aluminum ladder, long rubber gauntlets, assorted lengths of iron pipe, some iron rods of matching lengths and a couple of ten-pound sledgehammers.

"Get into your antislime gear," Nate told him, "and I'll show you how my idea works."

They both stripped off their clothes and pulled on the protective gear. Then they carried all the other stuff over to the dead whale.

By that time, it was time for new cigars and another beer.

Beck picked up a short length of the iron pipe and handed it to Liam. "Hold the end of it against the body," he said, picking up a sledge.

With a solid swing, he drove the pipe into whale meat, like a tent peg into soggy ground . One good whack put it in a yard. O'Toole twisted the pipe around and then they both pulled it out, leaving a two-inch-diameter tunnel bored into the whale.

"Perfect," O'Toole said, grinning around his cigar.

Beck used one of the iron rods to clear the pipe, ejecting a yard-long core of putrid meat. "Arrgh," he gasped.

Liam then paced off the length of the whale's back, figuring which parts were the thickest, estimating how many sticks it would take to do the job. The tunnels in the backside of the carcass didn't have to be very deep. They punched out the holes and Liam planted the charges, wiring them all together.

The going got really nasty on top of the thing. Not only was it slick and rubbery soft, but they had to use the really long pipes and pound hard to get them deep enough. They kept hitting ribs and getting stopped short. Beck fell off twice, sliding on his ass down over the belly of the beast. But he didn't hurt himself and he got right back on.

It was lunchtime when they finished. Funny thing, neither of them felt much like eating.

They stripped off the protective gear, wrapped it in the tarp and walked up the beach a ways, where they had a swim to cool off and cleanse themselves.

When they got back, they broke out the shovels and started moving sand. The steep slope of the beach was a big help. But it was murderously hot work. They drank a case of Tecate between them and didn't even get a buzz. They sweated it all out.

By nightfall they had finished. From the patio of Beck's cottage they couldn't even see the whale for the mound of sand they'd piled up behind it.

"Too bad we can't wait until daylight to blow him up," Nate said. "I'd sort of like to see what happens."

"If we wait, we lose the offshore breeze," Liam reminded him, as he screwed down the terminals on the old-fashioned plunger-type detonator. "There's one more thing...."

"Yeah?"

"How stable is the ground under this house? It's a long shot, but when you're dealing with as much TNT as we are..."

"It's on bedrock," Nate assured him.

"I think we'd better move inside. Just in case..."

They pulled the detonator into the house and took up secure positions in the living room.

Fifi lay on her back next to Liam, wriggling in what she hoped was an enticing manner.

"What a slut," he said, rubbing her tummy.

"Can I do the honors?" Nate asked.

"Sure." O'Toole pulled up the plunger and hit the on switch. "She's ready to rip."

Beck hunkered over the detonator, pausing to shut his eyes and mutter a short prayer. It wasn't hard to guess what he was wishing for. Then he shoved the plunger down. It made a grinding, mechanical noise until it hit bottom.

Outside, the night lit up, and the house rocked, floorboards undulating, rafters shaking. The explosion shattered and blew in every window on the sea side.

It took several minutes before they could hear what each other was saying.

"Well?" Liam said. "Shall we have a look?"

"Let me tie up the pooch. There's all that glass on the floor." That done, they carefully stepped out onto the patio. Beck gingerly tested the footing. It seemed to be okay.

"No blubber on the house," Liam said, obviously very pleased with himself.

"Can't see much of the beach," Nate said. "Too damned dark. Shall we go down and take a look?"

"Take a whiff, first."

He did. "It hardly stinks at all."

They hurried down to the beach, then much more cautiously approached a huge, still-smoking crater in the sand.

"It's gone!" Beck said, slapping Liam on the back. "The damn thing is gone!"

"SURE ARE A LOT of birds out there," Liam said, looking out the glassless windowframes at the water. "There's so many of them the sea looks white."

"Hey, they don't have it easy," Beck told him as he shook the contents of a skillet onto a pair of plates. He was cooking breakfast. *Huevos rancheros.*

"Let's eat out on the deck," he suggested, carrying the platter-size dishes in oven mitts. "Bring the *cerveza.*"

O'Toole picked up a couple of cans and two glasses. He popped the tops and poured while Beck adjusted the chairs and tiny table.

"What a morning!" Nate said, patting his dog on the head.

Fifi looking longingly at their breakfast, which was roughly on the same level as her wet black nose.

Without further ceremony Beck and O'Toole started to tie into the food.

"Man, there really are a lot of birds out there," Beck said, noticing them for the first time.

Thousands. Thousands of them, bobbing out there, picking up floating scraps of el whalo. Then something spooked them. A shark cruising under them, maybe.

They all took to the air at once in an explosion of madly beating wings.

"Wow!" Beck exclaimed around a forkful of food.

In the sunlight white wings and bellies were dazzling.

The gulls wheeled in a giant formation, doing a 360-degree turn over the land, over Beck's house.

As they passed above the house, it began to rain. A little at first. Then, as the main body of the flock flew directly overhead, a lot.

Not water.

Not hail.

Not brimstone.

Bird droppings.

They splattered their heads, their food; they plopped into their beer glasses.

"Aw, for Pete's sake!" Nate groaned, pushing back from his plate in disgust.

Then the gulls came around again.

"I don't believe this," Liam said as he was pelted once more. He made no attempt to cover his food or himself. It was far too late for that. Everything and everyone on the patio was covered with fresh guano.

Fifi, her head and back blotched with white, threw back her head and let out a miserable howl.

Beck shoved back his chair. It slid over the stone flags easily, for they were well-lubed. "They're coming around again!" he said. "Let's get out of here."

He got no argument from Fifi or O'Toole.

FOUR HOURS LATER, O'Toole, Beck and Fifi were flat on their backs some hundred miles away, around the swimming pool of the San Quintin El Presidente Hotel.

They were awakened from their Tequila Shooter stupor when someone rudely came between them and the sun, and stayed there. The someone in question cast a mighty wide shadow.

Liam groaned, pushed up on an elbow and, shielding his eyes from the glare, said, "Push off, buddy...."

Then he recognized who it was.

14

Barrabas lowered the slim volume to his chest and rubbed his eyes. As he did so, his fingers brushed the edge of the butterfly bandage that covered a shallow bullet track, a memento of Mr. Cheesy's Restaurant number one hundred.

He reached up and shut off the reading light. The plane was dark. Under the drawn window shades he could see daylight leaking in. He checked his watch. It was 6:00 a.m. They had been on the commercial flight, LAX to Mantuego, for nearly twelve hours. It seemed even longer—in his lower back and his hip joints. He wanted to get up and move around, but Nanos and Starfoot were snoring in the seats between him and the aisle and he didn't want to wake them.

So he shut his eyes and thought about what he had been reading.

The Great Mandelo, according to the book's introduction, penned by a local scholar, had lived his whole life in the preceding century, before the first manned flight, before radio, before automobiles. He was an itinerant farm laborer, a self-styled preacher with four wives, an influential adviser to the first self-elected president of Mantuego—one of many. Prior to the first president-for-life, the country had been a crown colony of a decayed European power. The power had given up the island after only a token fight. Mantuego was simply too poor, and had too few prospects to be worth the trouble. The administration costs alone were prohibitive.

Mandelo's words had lived on after his death and so had many myths surrounding his deeds. Barrabas had taken Nochenegra's suggestion and studied the poem "Ode to Servitude." It was indeed telling, whether or not it was as important as the dictator made out. If the piece had a point, a philosophy, other than being a paean to the natural beauty available to even the lowliest of Mantuegans, it was that bondage, both physical and socioeconomic, was in many ways an illusion. Though the message was complicated by allusions and metaphors, essentially it said of servitude, "Put on a happy face."

As Barrabas read through the book, which was a collection of poems, essays and tracts by Mandelo with biographical material inserted here and there, he found this same theme cropping up time and again. It was not a *total* acceptance of slavery and misery, it was an acceptance for the time being. It called for a confident patience.

As to the man's deeds, he had been a living dynamo. There seemed no end to things attributed to him. Though an impoverished man all his life, he somehow managed to achieve a movement of funds from the island's rich to the poor. He spent much of his time in the slum of El Infierno, working with society's outcasts. He was revered by Mantuegan prostitutes as a saint, even though he had never been canonized. According to the text, even nowadays it was rare to find a Mantuegan prostitute who didn't have some sort of picture or icon of Mandelo hanging over her professional bed.

"Under his fatherly gaze," said the text, "she believes that she will come to no harm and that her business will grow and prosper."

What did this all say about the Mantuegan people? That they were basically complacent, optimistic in the face of their own bitter circumstances, accepting of what was because it was only temporary? It was understandable that a people faced with crushing poverty would try to escape from it, would want to believe something better was coming. Such people were prime meat for an authoritarian dictator, an exploiter like Juan Carlos. It was no wonder that he found the dead philosopher's work so enthralling. The man's worldview was a recipe for subservience and subjugation.

Barrabas tucked the book into the seat pocket in front of him. He considered Nochenegra's reaction to the recent attempted assassination. The man had blamed the whole thing on the PFM, the Soviets, the KGB. He blamed everything on the Communists, all the time. Barrabas found it hard to believe that a bunch of guerrillas on an island tens of thousands of miles away would take the trouble to try to kill the exiled dictator. They had other, bigger fish to fry much closer to hand. If Soarez was as weak as everyone said he was, the PFM would be concentrating all their efforts on him, not worrying about a man who might try to return to power someday. Nochenegra's other Commie bogeymen seemed just as unlikely. The KGB, even if it knew about his plans, wouldn't give a damn. Juan Carlos flattered himself much . . . and often.

Which left an interesting question: if the Red Menace wasn't to blame for what had happened at Mr. Cheesy's, then who?

The list of candidates was long. Anyone who had ever done business with the president-for-life had to be considered a suspect. That included his own supposedly loyal generals back home, and a handful of multinational conglomerates and billionaire private investors who took a beating when he took a hike. Whoever was behind it, they knew what they were doing. The operation at Mr. Cheesy had been well conceived. It had only been thanks to a stroke of luck that anyone had escaped. Had they been closer to the blast they wouldn't have. The hit crew would have been able to move in and administer coups de grace to all and sundry.

The LAPD couldn't identify the dead attackers. They were thought to be foreign nationals, possibly South Americans, imported to do the hit. The investigation was stalled and probably would go no further.

Barrabas asked himself—and not for the first time on this particular job—if he was doing the right thing, if he had taken the right side. A choice of degree, of relative good and evil, was never easy for a man like him to swallow. He had already seen one country, one people he cared about fall to communism; one Vietnam was one too many. History had taught him that though some of the world's most oppressive authoritarian regimes had eventually turned democratic, a Communist country had never done so. Juan Carlos Nochenegra was bad, but at least it was possible for the Mantuegan people to go somewhere from his rule. There was hope for reform and improvement.

Barrabas shut his eyes and lightly dozed until the warning bell sounded. He awoke to a flashing light overhead. It was time to fasten seat belts for landing.

The four mercenaries stepped off the plane into stifling heat and humidity, though it was only eight in the morning.

"Welcome to Mantuego," Nanos said.

The sweat squirted from their skins as they walked across the tarmac to the terminal; the air was heavy in their lungs. The sky above was a glorious blue; in the distance palm trees waved, and farther away still, blue-green, jungle-clad mountains jutted up like mossy fangs.

They were met at the gate by a four-man military escort, who took them through to the baggage area, saw to their luggage and put them and it into an olive-green Suburban wagon. They were then driven from the airport and across town.

The tropical sunlight was blinding, but it could not hide evidence of the recent fighting. Along their route they passed burned-out buildings, shell craters in the road, bullet holes in the flamingo-pink stucco walls. The people they saw were shabbily dressed but bright-eyed, enthusiastic despite the ruin around them. Repair crews were hard at work on some of the larger structures. Next to where they labored in hard hats and swimming trunks, PFM graffiti decorated the walls.

They were driven past a broad area cordoned off with yellow tape. The smell of burned cordite hung heavy in the air. An apartment building had had its front third leveled, collapsed onto the street. They could see into the exposed floors, observe the pictures on the walls, the furniture. It was like looking into the backside of a dollhouse.

Men in surgical masks crawled over the ground-level heap of debris. In some places they were digging with shovels.

"Is that recent?" Hayes asked one of their escort.

The officer nodded. "Three nights ago, the PFM parked a car full of explosives right there. The building was the residence of several conservative representatives to our parliament. One of them was killed, the other two were not home at the time. They are still searching for bodies of the missing."

"Pretty heavy blast," Starfoot said, wincing.

"The PFM is not short on explosives. They've been using them regularly in the past weeks. It's part of their terror campaign designed to weaken the people's faith in Dr. Soarez. It seems to be working, from all accounts. That was the fifth attack in ten days."

The officer didn't seem very broken up about it.

"So, the government isn't taking any special security measures?" Barrabas asked.

"The good doctor is reluctant to establish and enforce a 10:00 p.m. curfew, and he refuses to order the necessary border checkpoints to keep the city secure. He says he doesn't want to turn Mantuego City into an island on an island."

"It sounds to me like you're close to being in a state of siege," Nanos remarked.

"The sooner Soarez admits to that the better, as far as I'm concerned," the officer told them. "The PFM have always taken advantage of any show of weakness. If we don't hard-line them soon, we're going to be in a hell of a fix."

The carryall stopped in front of the Mantuego Princess Hotel, a thirty-story, high-rise tourist trap near the bay. The place was nearly deserted; vacationers were staying away in droves because of the volatile political situation. Barrabas and the others checked in, showered and shaved, got into some fresh clothes and met the escort back in the lobby forty-five minutes later.

They were then driven to the grounds of the main army base, southwest of the capital. It was by far the most modern, most well-kept part of the city they had yet seen. Either it had been missed by rebel attacks or it had been subsequently repaired. The perimeter was ringed with triple high-wire fences, inside which jeeps patrolled. Machine-gun towers with klieg lights stuck up at even intervals. They rolled past the heavily fortified front gate onto a plain of asphalt. Everything had been paved for ten thousand yards. There was an airstrip, a control tower, hangar buildings, barracks, warehouses; all spotless, freshly painted. Troops marched in formation across the parade ground. Beyond them, helicopter gunships sat. Sounds of gunfire came from a nearby target range.

The Americans were taken to a three-story building, one of the few that were to be seen inside the base. The entrance was guarded by sentries with M-14s. Inside, the theme of Spartan comfort played heavy: linoleum floors waxed and buffed to gleaming perfection, blank walls, spotless unshaded windows, ash cans filled with nothing but clean sand. Furniture minimal. Couches and chairs made of molded plastic, no cushions.

They all rode in the elevator up to the building's top floor.

There things changed.

There was carpet. And wood paneling. And furniture that didn't break your butt.

Three generals waited for them in a conference room equipped with a large oblong table and a wet bar. Barrabas was introduced to Alvarez, Bonifacio and Del Rey—the three heads of the Mantuegan military establishment, men so powerful that even after the dictator's exile they remained in control of their little fiefdoms.

Alvarez was the oldest of the three. In his late sixties, he had a craggy face, and his nose and cheeks were blotched with broken capillaries. Bonifacio was heavyset, with an oily sheen to his face. His black eyes were as hard as rock. Del Rey, the youngest, was barely in his fifties. Suave-looking with a pencil mustache, he had a strong scent of cologne about him.

The Americans sat down around the big table after routine pleasantries had been exchanged concerning their air flight, the health of the president and so on.

"Your reputation precedes you, Colonel Barrabas," Bonifacio said, beaming. "Your career since Vietnam has been most colorful."

"And successful," Del Rey added.

Alvarez cleared his throat. "To the matter at hand, gentlemen," he said. "I know you must be anxious to begin. We are about to embark on a most ambitious and, in the history of our country, unprecedented undertaking. We put much value on your input."

"I take it you've already developed some preliminary plans?" Barrabas asked. When the generals nodded that they had, he said, "Before you explain them to me in any detail, I'd like to get an idea of the type of resistance you expect to meet and the anticipated locations of same."

Del Rey took the floor. "Resistance we categorize in two groups. First, those loyal to Dr. Soarez: Social Democrats, liberals, moderate conservatives. These would include but not be limited to the man's appointees—the head of the civilian police, local officials and the like. While only a few of these will take up guns, most will support those who do. This type of resistance we expect to find in and around government installations and in the middle and lower-class neighborhoods."

"I think it is important to note," Alvarez added, "that the large majority of Mantuegans will do nothing but hide in their houses until the shooting is over. They are sick of Soarez's failures, economically, politically and militarily, and would welcome back a strong and intelligent leader."

"So," Hayes said, "you are saying that Mantuego is a ripe plum, ready to fall into Nochenegra's lap?"

"Except for the PFM," Del Rey said. "They, of course, are the second and main focus of the armed resistance we will face. You can be sure that the moment fighting begins between elements of our forces and those of Soarez, the Communists will be out in force, and that they will join the Social Democrats against us. It will be their best and only chance to defeat us. If they do, it will be easy for them to destroy the weakened forces of Soarez."

"The PFM doesn't want Juan Carlos back," Bonifacio stated. "It is afraid of him and us."

"I think we get the picture," Barrabas said. "What's your basic plan?"

Alvarez took over the discussion, asking them all to rise and taking them over to a three-dimensional model of the island built atop a table. He picked up a wooden pointer and began.

"Our first action is actually three pronged. Three separate maneuvers undertaken simultaneously. We will isolate the palace with Soarez inside, cutting phone lines and road access; we will seize the media centers, television and radio; and we will block off all roads leading in and out of the city.

"That accomplished, we will close off the slum, El Infierno, by lining the opposite banks of the rivers with troops and machine guns. Troops will be ferried from the airfield base by helicopter to pockets of opposition. We will establish twenty-four-hour kill-on-sight zones here, here and here."

"So you are confining the battle zone to the area around the slum?" Starfoot said.

"We want to minimize damage to commercial interests, for obvious reasons," Alvarez explained.

Hayes shot Barrabas a furious look.

"When we have the situation under control, we'll take the palace," the eldest general finished. "Then we will give Juan Carlos the green light to land."

"How long do you figure it will take you to get control of the city, assuming everything goes right?" Nanos asked.

Bonifacio shrugged. "No more than eight hours," he answered. "If we start the operation at dawn, I see no reason why Juan Carlos can't expect to enjoy a late lunch on the palace veranda the same day."

"What do you think of the plan, Colonel Barrabas?" Del Rey asked.

"It sounds workable to me. I'd like to take a look at the city before I make further comments. Something might occur to me as an outsider that you might have missed."

"There is always that slight possibility," Alvarez admitted.

"If we could," Barrabas said, "I'd like to make our survey at once."

"Of course," Bonifacio said. "I will give your escort instructions. You can leave right away."

The same group of soldiers who had chauffeured them around earlier did the honors. Barrabas referred to a city map and told the officer where he wanted to go and what he wanted to see. As they drove, the officer gave them a running commentary on the multitude of evils the Soarez government had wrought. These included weakening the military to provide social services to the needy, cracking down on corruption and waste in same, letting the political opposition speak freely. Everything that the good Dr. Soarez had done, it seemed, only opened the door wider for the Communists, ruined the business climate and played pure havoc with the tourist trade.

To listen to the man talk and look out the window at the tattered but still vibrant town made Barrabas feel uncomfortable, as if he was visiting a person who was dying but didn't know it yet.

The more the officer talked the more dour Claude Hayes got. Even Nanos and Starfoot picked up on it.

"I don't see any food lines," Claude said.

"Excuse?" the officer replied.

"We heard there were food shortages and that the economy was in a state of collapse. I don't see any evidence of it."

The officer looked at Barrabas impatiently, as if he expected some help. He didn't get any. The white-haired man stared him down until he blanched and answered. "Well, of course, you wouldn't see it here," he said with a thin smile. "This is one of the better parts of town...."

Outside the carryall were bougainvillea-draped arbors, whitewashed mansions clinging to verdant hillsides.

"One of the parts you intend to protect," Nanos said.

"Who lives here?" Billy asked.

"The most important people in Mantuego. Military, business and, of course, the foreign investors."

"Somehow that doesn't surprise me," Hayes said. "Why don't you take us to one of the worst parts of town? I'd really like to see that El Infierno the general mentioned. I'd like to walk around inside it."

"I'm sorry but that's impossible. It's not safe."

"You guys have got guns," Billy said.

"We would be ambushed by the PFM before we got a hundred yards. Since Soarez took power the Communists have infiltrated the slum in large numbers. The only way for men in uniform to enter there now is in overwhelming numbers. They routinely kill the small patrols

we send in and throw the bodies in the river to wash out
to sea. We have to pick the mutilated corpses out of the
bay.''

As they drove by the seal-off points on the roads leading into the city, it started to rain. It was as if they were
suddenly in a different country. A country of delicious
coolness. The rain was torrential but didn't last long.
After half an hour, everything had dried up and it seemed
hotter and stickier than before.

They rolled downhill into the lower-class neighborhoods that would be the free-fire zone. Soarez likenesses
were stuck up on telephone poles, on the sides of buildings. He was a frail-looking man with thinning hair and
round, rimless glasses. He appeared scholarly. Intellectual. Kindly.

"Why haven't they ripped down the signs?" Nanos
asked the officer.

"Pardon?"

"If Soarez is so damned unpopular, why do the people leave the signs up?"

"He is popular with Communists and Communist
sympathizers," the officer explained. "I promise you, on
the day of the coup there will not be a single Soarez face
around here."

They passed through the downtown section, staying
several blocks south of the twin rivers and El Infierno.
The streets showed signs of being recently repaired, shell
holes filled in. The large commercial buildings had scaffolding up; repairs were still being made.

"That is the Mandelo Arch," the officer announced
proudly.

The structure in question stood on a concrete island in
the middle of a broad traffic circle. It was 150 feet high,

and actually not one arch, but two that intersected to form a giant M.

"At night when it is lit up, yellow like gold, it is most beautiful."

"Reminds me of something," Nanos said. "I can't quite put my finger on it."

"You de-serve a break to-day," Billy sang tunelessly.

Barrabas nudged him with an elbow and he shut up.

The tour ended at dark. Over Barrabas's protestations the officer took them all to a restaurant. He said he had been ordered to and he would get into serious trouble if he didn't. The food was just like what they had sampled at Juan Carlos's party—thoroughly inedible. They struggled through the meal, watching the officer and his men get tanked on pineapple-with-parasol drinks. None of the Americans drank anything alcoholic. They weren't left alone for a moment. If one of them went to the head, one of the soldiers went, too. If two of them went, two soldiers went.

It was after midnight when they got back to their hotel. By then the officer had sobered up enough to make arrangements to pick them up late the next morning. As they entered, Barrabas noticed four soldiers sitting in the lobby, looking very much out of place. When the mercenaries got into the elevator, two of the Mantuegan enlisted men rose from their seats and joined them in the car.

"Just along for the ride?" Nanos said to the back of the neck of the man standing in front of him.

The soldier did not respond. Maybe he didn't speak English. That was something none of them could count on. They all kept silent.

The soldiers got out on their floor. It was clear that the second shift had taken over the foreigner watch. When

Barrabas and the others went to their separate rooms, the soldiers took up sentry positions in the hall.

Barrabas shut his door and locked it. Then he walked to the sliding glass doors that opened onto his little sea-view balcony. The others were already clambering over the concrete porch railings—Hayes onto Barrabas's, Starfoot onto Nanos's and then both of them onto Barrabas's.

Some twenty stories below them, the lights of the city and the ships in the bay twinkled.

"Pretty peaceful, huh?" Nanos said.

They were all thinking the same thing.

Hayes put it into words. "Colonel, this island isn't a powderkeg. Powderkegs have a certain feeling to them. A kind of crackle in the air. Electric. Ozone. I think we've been handed a crock. None of what the generals said makes sense. None of what that jerk official tour guide said makes sense. None of what Nochenegra said makes sense, either. We've got to do some reconnoitering on our own to make sure, otherwise we could be handing these people here a hell of a lot more heartache and grief than they deserve."

Barrabas frowned. "As individuals we aren't in any position to judge the PFM threat."

"No, but we can talk to some people, maybe find out what really gives here. We can at least get a handle on how the Mantuegans feel about Soarez."

"I don't like the way we've been steered around so far," Nanos said, "and I sure as hell don't like the house arrest we're under."

Barrabas thought for a second, then said, "Okay, we'll go out and have a look around."

"Great!" Nanos said. "Nightlife."

"Not you," Barrabas told him. "Just me and Hayes. Have you got your Kevlar on, Claude?"

"Yes, sir."

"How are you going to shake the guys in the hall?" Starfoot asked.

"We aren't," Barrabas told him, "you are. You and Alex are going to go down to the bar for a nightcap. One at a time. About three minutes apart. Take the stairs. Act suspicious."

"In other words, just do what comes natural," Hayes said.

Barrabas was emphatic. "Make sure you get followed."

"What about the guys waiting by the elevator downstairs?" Nanos said.

"We'll worry about them."

"How're you going to get back without being seen?" Billy said. "I mean, if the generals find out, they're going to be pissed."

"We'll call your rooms from a pay phone," Barrabas said. "You can pull the same routine again."

Hayes waited by the hall door with the colonel while Nanos and Starfoot climbed back across the balconies to their respective rooms. They heard one door open and close down the hall, then the sound of footsteps quick-marching down the corridor toward the fire stairs. Some unintelligible words were passed—presumably between the two soldiers. Then running footsteps. The stairwell door banged back.

After a couple of minutes, the whole thing happened again. Except that the hallway guard tried to talk Billy out of his nightcap. A difficult task when you are giving up ten inches in height and a hundred pounds in weight, all muscle.

Barrabas and Hayes took the elevator down to the second floor and got out. The hallway was deserted. They hurried down the corridor until they found a room without a Do Not Disturb sign on the knob, and Hayes used a credit card to pop the lock. The room was empty. It had been a bad year for tourists. They then opened the slider, and jumped from the balcony to a sidewalk planter filled with nice, resilient redwood chips.

Then they ran around the corner and hailed a taxi.

"Take us to El Infierno," Hayes told the driver.

The man just stared at them.

Then Hayes said it in Spanish.

Comprehension wasn't the problem.

"You crazy or something?" the cabbie said. "There's nothing there for Americans. No nightclubs. No casinos. I know some great places. I'll take you. I'll show you."

"We aren't interested in the Mantuego-by-night tour," Barrabas said. "We just want to talk to some real people about what's going on here. About how they feel about President Soarez."

"And we don't want to listen to crap," Hayes told him. "We just got through with a sixteen-hour bullshit-o-rama session with guys in uniform."

"Are you journalists?"

"No," Barrabas said, "free-lance sociologists. And we've got a bug up our ass about getting to the truth."

"Humor us," Hayes suggested, shoving a wad of money in his face.

"El Infierno, it is," the taximan said, slapping down his meter and ripping away from the curb.

He stopped the cab at one end of a narrow wooden bridge. On the other side of it was a black hole. No electricity. They caught the swamp-gas smell of river mud . . . and high-density human occupation.

Hayes paid the man and they got out. They were the only people on the bridge. It shuddered under them as they crossed it.

At night the slum was lit by lantern and torch. The light flickered and wavered and cast wild shadows across the dirt streets. El Infierno proper had a smell all its own. Eau de Third World. A piquant combination of outdoor plumbing, exotic spices and burning garbage heaps.

And it had sounds.

Screams. River rush. Congas. Radio. Laughter. Babies crying. Dogs barking.

Barrabas and Hayes walked, taking it in. Slum people sat in the doorways of their huts, openings hacked in sheet tin and cardboard. There were no doors, no locks. Black plastic hung over the entrances to the shanties. Or old bedspreads. The people stared at the strangers, and with reason. Mantuegans were not usually large in stature. Comparatively speaking, Barrabas and Hayes were giants. And the slum dwellers, having a poor diet and nonexistent health care, had no body bulk, no muscle mass to speak of.

"I think we're a hundred yards in," Hayes said as they followed the winding lane.

The houses of El Infierno were so small, and on lots so tiny, that they reminded Barrabas of the rows of stalls at a swap meet. As there were no curtains over the window openings cut into the walls, it was possible to see inside. Rows of candles burned on wooden ledges. Broken mattresses lay on the dirt floors. And on the mattresses, many babies.

Hayes stuck his head into one of the shacks, spoke softly for a moment, then entered. He had a brief conversation with a woman whose four babies and toddlers crawled around her feet. Barrabas was fluent in Spanish, but the words were whispered so softly that he couldn't understand.

Hayes exited with a scowl on his face. "I hate this place," he said. "I bloody hate it." As they moved on, he continued. "Everyone in that house is sick. One of the babies has a high fever. The mother said Soarez is the only hope for her family. She showed me the free medicine she was given at the government clinic. She said the PFM isn't as strong as they seem, that they do bad things to scare people, but that there are no more than a hundred of them in the slum."

Barrabas said nothing.

They came upon what in El Infierno passed for a bar. It was a shack like the others, except it had a covered porch running the length of its front, and on the porch, on chairs with the stuffing exploded out and legless couches, were drunken men and women. All sweaty. All wild-eyed.

Barrabas knew it was not the wisest place to enter. He also knew that he couldn't stop Hayes, short of knocking him unconscious. More than that, he knew that he would have to follow because he could not desert him. Claude had witnessed enough human misery in his thirty-some years to drive an ordinary man insane. Enough to make a man pull the covers over his head and stay in bed forever. Claude Hayes had never run from anything in his life. He flat out didn't know how to do it. When he came upon something that terrified him, he did battle. He took no quarter. Poverty and disease had scared him pretty badly the past few years. And he had made them pay. Hayes was like a diamond. Hard. Cutting. True.

When they stepped under the doorway, everything inside the bar stopped. All talk. All laughter. All music. All breathing. It was a tiny room and packed with people.

"What do you want?" someone said in Spanish.

Hayes replied. "To talk."

"No, they want to die," said a man with a machete.

"Who are you?" a drunken woman demanded.

"That doesn't matter," Hayes said. "We want to know about Dr. Soarez. About what you think of him."

Perhaps because they were mostly ripped out of their skulls, and therefore brave as lions, perhaps because from the strangers' accents and appearance it was obvious they weren't spies for either the PFM or the Nochenegra side, the people spoke.

Everyone talked at once. There was no stopping them. They said that Dr. Emilio Soarez was the second coming, the reincarnation of the great Mandelo. That he was their true savior. That before him they had been caught between El Dragón—Juan Carlos's nickname among the peasantry—and the PFM. That they wanted neither.

"Do you know what it is to finally have hope?" one man asked. "To see a way clear of this place?"

"And the PFM?" Barrabas asked.

"That one is PFM," said the man with the machete. He pointed it at a thin man in a straw cowboy hat just slipping out the door. "He goes to tell his comrades. They try to make us do what they want, but only the weak-willed ones join them. *Los condenados*, people who live in the suburbs of hell, fear no one."

Barrabas finally had his answer. It had been sticking in his craw for days now—an instinctive, gut-level response to Juan Carlos, to the generals. Normally he trusted his instincts. This was not a normal situation. It evoked too many resonances of his past. Of Nam.

Hayes and the colonel left the bar. They continued down the narrow, rutted track, which wound through claptrap low rises and was bordered by an open sewer. The path ended in an open spot where a tall heap of rubbish smoldered. Mattress springs, tin cans, foam rubber billowed vile black smoke. It was a sort of primitive courtyard, bounded on all sides by shacks. Shacks that were jammed wall to wall, cardboard to plywood to sheet tin.

"I guess we'd better backtrack and try another way," Hayes suggested.

Barrabas opened his mouth to respond, but the words died on his tongue.

Footsteps. Behind them.

Many footsteps.

Stealthy.

He turned. Shadows moved at the fringes of the dim dancing light cast by the rubbish fire. Light that glinted off the blades of many machetes.

They were surrounded.

15

At about the same time, some twenty miles to the north, Walker Jessup was peering out the co-pilot's window of a rickety DC-3, looking for the landing lights that had been promised. He badly wanted to find the lights, for they were flying low and slow, and without clearance, an easy target for a Mantuegan attack helicopter.

"There it is," the pilot said.

Two rows of yellow fire points, torches, flicked on out of the pitch-blackness below them.

Jessup twisted in his seat and shouted back to Hatton, Beck and O'Toole, who were strapped into jump seats among the weapons crates. "We've got it!" he said. "Brace yourselves. We're going in."

The fat man was much relieved that they were finally on their way down to make the rendezvous. He had sweated rings around rings. In his opinion, nothing was worse than a night flight in a clunky old beater of an aircraft. Except maybe a nearly blind night landing. He gripped the bottom of his seat as the pilot banked, slowed and descended.

At the very last second, after he had already dropped below the level of the trees, the pilot hit his landing lights. The sudden glare picked up two lines of men holding crude, blazing torches, and the runway. Jessup wished he hadn't seen the runway. It was nothing but a field that had been recently cleared and more or less smoothed over. The DC-3 bounced and skittered, but came in without digging a wing tip or crashing nose first into an irrigation ditch.

"Piece of cake," the pilot said, after he had brought the plane to a stop. He taxied it 180 degrees, readying it for the takeoff, and then cut his lights.

The torches winked out as the men doused them, plunging the makeshift landing field into darkness.

Jessup unbuckled his seat belt and turned for the rear of the plane. This was to be a quick hit-and-git. They were to land, dump the matériel and get the hell out before the Mantuegan military could move in.

The others were already up by the time the Texan got to them. Beck was opening the side door. It slammed back. Outside the night was oppressively humid. Jessup pushed past O'Toole to the doorway and leaned out. There were a lot of men below. He could not see faces, only vague outlines. "Who's your leader?" he said.

"Me," came the reply. "You are Americans?"

The question seemed odd, as did the man's tone of voice. As if he was truly surprised. And pleasantly so.

Jessup turned on a flashlight and swept it over the men standing beneath him. He had himself quite a shock. For one thing, there were about sixty AK-47s pointed at him; for another, the men doing the pointing were all stripped to the waist, in red headbands, with long straggly hair.

They sure as hell weren't FSI.

There was only one other possibility.

Jessup reacted at once. He clicked off the flash and threw himself down inside the plane, shouting for the pilot to get them the hell out.

The pilot hit his starters and the engines caught right off. The plane began to roll away from the crowd on the field. The runway ahead was pitch-black as the DC-3 lumbered along, rapidly picking up speed.

"Mother of God," Liam groaned, leaning into the cockpit, seeing what the pilot was seeing out the front window.

That was nothing at all.

Over the roar of the throttled-up engines gunshots rang out and the plane lurched wildly. It suddenly had no tires on its landing gear. It wobbled dangerously, wings seesawing up and down.

Too dangerously.

"Can't do it," the pilot said, shutting down the engines. "No way. Goddamned suicide."

"What's going on?" Dr. Hatton demanded of Jessup.

The Texan mopped his brow with a huge handkerchief. "We've got problems," he said as the aircraft came to a stop.

After a minute or two, fists and rifle butts pounded on the underside of the plane's hull.

"Come out!" someone shouted from below.

"We've got guns," Liam said, popping the top off the nearest crate. "We can fight...." He picked up a spanking-new Kalashnikov. "What the fuck!"

"How're you going to fight?" the pilot asked. "You're sitting on enough high-test fuel to blow us to hell and back. One spark, man, and she blows."

"Come out or we'll come in," called one of the men outside.

"All this shit's ComBloc," Beck said, checking the contents of the other crates.

"Who the hell are we working for, Jessup?" Hatton asked.

Jessup was speechless.

"Come on," Beck said, "we might as well go out and get the bad news."

They lowered the gangway ladder and descended, hands on top of their heads.

From the darkness came the sound of truck engines starting up. The SOBs were marched at gunpoint to the edge of the field and made to lie down on their stomachs while the plane was unloaded. It took about five minutes. There were a lot of helpers.

Jessup was trying to figure out what the hell had happened. The guerrillas were clearly expecting the shipment. They were prepared to assist with the landing—at just the right time—and to move the stuff once it arrived. It was possible that they had waylaid and disposed of the FSI men who should have been the ones collecting the weapons. Very remotely possible. That didn't explain the type of weapons he had delivered, which had come as a complete surprise to him. He was expecting to pass out M-16s, not AK-47s. Jessup had a powerful feeling that he had been had—in spades.

When the loading of the trucks was complete, the Americans were ordered up.

The man who had spoken to them before spoke again. "Take that one," he said, "the pilot, and put him back in the plane."

The pilot was set upon by four men and jerked away from Jessup and the others before they could do anything to help him.

"What's going on here?" Jessup demanded.

"Get in the back of the truck," the man ordered.

Twenty AKs ringed them.

The odds were suicidal.

They got in, guarded by five armed men. As the truck took off, bounding over the ungraded part of the field, the DC-3 exploded. A thunderous bang, a flash of orange light, and the plane flew apart.

"You bastards!" Beck said.

For his trouble he got a gun butt smack in the middle of his face.

The ride didn't take long. Jessup couldn't see much out the open back of the truck. The headlights of the following truck illuminated the sides of the road when they went around a turn. All he saw was bush, trees tightly packed. He tried to keep himself oriented, but lost track of their direction after a dozen turns.

One of the turns sent them down a road so narrow that the foliage brushed the sides of the truck and scraped the roof. Then the convoy stopped.

The Americans were ordered out and forced to stand against the mud wall of an outbuilding while the guerrillas moved the boxes of weapons from the trucks to a previously prepared hole in the ground. It was high tech, shored up with timbers.

After the crates were laid down, the top of the hole was covered with boards, sheet plastic and a layer of dirt.

The trucks then turned around and left.

"At least I don't see another hole around here," Beck pointed out, "for us."

"Why would they bother digging?" Liam asked. "They could take us out in the bush and dump us anyplace."

"Hold that happy thought," Lee said.

The leader of the guerrillas told them to march, single file, with their hands on their heads. They followed a slender and apparently little-traveled trail. The bush was so dense on both sides of them that escape into the trees was impossible. As they walked they came to several forks. Jessup tried to keep track of their path, the distance they had gone; it kept his mind off what he was sure was coming.

For a while they climbed uphill, then moved off the path. Two of the guerrillas continued on, to leave a trail for pursuit, if any materialized.

The guerrillas took them to a cave in a hillside. Its entrance was hidden by brush and vines. When they were pushed inside, a piece of fabric, a light-proof cloth inner door, hit Jessup in the face.

Someone lit a match, then a Coleman lantern.

The cave was no more than ten feet deep.

The leader indicated with his assault rifle that they should all sit with their backs to the wall. He was extremely short and widely built.

"I am El Ticón," he announced. "Co-commander of the PFM. Welcome to Mantuego."

Dr. Lee checked Nate's face. He had a nasty contusion above his right eyebrow.

"We didn't expect such a wonderful gift," the leader told them.

"You mean the weapons," Jessup said sourly.

"No, the guns and munitions were as promised," El Ticón said. "You're the surprise. Previous deliveries have been made by Cuban friends. Are you CIA? Who hired you? What do you know of the arms-supply operation?"

"We don't know anything," Jessup returned. "If we had, do you think we would have been so stupid as to land in that field?"

El Ticón pulled at his sparse goatee. "Perhaps it is some kind of trick. Perhaps the weapons are sabotaged."

"Then we sure as hell wouldn't have delivered them knowing that. We were tricked."

"How and by whom?"

Jessup could feel the eyes of the mercenaries burning into his neck.

"Yeah, fat man," Liam urged, "tell us a story."

Jessup shivered. Did it really matter now if he told the PFM leader the truth? Or as much of the truth as he knew? He had a sinking feeling about the weapons transfer: that it had been going on for some time and that the Cubans were never really behind it. He decided to play it as coy as he could without incurring the man's wrath.

"You were supposed to be FSI," he said.

The leader laughed. "If that is true, you must have had a terrible shock."

Jessup tried to smile.

"Who hired you?" El Ticón demanded.

This was the touchy part. "An intermediary of Juan Carlos Nochenegra."

"But not the Cubans?"

The man didn't seem all that surprised.

Jessup responded by asking, "You know about Nochenegra?"

"We have known from the second shipment," El Ticón said. "Juan Carlos thinks we are idiots. All we had to do was check with officials in Cuba and Angola. They refused us help more than once. We thought it strange that they should suddenly come around. We know who is sending the guns and we don't care. Actually it is more appropriate that Nochenegra provides the weapons that will enable us to liberate the island. The slave master ends up freeing his slaves."

The cloth hanging in front of the cave entrance swung back and another man entered. He was tall for a Mantuegan, with a full black beard and a camou beret.

"So, these are the Americans," the new arrival said, looking them over. He eyed Dr. Hatton a long time. "And a pretty woman, too. Was she the flight attendant?"

El Ticón said to the prisoners, "This is Major Zed, my co-commander." Then to Zed, "This changes the plans, no?"

"For the better."

Major Zed hunkered down practically nose to nose with Lee. "You see, we planned to assassinate that imperialist puppet Soarez tomorrow. We intended to take credit for the killing ourselves. Now things are different."

Dr. Hatton stared the man down, never blinking.

He pulled back and said, "We will forgo the glory in the service of our cause. What will the people of Mantuego do when they hear that their simpering elitist president has been murdered by agents of the American government? Agents undoubtedly working for the return of the hated Nochenegra? They will flock to us and we will be victorious."

"Except that we aren't going to kill Soarez," Lee Hatton said. "We'll all die before that happens."

"No," Major Zed said, "you'll die afterward."

16

There was no doubt in Barrabas's mind who the guys with the cane choppers were.

PFM.

The Communist who'd run out of the no-name bar had gone and brought back some pals. The odds purely stank. They were fifteen-to-one against. Like a pack of sharks, the guerrillas circled the ramshackle courtyard, keeping to the shadows.

Hayes and the colonel stood shoulder to shoulder, their backs to the burning rubbish heap. They watched, knees bent, bodies poised, ready to respond to the coming attack.

The PFM were in no big hurry. They were sure they had their quarry trapped, helpless—as good as dead. They had obviously run this same routine before with success. They wanted to enjoy its unfolding. Slowly, they closed in, some of them rushing, feinting, then retreating.

"Quite a brave bunch of *pinche putos*, aren't we?" Barrabas said, faking a sudden rush of his own and watching them melt back into the darkness. The white-haired man was pumped with adrenaline, but he wasn't afraid. He wasn't afraid, because he refused to allow fear to enter his mind. He made no room for it. His whole attention was focused on one thing: how many of the bastards he could kill.

It was more than a bizarre, even perverse sort of optimism; it was a kind of personal creed. In any potentially lethal situation, no matter how lopsided the odds, there was the opportunity, the "license," for both sides to commit mayhem. Nile Barrabas made it a matter of course to take advantage of such opportunities to the fullest.

The PFM didn't appreciate his obscene reference to their station in life. They shouted taunts back at him in Spanish and Pidgin English; they whistled and hooted.

It was all performance.

An intended distraction.

When the rush came, Hayes and Barrabas were ready for it.

It came from behind, from over the top of the burning rubbish pile: three shrieking guerrillas stormed over the smoldering hummock with machetes waving.

As Barrabas pivoted to face the attack, a blade slashed across the front of his neck. He felt the breeze of it as it swept inches from his throat. Instead of backing up, he lunged forward, inside the man's guard. He fired a full-force blow to the side of his attacker's head. A blow with plenty of hip and leg in it. It still wasn't enough to knock the guy out—he had a hell of a hard head—but it was enough to stun him and momentarily weaken his grip on the well-worn machete.

Barrabas ripped the crudely forged weapon from his hand. As he turned to help Hayes he was struck from behind. The heavy blow fell across the middle of his back and drove him into a half crouch. Pain numbed him for a second, all the way to the soles of his feet. Without the Kevlar, he would have been numb for the rest of his life. The machete would have severed his spinal cord. He spun without rising from the low stance, back-slashing his own blade at thigh height. It chunked into something solid. Something that screamed blue blazes.

He jerked the machete back from the man's leg. Blood gushed from the bisected quadriceps and the guerrilla tumbled backward into the fire.

The man Barrabas had punched made no move to help his fallen comrade. He staggered, half crawling to the safety of numbers.

Hayes had taken care of his opponent, as well. Barrabas had missed the blow-by-blow, but it looked like the man on his face in the dirt had a broken neck.

The Americans waved their captured weapons menacingly, driving back the PFM who had tried to move in while they were occupied. Barrabas glanced behind them at the fire. It wasn't a signal that the Communists could recognize, but Hayes did, at once. It was time for an intelligent retreat. They turned and scrambled over the burning heap, running across the shambles of a courtyard.

The men on the other side of the fire panicked at the sight of the big men waving long knives, and they scattered, blundering into those running around the fire to pursue.

They gave Barrabas and Hayes a few extra seconds.

The colonel and his comrade sorely needed them.

In front of the Americans there was no apparent exit. Only an unbroken row of shacks jammed wall to wall. Had they been made of brick or had they been wood frame, Barrabas and Hayes would have been done for. But the colonel knew what he was doing.

He led the way, charging through the doorless doorway of a cardboard shanty. Inside, a man and a woman were frantically coupling by candlelight. The lovers froze on the ratty mattress, their eyes full of terror, when they saw the two huge men burst in.

They had nothing to fear; however, the same was not true for their corrugated-paper house.

Barrabas charged straight to the back wall and began hacking at it, slicing great rents in the cardboard. Four strokes and he was through it and also through the abutting cardboard wall of the house behind.

He shouldered through the opening; Hayes was right on his heels.

They slipped into a much more elaborate domicile. It had a filthy shag throw rug on its packed dirt floor. A skylight of clear sheet plastic. Orange-crate furniture. Six naked children huddled in panic against the wall.

The Americans barged on through, out the doorway, out onto another winding lane. Barrabas didn't hesitate over direction. It didn't matter which way they went. They had no idea of the street plan, if any, of the slum.

He sprinted down the narrow alleyway, trying to put some distance between them and their pursuers. They could hear shouts behind them. The PFM had broken through into the street. Barrabas had to work hard to keep ahead of Hayes. It was no wonder: the black man was eight years younger than he was. But ahead he stayed. The white noise, the rushing sound of the river was growing louder; he could hear it over the thudding of his heart, the slap of his shoes on the path.

As they rounded a turn, they saw four men with machetes standing in the middle of the dimly lit lane. The guerrillas were waiting for them. Barrabas realized at once what had happened: the Communists had split up their forces to cut off all possible routes of escape.

Still running, Hayes looked at Barrabas. It was do-or-die time. They charged, machetes overhead.

This was no delicate contest of musketeers, no waving of elegantly forged, wire-thin blades. This was a meat-market hack-a-thon. In the dusty dark, there were no capering titled gentlemen pulling tricky ballet moves, quoting poetry, sniffing at nosegays.

This was close-quarters combat.

Close enough to catch the reek of liquor and garlic on the opponent's breath as he swore and spit.

Steel clanged on steel, spraying showers of fat sparks, sending jolting, nerve-numbing impacts up arms. Steel on steel screeched a thin, shrill counterpoint to the grunts of the combatants.

Barrabas drove his men back with broad back-and-forth slashes of his machete. He knew they had to go down. He and Hayes could not simply run past them. That would offer them a shot at their backs. A machete swipe from behind could clip an Achilles tendon and end one's running days in a hurry. In this case, it would end their days, period. If they couldn't flee, they would be chopped to death.

He saw the fear growing in the guerrillas' eyes as they realized how strong he was and how demonically determined. They fought back like cornered rats: frenzied, all-out. They blocked his ringing blows and tried to counterpunch, to slash him, any way, anywhere.

From behind him one of the men Hayes was fighting let out a squeal of agony, followed by an equally high-pitched cry, "¡Aieeeee madre! ¡Madre mío!"

Barrabas dodged an overhead swipe and countered with a full-power sideswipe. The blade bit into flesh at the shoulder. It slid easily through tendon, gristle and muscle all the way down to the bone socket.

The guerrilla wailed, dropping his weapon, clutching his spurting shoulder. Blinded by pain, he staggered to the side, and in so doing inadvertently blocked his partner's next swing.

Barrabas took advantage of the opening. He reverse-pivoted, building up momentum, and slashed at the man's head. The blade cleaved the guerrilla across the face, from cheek to cheek just under the eyes, cutting his nose in half crosswise, opening a horrendous gaping wound.

The man collapsed to his knees, clutching his ruined face and shrieking.

Barrabas turned in time to see Hayes trying to lever his machete free from the top of his second opponent's skull, where it was securely stuck.

Behind them—close behind—came shouts and the sound of running feet.

"Leave it!" Barrabas shouted, grabbing Hayes by the arm and pulling him away. He waved Hayes on. It sounded as if the entire contingent had regrouped and was after them.

The Americans ran blind down narrow, twisting streets as the pursuers steadily gained. The guerrillas were used to moving in humid ninety-degree-plus temperatures; they were just getting their second wind. Barrabas knew that it was only a matter of time before he and Hayes were run down by the PFM or run into another dead end.

The river sound to their left was so loud it was almost palpable. Ahead on that side, Barrabas saw an opening in the unbroken line of shacks, a gap caused by a fire from the previous riot. It was three shacks wide.

"This way!" he told Hayes.

They ducked through the vacant lot, and looked down on the black, sliding width of the Letargo. It was moving by at a rapid clip. They had no choice. Barrabas chucked his weapon aside and slid down the steeply eroded bank. He and Hayes reached the water at the same moment, just as the PFM arrived above and behind them.

Barrabas splashed out to his waist in the cool water, feeling the tug of the current, then he dived in. He was instantly swept away by the flow. There was no point in fighting it; he couldn't win. He bobbed, treading water, as he was carried pell-mell downstream. He couldn't see Hayes ahead or behind him. "Claude!" he shouted. He got no reply.

He could see the tops of the downtown high rises. He was really moving. The water was full of debris, snags, deadhead logs. He tried to get close to the far bank and couldn't. He was caught, stuck in the middle of the flow, the strongest current.

Then he saw the beach. The river mouth. Both came and went.

And he hit tidewater. The current was still too strong for him to fight. It drove him farther and farther out into Mantuego Bay. He could see the lights of the city behind him, growing smaller, fainter. He had to do something and fast. His best bet was to swim perpendicular to the current and hope he could get past its influence.

As he started to swim, someone called his name.

"Claude?" he shouted back. "Where the hell are you?"

Barrabas heard the sound of splashing. Then he saw a dark form coming toward him.

Hayes stopped a yard from him and dog-paddled. "We got quite a swim ahead of us, Colonel."

Barrabas looked at the distant lights. "Yeah, loser buys, okay?"

17

Liam spent an uncomfortable night on the dirt floor. It wouldn't have been so bad but he couldn't use his arms for a pillow. The PFM had figure-eighted his thumbs together with stainless-steel wire. He hadn't been singled out for special treatment; they all had been bound the same way. After six hours of such restraint, not only did the tips of his thumbs ache horribly from having the circulation cut off for so long, but the nerve pain radiated from them all the way up his arms and into his shoulders.

O'Toole knew he could have broken the bonds. He had the physical strength and the willpower. But it would have cost him both thumbs. And that would have severely limited his options. It would have made it impossible for him to make a fist, to hold a gun or a knife. Crippled in that way, he couldn't improve their situation.

The other option open to him was to slip his connected hands under his buttocks and legs and at least have them out in front of him so he could use them to pound or, even better, to strangle. It was the kind of move he would only get to use once. He had to make sure it counted for something.

The odds were too long as things stood now.

He lay there pretending to be asleep, listening to Jessup snuffle and snore. O'Toole was not bothered by mixed feelings about the fat man. He wanted to kill him. He kicked himself for not talking the others out of the mission when he had the chance. They should have known better than to take the sneaky pete's word for anything. In retrospect, it seemed obvious it was a setup: Barrabas supposedly in big trouble and the job needed to help him out so easy, so quick and so lucrative.

Liam was imagining interesting ways of almost killing Jessup when their captors entered the cave bearing breakfast.

The PFM guerrillas prodded them awake with boot toes.

O'Toole and the others struggled up to sitting positions against the wall.

One of the PFM underlings had a net bag full of mangoes, which he inverted on the dirt in front of them. *"El desayuno,"* he said.

"How are we supposed to eat them?" Jessup demanded in fractured Spanish.

"Como perro," the man said. "Like the dog."

Beck shook his head. "I'd rather starve."

"Me, too," Lee agreed.

Jessup eyed the ripe fruit as if he hadn't eaten for a week. He shuddered and slumped back against the wall. "No way, José," he said.

Liam grinned. "Look at it on the bright side, Jessup, at least you won't be hungry for long."

"Nor you thirsty," he countered.

The smile melted from the Irish-American's face. That was hitting below the belt.

The curtain over the cave entrance pushed back and Major Zed entered. "We go now," he said, ordering the prisoners to their feet.

Jessup needed help. It took three men to right him.

They were taken out of the cave and led back down the hillside to the site of the previous night's arms cache. The hole that had been so carefully covered was now exposed, earth mounded to one side, plastic and boards tossed away. The pit was empty.

"Don't worry," Major Zed said as they skirted it, "at this very moment, El Ticón is busy distributing the munitions to people who will put them to good use."

Liam wasn't worried, but he kept his mouth shut. And his eyes open. He could tell the others were thinking the same thing—that between now and whenever the PFM planned to execute Soarez was all the time they were going to have to turn the tables and get away. Their lives depended on whatever angle they found in the next few hours; they couldn't afford to miss anything.

Parked at the end of the two-rut road where the trucks had pulled in the night before was a white, official-looking van.

As they walked around it, Liam saw three bare butts in the high grass to his right. Three dead guys lying face-down in a row. Stripped naked and dumped like garbage. The side of the van had an insignia and a logo that said it belonged to the Mantuegan Ministry of Justice.

While they stood by the van, Major Zed and two of his colleagues stripped down to their khaki undershorts and put on the dead policemen's uniforms. They had their weapons, too. Three Uzis.

"Get in the back," Major Zed told the captives.

They were shoved into the rear of what was apparently a convict-transportation van. There was a wire-mesh wall between them and the driver and co-pilot, and over the back windows. In the back there was one seat, for an armed guard who rode shotgun. The prisoners sat on the sheet-metal floor.

As the van roared out of the clearing, the Americans took quite a bouncing. The ride smoothed out considerably once they hit the main road to town. Major Zed, who was riding shotgun, said, "This reminds me of a story. Do you know the writings of the philosopher Mandelo?"

Under any other circumstances Liam would have maintained resolute silence, but not now. He wanted to draw the man out any way he could, to try to find a weakness. "Never heard of him," he said. "A local boy?"

"Your ignorance doesn't surprise me," Major Zed said with a sneer. "Neither does your smugness. I take pity on you. Mandelo was a true prophet; he foresaw everything that has come to pass in Mantuego for the past eighty-nine years. He predicted the founding of the PFM. He predicted the downfall of Nochenegra. 'The last tyrant,' he called him. And he predicted our final victory."

Liam was amused. "Gee, I didn't know you hard-line Commies went in for crystal balls and such."

Major Zed glared at him. "Mandelo was not a fraud. He was a social scientist, a keen observer of human nature. Some of the more reactionary segments of this country claim to believe that he was a holy man; they even wanted to make a saint out of him, but we know who he really was and what he stood for. It is clear from his writings that he was a Communist and a man of the revolution. The corrupt oligarchy has perverted the purity of the manifesto and his vision to suit their own ends."

"You said something about a story?" Beck prompted.

The major nodded. He licked his lips and began. "Mandelo once wrote about a colony of rats in a cane field. The cane had been harvested and it was time to burn the field in order to fertilize the next year's crop. The rats anticipated this event—it happened every year—and they were ready to flee ahead of the blaze set by the cane cutters. The farm foreman, who hated rats more than anything, had seen this phenomenon many times before, and was determined to rid the field of rats. To accomplish this he set two fires, instead of one. The initial blaze was a trick to put the rats in motion; he set it at right angles to the direction of the prevailing wind. When the rats began to run, he torched the windward end of the field. Flames swept through the slash so quickly that only the fastest, strongest, smartest rats made it to safety on the other side. All the others were consumed.

"That winter the fast rats did not suffer, there being much more food to go around. In the spring they bred in profusion. They overran the cane field and moved into the farmhouses, where they proved to be almost impossible to exterminate."

"How exactly does that apply?" Lee said.

"Don't you see? The PFM are the smart rats. Those of us who have survived are formidable, indeed. And we will go on to conquer."

"Did you follow that?" Liam asked Dr. Hatton.

"Clear as mud."

"The story would make a nice animated feature," Beck remarked. "A Marxist *Watership Down*."

"It seems to me," Liam said, "that we could just as easily be the smart rats."

Major Zed laughed. "You don't look very smart to me, tied up like a bunch of pigs for slaughter."

"So, you're not afraid of us?"

"Afraid? Ha!"

"I rest my case."

The PFM commander frowned. "Shut up," he said. "Talking to you is a waste of time."

Lee winked at O'Toole.

A short time later the van stopped. Major Zed said to his men, "We will take no chances. Come around and help me."

At gunpoint the prisoners were gagged. Then they were forced out into the sunlight, which was reflected off a concrete drive and the concrete walls of a tall building beside it and off the asphalt of a large parking lot. A concrete ramp led up to a steel door. There was a sign over the door in Spanish, identifying the access as the Ministry of Justice Prisoner Entrance.

Liam figured their break was going to come soon. There would be guards inside the door who might recognize the PFM leader or check IDs. Or maybe they would pull down the gags. The Ministry of Justice meant trials. Courts. Dockets. He was feeling pretty up, all things considered, as they passed through the steel door.

That up was short-lived.

The armed security men working the door didn't ask any questions. They didn't ask to see paperwork. They didn't even ask where the prisoners were being taken. One of them just gestured with a thumb for the entourage to pass on through the checkpoint.

Then Jessup had a brainstorm. He sat down on the floor, and refused to budge.

While the PFM imitation guards held the other Americans at gunpoint, Major Zed and the two real security men tried to get Jessup to his feet—something much easier said than done. When pulled upon, the gagged fat man went limp—and 380 pounds is a lot of deadweight, especially when you can't get a solid hold underneath it.

On balance, Liam concluded, it was a nice try on Jessup's part, but the best they could hope for was multiple hernias.

None came.

They pulled back and Major Zed kicked Jessup in the lower back, the others following his lead.

A security man snarled at him to get a move-on, and they laughed as they brutalized Jessup, until he realized it was pointless. He rolled to his knees, then staggered up.

Zed booted him forward, almost causing him to fall again, as he bounced off the wall, then caught himself.

Liam wanted to bounce Zed. He wanted to do it because the guy was a creep. A sicko. To bounce him until his brains splattered the wall. He wasn't a soldier, a professional; he was a bloody psychopath with a mission ordained by some dead-as-a-mackerel local Shakespeare. O'Toole knew about writers, being one. He knew that writers didn't always mean what they said, didn't always know what they were saying.

He wondered if Mandelo would be turning over in his grave if he saw to what ends his ideas were being used. No, Liam decided, he'd probably be more interested in collecting a century of back royalties.

DR. HATTON WAS RELIEVED to see Jessup get up. That extra padding in his buttock region had come in handy. A less substantial victim might well have been crippled for life by those kicks. As it was, if Jessup survived the morning the PFM had planned for them, all he'd have would be some deep bruising.

That "if" was pretty big, too.

They were well on their way to oblivion and still no escape opportunity had presented itself. Hatton was prepared to do damage to their captors, even with her hands tied behind her back. She could fight well enough with her feet alone. But balance was a real problem with your arms fixed behind you. Once you lost it, you couldn't recover. There was a point, of course, when it didn't matter whether you fell or not, you were going to get blown away, anyway. That point, it seemed to her, was looming large on the horizon.

They were force-marched up a stairwell. As they climbed five full flights of steps, Jessup had a hell of a time. Not just because of his weight, either. He could only breathe through his nose, for his mouth was blocked by the gag, and he couldn't get enough air. His face had turned beet-red by the time they stopped at the landing to the fifth floor. One of the phony guards opened the door and they were shoved through.

Into a hallway. Then the major ordered a change in formation. Major Zed took up a position directly behind Jessup, who was pushed into the lead. Lee and Beck were made to walk shoulder to shoulder with a PFM man behind. Then came Liam, with the last guerrilla at his back. All three PFM had their stolen Uzis out and up and pressed into the middle of their prisoners' backs.

Up until that moment Dr. Hatton hadn't really believed that Zed could successfully penetrate the Mantuegan president's security. Now, she saw that he could.

Down the hallway, four armed security men stood guard at the entrance to a hearing room. Lee could see what was about to happen. There was nothing she could do. The gun jabbed at her back and forced her ahead.

As Major Zed approached the presidential bodyguards, he angled Jessup slightly in their direction, using the man's tremendous bulk to block their view of him as he brought his Uzi to bear.

Lee flinched at the sound of full-auto gunfire in the close space. Flame leaped from the muzzle of Zed's Uzi and the security men slammed back against the wall, twisting, turning as they were ripped by 9 mm lead.

It was over in a couple of seconds.

With the security team down for the count, there was nothing to stop the PFM assassins. Zed booted Jessup through the hearing-room door, to test the waters, so to speak. When there was no flurry of answering gunfire, he charged in after him. Major Zed was already shooting by the time Lee, too, was shoved into the hearing room.

She saw a long polished wood table ringed with padded chairs. Most of them were empty, but some held dead men, their faces shot off. The air in the room was an unbreathable mixture of gunsmoke and misted blood.

Major Zed fired into the backs of a retreating pack of judges, ministers, presidential advisers. They were screaming in panic, trying to get out the narrow door at the far end of the room. Under the waves of Uzi slugs, the men dropped away from the door like fanned pages of a book.

A second PFM man knocked Liam to his knees and opened fire as well. The third guerrilla joined in.

The Mantuegan officials died clawing at one another, trying to wedge through the already jammed door.

Then the shooting stopped.

"Soarez?" Major Zed shouted, storming the pile of bodies, kicking them aside. "Where is Soarez?"

The other PFM men pushed the Americans ahead, toward the heaped corpses.

Beyond them, on the other side of the door, Lee saw an anteroom. In it was a small man with glasses. She recognized Dr. Emilio Soarez from the news stories she'd read. He wasn't cowering. He didn't have his hands raised to protect himself. The expression on his face as he looked into the smoking barrel of Major Zed's Uzi was impossible to read.

"Die, bastard!" Major Zed snarled. The Uzi chattered in his hands, blowing holes through the president and the wall behind him. As red blotches spread across Soarez's chest, he slumped to a sitting position on the floor. The bullet-pocked wall behind him glistened red.

Lee felt a crushing blow to the back of her head and she went down. Blinding white light flashed inside her skull, fading almost in the same instant to impenetrable black. She was unconscious before her knees hit.

She awoke to someone shaking her. She put her hand to the back of her head. It came away wet.

"Doc, come on, snap out of it!" Liam was saying.

She sat up, her head reeling.

"They knocked us all out and then cut us loose," Beck told her. "They wanted us to be found here with him."

"Soarez?" she said, pushing O'Toole away. She crawled over to the body. The man still had a pulse. "He's still alive. Jesus! Get some help. Hurry!"

Liam, Nate and Jessup ran out.

Lee worked fast. She stripped off the president's coat, then ripped his shirt off so she could see the nature of his wounds. Soarez had three chest hits, all of them high, a couple of inches below the clavicle. Two were superficial through-and-throughs; the third had to be a miracle miss or he'd have been dead already. It was center chest.

As she was making a compress from his shirt to stanch the flow of blood, Soarez came to. He looked at her and smiled. He tried to say something, then he faded out.

Gunfire bellowed from the hallway outside and then the others came rampaging back.

"We've got to go," Jessup said. "They're shooting at us."

"They've got our number," Beck said. "Zed must've made sure of that before he left."

"Come on, Doc!" Liam growled. "We can't stay." He made motions as if he was going to grab her around the waist and pick her up bodily.

"All right," she said, getting up. "He's going to be okay, anyway. He's one lucky sucker."

Beck threw a chair through the glass in one of the room's windows and they all climbed out on the fire escape, then scrambled down it.

As they ran down the alley, autofire barked at them from above and behind, screaming slugs skipping off the concrete. They made it around the corner to the front of the ministry.

Liam didn't pause. He dashed out into the stopped traffic, reached into the first open driver's window he found and jerked the hapless driver out through it, tossing the man aside. He opened the door and got behind the wheel of the late-model Buick station wagon.

By that time, the others were jumping in.

Before they had the doors closed, he stomped on the gas, driving up on the sidewalk, clearing it of pedestrians. He bounced back onto the street when he reached the corner.

The road ahead was clear and O'Toole highballed it.

"Do you know where you're going?" Beck asked, hanging on to the back of the front seat.

"A-way," O'Toole answered. "Far a-way."

18

Barrabas and the others got the word about Dr. Soarez as they were returning to their hotel rooms after breakfast. They had spent the early morning talking about what Barrabas and Hayes had learned the night before. After the discussion, all had been in agreement that it looked as if they had come down on the wrong side of the struggle. The problem was what to do about it.

Starfoot had suggested they play along until they could get safe passage out of the country, then desert the project and go public the moment they reached the States, thereby ruining the element of surprise for Nochenegra and his generals, and giving Dr. Soarez the opportunity to arrest them and shut down the planned coup.

Hayes advocated a more active and direct role in destroying the dictator's chances for a return to power. He wanted to go straight to the current president, lay the cards on the table and then help the man break up the cadre.

Barrabas leaned toward the latter choice. And in the end, they were all convinced that it was the way to go.

All of their discussion and decisions became moot when the television in the hotel bar blared the bulletin that Dr. Soarez had been shot in an assassination attempt at the Ministry of Justice.

The mercenaries, like the early drinkers and hotel workers, stood in stunned silence and stared at the set. There were no video pictures yet, just words spoken over a station logo. The attack had taken place during a select committee hearing on constitutional reform. It was described by the bulletin reader as a massacre. Automatic weapons had been used at extremely close range. Fifteen of those present were known to be dead. Many more had been wounded critically, among them President Soarez. No other news of his condition was available. Units of the army and police were at that moment chasing down the killers. The announcer promised more details as they came in, then proceeded to repeat the story he had just read.

All around the mercenaries people broke into tears. Some of them were furious—none more so than Claude Hayes.

"The dirty, chickenshit bastards!" he exclaimed. "Goddamn them all to hell!"

"We can watch this upstairs," Barrabas suggested, putting an arm around Hayes's powerful shoulders. "I think it'd be better if we did."

"Yeah, come on, Claude," Nanos said.

They took the elevator up to their floor and all entered the colonel's room. Hayes could control himself no longer.

"Damn, we blew it!" he said. "You all know we blew it! Soarez was the only hope this fucked-up country had. The only one standing between Nochenegra and the PFM. What choice have these poor people got now? What choice have *we* got?"

"We know, man," Starfoot said.

"It sucks," Nanos agreed.

Barrabas turned on his room's TV. The station had video now. It was broadcasting shaky pictures of the aftermath of the slaughter. A conference room in shambles. Chairs overturned. Blood sprayed on the walls. The camera panned to the hallway outside. Lining one side were bodies covered with plastic tarps.

The reporter live on the scene cornered a security man and shoved his microphone in the man's face.

"What can you tell us about this tragedy?" the reporter demanded.

The security man tried to slip away, but the newsman grabbed him by the back of the shirt. "Our elected president has been shot!" the journalist shouted at him. "We deserve to know what happened!"

The guard winced at the camera. "I saw them," he said. "There were at least four. They had submachine guns." The man paused to swallow, which infuriated the reporter.

"And?"

The guard took a breath and then dropped his bombshell. "They were Americans."

Even the reporter was stunned. It was several seconds before he could follow up. "Americans involved in the assassination of President Soarez?"

"I saw them," the man said with conviction.

"Holy shit!" Nanos exclaimed. "What is going on here?"

The TV cut to another reporter in another location interviewing the chief of police.

"On the face of it," Starfoot said, "I'd say that the boys from Disneyland decided Soarez couldn't be trusted to keep the PFM forces at bay, so they decided to adjust the balance of power accordingly."

Barrabas lowered the volume on the set. "A little strange that one of our intelligence agencies would hire hit men who could be so easily identified as Americans, don't you think?"

"You're saying what?" Nanos asked. "That the CIA wasn't involved in the assassination? Or that these Americans weren't the ones who did it?"

"I'm saying it's more complicated than it looks."

"And it complicates the hell out of our situation," Starfoot said. "It was one thing to back Soarez when he was strong and in control, but what about now? If he dies, we've got no choice but to swing back to Nochenegra and follow the original game plan. You know that in light of developments the PFM is going to make its move real soon."

"The middle of the road has been taken away from us," Nanos said.

"Man, it could have been anybody who pulled the hit," Hayes said. "Anybody."

"Hold it, guys." Barrabas turned the volume back up to catch an update.

"We have a bulletin just in from the hospital," the station anchorman answered. "President Soarez is in critical condition, with three gunshot wounds to the chest. He is in a coma. Hospital spokesmen refuse to comment on his prognosis."

"Great! Just great!" Hayes said. "He might as well be dead for all the good he's going to be able to do."

Barrabas stood up. "Claude is right. Soarez is out of the picture. Even if he pulls a miraculous recovery both Nochenegra and the PFM will seize the chance to take power." To Hayes he said, "I know how you feel about Juan Carlos, and we all agree with you that he's scum. But if the alternative is a Communist dictatorship..."

"We have no other alternative," Hayes said bitterly. "But if I find out that Nochenegra had anything at all to do with this hit, I swear to God, I'm going to tear his lungs out with my bare hands."

Nanos gave Starfoot a deadpan look. "I'll fight you for his liver," he said.

Through the open balcony door they heard sounds like strings of firecrackers going off. A distant pop-pop-pop-pop.

"It's started already," Barrabas said.

They walked out onto the balcony. The view still looked so deceptively peaceful—blue sky, azure sea, serene mountains.

Then a hard knocking on the room door brought them in from the balcony. It was their escort. "The generals wish to see you at once," said the officer in charge.

Out in the street in front of the hotel, they could sense the panic setting in. People were running, cars speeding. Everybody was suddenly late for a very important date. Everybody wanted to get to ground before the shit hit the fan.

The mercenaries jumped into the Army carryall parked at the curb out front. The driver pulled away, his shoulders braced up around his ears, as if he expected something very hard and very heavy to come down on his head.

"Look over there," Nanos said.

To their right, the upper half of a building was burning, flames leaping into the sky, spreading a pall of dense black smoke. A few doors down, a mob of looters smashed the ground-floor windows of a department store with jagged chunks of concrete. Some of them were already leaving the scene with armloads of merchandise.

As the carryall passed, the looters turned away from the department store and hurled curses at them. Then they were throwing more than words. Heavy pieces of concrete slammed into the side of the vehicle, spider-webbing the windows, denting the hood and the roof.

The driver floored the gas pedal and redlined them out of there.

"They sure didn't waste any time going wild in the streets," Starfoot remarked.

"The criminal element is always ready to take advantage of a crisis," the officer said.

Barrabas found it hard to believe that nine- and ten-year-old kids dressed in rags and their stick-figure parents could be considered a "criminal element."

They drove quickly out of the downtown section of the city, and as they climbed off the lowland plain, more police and troops were in evidence. The battle lines had already been drawn. And decisions had been made as to what—and who—was important and what—and who—was not.

When they arrived at the army base they found it on full alert. Men in camou fatigues with M-16s were running all over the place. Six-by-six trucks loaded with armed personnel were rolling out the gates as they rolled in. Behind them, jeeps towed heavy machine guns and howitzers.

The carryall stopped in front of the command HQ. Barrabas and the others were hustled upstairs to a room they had been in before. Waiting for them around the three-dimensional representation of the island were the three generals. The model of Mantuego had colored pins and flags stuck in it—markers that had not been there the day before.

"You have heard the news?" Alvarez asked, indicating the TV set in the wall unit behind him. It was showing pictures of the rioting in progress, and running a warning for people to stay indoors and away from windows.

Barrabas nodded. "Are the rumors true that Americans were involved?"

Del Rey answered. "As you can well imagine, everything is so sketchy at this time, it is hard to say."

The three generals looked smug as hell.

"Were you involved?" Hayes asked point-blank.

They regarded him with suspicion.

"If we're supposed to be coordinating between you gentlemen and Juan Carlos," Barrabas said, "then we have the right and you have the duty to keep us informed of any and all steps you intend to take."

Bonifacio tried to make amends. "It was none of our doing, I assure you. If we had had any such plans, we would have kept you fully up to speed."

"Whoever did it—and I think it was probably the PFM—couldn't have picked a better time," Alvarez said. "Which brings us to the point of this special meeting. We're going to have to move up our timetable radically."

"From the troops barreling out of here, it looks like you already have," Starfoot said.

"We had our contingency plans for a national emergency, of course," Alvarez explained. "We are merely implementing them. I'm talking about moving up the timetable for Juan Carlos's arrival. We would like him to be here tomorrow."

"You can consolidate your position in the next twenty-four hours?" Barrabas asked.

"No problem," Del Rey said.

"Can you get our man here by then?" Bonifacio asked.

Barrabas nodded. "If I call him now, I think it can be arranged. The only difficulty I see will be with his beach landing. We haven't set up the necessary ship-to-shore

transportation. We're going to have to get that together
in a hurry."

The generals smiled.

"That won't be necessary," Alvarez said. "There's
been a change of plans in that regard. Under the press of
circumstances we believe the interests of the nation would
be better served if Juan Carlos simply landed at the base
here. He can ride in a victory cavalcade to the palace.
That should soothe his need for pomp...."

"You can make him see that it's in his best interests,
too," Bonifacio urged. "We're considering his safety as
well."

Barrabas found the prospect of talking the dictator out
of his long-fantasized, MacArthur-type return to power
a highly revolting proposition. It would be like coddling
a spoiled, evil child. He was going to have to listen pa-
tiently to the egotistical bastard's tirade.

"Where's the phone?" he asked.

Del Rey led him over to the wall unit. Above Barrabas's head, on the TV, a section of the slum of El Infierno was burning.

He dialed the number, and as he waited, the picture on
the TV screen changed. A harried-looking studio
anchorman shuffled papers in front of him.

"Attention," the newsman said, "we have just received a copy of a description of the attackers of
President Soarez. The police and military are looking for
three men and a woman, all of them presumed to be
American. One of the men was extremely overweight.
Another man had red hair, five foot eleven inches. The
third man was shorter and thin. The woman wore her
black hair cut short; from a distance she could pass for a
man. If you have any information on these people, please
contact the authorities at once."

Barrabas put his hand over the mouthpiece and looked at Hayes, Nanos and Starfoot. They were staring at the screen with grim faces.

The descriptions sounded alarmingly familiar. It was almost too coincidental.

An off-camera figure passed the newsman a sheet of paper. He read it quickly and looked up, very excited. "Just in," he said, waving the paper. "This station has just received a copy of a home movie shot by a tourist in front of the Ministry of Justice immediately after the attack on the president. It is said to show the escape of the killers. We'll all be watching this for the first time. Please roll the film."

After a long pause, the Ministry of Justice, huge, white, stark, filled the screen. On the front steps tiny figures in Bermuda shorts and straw hats waved for the camera. Then the camera jerked around to the right. It caught four people running around the side of the building. The camera panned with them. A red-haired man was in the lead. He ran out into the stalled traffic, approached a station wagon and yanked the driver bodily through the open window. Then the other suspects got into the car and it roared off.

"That was amazing!" the reporter exclaimed. "Back it up, please. Let's see it again. Slow it down some, maybe we can make out their faces."

Barrabas ignored the voice coming out of the phone in his hand. He looked at his men. They were looking at him. They didn't need to see the film again. They already had made a positive ID.

Under his breath, Nanos said, "Holy shit!"

19

The senator watched Juan Carlos's face run the entire gamut of human emotions, from wild elation, through shock, horror and despair, then to fury as he spoke via cable link to the Democratic Republic of Mantuego.

"What do you mean I can't land on the beach?" he howled into the telephone's mouthpiece. Then, in a hissed aside to the lawmaker, he said, "The imbeciles want me to fly in, to land at the army base."

The senator swallowed hard. He, too, felt shock and despair. And fury.

"They say it isn't safe for me to arrive by ship."

Dammit, that was the whole point, the legislator thought bitterly. He had been the one who actually planted the seed in Nochenegra's mind about wading ashore in triumph. A subtle mention of the glorious return of General Douglas MacArthur to stir his interest, then a timely showing of the historic footage, and Juan Carlos, the infantile, the predictable, had been hooked solid. Nochenegra had said he wanted schoolchildren a hundred years after he was dead to be shown the movies of his triumphant return. They would memorize the date, the time.

The length of the barrel of his big shiny gun.

It would have been so easy for the senator to arrange for an accident to happen between the time Nochenegra left the mother ship and the time he hit the beach in the amphibious landing craft. The senator had much favored an explosion halfway to the beach, a great fireball at sea with no chance for survivors. He had simply been waiting for the details to be set so he could have the bomb planted.

Now he would have to improvise another plan, if there was time before the dictator left the States.

"I know it's a great disappointment to you," the lawmaker said with oily sympathy, "but the important thing is for you to assume power again."

The dictator nodded grimly. He returned to his phone link with the island. "I understand," he said into the phone. "Yes, yes, I understand. I'll have Ortega settle the flight details at this end. He'll call back and give you my estimated time of arrival."

The president-for-life started to hang up, then caught himself. He had almost forgotten in his excitement. "Please inform the generals that Colonel Enriquez is en route to Mantuego at this time," he added. "He should arrive within a few hours. I trust he'll be given every cooperation. He'll be organizing his FSI forces to aid my return to power."

With that, Juan Carlos hung up.

"Such good news coupled with such bitter news," he said, throwing up his hands. "The only thing better than having Dr. Soarez get shot, would be having the chance to do it myself. And they say Americans were involved in the attack on him."

"Americans, really?" The senator covered his surprise with a quip. "Anyone I know?"

"I sincerely hope not," Nochenegra said. "That could prove highly embarrassing."

"I was only joking."

"So was I. It really doesn't matter who shot the bastard. I'll be in power before the truth can embarrass anyone. I leave for Mantuego tonight."

"So soon?"

"My country calls," the dictator declaimed. "Where is Luisa? I must tell her the good news."

The senator watched him leave the room. Maybe it was for the best that the beach landing had been scrapped. A violent explosion at sea, while aesthetically satisfying, it had to be admitted, lacked something necessary to the smooth transfer of power. It lacked certainty. It would be much better if the dictator's body could be shown to the Mantuegan people on television, pictures of it plastered over the front page of the newspaper. They had to know that he was really dead.

The senator motored over to the phone that Nochenegra had put down and started to call the island, to make final arrangements. He thought better of it. The phone was not secure. He replaced the handset. He would wait until Juan Carlos was in the air and call from his hotel.

LUISA WAS in a broom closet in the Bel-Air mansion.

Her interest in brooms and dustpans and such had never been all that keen.

But her interest in other things had never been hotter.

Lieutenant Ortega was in the closet with her—with her in every sense of the phrase.

She, naked but for her requisite high heels, stockings and garter belt, and Ortega, clad only in his jungle boots, squirmed and thrashed among the mops and brooms and buckets, rattling them in the throes of passion.

Anyone passing in the hall outside the closet would have thought an earthquake was in progress. No one passed, however, and the earthquake eventually crescendoed.

Ortega held his sweaty mistress close and said, "This is so foolish, so dangerous, my darling. Anyone could walk in on us here."

Her eyes shone brightly. There was, she thought, something to be said for danger. It was not as thrilling perhaps as the bear suit, but then again what was? At any rate, it made a nice change of pace.

"When we return to Mantuego, it will be different," he told her. "Juan Carlos will be so busy with the presidency he will not notice where you go or what you do. We will be together any time we want."

Luisa kissed him lightly on the cheek and extricated herself from his embrace. Lieutenant Ortega was a beautiful man, an ardent and enterprising lover. He filled a yawning void in her life. Juan Carlos didn't care for her; he never had, really. She had always been an ornament to him. To his presidency. He was much more interested in wielding power over the Mantuegan masses than in making her do things—things she didn't want to do but that she loved doing. She had come to the opinion that there were two types of men on the planet, those who loved women and those who loved power. In order to satisfy her need for extensive creature comforts and broad-spectrum sexual excitement she decided she had to have one of each.

Ortega covered her mouth with his and gave her a hard, passionate kiss. When he drew back, he said, "Again, my darling! I must have you again."

Luisa giggled and buried her face in his chest. "No, darling, we can't. Juan Carlos will be looking for me. I must go."

She tried to push away. He held her fast. "Later, then?" he said.

"You are such a greedy devil," she said. Then she relented. "Meet me in the pool house during cocktail hour. I can slip away for a few minutes."

"Wonderful," he said, kissing her neck. "Marvelous."

She pushed him away. "There's just one thing, though."

"Yes, darling, anything."

"Wear the skin-diver suit...."

JUAN CARLOS LOOKED high and low for his wife. He could find her in none of her usual haunts: the lavish marble bathtub, before her dressing room mirror, in the shoe pavilion. She was not to be found. In the end he sent servants to do the hunting and adjourned to the private office off his bedroom to wait for her to be brought to him.

As he sat down behind his desk, he noticed the file Colonel Enriquez had left for him prior to his departure. He had been putting off opening it. It was a powder-blue envelope, an FSI envelope, and it had For Your Eyes Only stamped in red letters across the front and the back.

He broke the wax seal with a letter opener and dumped out the contents of the envelope onto his desk top. Typed reports slid onto the green blotter. And color photographs.

He picked up one of the latter, and looked at it without understanding at first. It was hard to decipher the outline of honey-brown bodies on the tangled satin sheets.

Then his blood ran cold.

How could she have?

How could he have?

There was no question that Juan Carlos would kill them both for their betrayal.

The only question was when.

20

"It's gaining on us!" Nate exclaimed. "Can't you go any faster?"

Liam grunted. His right foot ground the Buick's accelerator pedal flat against the fire wall. O'Toole cursed whatever gas-economy-conscious wimp had ordered the heavy car with nothing but a V-6 to push it. He cursed the dealership that had sold it, the company that had shamed all of Detroit by letting it roll off the production line.

This Buick, this chromed, blue metallic behemoth, was gutlessness incarnate. It lumbered and complained when it was pushed beyond its meager limits, engine over-revving, lifters clattering, transmission whistling.

About a hundred yards behind them on the two-lane highway, its siren wailing, pursuit lights flashing, headlights blazing, a white-and-black Mantuegan police car was definitely gaining.

The highway cut through plantation country. Broad, flat rectangles of cultivated fields were interspersed with groves of tall trees. The road swung back and forth in a series of lazy, half-assed curves. As undemanding as the track was, the Buick's mush-bucket power steering couldn't nail it down; the car kept slip-sliding back and forth across the center line. The speedometer said they were doing 95. It handled more like 150. Whatever its true speed, the top-ended station wagon floated over the road, drifting in and out of control. Liam gritted his teeth. The discrepancies between the steering and the car's course gave him a spooky, eerie feeling. It tied his stomach in knots. He could visualize a sudden gust of wind sending them off the tarmac and into the roadside ditch.

"Do something, O'Toole!" Jessup shouted.

Liam answered out of the side of his mouth. "The only way I can make this unredeeming shit pile go any faster is if you jump the fuck out."

"Look out for that guy," Lee said.

Ahead, there was a car in their lane. It was going fifty but it looked like it was stopped dead. Without easing up on the gas, Liam swerved around it, into the oncoming lane—where they faced another car! The distance between them could have been measured in inches.

"Oh, my God!" Beck groaned, clutching at the seat back with both hands.

Liam held a true course, keeping the road's centerline aimed right down the middle of the Buick hood ornament. It was over in a heartbeat. They passed within inches of both cars. Then they were around and Liam cut back into his proper lane.

The slowpoke, now behind them, swerved onto the shoulder to let the cop car pass.

"Shit, you had to be a good citizen, didn't you?" O'Toole snarled into the rearview.

The cop car roared up behind them and tried to pass.

No way was O'Toole going to let that happen. As the police car swung out into the oncoming lane, so did he, blocking its path with the Buick's broad butt, almost forcing it onto the opposite shoulder.

"That fixed 'em!" Beck said.

Not for long.

The police car came up behind again. The cop riding on the passenger side rolled down his window and leaned out. He had a revolver in his hand. He started shooting.

As bullets crashed through the station wagon's back window and thumped the rear door, Liam took evasive measures, swerving, juking. Scary was relative—mushed-out steering seemed safer than the freight-train whine of full-metal-jacketed slugs sailing past his window.

The cop hanging out pulled back inside, probably to reload. As he did so, the police car accelerated, slamming into the Buick's rear end. The impact sent the station wagon briefly but completely out of control.

"Oh, shit!" O'Toole cried, struggling to get it back, spinning the useless wheel until the tires bit and wrenched them out of the sickening fishtail.

"Here they come again!" Jessup shouted.

Liam looked in his rearview as the police car homed in on the Buick's backside. He could see the cop driver. The jerk was laughing his head off.

There was a bone-jarring jolt as the cruiser's front bumper made solid contact with their rear end. And then they were airborne. All four wheels off the ground. Flying at ninety-five plus miles per hour.

They landed with a crash. Again O'Toole almost lost it. They were heading straight for the ditch, sideways, when, swearing a blue streak, he managed to recover.

"Do something, O'Toole!" Hatton said.

Liam rounded a turn and on the straight-as-a-string road ahead saw the back end of a semitruck and tractor rig dead ahead. He didn't pull out to pass, he barreled down on it. The cops surging up on him from behind for another wallop couldn't, or didn't, see it.

"O'Toole!" Jessup cried, pointing at the looming solid wall of the truck trailer.

Liam waited until the last possible second, then cut hard over into the oncoming lane and around the truck's rear end.

They didn't see the crash but they heard it. Shattering glass and shredded sheet steel. The cop didn't even have time to hit his brakes.

When O'Toole checked his mirror, he saw the truck slowing to a stop.

"Great driving," Nate told him.

Dr. Hatton wasn't so enthusiastic. "The cop had a radio," she said. "They know what road we're on. They'll be moving in to intercept."

"I know, I know," Liam said. "We've got to find a turnoff, and quick."

"There!" Beck said, pointing at a one-lane dirt road that crossed an open field and led to the edge of the jungle, which went from flat to steep in a matter of a few hundred feet.

O'Toole slowed and turned. But as he sped up again, heading for the jungle as fast as he could go, a helicopter gunship swooped down on them.

One second the sky was clear, the next it was full of howling death. The road before them disappeared in a hail of minigun fire. When the chopper swept past and the car rolled through the clouds of dust, its hood was riddled with bullet holes. Even as O'Toole gawked, flames shot up through the 7.62 mm perforations.

"It's making another pass!" Lee said.

O'Toole had no intention of playing chicken with a goddamned minigun. He swerved off the road and into the ditch, still rolling. Slugs slammed through the roof of the car, just clipping the back end. The Buick hurtled on, tilted on a forty-five-degree angle to the right.

He hit the brakes and brought it to a stop under a tree at the edge of the bush.

"Out!" he ordered.

He didn't have to say it twice.

Even Walker Jessup moved with unusual grace and speed.

Lee took the point, ran up the other side of the ditch and into the shrubbery next to the tree. There, she found a trailhead of sorts. It was a narrow break in the almost solid wall of jungle, a little-used path that required a machete—and they, of course, had none.

As the helicopter droned in for another pass, they plunged into the seam in the forest. After that, the going got rough. Creeping vines and a profusion of thin branches slowed them down. The canopy of trees, dimly visible overhead, was easily two hundred feet above them. Hanging from the trees were vines as thick as a man's arm. The bases of the trees were choked with smaller, broadleaf plants and seedlings. The light filtering down through the canopy was yellow-green. The heat and the lack of air circulation made walking a perfect bitch. As they moved along, they had to duck under, and hold out of the way, the various green obstacles. When they started to climb the incline at the foot of the mountain, Jessup started huffing.

All of them, Jessup included, had felt relieved to be out of the car and on their own two feet. But Jessup's relief dwindled as the incline steepened suddenly.

Lee called for a stop.

"We got nowhere to go but up," Beck said.

"You okay, Jessup?" she asked.

The fat man nodded, trying to catch his breath.

Overhead, out of sight on the other side of the canopy of trees, a helicopter passed. Slowly. Searching.

"We've got to keep moving," Liam urged. "If we can stay ahead of them until dark, we've got a fighting chance."

"We've got to get off this trail," Lee said. "As long as we stay on it, they're not going to have any trouble hunting us down."

They all looked at the track ahead. At this point there was only one path possible, and it led almost straight up, via a series of tight switchbacks.

Lee started off again. The others fell into step behind her. No one spoke. They had to concentrate on their footing and conserve their energy.

They had climbed about five hundred feet when the air suddenly seemed cool. It was an astounding change. They stopped and looked up. The sky through the maze of branches didn't seem so bright.

Then it began to rain. Hard.

It was as if faucets had been turned on above them. The raindrops funneled through breaks in the trees, running down branches, gathering mass, pouring down trunks.

The Americans stood under the minicascades, drinking, soaking. The torrent quickly saturated the trail, making a streambed out of it.

After the storm passed over, Lee waved them on. They had to take advantage of the break in humidity while it lasted.

They climbed for another half hour. The delicious coolness gradually faded, until at the end of that time, it seemed even hotter than it had before.

Jessup begged for a rest. "I have to stop...can't go on."

They pulled up on some rock outcrops covered with moss. They were all pretty beat. The Texan was hammered. He sat down as if he had no intention of ever getting up.

Liam watched him wheeze for a while, then said, "So, Jessup, how about telling us the real skinny? What the hell happened at the plantation? How did you manage to get us into this godawful mess?"

"What good is hassling over all that going to do now?" Lee asked.

"I want to know."

"Me, too," Beck added. "I want to know who sold us down the river."

Jessup looked each one in the face. He knew that any of them could have killed him plenty quick. He wasn't afraid of dying, especially on a day like this one. He was a better man than that. "I guess I owe it to you," he said.

He mopped his face with his handkerchief. "Before I start, I want to point out the obvious. I'm in the same boat as you. I got suckered, too."

"Talk," Liam told him.

"I was led to believe that the arms-transport operation was sponsored by the U.S. government."

"Shipping guns and munitions to Communist rebels?" Lee said. "An official sanctioned operation?"

"No, it was an unofficial sanctioned operation. At least that's what I was told. As for the guys who met us at the plantation, they were a big surprise to me, too. They weren't supposed to be Communists; they were supposed to be supporters of the deposed dictator, Nochenegra. I was told the States was afraid that Soarez was going to cave in to the PFM, so they were throwing support to Nochenegra. I had other evidence to back up that story, but now it seems suspect, too."

"What other evidence?" O'Toole asked.

Jessup looked at his shoes. "Barrabas is here."

Beck blinked. "On Mantuego?"

Jessup nodded. "The same person who hired me to deliver the arms hired Barrabas, Hayes, Starfoot and Nanos to help the dictator return to power. They're supposed to coordinate between the man in exile and his local backers. I was told that that, too, was an official unofficial operation."

"Who is this guy?" Liam said.

"The senator."

"Our old friend," Nate said.

"I had no reason to doubt him."

O'Toole shook his head. "No reason aside from the fact that he's a total sleaze."

"We've all worked with him before and never had a problem like this," Jessup said.

"Maybe we've been damned lucky," Hatton said.

Jessup wrung out his handkerchief, rolled it up and put it back around his neck. "For the life of me, I can't figure out the senator's angle in all this," he said. "It's driving me frigging crazy."

"Do you think he's sold out the colonel, too?" Lee asked.

"Who knows?"

"That dirty old man has got a lot of questions to answer," Beck said.

"I just hope we live long enough to put them to him," Liam added.

"We'd better get rolling." Lee got to her feet.

They pushed up the slope again.

The climbing got harder the higher they went. Not only did they have to deal with the slope, but with the slimy mash of rotted leaves that covered it. By the time the last guy in line reached any given point on the trail, the three others before him had slid, slipped, scrambled, and in the process polished it to glasslike slickness. O'Toole ended up on his butt every forty feet or so.

It got so regular that he didn't even bother to curse.

As he was dragging himself to his feet yet again, a helicopter passed almost directly overhead. The noise of its rotors moved slowly up the side of the mountain.

Liam stopped them at once. "I really don't like the sound of that," he said. The chopper was still droning on. Steady now, as if it were hovering. "Hey, Beck, how are you at climbing trees?"

Nate looked up at a towering mossy trunk. He had to crane his neck way back to do it. His Adam's apple bobbed. The top of the tree disappeared in the dense jungle canopy. But not before it swayed, gently in the breeze up there, as if the upper third was made of green rubber.

They were all waiting for him.

"I'm great," Beck lied.

"Then scoot up there and have a look-see."

Beck, with a leg up from O'Toole, shinnied into the lower branches. The branches were quite sparse at the tree's base and there were long distances between them. He had to stretch hard to reach from one to the next. He didn't look down. He knew he was lost if he so much as peeked. He refused to admit that anything existed above or below the limits of his ability to stretch, and confined his full attention to those roughly six-and-a-half feet. He had plenty to deal with. The trunk was slimy to the touch and his feet kept slipping off the branches.

As he worked his way up, the branches became more numerous and closer together, so the going was actually easier. Unfortunately, the top of the tree was also more pliant. It swayed back and forth under him alarmingly, like the mast of a sailing ship in a storm.

Nate was really swinging. The arcs were seven or eight feet across. For an instant he just hung on and shut his eyes. His head swam. He knew his mother would have dropped stone-dead if she could have seen him. Who the hell was he kidding? He would have dropped dead if he could have seen him.

He moved up. The higher he went, the more extreme the swing. There was wind up there. Sunlight streamed through the canopy. He kept thinking, just one more step and he'd be high enough to see over the tops of the other trees. But of course he had to take one more. And one more.

Finally, when he could see the top of his tree some five feet above him, he climbed onto some exceedingly springy limbs into pure sunlight.

From there he could see over the tops of the much smaller trees downslope. What he saw was not pleasing. Another helicopter gunship was flying right at him. He ducked into the foliage as the chopper flew past, then popped up again to see where it was headed.

The damned thing flew uphill about a hundred yards, then dropped down among the trees and disappeared.

"Oh, hell!" he groaned.

It didn't take a genius-level IQ to know that the helicopters were landing somewhere uphill from them—that they were about to be overrun by troops from above.

Beck looked down.

And was sorry.

The world spun crazily.

The jungle floor was so far down he couldn't see it. Gritting his teeth, he confronted the vertigo. He couldn't surrender to it. He had to get down safely to warn the others.

He forced himself to look up. Then he started down. One step at a time. By the time he reached the ground he had lost five pounds in sweat.

"The choppers are landing someplace up there," he told the others. "Probably unloading troops."

"We could go down," Jessup suggested.

"No," Lee said. "The men above are fresh. They'd run right down our backs before we got very far. And besides, there's probably more of them coming up the trail behind us."

"We're caught," Jessup said.

Liam scanned the steep slope around them. "Look, our only chance is to move off the trail and take cover. We let the troops descending pass by, then try and reach the LZ above. Maybe we can commandeer a chopper."

"Can anybody here fly one?" Jessup asked.

There were blank looks all around.

"Hey, I'm willing to give it a try," Beck volunteered.

"We'll cross that bridge later," O'Toole said. "Move off the path, space out, bury yourselves in leaves, mud, anything. And be careful. Don't leave any trail behind. I'm going to sneak up the hillside and see what I can see. I'll holler for you to come out when it's all clear."

With that, Liam shouldered his way into the underbrush and started a grueling hands-and-knees ascent.

21

Barrabas had seen more than his share of wars begin. They usually started with anger, an act of aggression, a boundary violated. The men who fought reflected that first cause; they were pissed off.

Not in this case.

The soldiers of Mantuego acted as if they all had tickets to a World Cup soccer match. Bright smiling faces. Joking and cutting up as they climbed into the camouflaged six-by-sixes.

It made Barrabas want to grab them by the throats and give them a hard shaking. War was not something to be taken lightly. Especially not civil war. He knew.

He knew but he did nothing, said nothing. He was just an observer, an adviser. He hadn't been paid to take up arms, and under the circumstances, unless caught in a potentially lethal situation, he wouldn't.

"This way, Colonel," said Enriquez, gesturing toward a line of loaded trucks. The FSI chief was resplendent in his tailored pale blue uniform. The men in the indicated trucks were also in pale blue, his resurrected Gestapo. Enriquez hadn't wasted any time once he'd arrived. To the irritation of the generals, he had commandeered weapons and transport, acting like a prima donna.

Barrabas waved Hayes, Nanos and Starfoot after him. They followed the rotund secret-police chief to a truck and got into the back where twenty-five or so grinning soldiers sat waiting.

"Kind of takes me back," Billy said, eyeing the men around him.

"Yeah?" Nanos said. "To where?"

"Cub Scouts."

The truck started off with a lurch. Barrabas tried to get comfortable, leaning his back against one of the inner ribs of the Conestoga top. He could hear automatic-weapons fire in the distance, and every now and then the scream of howitzer rounds, followed by muffled explosions. The war for Mantuego had started, all right.

And according to news reports his people had set off the chain of events. His people operating on their own, independently. Barrabas could imagine Walker Jessup involved in something as dirty as the assassination of Dr. Soarez, but not Lee Hatton, not O'Toole, not Beck. Such a thing went against their grain. It had to be some kind of ghastly mistake. With ghastly consequences. At last report, they were being chased as they "tried to link up with their PFM comrades in the mountains." Their capture was "expected soon."

Most infuriating was the fact that there was nothing Barrabas could do to help them. There were too many unknowns, too many miles between where they were thought to be and where he was now. The political and military situation in the capital had deteriorated to the point where, as much as it galled him to admit it, he was absolutely helpless to act outside limited parameters— boundaries not of his making. No way could he disengage from the current scenario with Enriquez without bringing all holy hell down on himself and his crew. And, realistically, with slim hope of results. Hatton and the others were all excellent fighters, with combat experience on every continent. He had faith in their ability to survive. That didn't make the circumstances any easier for him to take.

The convoy of FSI troops rolled out of the base, then turned downhill, heading for the lower-class ghetto. The closer they got to it, the louder the gunfire. They could smell smoke. They took no incoming fire, but the shooting was only a block or two away as they screeched to a stop.

Enriquez ordered everyone out.

The neighborhood of tiny, single-family stucco houses was in flames. The cars parked on the street were burning as well. Troops loyal to the generals were moving through like a whirlwind, destroying everything and everyone in their path.

"You know what to do," Enriquez told his junior officers. "We will work our way north and link up with regular army units at the main post office. Get on with it!"

The underlings barked commands to their enlisted men, then took off down the street, leapfrogging from house to house on both sides.

"Gentlemen," Enriquez said to the Americans, chambering a live round in his Uzi, "please follow me..."

The FSI troops kicked in front doors and disappeared into the houses. Seconds later autofire raged from within. As the blue-uniformed men made their exits, they tossed hand grenades. Houses on both sides of the street rocked, windows blew out, flames flickered from within.

Enriquez pushed aside one of the assault-team leaders. "I will take this one," he said, storming up the walk to the little house's front door. As he did so, he waved the troops on his heels to go around to the rear of the building. He put his back to the wall and shouted at the window next to his left arm, "Surrender, Communist pigs. Surrender or die!"

The window burst out as a single shotgun blast boomed.

Barrabas and the others took cover beside the smoking wreck of a car.

Enriquez didn't turn and fire through the shattered window. He kept his back to the wall. After a few seconds the shotgun bellowed again, sending a long orange flame licking out of the shadows behind the curtain.

Then the inside of the house flashed as hand grenades tossed by the rearguard troops exploded. The man with the shotgun came flying out the window, blown off his feet by four or five simultaneous grenade blasts. He and his weapon landed at Enriquez's feet. The man's back had been reduced to bloody hamburger.

Barrabas rose and walked over to the tiny front porch. The others followed.

"One less PFM bastard," Enriquez stated proudly.

"Hell of a piece the guy had, huh?" Nanos squatted down. "A single-barreled, single-shot twelve-gauge."

"Real firepower," Billy said.

Before anyone could stop him, Hayes ducked through the open window and climbed into the house.

"Where is he going?" Enriquez demanded. "He's not allowed in there. I'll have him shot."

Barrabas seized the FSI colonel by the shoulder. His steellike fingers dug deep into the man's doughy muscle. "Wait a minute," he said.

Enriquez, caught like a rat in a trap, twisted around and glared up at him.

"My man Hayes," Barrabas said, "is a little headstrong and curious. That's the way I like him. He'll be out in a second, no harm done."

"You are under my orders here, Colonel," the FSI man said. "And I order you to keep your men out of the action and well back."

"I understand." Barrabas released him. "I'll make sure we keep out of your hair from now on."

When Hayes came back through the window, the expression on his face was one of pure loathing. He said nothing. He refused to meet the eyes of his comrades-in-arms.

All along the shabby street, houses were being assaulted and blown up by the men in powder-blue.

Enriquez's walkie-talkie crackled. He removed it from his belt, and turning away from the Americans, listened, then spoke briefly into it.

"This way!" he shouted to his men. He trotted up the street, calling them away from their search-and-destroy fun and games. When he had gathered them all back, he addressed the squad leaders. "The guerrillas have taken the post office," he said grimly. "We must advance at once and engage them. On the double!"

Two abreast the FSI troops jogged down the middle of the street. Barrabas and the others ran along the side of the road, keeping back.

"There are supposed to be guerrillas in this neighborhood?" Billy asked the colonel's back. "And these guys are doing formation drills in the center of the street?"

"There aren't any fucking guerrillas," Hayes said. "That poor bastard back there was just trying to protect his home and his family. A wife and three kids. I found them in the back room, all blown to hell."

"Jesus!" Nanos groaned.

"We've got to stop these guys, Colonel," Hayes said. "This is murder."

Barrabas said nothing. He was torn between the bitter truth of what Hayes had said and the bottom-line goal of the mission: to keep the PFM from taking power. He wanted to kill Enriquez, no doubt about it. The man was a butcher. But killing him would jeopardize the mission. The lesser of the two evils had to prevail.

"Colonel?"

"What can I tell you, Claude? What do you want me to say? The whole thing stinks, from top to bottom. Nochenegra is a world-class motherfucker. He deserved to get his ass kicked out. The people here seem to genuinely love Soarez. We've been lied to by everybody with something to gain from Soarez's fall. And somehow Hatton, Beck, O'Toole and the fat man are hooked up in the assassination attempt, and at this very moment they're getting their butts run ragged by combined police and military units. We've got to hang in until we can see some way to make things right. Blowing away that shithead Enriquez isn't going to help us. At least not yet."

Hayes shut up. Barrabas could feel the anger and hate boiling off him; he empathized. His own frustration was reaching the breaking point.

The main post office stood on a corner of a broad intersection. Stone-faced, pillared, linteled, it looked as if it had been ripped out of Des Moines and planted there. Except that there were dead bodies all over the sidewalk, and more bodies littering the long flight of stone steps leading to the entrance. A car was overturned out front.

As they approached, men hiding in the shadows behind the pillars opened fire. No shotguns these. Steel-jacketed slugs whined over the mercenaries' heads and forced them to their bellies and the slim cover of a drainage ditch.

Enriquez's men, confronted by real danger, real opposition, faltered in their resolve. Instead of holding together, working as a team, they scattered in all directions, shooting back wildly. Enriquez and a half dozen of his boys in blue took cover behind the rolled car.

"We could be here all day if they don't get off their butts," Nanos grumbled.

Then the men behind the car primed and chucked hand grenades at the building's entrance. They flew in soft arcs and dropped clattering among the shooters in the shadows. Two grenades were instantly kicked back, bounding down the stairs. Then they all went off with a thunderclap report. Smoke gushed from between the pillars.

"Did they get 'em?" Billy asked.

"I thought I saw three make it to the doorway," Barrabas replied.

The explosions and Enriquez's rallying shouts brought the FSI out of hiding. They rushed the stairs, spraying the entrance as they ran.

"That's dumb," Nanos muttered. "Very dumb."

His assessment was validated in short order. When the troops were two-thirds of the way up the steps, a grenade hurtled from the entrance and landed in their midst. They surged away from it, fleeing in all directions, leaving a widening empty space on the stairs.

The empty space suddenly filled with fire and heat and flying metal.

The FSI troops closest to the blast dropped as if their strings had been cut. Those who had been faster, quicker off the mark, only staggered. And the fastest, those who managed to dive over the side railings, were unhurt.

Enriquez barked an order from his secure position. Troops climbed the opposite ends of the portico, and set up a heated cross fire that drove the insurgents back from the inside of the entryway.

With the approach to the building under control, Enriquez and the rest of his men charged up the stairs.

The Americans got to their feet.

"We're not going to do like he said and stay out of it, are we?" Nanos said.

"No way," Barrabas replied, pulling his Browning Hi-Power from its cross-draw sheath. "We go in after them, but slow and careful. Shoot only if you're given no other choice. Make sure of your targets."

"Do we have the green light on folks in powder-blue?" Billy said.

"You have the green light if you're fired upon. Understood?"

They nodded. Guns in hand, they sprinted for the foot of the stairs, running around an obstacle course of fallen Mantuegans, none of whom appeared to be anything but unarmed and brutally slaughtered civilians. When they reached the stairs they could see bodies in uniforms. Not FSI colors, but khaki. The corpses were in contorted positions, and all around them, splattered with blood, were pieces of paper.

Envelopes. Small packages. Advertising circulars.

Hayes bent over one of the dead men. He read the words emblazoned on the man's shoulder patch. "Postal Service, Democratic Republic of Mantuego."

"Must've gotten caught in the attack," Billy said. "Poor bastards."

"On your toes," Barrabas reminded them as they reached the entrance level.

The FSI men were gone, already sweeping the inside of the building for guerrillas. The staccato sound of autofire echoed from within. Nine-millimeter room-brooms, hard at work.

Barrabas went in first, gun up and ready. There were more bodies in the hall, postal workers and patrons lying on the cool linoleum in pools of their own blood. Avoiding the puddle, he knelt over a woman in a flower-print dress.

"Who shot them?" Hayes asked. "The guerrillas or the FSI?"

Barrabas could only shrug. It was impossible to say. The woman still felt warm to the touch, but she was very dead.

Gunfire and screams erupted ahead, up a broad staircase that led to the second floor. Then a body fell from the landing above, crashing to a heap on the steel-edged treads. It thrashed as it dropped, but upon impact it was still.

"Come on!" Barrabas waved the others after him.

They dashed down the corridor, checking doorways as they passed, making sure the rooms were empty so they wouldn't be taken from behind.

When they reached the body on the stairs, Barrabas didn't even try to find a pulse. The man's head was cracked open, and what had been in it was running down the steps. He was in a postal worker's uniform.

More shots rattled from above.

Barrabas took the stairs three at a time, pausing at the landing until the others could cover for him, then charging to the top. He knelt there, right shoulder to the wall, sighting down the Browning, until Hayes, Nanos and Starfoot joined him.

He advanced in a crouch, skirting the nasty twenty-five-foot-long blood smear where the dead man below had been dragged along the floor before being thrown over the railing.

To the right was another hall. From it, gunfire raged, then stopped.

They approached the corner cautiously. Barrabas peered around it and saw, some fifty feet away, at least twenty FSI men and their leader, Enriquez, standing on both sides of a pair of heavy doors. Even as he looked, gunfire barked again, bullets splintered through the doors—from the inside out—and ricocheted down the corridor in both directions.

The FSI men didn't seem perturbed by it. They hunkered down until the shooting stopped, then one of them pulled the left-hand door back, using a lanyard dropped over the knob. An FSI man on the other side then backhanded something into the room.

With a rocking boom the grenade detonated. Smoke billowed out into the hall. The assembled FSI broke into fits of coughing and laughing, which were answered by more gunfire from inside.

Another grenade was tossed in. Ka-boom!

Barrabas deduced that the guerrillas had barricaded themselves in the room and were making a last-ditch stand. The FSI, instead of getting the thing over with, rushing the room or chucking in a half-dozen grenades, were toying with their trapped enemy.

As Barrabas turned back to his men, he saw a guy with a gun slinking across the hallway in the distance, then opening a door. The guy was not in powder-blue. Barrabas reasoned that he must have escaped from the room the FSI were bombarding.

The white-haired mercenary raced after him, slowing only as he reached the end of the hall. He found the door the man had entered standing ajar. Barrabas waited for the others to back him up, then dived at the door, banging it back, rolling into the room. He came up on one knee, his handgun tracking.

The fleeing man was halfway through the room's window. His weapon was on the outside. He couldn't turn and fire. He was dead in the water.

"Drop it," Barrabas said.

Hayes, Nanos and Starfoot rushed in and drew beads on him, too.

The man lowered the Uzi he carried and let it fall on the fire escape platform.

"Back inside, quick," Barrabas told him.

A vicious glare in his eyes, the man obeyed.

"He's a goddamn mailman," Nanos said.

The Greek's statement was punctuated by another grenade blast from the other side of the building.

"Or PFM in a mailman's uniform," Billy offered.

"I'm no stinking Commie PFM!" the postal worker snarled back.

"Then what were you doing with the submachine gun?" Barrabas asked.

"I was fighting for my country. Like the others. Fighting for democracy. Against the damned FSI butchers. I'm loyal to my president."

"Soarez?"

"Of course, Soarez. We postal workers armed ourselves when we got the news that the military was going to try and take over. Mantuegans suffered too much and too long to give up a real chance at democracy without a fight. We're all ready to die for it, if we have to."

"Yeah, but some are more willing to die than others," Nanos quipped. "It looked to me like you were running out on your buddies back there."

The mailman shook his head. "Only one of us could get out safely. We drew straws for it. Someone has to escape to spread the news of the massacre, otherwise many brave people have died misunderstood and in vain." He looked at them defiantly.

Barrabas lowered his weapon. The others did the same.

"Who are you?" the postman demanded. "You're not FSI. You're Americans! CIA! Part of the team that tried to kill Soarez!"

Another grenade boom rolled down the hallway, rattling doors and windows.

"Easy, buddy, we're just tourists," Billy said.

The postman was not convinced.

"We have no interest in harming your president," Barrabas told him.

The man smiled. "You can't harm him, now."

"He's not dead, is he?" Hayes said.

"No, he's rallying," the mailman said. "And expected to regain consciousness soon. The Mantuegan people won't allow another attempt on his life. They have swarmed to the hospital. Haven't you seen the TV? There are two hundred thousand supporters in the streets around the complex. No army truck, no soldiers can get within three hundred yards of the building where he's being treated. No one is being allowed in or out. Armed loyalists are guarding the corridors."

"I'll be damned," Nanos said.

"And they'll stay there until the crisis is over," the postman said with conviction.

If Barrabas had any lingering doubts about the feelings of the Mantuegans for their duly elected president, they were long gone. Claude Hayes, who hadn't had any doubts, period, looked happy and damned proud of the little mailman and his do-or-die cohorts.

Shouts from the hallway outside and the sound of running feet coming their way put Barrabas in mind of the danger the postman was in.

"You'd better get out of here," he said.

The man didn't move. He stood there in astonishment.

"Go! Quick!" Hayes told him.

The mailman flashed them a smile and ducked out of the window.

They could still hear his shoes clunking on the fire escape steps as the door to the room burst in and a trio of FSI men entered, their SMGs at waist level.

"What's happening?" Billy asked, standing between the troopers and the window. His broad shoulders completely blocked their view of the fire escape.

But they didn't muffle the sounds of running feet.

"What's that?" one of the FSI men asked. "Someone's getting away!"

The trooper lunged for the window, half stepping out onto the landing, bringing his Uzi to bear on the figure hightailing it down the alley.

Before he could fire, Billy turned, his wide back again blocking the view of the others, and gave the guy a push. It was meant to be a little shove to knock off his aim, but Starfoot got a bit carried away. Actually, he got a whole lot carried away. The FSI man went flying ass over teacup over the fire escape railing. He screamed all the way down.

"Oops," Billy said.

"You pushed him!" one of the other FSI men shouted. He raised his Uzi.

"Fuck!" Nanos pointed the Beretta at the man's chest and fired in a move so practiced, so down-pat that it was a blur.

The FSI man slammed against the wall and slumped, rag doll limp, to the floor. His sole surviving comrade tried to bring his weapon to bear, but two shots—one from Barrabas, one from Hayes—transfixed his torso. The Uzi went flying. The FSI man went down.

Barrabas kicked the door shut. "Out the window with them," he said, grabbing the man he'd shot by the back of the collar.

They passed the bodies through the window to Billy, who tumbled them off the fire escape landing.

Starfoot was just climbing back in, when the door opened again and Enriquez and a handful of others rushed in.

"What are you doing here?" the FSI colonel demanded. "I told you to stay outside."

"Hey, it sounded like you guys were having fun," Nanos told him. "We didn't want to miss out."

"I hold you responsible," Enriquez said to the mercenary leader.

"We tried to save some of your men from their own stupidity." Barrabas indicated the window with his thumb. "They were chasing a guerrilla who took the fire escape. They were so eager to catch him that they didn't take basic precautions to cover each other. They got caught in a cross fire halfway down. We shot back but missed. And it was already too late to save your troopers."

Enriquez stepped out onto the landing and looked down. He was back in a moment. He pointed a finger at the men standing around in the room. "Let this be a lesson to you all," he said. "That could be you splattered all over the alley if you disregard your training."

The FSI men looked suitably impressed.

"Come on," Enriquez commanded, "we have the outbuildings to sweep before we're through here."

Barrabas and the others followed the FSI colonel out of the room. As they did, Enriquez turned back to them and said, "I want you to know that I appreciate what you did in there."

"Think nothing of it," Barrabas told him.

"Any time," Hayes added.

22

Liam O'Toole lay on his belly not three feet from the right boot of the man in charge of bringing him to justice. He was close enough to count the boot's frigging eyelets. Liam had crawled up the slope, making his own trail through the pungent slime of rotted greenery. Cut, bruised, bathed with sweat, he nestled in the dense undergrowth just below the lip of the dirt road that crossed the narrow, tortuous jungle path they had spent so many hours climbing.

The troop-carrying helicopters that had passed overhead had landed on the road. The man in command of the pursuit had driven up.

Driven, while his quarry toiled and sweated, thinking they were ascending the back of beyond.

That's what happens when you go hiking without a map, O'Toole told himself.

On the road to his right, the search teams were assembling. Liam saw that they were sporting American-made infrared spotting scopes on their M-16s. His heart sank. If the others hadn't moved far enough off the trail, or if they had left some clue, a broken branch, a footprint to follow, they wouldn't stand a chance.

Liam was racking his brain, trying desperately to come up with something when the radio in the car above him crackled and bleeped. The commanding officer opened the car door and spoke into the hand mike. Though O'Toole's Spanish was limited to the vocabulary necessary for getting drunk and getting laid, in that order, he could tell from the surprised tone of the man's voice that something big had happened.

The officer slammed the car door and walked quickly away.

O'Toole considered slipping out at once and trying to steal the khaki four-door sedan. He figured that if he could drive it away he might lead off pursuit from the others. He drew himself up a bit, preparatory to making his move.

And saw the troopers returning en masse from the boonies.

They were pulling out.

All of them. Piling back into the choppers. The starters whined, rotors turning sluggishly, then the engines caught, and in a few seconds, the helicopters were lifting off the road and wheeling away in a cloud of dust.

Evidently, much more serious shit was going down elsewhere.

The commander returned to the driver's side of the car. Another soldier, a subordinate, got in the passenger side and shut the door.

Liam wanted the car. He had to have it. Even if the search teams coming up the hill had been pulled off the hunt, too, he, Hatton, Beck and Jessup would be stuck up here. And if the searchers hadn't been pulled off, it was just a matter of time before they would overtake their prey.

The SOBs had to have wheels.

When the commander opened his door, Liam lunged out from the undergrowth like a tiger. He tackled the officer just behind the knees, sending him slamming into the side of the car.

The junior officer sitting on the other end of the sedan's bench seat was stunned by the suddenness of the attack. Too stunned to do more than let out a yell.

Liam grabbed for the commander's holster as he pulled the man down to the ground. Come on, you bastard, he thought. Come on. He unsnapped the flap and jerked free a blue-steel .38 service revolver.

The underling had his own weapon out by that time, but he couldn't shoot without endangering his superior. He had to bail out of his side of the car.

Liam had meanwhile rolled away from the commander. He could see the feet moving to his right under the car, heading for the trunk. He threw himself into the open driver's door, his knees landing on the seat. His gun-hand thrust over the top of the seat back. The junior officer was a dark streak on the other side of the rear window, rounding the back bumper. O'Toole led him and fired. Four times in rapid succession. The concussion in the enclosed space was earsplitting. The back window suddenly went opaque around a quartet of crusty holes. And the subordinate, a shadow on the other side of the ruined glass, twisted and took a funny fall, out of sight.

Liam hopped out of the car and cautiously approached the rear end.

The poor bastard was on his back in the dirt, legs pumping, hands clawing at his chest. He had his mouth open and he was gasping for air.

"Jesus," O'Toole said, taking aim at the man's head to put him out of his misery.

Before he could squeeze off a shot, he was tackled from behind. The commanding officer punched his kidneys, the back of his head, then grabbed for the gun.

"You dumb fuck," Liam growled as they rolled off the road and into the brush. The slope dropped off precipitously. They turned over several times, and when they stopped they were nose to nose and the handgun was between them. Both of them had their hands on it. O'Toole's index finger was inside the trigger guard.

The officer squeezed and the double-action revolver's hammer inched back.

It was aimed straight up.

An inch or two either way would determine whose head got blown off.

Liam's powerful forearms strained, bending the muzzle away from his face.

The gun went off with a stunning boom. O'Toole felt the searing heat and the blast, and for a second wasn't sure if he hadn't been the one hit. Then he blinked the burned cordite out of his eyes and looked into the face four inches from his own.

The eyes were all wrong. One was aimed straight up; the other was looking away at a right angle. Under the man's chin was the entry wound. The exit was as big as all outdoors on the top of his head. Between the two points was mush.

Liam shoved the quivering corpse away and scrambled back onto the road. The younger officer no longer needed a coup de grace. O'Toole rolled the body into the brush, then found the point on the road where the trail crossed it. He trotted downhill until he figured he was within hailing range of his friends.

"Yoo-hoo!" he said.

He got no reply.

"Yoo-hoo!"

"Is that really called for, O'Toole?" said a pile of moldering compost next to a boulder. The pile stood and shook itself and became Nate Beck. Then Lee and Jessup wandered in from either side of the trail.

"Yoo-hoo!"

The Americans looked at one another. None of them had spoken.

"Yoo-hoo!"

They looked down the hill where the cries had come from. They could see nothing but bush.

Autofire stuttered from below and 5.56 mm tumblers whacked the tree trunks beside their heads.

"This way!" Liam said, leading them up the hill.

Having rested, Jessup was now in better shape. Getting shot at improved his performance immeasurably. Even so, the troops below were gaining.

The Americans burst out of the jungle and onto the road. O'Toole waved them to the waiting khaki sedan, and slipped behind the wheel while the others jumped in. They were off in a cloud of dust, headed downhill before the first of their pursuers reached the road.

"Ha-ha!" Liam gave the steering wheel a smack.

"How did you get this car?" Lee asked.

"Leprechauns, me darlin'," he said. "I made me a deal with the little people."

"Little people, my butt," Jessup said. "This is a military vehicle."

Liam explained events to them as the car sped down the dirt road. When he was through, Jessup said, "We've got to find a way off this island and quick."

"What about Barrabas and the others?" Beck asked. "Shouldn't we try to link up first?"

Lee had the same concerns. "I don't like the idea of leaving Mantuego without them. For all we know, the senator royally screwed them over, too. Come to think of it, that's pretty likely."

"Barrabas isn't in half the shit that we are," Jessup said. "He's working for Nochenegra and the senator is on Nochenegra's side, has been for twenty years. Do you know what they do to people convicted of murder here?''

The others shrugged.

"It's the one truly democratic feature of Mantuegan life," Jessup told them. "When it comes to capital punishment, Everyman is the executioner. They stone murderers to death in the city park."

The mercenaries remained unconvinced.

"There's another downside to making contact with Barrabas," Jessup went on. "What do you think is going to happen if the authorities connect us with him? They're going to put two and two together and come to the conclusion that we were in on the operation together—all of us working for Nochenegra. Nochenegra, who would benefit enormously from Soarez's assassination. If we go anywhere near Barrabas, we put his life and the lives of the others at a terrible risk."

"You may be right," Beck admitted.

"No, I *am* right," Jessup said. "The best thing we can do for the colonel and the best thing we can do for ourselves is to get the hell out of here as fast as we can."

"The airports are going to be sealed off," Liam said. "You can damn well bet on that."

Though Lee Hatton obviously disliked the whole idea, she, too, came around in the end. "We'll have to go by boat," she said.

"Boat?" Beck exclaimed. "We're a week's sail from anywhere hospitable."

"We're not going to take a rowboat," Jessup said. "If we can make it down to the bay after dark tonight we can liberate a ship big enough and fast enough to get us safely away. Once we get a few hundred miles out to sea we'll be all right. They won't bother to hunt us past that point— assuming that they even figure out that we've left."

LIAM AND THE OTHERS spent a tedious afternoon moving from one place of hiding to another. They parked the car in various shady glens, dead-end roads, abandoned farmyards. Whenever a helicopter passed overhead or a donkey cart rolled by, they upped stakes. When they traveled, Hatton and Jessup hid under a blanket behind the front seat.

All day long they could hear the battle for the capital city raging in the distance. If the sounds were any indication, it was a struggle waged mostly in calibers thirty and smaller, with an occasional, brief, all-out artillery barrage thrown in for good measure.

By the time the sun set, they were a jumpy bunch, eager to get on with it.

O'Toole took one of the main north-south roads that led into the city. They could just make out the city's lights in the far distance. Every now and then a flare would go off over the downtown section, a miniature sun that illuminated it until the light source drifted down, out of sight.

They came around a bend in the road and Liam almost rear-ended a car stopped in front of him. He had to hit the brakes hard to keep from tapping it, and stopped with only a couple of inches to spare.

"Watch it, for crying out loud!" Beck said.

It wasn't really Liam's fault. He had no way of anticipating the massive traffic tie-up. Blazing taillights stretched before them for a good half mile. At the beginning of the jam, visible as the road curved right and down, was a row of bright white lights, set up on the shoulders of the road. Between them was a makeshift security checkpoint. Two six-by-sixes had been parked across the highway, perpendicular to the flow of traffic. There was about twenty feet between the trucks and they were parked one ahead of the other, turning the once straight road into a sharp zigzag that a car traveling at any kind of speed could never make.

In the glare of headlights and klieg lights, they could see armed troops stopping and searching each car as it came up to the barrier.

"We don't want to take this route," Beck said.

"Let's get out of here," Jessup added.

Lee made it unanimous. "Turn around!"

O'Toole swung his arm over the seat back and craned his neck around to look behind them so he could back up. As he did so, another car pulled up, cutting off his route. They were trapped in line. "Shit!" he said. Then he slammed the sedan into reverse. "Hang on."

Liam tromped on the gas, and the sedan lurched backward, smashing into the car in back. Both vehicles jolted at impact; the rear car's headlights crashed out. It was knocked back five feet. Then Liam jammed the sedan into forward gear, tramped hard on the pedal and bashed the car in front. More squealing of steel, more breaking of glass.

"Go!" Hatton said. "You're clear!"

O'Toole cranked the wheel hard over and cut a wicked, rubber-burning 180-degree turn, whipping over into the opposite lane of traffic. Both of the driver-victims honked their horns at him as he peeled away. Their adenoidal toots sounded a good deal more cheerful than the circumstances called for.

"What the hell are we going to do now?" Beck said. "You know they've blocked off every major road into the city just like that. The place is a goddamned battle zone. The last thing the government wants is guerrilla reinforcements filtering in under cover of darkness."

"We'll have to find a minor way in," Liam said, searching the dim plain around them. He could make out a checkerboard of tilled fields, bordered by wire fences. "I've got an idea." He pulled over onto the left shoulder of the road, opened his door and got out. There was an open drainage ditch between the edge of the road and a three-strand wire fence that bordered the nearest field.

"Don't even think about it," Beck told him as he stepped up alongside. "If you drive down into that ditch, you'll never get out of it. The curve is too steep. Your back end will hang up before you can cross it."

"I wasn't thinking about driving down into it," Liam said. "Why don't the rest of you people get out of the car for a minute?"

"What are you up to, O'Toole?" Jessup asked.

"Just stand on the other side of the road over there and pray."

"He's going to jump the ditch," Lee announced.

"The ditch and the fence," Liam avowed.

"You're out of your mind," Jessup said. "If you blow it . . ."

"We've got nothing to lose," he told the Texan. "If I blow it or if I don't try, we're still going to have to walk into the city to avoid the checkpoints."

Beck, Hatton and Jessup walked across the road. O'Toole got back in the car and pulled away. He drove a quarter mile up, giving himself plenty of room to pick up speed. Then he turned the car around. He waited on the shoulder until there was no traffic coming either way, then he floored it.

The sedan's speed rose slowly at first, then as the transmission shifted up, more quickly.

"Come on, sweetheart," Liam said, coaxing the car along. "Give me all you got."

It was doing seventy-five when he veered it off the road. For a split second he was weightless, clinging to the steering wheel, as he stared up at the stars. Then the car's nose dropped. The front just cleared the top of the fence; its rear wheels came down on it, flattening it. The sedan landed on all four wheels with a jarring crash. O'Toole sank deep into his seat, then bounced up again. His head bashed into the roof, despite his seat belt.

The car kept on rolling across the field.

Liam stopped it some thirty feet from the ruined fence.

"Great driving!" Beck said as he and the others got back in the car.

"Where'd you learn to do that?" Jessup asked.

"Self-taught," Liam said.

"Really?"

"Yeah, just now."

Headlights off, the car crawled through the dark field. O'Toole made Beck get out and sit on one of the front fenders to make sure they didn't drive into something they couldn't get out of.

It was slow going but in everybody's opinion it beat walking all to hell.

Liam angled them away from the row of taillights stopped at the highway.

"I sure wish we had a map," Lee said.

"We're going the right direction," Jessup assured her. "All we have to do is turn right once we get to the city. We can't miss the bay."

They drove through a dozen pastures linked by closed but unlocked gates. When they came to one, Beck would hop off the fender and do the honors. The only living creatures they saw were a herd of cows sleeping around a watering hole made out of an old bathtub.

When they reached the last gate in the line, the one between them and a dirt road that led in the direction they wanted to go, they found it locked.

Beck tried to break the padlock with a chunk of rock and couldn't do it.

"Everybody out again," Liam ordered. When they had made their exits, he started to back up.

"You're really getting into this, aren't you, O'Toole?" Lee said.

He just grinned as he went another hundred feet in reverse. She was right. There was something special about taking someone else's car and crashing it through solid obstacles.

He revved the sedan's engine and dropped it into gear. He hit the gate at thirty. The gate went flat and the car bounded out onto the dirt road.

When the others had rejoined him, he drove down the dirt road a ways, headlights still off. He drove slowly, looking around for witnesses, for pursuit. There was nothing. He turned the lights on. The narrow street came into view. It was lined by treeless, grassless dirt lots, on which every fifty yards or so was planted a prefab house.

Retirement real estate.

The population density started to pick up as they neared the outskirts of the city. Finally they came to a streetlight.

The sounds of fighting were close, only five or six miles away.

"Let's give the action a wide berth if we can," Jessup suggested.

"Sounds good to me," Liam said. He turned right and headed in the direction of the bay.

They'd gone about a mile when headlights flared in the opposite direction.

"Duck down," Liam told the back-seat passengers.

A pair of army trucks rolled past.

O'Toole checked his mirror. The trucks kept right on rolling out of sight.

"Actually," Beck said, "we couldn't have picked a better car to be out in. There's got to be a shoot-on-sight curfew in effect. The army boys think we're one of them."

"As long as we don't get stopped," Lee said. "Or they get a close look at us."

Beck spoke up. "Isn't there supposed to be a river around here somewhere? Maybe it's over there."

He pointed at the left-hand side of the road, which was heavily treed. On the right side were more fields. The sedan's headlights caught the back ends of a row of vehicles parked along the right shoulder.

Olive-drab vehicles.

Troop carriers and jeeps.

"Hey, O'Toole," Beck said, gripping the dash.

The headlights swung over men in uniform standing in a break in the trees on the left side of the road. In front of them were sandbagged machine-gun emplacements. Beyond them was the river, inky, sinuous.

The soldiers stared at them as they drove past. One of them shouted for the car to stop. *"¡Alto!"*

Liam goosed the gas instead.

They had to forge ahead now. They were committed. What with the six-by-sixes parked on the side of the road, there was no place for them to turn around. And if they did, they'd have to pass by the same troops.

Gunfire erupted from behind them. Slugs thwacked into the trunk lid.

Liam looked into the rear mirror and saw headlights swing out. "Dammit!" he said, putting the pedal to the floor.

Ahead, the road became indistinct. It blended into a broad apron of hardpan. On it were parked four more trucks, and a goodly number of troops.

Without a pretense of a challenge, the soldiers started shooting at them. The center of the windshield spider-webbed.

"There's a bridge!" Beck shouted. "To the left!"

Liam cut the wheel hard over, skidding on the dirt, then rocketed for the narrow span that crossed the river and ended in the slum of El Infierno.

"We're going to make it!" he bellowed. "Goddammit to hell, we're going to make it!"

The car thudded over the bridge's loose floorboards. The bridge was barely wide enough to accommodate the vehicle's wheel span.

Then, over the noise of the tires on the boards, over the autofire blistering at their backs, another noise. A groaning that grew louder and louder. And then a solid crack.

As the bridge collapsed under its weight, the car began to slide left and fall.

"Oh, shit!" Liam cried. The sedan still had plenty of momentum going for it. It twisted in midair, passing over the sluggish river, falling, crashing on its side onto the mud flat beyond. It spun as it hit, turning its underside to the far bank from which it had come.

It took a few seconds for the occupants to regain their senses.

"Is everyone all right?" Liam said.

His question was answered with grunts and groans.

O'Toole kicked out the fractured remnants of the windshield and crawled through onto fragrant muck. When he put his weight down, his legs sank in up to his hips.

Then the searchlights from the opposite bank kicked in, spotlighting the car and the area around it for a good thirty yards.

At a shouted command, the army boys opened fire. A hail of bullets whacked the underside of the car, ricocheted off and skipped over the sea of mud between the Americans and the shantytown.

Liam clung to the sedan's roof, wishing to hell he was someplace else.

Anyplace else.

23

Nile Barrabas stood out on his hotel-room balcony watching Mantuego City do a slow burn. A Third World meltdown. He had cut his room lights so he wouldn't be backlit, a tempting target for a bored sniper on either side of the conflict.

The battle for control of the capital hadn't been as easy as the generals had predicted. They had met determined and forceful resistance not only from elements of the PFM guerrillas, but from civilian police units and from bands of private citizens.

Flares floated down over the north end of the city, bathing it in brilliant white light.

It was a free-fire zone.

Heavy fighting had been going on there all day, the rattle of small-arms fire an irritating constant. It wasn't the only hot spot, but it was one of many. The cadre's forces, despite superior numbers, training and firepower, had been unable to contain the opposition the way they had wanted to. They had been compelled to move in force into the high-priority zones, which housed industry and the estates of the wealthy, in order to keep them from being overrun. As a result of the necessary reallocation of manpower, large sections of the capital were seriously undersupported, in effect written off by the military. The opposition, especially the PFM, had that part figured out early on.

The city below was in chaos. Everywhere factions of combatants were running. Dog packs in the streets, waging hit-and-run warfare against anything that moved.

Sirens ripped the air.

Explosions echoed down deserted streets.

Barrabas felt sorry for Mantuego, for its people.

This coup was a botched job, an execution where the doomed man has to be hanged, or shot, or injected over and over again because he continues to struggle, to survive, to suffer.

The only thing the generals had nailed down in twelve hours of combat was the capture of the presidential palace. It wasn't exactly a feather in their caps. As the president wasn't there, there had been little resistance. They hadn't been able to do anything about Soarez. The mob outside his hospital was still there and it wouldn't let them in.

Barrabas squinted into the darkness.

Somewhere out there Lee Hatton, O'Toole, Beck and Jessup were running for their lives. There hadn't been any news reports on their whereabouts since the military had taken over the radio and TV stations. He had to assume that if they had been captured they would have been paraded before the cameras, dead or alive. It was even possible that they were already off the island, that they were back in the States. Possible but unlikely. Whatever their mission on Mantuego had been, he was certain it wasn't to assassinate the president. That meant that they had probably been tricked, trapped. That meant that they probably didn't have an adequate escape route set up in advance.

It fried him that there was nothing he could do to influence the outcome for them.

Hell, he was kidding himself. He couldn't do anything for anyone. Fate had taken it all out of his hands.

In seven hours Juan Carlos Nochenegra was going to land at the army base and the Mantuegan people would slip back under the yoke of the dictator's tyranny. Maybe Nochenegra could consolidate the country. Maybe he could defeat the PFM. Maybe he could be convinced to someday allow democratic reforms.

A lot of maybes.

And given the man's past performance, very doubtful maybes at that.

Barrabas wondered what Mandelo would have thought of the night's goings-on. Would the great philosopher have found something intrinsically good in the evil that boiled unchecked in the city streets below?

Barrabas didn't doubt it. There was always another side to a problem, a silver lining—if you took the trouble to rationalize it.

A heavy barrage of autofire erupted from the darkness on the other side of El Infierno.

Barrabas grimaced. Put on a happy face, my ass.

24

When the savage torrent of machine-gun fire finally stopped, Liam pulled himself back to the opening where the car's windshield had been and stuck his head inside. "Everybody out," he said. "This tub is sinking."

It was true. The sedan had begun to settle into the soft muck. Already the pungent stuff was oozing over the lip of the destroyed windshield and into the passenger compartment.

Beck slithered out over the dashboard and slid arms first into the mud. "Yuck," he said, fighting to right himself.

"Come on, let's move," O'Toole said.

Jessup and Hatton were still in the back seat. With great difficulty the broadly built Texan slipped around the top of the front seat. The mud level had risen to touch the side of the steering wheel.

Jessup regarded the gap that had once held the windshield. "I don't know if I can get through it," he said.

"Come on, you're not that big," O'Toole told him.

"Go for it," Beck urged.

With agonizing slowness Jessup dragged himself over the dashboard. He got his head and shoulders through the opening. Beck and O'Toole grabbed him by the arms and pulled. He came real smoothly for a foot or so, then he stopped short.

"Ooof," he said.

"Push, Lee," Beck said. "Get in behind him and push."

She climbed over the seat back and put her shoulder to his behind. He wouldn't budge.

"Brace your back against something and use your legs," O'Toole suggested.

Lee quickly readjusted herself.

"Oh, God," the Texan moaned as he inched through the opening. Once his middle cleared there was no stopping him. He slid the rest of the way out with a rush, landing on Beck and O'Toole, knocking them both back into the mud. While they thrashed about, he fought for a handhold on the car.

Lee slipped out and joined them with no sweat.

In seconds they had all sunk up to their armpits in the lukewarm mud.

"What now?" Beck asked.

"Maybe they'll let us surrender?" Jessup said. "I don't know about the rest of you, but I don't feature drowning in this shit. I'd rather be stoned."

"Me, too," Liam said. "To tell you the truth, I wish I was stoned right now."

"Hey! We give up!" Jessup cried.

At his shout, the troops on the other side of the river once again opened fire. From positions spaced along the bank, a half-dozen heavy machine guns roared, pounding hot lead against the undercarriage of the car. The whole damn thing vibrated and rocked from the fury of the onslaught. The underside of the sedan was no longer impervious to the concentrated firepower. As slugs smacked the car's bottom, hitting weakened spots where previous bullets had struck, they passed through, striking the roof at greatly diminished velocities and rattling around inside the passenger compartment.

After what seemed a long time, the shooting stopped again. Gunfire echoes rolled away into the distance.

Clouds of milky cordite smoke swept over the river, over the car, and into El Infierno.

Lee followed the path of the smoke, looking back behind them at the slum. At the houses on stilts perched above the mud flat. In the shadows under them, there was movement.

"Uhh, Liam," she murmured without taking her eyes off whatever was stirring in the darkness.

From the direction of El Infierno came a series of single rifle shots. Bullets whined over the Americans' heads. Each shot was followed by the tinkling sound of breaking glass and the sudden winking out of one of the army searchlights.

The machine guns opened up again. Raining death on the cardboard shanties. Then the last light was shot out and the whole area plunged into blackness.

The boys behind the MGs stopped shooting.

The silence was eerie.

"Uhh, Liam," Lee whispered.

He shushed her.

She poked him, hard, and then pointed at the slum. Faintly visible in the starlight, men crawled on their bellies over the top of the mud. Crawled toward them.

When Liam finally saw what she was getting so excited about, his first thought was the same as hers: they were PFM. Not that he cared at that moment. Whoever they were, they were coming to help.

On the far side of the river truck engines started up. Then headlights switched on, broad white beams swinging over the mud flat as the trucks were maneuvered into position along the bank.

The second the mud-bound car was illuminated, the machine guns began anew. One of the crawlers got caught in no-man's-land. The muck in a wide circle around him was stippled by impacts. He must have been hit by fifty slugs; he was literally pulped by them. His blood ran in a black trickle over the surface of the mud. His companions made it to the cover of the car.

"You guys got yourselves into a terrible fix on our account," Jessup told their would-be rescuers.

As he spoke, a very slow rocket arched up from the shantytown, a rocket with a long orange tail. It landed with a crash on the other side of the river, on the hood of one of the trucks. With a whoosh the Molotov cocktail exploded. Men screamed. Then from the ghetto more single rifle shots barked, picking out the truck headlights one by one.

The MGs raised their sights to probe for the source of the attack, but before they could locate and negate it, two more firebombs sailed overhead on high, wobbly trajectories.

Across the river more trucks caught fire. Men caught fire, too. One of them ran along the riverbank, trailing a cape of flames four feet long. He threw himself into the river and was instantly swept away.

When the last headlight was shot out, the men from the slum started to push three of the four Americans out across the mud. Beck, Hatton and O'Toole, but not Jessup.

When the Texan protested, the men slipped one end of the rope they had brought around them, tying it securely under his armpits. The leader of the group told him to wait until they got to the pilings across the mud flat and then they would all pull him to safety. "You'll never make it across any other way," the man explained.

Liam, Lee and Nate belly-crawled with the slum dwellers over the flat to the shadows under the elevated shacks.

"Now we must pull your large friend across," the men's leader said. "We must pull very fast and very steady or he will sink in over his head."

They all took hold of the rope, now slimy with mud, and on a counted signal, started hauling for all they were worth.

For a minute Jessup thought he was going to be torn in half. Then his feet came out of his shoes and he slipped up on top of the mud. Holding on to the knot with both hands, he slid along the surface in rapid pulses. In a couple of minutes he reached the safety of the shadows.

The slum dwellers then took them deeper under the shacks, to a ladder propped up in the mud. They climbed into the house above, and the ladder was pulled up after them.

"Come," the leader said, "we must not stay here. We must move on quickly."

They were led out of the cardboard-walled shack and over a very shaky walkway on stilts. The plywood scrap under their feet sagged and creaked at every step. They were coated with mud pretty much from head to foot, and as they walked it began to dry on them.

Finally, after traversing a puzzle maze of walkways, they got to solid ground in the older part of El Infierno. It was the kind of place Lee Hatton had seen too many of. They were taken into a hut made of sheet tin. A mansion, relatively speaking, its single room was all of ten by ten.

There they were given water to drink.

"Would it be possible for us to clean up a bit?" Jessup asked.

The leader apologized. "I'm sorry. I know it must be uncomfortable for you, but there is no way to wash off the dirt. Our only running water comes from the rivers on either side of us. The army has lined the banks of both the Sueño and the Letargo with machine guns. They're shooting anyone from El Infierno who goes near the water. They don't want anyone to leave."

One of the other slum dwellers stepped in front of them and said, "You are the Americans, the ones the police are chasing?"

Liam grimaced. "You aren't PFM by any chance, are you?"

"No," the man replied. "We are supporters of Dr. Emilio Soarez."

The Americans glanced at the machetes ringing them. There was no way out of the tiny room.

"You look worried," the man said.

"Don't we have reason to be?" Lee asked.

"Dr. Soarez has recovered consciousness," the man explained. "He has issued a statement about who attacked him...and who helped him. You are the ones who saved his life. We, the people of Mantuego, are very grateful."

"I think we can call the score even," Lee said.

"You saved our lives, too," Beck said.

"Not for long, I'm afraid," the man told them. "The military lines the banks of the rivers for a reason other than to contain us. They are keeping us trapped here so that when they blow up the dams on the Letargo and the Sueño, we will all be washed into the sea."

"Why would they do that?" Lee asked.

"They are holding the entire slum of El Infierno hostage. They are demanding that all hostilities cease, that the opposition surrenders, or they will carry out the threat. The deadline is tomorrow at noon."

"We've got to do something," Beck said.

"Yeah, but what?" Jessup exclaimed.

"There's no way to sneak out of here and get to the city?" Liam asked the leader.

"No way. The army has El Infierno sealed off from above the point where you crashed your car, all the way downstream. There are even troops stationed at the tidewater. We are cut off completely."

"Damn!" O'Toole said. "If we could just find a way to get out of here, we might be able to link up with the colonel and stop the dams from being blown."

"The colonel?" the leader questioned.

"Barrabas," Jessup said. "One of our people here on the island."

"Another American? Big, white-haired?"

"You've seen him?" Lee asked.

The leader nodded. "And a black man, too."

"Hayes," O'Toole said. "That'll be Hayes."

"They fought the PFM here last night. We have heard conflicting rumors about them since. It was first believed that they were working for the cadre. But this afternoon they helped a man escape from the FSI. Their loyalties are unclear."

"Only because the situation is unclear," Lee said. "They are as straight as they come."

Jessup asked, "Have you heard any rumors about the return of Nochenegra?"

"Yes," the leader said, "there have been rumors for weeks now. We have heard that special preparations have been made at the army base for a secure landing. The word is that El Dragón may be coming back as early as tomorrow morning."

Beck nudged O'Toole. "Then Barrabas and the others will be there. They'd have to be there to greet him. They're supposed to be the coordinators."

"We've got to get out of here and connect up by early tomorrow," Liam said.

"But how?" Jessup said.

"Let me think out loud," Liam said. "The slum is sealed off because the army wants the opposition to surrender. It won't let anyone out until that happens."

"We know that," Lee said.

"Do we?" O'Toole asked. A broad grin suddenly spread over his face. "Is it true? Or will the army let certain people out? Certain special people with a special purpose?"

"What are you getting at?" Jessup said.

"They want surrender, right? Well, someone has to be allowed to leave the slum to do that. Some authorized contingent has to be allowed to leave to even discuss the terms of surrender, if any. Where will the contingent be taken? Why, to the command center at the army base."

"So, we're going to do the surrendering." Jessup nodded in agreement.

"Not we," Liam said. "I'm afraid this is a job for me and Beck only."

Lee started to protest, but he shouted her down. "If you and Jessup come along, the two most easily recognizable members of the supposed Soarez hit team, we aren't going to get more than a few steps beyond the walking bridge before the soldiers start shooting."

"He's right," Jessup said.

Dr. Hatton glared at the fat man. "Yeah, I know," she said, "but I don't have to like it."

25

Beck and O'Toole walked down the dirt lane that wound wormlike from the heart of El Infierno. The light of dawn was blood-red with the pall of smoke that overhung the city. The mercenaries were dressed in clothes borrowed from the slum dwellers. They both wore shabby straw hats; both carried white flags tied to sticks.

"Just keep your mouth shut, no matter what happens," Nate reminded Liam.

"No problem," O'Toole said. "You're the official spokesman."

The winding lane ended in a rickety footbridge. On the other side of it they could see the riverbank, and beyond that, the city. On the roadside above the river, rows of trucks and jeeps were parked. Guys in camou fatigues were standing around, eating their breakfast. Down low on the banks were sandbagged MG emplacements.

Before they even set foot on the bridge the Americans started waving their white flags.

"We give up!" Beck shouted in Spanish across the river. "We surrender!"

They waved and walked on. They got about halfway over the bridge when the nearest MG position bellowed. A line of slugs cut across the plywood planking less than twenty feet from where they stood.

"Got the distance lined up pretty good," Liam said out of the corner of his mouth.

"Shut up," Beck said. Then to the soldiers across the way he shouted, "We are representatives of the PFM. We want to discuss surrender with the generals."

They began walking again.

The MG stuttered. Bullets skimmed off the bridge.

They froze. They could see an officer running down to the MG. He clapped a hand on the gunner's shoulder and the shooting stopped.

"Come on across!" he shouted back. "Keep your hands in the air."

Beck and O'Toole advanced, waving their flags the whole time. They both got an itchy-twitchy feeling as they stepped over the bullet-riddled planks.

The moment they reached the other side they were set upon by a dozen or more government soldiers.

"We surrender," Beck told them.

The soldiers weren't all that interested in what a pair of red terrorists wanted to do. They slapped them down for weapons, *slapped* being the operative word. Once it was clear they were unarmed things got worse.

"Dirty Communist pigs!" one soldier snarled, giving Beck a shove.

"Kill the bastards!"

It was a free-for-all. Free for them, anyway.

Beck took a boot in the belly and then someone punched him in the kidneys. He sank to his knees, gasping for breath.

Liam, too, was getting the hell kicked out of him. Three soldiers were booting him in the ribs.

God, don't let's say anything, Beck prayed. Liam's whorehouse Spanish, if he could dredge it up under the circumstances, would be a dead giveaway that they weren't who they claimed to be.

The officer finally arrived on the scene and pulled his men back. Then he had a crack at the messengers of surrender. Grinding in the boot, as it were.

They didn't fight back.

When the officer had tired himself out, he told his men to drag the PFM representatives to their feet. The soldiers held their arms twisted behind their backs.

Beck looked at Liam. He smiled back, showing bloody Chiclets.

"We speak for the PFM combatants," Beck told the officer. "We are ready to surrender."

"Decided that you didn't want that shithole you call home washed into the sea?" the officer asked.

Beck decided the best policy was to ignore him. "We would like to meet with the cadre and discuss terms."

"Maybe I'll just keep you here until, say, five minutes after noon? I'd sure hate to miss the show. And my men have been waiting here all night to get the best seats."

"I wonder what the generals would think of that point of view?" Beck asked.

The officer punched him in the face.

Nate spit a gob of blood in the dirt. For a second he thought the officer was going to hit him again, but the guy changed his mind.

"Bring a car around," he told his men. "And I want you to radio ahead that we are coming with the very important representatives of the PFM."

They were trundled into the middle seat of a four-wheel-drive carryall. The officer rode as a passenger in the front seat. Two soldiers sat in the rear bench, their automatic pistols drawn and pointed at the backs of Beck and O'Toole's heads.

So far so good, Beck thought.

BARRABAS, HAYES, NANOS and Starfoot stood on the army base airfield, inspecting the welcoming arrangements for the returning president.

"Kind of understated, isn't it?" Billy said, looking wonderingly at the tiny reviewing stand, the paltry display of Mantuegan flags. In front of the reviewing stand was a lectern with a couple of microphones on it. Parked to one side was a mobile video unit. The most impressive part of the setup was the hundred-piece marching band from the base. All dressed in snappy white uniforms, they were standing around, tuning up, getting in the mood to Sousa.

"Maybe the generals are saving up, maybe they're going to do it up big at the palace?" Nanos suggested.

"I know one thing," Hayes told them. "Juan Carlos is going to be bummed. He expects half the city to be here, cheering his glorious return."

"He also expects the city to be his," Barrabas said. "Which isn't exactly the case."

"What the hell will he do?" Starfoot said. "Turn around and go home?"

"No, but you can bet he'll make life miserable for everyone," Nanos predicted.

"There hasn't been any news about O'Toole and the others?" Hayes asked.

"No news is good news," the colonel said. "If the people chasing them are as competent as the ones doing the fighting down in the city, they're probably in L.A. by now."

"Here's hoping," Billy said.

Two troop trucks pulled up beside the reviewing stand. Men piled out, their uniforms gaudy even by Mantuegan standards. They wore chromed helmets, maroon shirts, goldenrod-yellow jodhpur pants and high black boots.

"It must be the Mantuegan honor guard," Nanos said.

"Are they going to give him a fifty-gun salute?" Billy asked.

"Probably," Hayes said without enthusiasm.

A jeep drove up beside them, with General Bonifacio sitting in the back seat. He, too, had changed into something more flashy. He looked like a doorman at a fancy New York hotel, except that he had enough fruit salad on his chest to choke a chimp. Gold ropes and fringed epaulets completed the fashion statement.

"I have just had word from the control tower," Bonifacio announced. "The president's plane is due in any second."

Barrabas nodded. It couldn't happen soon enough to suit him. He couldn't wait to get this bit of operatic farce over with and get the hell out.

"We have put some extra chairs behind the lectern for you and your men, Colonel Barrabas," Bonifacio said. "We felt that you should sit in a place of honor, at the right hand of Juan Carlos, for the people of Mantuego to see. You deserve much of the credit for the coming of this glorious day."

"That's very kind of you," Barrabas said.

The general eyed the hardware the Americans were packing. "Perhaps it would look better for the cameras if you weren't wearing those," he said, indicating the autopistols hanging below their armpits.

Barrabas shook his head. He wasn't going to give up his Browning for anything. "We'll be sitting down," he told the general. "They won't even show."

Bonifacio didn't press the issue. "Now, if you will excuse me, I must see to a few last-minute details."

They watched the jeep roar away.

"Sitting next to that bastard Nochenegra is one honor I'd like to skip," Hayes said.

"We've got to play the game a little longer," Billy told him. "A few more hours and we're out of here."

"I'd sit *on* him for a ticket on the next flight to L.A.," Nanos confessed.

"Hey, Colonel," Billy said.

Barrabas wasn't paying attention to them. He was looking at the honor guard. At the flat-black M-16s they carried. He was getting a funny feeling—a kind of tickle inside his head, in a place that couldn't be scratched. The honor guard was loading up, cracking magazines into their assault rifles. For guys about to touch off a festive national occasion they seemed uniformly taciturn.

"Colonel?" Starfoot repeated. "Is something wrong?"

Barrabas grimaced. "I don't know yet," he said. "I want you guys to stay close and alert from the minute that plane's wheels touch ground. Got it?"

"Sure, whatever you say," Nanos said.

FROM AN ALTITUDE of eight thousand feet, Juan Carlos looked down upon his island jewel—dark green like an emerald at its core, fanning out to the pearly white of its sand beaches, to the pale lapis-blue of its placid bay. He felt more than pride at the sight. He felt justified. Vindicated. The months of his exile had proved to the whole world that Mantuego could not survive without him, without his leadership.

The change in plans, the landing at the base airfield instead of the beach, no longer bothered him. In the excitement of the moment he didn't care where they plopped him down. As long as the cameras were there to film it, what difference did it make?

The first-class section of the chartered 727 was practically empty. On the whole aircraft there were only twelve people, including the pilot and flight crew. Luisa sat across the aisle and up a few rows. She was being attended to by a Hollywood makeup artist imported for the occasion. Lieutenant Ortega sat directly across from Nochenegra.

Juan Carlos was in such a buoyant mood he didn't even think about the pair's infidelities.

The makeup artist, having finished with the first lady, moved on to the main event.

"And how are we feeling, *Presidente*?" the woman asked as she carefully lifted off his sunglasses. "A few itsy-bitsy butterflies?"

Juan Carlos shrugged. "Don't put too much blush on my cheeks," he warned her. "I don't want to look like Howdy Doody."

While the woman worked with her brush and paint pot, Nochenegra thought about Mandelo, about his revered place in Mantuegan society. There would soon be another star in the firmament. His. The night before he had been studying what had come to be known as Mandelo's "Tirades," a series of loosely connected essays on the woes of mankind. The general theme of the collection was that misery is necessary for personal development. Nothing, the dictator thought, could be truer. In his own case, the misery of forced exile had made him grow enormously. He was determined not to make the same mistakes again.

No more Mr. Nice Guy.

He would strengthen the FSI even further, granting them unprecedented powers of search and detention. He would clamp down on all forms of dissent. Wage genocidal war on the PFM.

"There," the makeup lady said. "You're perfect."

Juan Carlos put his sunglasses back on. Of course he was perfect.

The plane banked over the city. He could see the wounds the civil war had inflicted. Blackened gashes cut across the downtown district. Entire blocks in the poorer sections had been reduced to rubble.

The common folk had learned their lesson, though. They would not be bad children again.

The Fasten Seat Belt sign blinked on over his head. He buckled up. As the air brakes cut in, his stomach lurched. Maybe he was an itsy-bitsy nervous.

They cleared the perimeter fence of the army base and eased down on to the field for a landing.

Through the plane's intercom the pilot addressed him. "On behalf of the crew of this aircraft, I would like to welcome you back home, President Nochenegra."

All seven of them applauded and cheered.

Juan Carlos watched out the window as the plane taxied down the runway, turning off near a complex of hangar buildings where smaller military aircraft were serviced and stored.

"On this side, Juan Carlos," Luisa said. "They are all on this side."

Nochenegra got up from his seat and moved across the aisle.

All?

His heart settled somewhere below his ankles. There were fewer than two hundred people in attendance. Half of those were either in the military band or the honor guard. Where was everybody? Where were the cheering masses? The adoring children so eager to accept his crumbs?

"It's because of the fighting," Ortega said. "They must have had trouble organizing because of the fighting."

It was no excuse as far as the dictator was concerned. He had expected no less than a thousand times the number of well-wishers. Still, there were cameras. He could see them. If he allowed himself to throw a tantrum the way he wanted to, he would spoil the day entirely. On film or videotape no one would ever know how few witnesses there were to his return. He still had his chance to shine for posterity. For the grubby-cheeked schoolchildren of the twenty-second century.

He drew himself up to his full height. "Ortega," he said, "my weapon."

The lieutenant hurried to fetch the hog-leg Smith & Wesson. Juan Carlos stood still as the holster was draped over his back and shoulders. Then his high, white officer's hat—the brim covered with gold encrustations—was placed on his head.

"The gangway is ready, sir," the pilot informed him. "Anytime you're ready."

Juan Carlos nodded. "Luisa," he said. "You will walk behind me."

She swung into step after him.

Nochenegra stepped out into the bright sunshine and the familiar humidity of his native land. The military band stood in formation at the foot of the gangway. The moment he appeared the bandleader raised his baton and started them up. They played "Hail to the Chief" at a speedy clip.

Juan Carlos waved to the people below, smiling fiercely. Milking the moment. His generals, resplendent in their best uniforms, waited for him at the foot of the gangway. As he started down, they began to applaud and cheer.

It wasn't the way he had pictured it in his mind's eye, but it was good. It was very good.

At the bottom of the ramp, he shook hands with Alvarez, Bonifacio and Del Rey. Colonel Enriquez was there, too, beaming with pride. Portable video cameras recorded it all.

"You have been sorely missed, *Presidente*," General Alvarez told him.

"Sorely," Bonifacio chimed in.

"It feels good to be home," he said right into the camera.

"Please, *Presidente*," Del Rey said, gesturing toward the lectern, "say a few words to your loyal supporters."

"Of course."

As they walked to the reviewing area, the band marched behind, playing at top volume. Luisa was gorgeous, as always, waving and smiling as if it was her one joy in life.

Waiting for him near the podium was the American mercenary Barrabas and his crew. Nochenegra warmly shook the man's hand. "A wonderful job, Barrabas," he said. "All of you have done superbly."

The white-haired man congratulated him and then backed away to the rows of folding chairs behind the lectern.

"Please, everyone sit down," Juan Carlos said into the microphones. His amplified voice was a booming command. When the band music stopped he could hear the distant gunfire.

The band stood in neat ranks to his left. To his right was the honor guard with its Mantuegan flags and chromed helmets. A riot of color.

"This is the most wonderful moment of my life," Juan Carlos began. "A return to my homeland, to my people. To the nation that needs my leadership. Through the dark times, the doubts, the disappointments, it was the anticipation of this moment that carried me through."

The honor guard commander barked an order. Like mechanical men, the honor guard jerked to full, straining attention.

"The philosopher Mandelo once wrote that anticipation is the progenitor of actualization...."

A second command was issued and the honor guard shouldered their M-16s, aiming them skyward.

"...I stand before you, living proof..."

The third command should have been "fire." Instead, it was a signal to change point of aim. All fifty rifles swung in the direction of the man behind the podium.

Juan Carlos's mouth went dry. The words he was about to speak dried up, as well, dried up and blew away. He was for an instant completely paralyzed.

A split second before the honor guard opened fire, something slammed the dictator from the side. The blow knocked him to the ground. A heavy weight on top of him kept him down.

Then the lectern was gnawed by a wild spray of bullets. Nochenegra tried to get up but the weight, the person on top of him, would not let him. He struggled in panic, twisting around, looking into the grim face of Nile Barrabas.

The marching band, standing so close to the focus of the gunfire, laden down as they were with tubas and bass drums, panicked also. Like turkeys caught in a rainstorm, they ran in all directions. Most of them ran into the kill zone and were chopped down by the honor guard's full-auto fusillade.

The band's blunderings did, however, divert the attention of the president's would-be assassins for a moment. When Barrabas let him up, Juan Carlos pulled his long pistol from its sheath and sent a .44 Magnum hollowpoint sailing in the direction of his traitorous generals. Then he took to his heels.

As he did so, he saw Barrabas and the other mercenaries gamely exchanging fire with the death squad.

He dashed past the rows of folding chairs, many now toppled and folded as were their former occupants. Lieutenant Ortega and Luisa were about thirty yards ahead of him, sprinting for the nearest hangar. There was no other cover available.

Juan Carlos followed them through the hangar's side door. Then he turned back, and sighting against the door frame, fired several more shots in the general direction of the reviewing stand. His fury slightly abated, he entered the hangar. Lieutenant Ortega had a man in khaki cornered against the tail of a twin-engined plane.

"The plane is gassed and ready, *Presidente*, but he won't fly us. He says he's scared."

Juan Carlos rammed the barrel of the Smith & Wesson down the front of the pilot's pants. "Now, he's scared."

NATE BECK HAD CONVINCED himself that they weren't going to get through the base's front gate. He was certain that they would be stopped, taken aside, thoroughly interrogated, maybe even tortured before they were allowed on the grounds. As it turned out, he had nothing to worry about.

The officer's men had phoned ahead. They were expected. The generals were eagerly looking forward to the meeting.

That was not so much of a surprise.

From what Beck had heard in the slum, and from what he had seen in the streets of the city on the way over, the army of Mantuego wasn't faring all that well. The generals were desperate for a quick way to end the hostilities, since they couldn't seem to do it militarily. If they suffered more serious battlefield losses, the generals would be facing a mass desertion of their troops.

After the gate sentries waved them through, the driver of the carryall headed across the tarmac in the direction of the base's airfield where a jet transport was parked. The area around the plane was full of people. A microphone squealed. He tried but he couldn't understand what was being said to the assembled crowd.

"Do you know who has just arrived?" the officer asked him.

Beck shook his head.

"A longtime friend of the PFM, Juan Carlos Nochenegra. Imagine the fun he is going to have with your kind once he's back in the saddle."

At that moment a horrendous barrage of automatic-weapon fire erupted from the direction of the plane. It so startled the driver that he swerved the car.

The soldiers holding guns on Beck and O'Toole broke concentration to look. "What is it?" one of them cried. "What's happening over there?"

The officer could see and he was speechless.

Liam and Nate made their move. They turned and grabbed the muzzles of the guns at their backs. For an instant they struggled in silence. The soldiers were too startled to do anything but fight for control of their weapons.

Then one of them let out a yelp.

The officer turned over his seat back to face the rear.

And the pistol Beck and the soldier were tugging over discharged.

An earsplitting crack.

The officer got worse than an earache. He was right in the line of fire. His head exploded out the back, spraying the dash and the inside of the windshield with pink.

O'Toole socked his man in the face four times in quick succession, while holding the man's gun away with his left hand. The soldier let go of the pistol and slumped back to his seat.

The driver of the carryall had meanwhile slammed on his brakes. He bailed out of the vehicle while it was still rolling and took off across the asphalt as fast as he could run.

Nate jumped into the driver's seat and got the car stopped. Liam held the captured gun on the two soldiers.

"Open the back gate," he told the guy who was conscious. "Drag your buddy out. Go on."

The soldier opened the back gate, all right, but instead of helping his knocked-out comrade to safety, he skedaddled.

"Hey, you dumb…" Liam started to yell. "Aw, to hell with it." He climbed over into the rear and dumped the guy out on the pavement.

When he turned back, Beck was trying to muscle the dead officer out the passenger door. It was a little difficult since the guy still had his seat belt on.

"The belt, Genius," Liam said, reaching over and giving it a snap. "Try it without the belt."

Beck grinned sheepishly. "Yeah, that would help, wouldn't it?"

The officer thudded softly to the tarmac.

Ahead of them, the gunfire was nonstop. They could see people running and people down.

"Do you think Barrabas is in the middle of all that hoo-ha?" Beck said.

"Knowing Barrabas, that's a pretty dumb question. Where the hell else would he be?"

Beck dropped the carryall into gear and floored the gas.

The cavalry, all two of them, was on the way.

BARRABAS GOT that tickle inside his head again when he was watching the generals with Nochenegra. When the dictator had his back to them, the senior staff officers gave each other *looks*. Not boy-are-we-glad-he's-back looks. Not wow-this-is-a-great-day-for-Mantuego looks. Not even jeez-what-a-boring-bastard-he-is looks. These were man-oh-man-do-we-have-him-by-the-balls looks.

The generals didn't stand close to him, either. They filtered off to the sides, then slipped over by the reviewing stand.

The tickle became a major itch when the honor guard started to do their fifty-gun salute in the middle of the president's arrival speech. That was so wrong it made his teeth ache.

Barrabas was up and moving on the third command. In his guts he knew those M-16s were not going to stay pointed skyward. He didn't even consider the fact that he might be wrong, the embarrassment if he blindside-tackled the president of the country in midsentence. He knew he was right.

And he was.

Out of the corner of his eye he could see the rifles dropping, swinging over.

He hit the dictator hard and drove him down behind the podium, just as it was turned into splinters.

When he landed on the ground, and the bullets started flying, Barrabas realized that he had saved the bastard's life again. He hadn't intended to do that. But it hadn't been a conscious choice. Everything had happened too fast. It had been an instinctive response. See somebody about to eat it and step in to help out. If he had been given time to consider the pros and cons, he would've had to do it the same way. Nochenegra was garbage, but he was all that Mantuego had.

In that same instant, he also realized something else, something equally as important. The generals had made a point of putting him and his men behind the dictator. In the line of fire. They were targeted for the hit, too.

As the band blundered into the withering volley, stumbling, knocked cockeyed by waves of 5.56 mm tumblers, Barrabas cleared his Browning from shoulder leather.

The dictator was struggling under him, wanting up. Barrabas rolled aside, coming up on his knees. He two-handed the Hi-Power, firing into the packed mass of the honor guard.

Juan Carlos dragged out his own hand cannon and let one rip. Then he scuttled off to safer ground.

Leaving Barrabas and his men to fight on alone.

The fallen band members made a kind of bulwark the SOBs could fire from behind.

Hayes, Nanos and Starfoot moved up beside Barrabas, blasting away with their own 9 mms.

The chromed helmets of the honor guard made great targets. When a niner slammed into one, it made a dull clunking sound, a cowbell sound. There were a lot of clunks.

The situation changed as the ranks of the honor guard were thinned by the mercenaries' fire. They got smart. They spread out. They slid over to the cover of the reviewing stand. Some of them even discarded their helmets.

As soon as Barrabas saw them ducking away, he knew it was time to retreat. "Let's get out of here." He waved his men back.

They leapfrogged to the underside of the 727, taking cover behind the landing gear.

A salvo of slugs pinged off the struts, then the big tires blew out and the plane sank down onto its rims.

"There goes Nochenegra." Hayes pointed at the hangar.

They watched the little man disappear inside.

"It looks like the best cover around," Barrabas said. "By twos. Billy and Nanos first."

While they sprinted across the tarmac toward the hangar, Barrabas and Hayes laid down a field of covering fire. Neat, precise single shots, keeping the chromed heads down behind the reviewing stand.

When Billy and Nanos reached the side door, it was their turn to give cover. Barrabas reloaded, nodded to Hayes, and they took off. No looking back. Just a flat-out dash. Slugs freight-trained past their heads as they pumped for the finish line. The chrome domes of the honor guard had realized that their quarry was getting away and they were trying to do something about it, even at the risk of their own lives.

Barrabas and Hayes skated through the open doorway; Billy and Nanos pulled back to allow them by.

Barrabas looked up to see that the other side of the hangar was open, a King Kong-size doorway rolled back. Through it a twin-engined Army recon plane was coasting. The props were throwing up a gale.

"Nochenegra?" he shouted to the others.

"Didn't see anyone get on the plane," Nanos shouted back. "But he's nowhere else in here. He has to be on it."

Barrabas watched the camouflage-painted aircraft zoom away, rolling toward the runway, away from the fighting. It lifted off and disappeared, banking toward the sea.

"The bastard got away," Hayes said.

"Shit, they're coming after us!" Billy swung back into a firing position against the jamb. His big stainless Smith & Wesson auto bucked against his two-fisted grip.

Barrabas saw the oncoming maroon-and-yellow hordes and cursed. Beyond the hangar was the vast open space of the airfield.

As the song said, "Nowhere to run, nowhere to hide."

26

When the army carryall came screeching in through the open hangar door behind them, the mercenaries turned as one, bringing their pistols to bear on the driver's side of the front windshield.

Both the driver and the red-haired passenger suddenly leaned out of their respective windows, yelling like banshees.

What they were yelling was "No!"

"Son of a bitch," Billy exclaimed. "It's O'Toole."

Barrabas and the others lowered their weapons and ran over to the carryall. There wasn't time for chitchat. They climbed in and Beck peeled out of the hangar, rubber smoking off the tires as they churned across the slick concrete floor.

Nanos, who had jumped into the passenger seat beside Beck, looked at the mess on the dashboard and windshield and made a face.

"Sorry about that," Nate said. "No time to run it through a car wash."

"Man I hate an untidy car."

"Listen, Colonel," O'Toole said as they made a wide arc around the control tower away from the scene of the attack, "We've got to move fast or our friends the generals are going to blow the dams on the Sueño and the Letargo and wash El Infierno halfway to China."

"Explain," Barrabas said.

Liam did, very quickly, leaving out all extraneous detail.

When he was through, Barrabas pointed over the seat at a three-story building across the parade grounds. "There!" he said. "The generals' HQ is there."

Beck veered in that direction.

"These guys have got to die," Hayes said.

"Agreed," Barrabas said, "but first the dams. We've got to locate and neutralize the explosives. That means keeping the generals alive. Understand?"

The carryall barreled down on the HQ building. The sentries normally out front were nowhere in sight. Beck skidded to a stop outside the entrance.

"Let's do this quick and clean," Barrabas said as they exited the vehicle.

They ran for the glass front door, guns up and ready. It got messy in a hurry.

A pair of sentries popped up on the other side of the doors, their M-16s braced at hip height.

The soldiers of Barrabas reacted as if it was just another extreme-close-range drill. They fired into the doors from a yard away, splintering them, blowing the guards back ten feet in the spray of lead and glass. The sentries crashed to their backs and stayed down.

"Come on! This way!" Barrabas stepped over the bodies and hurried to the elevator. No way would they ride in it up to the third floor. If there was someone waiting for them up there it would be a death trap. Barrabas didn't want it to be an escape route, though. He pushed the button. When the doors opened on an empty car, the mercenaries lowered their guns.

"Drag that guy over here," the white-haired mercenary told the others.

They dumped the body across the floor of the elevator, blocking the door, effectively freezing the car on the ground floor.

"We'll take the stairs," Barrabas said.

They moved quick and sharp, advancing in half-a-flight rushes, maintaining constant cover for one another. When they got to the door to the third floor, Barrabas opened it a crack and peered out.

He couldn't see anybody.

He could hear movement, though. It was coming from the conference room.

He slipped through the door, running in a crouch to the opposite wall. He covered for Hayes, who came out next. Then all four of them advanced to the conference-room doorway.

The door was ajar.

Barrabas put the sole of his boot to it and charged in.

Generals Alvarez, Del Rey and Bonifacio looked up in astonishment from the long table. Alvarez reached for the M-16 by his right hand on the table.

"Don't!" Barrabas said.

The general was already shooting, firing wild and full auto, trying to substitute rounds per minute for accuracy.

Shortcuts never work.

The mercenaries all fired back at once.

The general's spare frame was lifted bodily from the floor and slammed against the wall unit. His head in ruins, his fruit salad chest suddenly marmalade, he toppled to his side.

Del Rey seized the opportunity to unholster his own side arm. He got off a single shot from the revolver before 9 mms made through-and-through tracks in his lower face and throat. He bubbled from his new orifices, his eyes full of horror, then full of nothing. He flopped dead across the table.

"Don't shoot!" Bonifacio cried. He waved his hands high in the air. He was looking down four smoking barrels.

"Give us a good reason," Hayes said.

"Whatever you want," Bonifacio told them. "It's yours."

"We want to know about the plan to blow the dams," Barrabas said. "Who, when, where?"

Bonifacio stumbled all over himself in his eagerness to cooperate. "It wasn't my idea. Believe me, it was theirs. And Enriquez's. I wanted nothing to do with it."

"The dams are supposed to be destroyed at noon," Liam said. "We don't want that to happen."

"If it happens we can guarantee you will be a very sorry sucker," Nanos threatened.

"But Enriquez, he has just left to handle the detonation personally," Bonifacio said.

"Left? How?" Barrabas demanded.

"Helicopter. No more than two minutes ago."

"Grab him," Barrabas said.

They hustled the general down the stairs and into the carryall. The scene outside had further deteriorated. Fleets of ambulances were ferrying the wounded away. Gunshots were still ringing out inside the base perimeter.

Beck drove up beside a gunship parked on its own pad. Bolted in the front of the right-hand bay door was a 7.62 mm minigun. They dragged the general in through the other side.

"Can you fly it, Billy?" Barrabas asked.

"No sweat," he replied, looking over the instruments. He started flipping switches, then the starter whined. "Come on, mama," he coaxed. The engine caught and the rotors started churning.

Billy lifted off and banked away from the base.

Hayes and O'Toole held the general between them in the cargo bay.

Starfoot gained altitude until they could see the twin rivers sliding through the plain below. Billy made a straight-line course to intercept them.

As they flew, Barrabas gestured for Hayes and O'Toole to bring the general closer, so he could talk to him.

The man looked plenty scared.

"Which dam is Enriquez going to be at?" Barrabas asked.

"I don't know," Bonifacio whined, his eyes tearing from the wind ripping through the open bay door.

"If you don't want to take a swan dive," Liam said, giving him a little push toward the exit, "you'd better figure it out, but quick."

"He could be at either one. The explosives can be detonated from either site."

"Cute," Hayes said. "That's real cute."

"Which one do you think he'd go to?" Barrabas repeated.

Bonifacio shook his head. "They are equally distant. I don't know."

Barrabas frowned. "Anybody got a coin?"

COLONEL RIBAN ENRIQUEZ had been looking forward to this hour for a long time. As far as he was concerned, El Infierno was a cancer on the body of his nation, a source of corruption and disease. Moral and political issues aside, he was anticipating a thrill royal at pushing the button and watching the big earthen dams just slide away, the towering walls of water coursing out of the mountains. It was also going to be a thrill knowing that some 100,000 people would be washed into the bay.

He had planned things so he could be at both ends of the calamity, so he would miss nothing. As soon as he touched off the blast, he would climb back into his helicopter and head downstream for the slum. He would arrive just ahead of—and 150 feet above—the wall of water, just in time to see the havoc he had caused with a touch of his little finger.

He stood on the dam and peered over. It was three hundred feet down into the gorge. Behind him was Lake Letargo—the backed-up headwaters of a once mighty river.

It was a pity that things at the airfield hadn't gone as planned. With Juan Carlos still alive, and free, things could be very complicated. Indeed, everything seemed to be going wrong for the cadre. They had tried to do too much, more than their abilities permitted.

It was Enriquez's policy to work within his limits, intellectual and physical. To handle things directly—like the hostaging of the slum. A simple solution to the problem of the army's failure to win on the battlefield. Some would even call it an elegant solution.

That it hadn't worked was not his fault.

Actually, it was better that it hadn't worked, because now he was free to push the button. He had left straight from the mess at the base so the opportunity wouldn't pass him by. He didn't have to worry that the men he had stationed to guard the explosives and detonators might take it upon themselves to do the honors. They were petrified by the very idea.

It took a real man to conceive of such things, a hero to act them out.

He checked his watch. It was time to do the thing. He walked back across the dam to where his helicopter idled. The pilot sat waiting, ready for an instant takeoff. His FSI men loitered around the side of the chopper, not looking one another in the eye.

Enriquez picked up the detonating device. It was a very sophisticated instrument. It worked by radio waves. It could precisely synchronize the two explosions, delaying the one on the Letargo until the signal to the Sueño arrived. It was very important to the symmetry of the thing that both dams blow at once, that the maximum amount of water reached the slum at the same moment.

He removed the manual safety clip.

The FSI men muttered and crossed themselves. Then they all, unbidden, climbed into the helicopter.

"El Infierno," Enriquez said, holding the detonator button out in front of him, "go to hell...."

As he was about to press down, a helicopter swooped up from the gorge, stopping, hovering just over the middle of the dam.

"No!" Enriquez cried. "You can't. Get away!"

The helicopter pivoted and landed on the dam.

"Idiots!" he snarled, putting the detonator down. He turned to his men and said, "Don't any of you go near that button. If you do I will shoot you myself."

With that he stormed off, heading for the helicopter that had, for the moment, ruined his fun.

THE MEN IN THE HELICOPTER were sweating bullets until they saw Enriquez heading across the riprap for them.

"Here he comes!" Nanos cried.

"That's two lucky guesses today," Barrabas said.

"Hey, the coin toss was luck," Starfoot said. "But you had Enriquez pegged but good. No way would he blow the dam with an army chopper sitting on it."

"Some guys have a deep and abiding respect for government property," Liam said.

Enriquez shielded his eyes from the sun, squinting as if he couldn't see into the cockpit. "Get out of here!" he shouted. "Take off at once. That is an order."

"Fuck you," Billy said.

The FSI chief took one look at the men inside the chopper and turned tail. He knew that they knew that they were supposed to be dead by now. For a man carrying quite a few extra pounds, he could really move when he had to.

"If he gets to the detonator," Billy said, "it's going to be nasty."

"Yeah, somehow I think he'll sacrifice the chopper this time," Nanos said.

"Take us up, Billy," Barrabas said.

Starfoot lifted the helicopter into the air and swung out over the gorge, coming around a full 180 degrees to face the running Enriquez.

"He seems determined," Billy said.

"Yeah, determined to die." Barrabas motioned to the Greek who was manning the minigun.

"Whatever you do, Alex," Hayes told him, "don't hit the detonator."

"Are you kidding? I'm a frigging brain surgeon with one of these."

As Billy brought the gunship in for a pass, the brain surgeon cut loose with a three-thousand-round-per-minute burst. He stitched a line of .308-caliber lead across the width of the dam, raising a cloud of dust and rock chips. It was a line drawn between where Enriquez was and where he was headed.

Billy cut back sharply and came in low and slow. They couldn't hear what Enriquez was saying but they could see he was shouting at his men.

"He's trying to get them to hit the button," Barrabas said. "And they aren't having any of it."

"Shit, he's going for broke this time," Billy said.

Barrabas had given the man his chance—more of a chance than he deserved. He turned to Nanos and made a throat-cutting gesture.

"Gotcha, Colonel," Nanos said.

As the ship came by again Enriquez was dashing for the detonator, head down, fists pumping.

"He ain't gonna make it," Hayes said.

The brain surgeon's hands swung the mini around, his thumb tripped the trigger button. Hell roared out the bay door.

Colonel Riban Enriquez was swallowed up in a cloud of dust, lifted and flung like so much hamburger over the edge of the dam. His body bounced off the dam's face and disappeared into the gorge.

The helicopter on the ground took off.

"What do you think, Colonel," Billy asked. "Will they fight or run?"

The Indian maintained his position, keeping Nanos angled so he could nail the other chopper.

There was no need. The second ship ran.

"Take us up a little higher," Barrabas said.

"But Colonel, what about the explosives?" Hayes said. "Don't you want to get down there and disarm them?"

"It'll wait for a minute or two. There's one more thing we need to find out from our distinguished guest."

Barrabas climbed into the chopper's cargo bay and confronted Bonifacio.

"Who made the decision to include us in the hit on Nochenegra?"

Bonifacio looked desperate.

"Whose decision was it?" Barrabas grabbed him by the neck and hauled him over to the edge of the bay. He made him look down. "Either you tell me or we're going to see whether pigs can fly."

Bonifacio's eyes were shut tight. He nodded.

Barrabas jerked him back.

"The same man who hired you," the general said. "It was at his special request. He said it was personal."

Barrabas looked at the grim faces of his men. Yeah, it was personal, all right.

27

Juan Carlos sat behind the desk of his private office, playing with his stainless-steel Model 629. He took out the bullets, counted them, put them back in. He spun the cylinder. He looked down the barrel.

He put the muzzle to his temple.

So many choices in life. To live or die. To kill or to let live. It was hard to make up one's mind.

Nochenegra had suffered a series of terrible and humiliating defeats, in both his personal and public lives. He couldn't get them out of his head. And he had to. He had to put some of the awful burden to rest.

He cocked the Smith & Wesson's hammer. How cold the barrel felt against his skin. Like the touch of death's finger.

LIEUTENANT ORTEGA PULLED the legs of the bear suit up over his knees. Damn, the thing itched. As if it had hair on the inside, too. He paused to scratch his thigh. Then he dragged the legs the rest of the way up and shrugged into the arms. The suit was heavy, too. And it had odd lumps inside. It was the skin of a real bear. The lumps were real bear lumps. Luisa thought that made it easier for him to get into character.

Luisa was a strange woman. Strange but unforgettable.

When he thought about his life before Luisa it was gray. Oatmeal. She had infused him with spirit, joy. She was a skyrocket in flight. The best he could do was to tag along behind and below her, taking what paltry thrills he could from the twinkling fallout of her incandescent trail.

Since their return from the fiasco in Mantuego, Juan Carlos had locked himself away in his room, brooding over his lost presidency, his failed power. That was fine with Ortega. It meant that he could have Luisa all to himself.

He pulled the bear head down over his own and adjusted it so he could see out the eye holes.

He let out a practiced roar and waved his claws in the air menacingly.

He could feel himself starting to get excited. She had trained him to do that. To do tricks like a poodle. She had perverted his instincts to satisfy her own perverse needs. Ortega knew this and he didn't care. He was willing to be molded by the likes of her. He was soft clay in her slender hands.

Maybe, in the aftermath of Mantuego, old Juan Carlos would go morbid on them. Maybe the loss of his island would turn him suicidal. Maybe he would do the world a favor and do himself in. Then Luisa would be free and rich, and they would be free to live and love the way they wanted to.

It was not such a hopeless fantasy, he told himself. Even if the dictator didn't kill himself, he wasn't young. He could die of natural causes well before she did.

Then Ortega heard the door open in the outer room.

So soon! he thought. And he hadn't even picked out a hiding place yet.

He hurried to the closet, decided against it, then went into the bathroom. He pushed back the shower curtain and stepped into the tub. Then he closed the curtain.

Luisa loved it when he jumped out of the shower, roaring his lungs out, waving his arms about.

He waited, hardly breathing, every nerve tuned to listen for the footsteps approaching.

The door to the bedroom creaked open.

Yes, my darling, he thought. A few more steps. A few more dainty steps and your curiosity will do you in, as always. The thing you fear most, and the thing you love most, will most certainly pounce.

Sweat began to trickle from the top of his head where the bear head rubbed his skull. It ran down the back of his neck, then down his spine. He shut out the mental image. I am a bear, he told himself. Bears don't sweat. I am a hungry bear.

He strained to hear the sounds of movement, but there was nothing. Luisa loved to torture herself with the anticipation. She would stop and fantasize, mulling the possibilities over and over in her mind before she reached out and jerked open the door or threw back the curtain.

Then a sound!

A step over the bathroom threshold.

Ortega readied himself to roar. Soon, my darling, he thought. Soon, you will face the fanged terror.

A shadow was dimly visible to him through the opaque plastic of the shower curtain.

Ortega saw a hand reach out to grab the edge.

The curtain rings shrieked across the rod as the curtain was flung back. Ortega threw up his shaggy, beclawed bear arms, and let out a ferocious bellow.

The joyous cry died away in his throat.

Instead of coming face-to-face with his lady love, he was face-to-face with a stainless-steel Smith & Wesson Model 629.

"Well, well," Juan Carlos said, "what have we here? A bear in the bath?"

Ortega tried to laugh inside the costume. It had a hollow ring to it.

"It's open season on bears, you know."

"*Presidente*, it is I, Ortega," the lieutenant said. "I am only playing a little joke."

"I know who it is," Nochenegra said. "And I know who the joke is on, this time."

Ortega started to remove the bear head.

The crisp clack of the Smith & Wesson's hammer locking back made him drop his hands.

"It is hot inside this suit, *Presidente*. And I am tired of the game."

"The game? Or my wife?"

The lieutenant stared down the barrel of the .44 Magnum, his mouth suddenly dry. He could see the cupped noses of the big hollowpoints in the cylinder. "I don't understand..."

"I have been watching you and Luisa for a long time," Juan Carlos said. "Watching like a cat, interested, playful, trying to decide what and when."

"What and when...?"

"A proper punishment and when it should be administered."

"I'll go away," Ortega promised. "You'll never see me again. She'll never see me again."

"Yes, you will. You will go away today. Right now. And forever. Out of the tub."

Ortega obeyed. "Just let me pack a few things...."

"You have a fine suit, already, a coat to be proud of...." Nochenegra put the muzzle to the middle of his back. "Now you are going to walk ahead of me out into the garden."

Ortega didn't protest. He walked out of the room, into the hallway, down the stairs to the first floor and out into the garden.

"Can you run in that costume?"

"Run? Not very well, *Presidente*."

"That's a shame, because I am going to count to three and then start shooting. One..."

Ortega didn't ask for explanations, clarifications or modifications. He took off like a bear out of hell.

"Two..."

The suit was baggy in the crotch and prevented him from taking his full stride. Still, if he could just make it to the garden maze, he thought, if he could just...but his legs were going all soft and mushy from fear.

"Three..."

The Smith & Wesson barked.

Ortega's right leg blew out from under him and he crashed to the paving stones. For a second it felt as if he had no leg at all. Then he wished he had no leg. The shock of the huge bullet's impact racked his whole body.

He fought down the haze of pain and looked back. Juan Carlos was coming, holding the big pistol in the air.

"Help!" he cried. "Somebody help me!"

It suddenly occurred to Ortega that he was really going to die here and now. He didn't want to die with the stupid bear head on. He grabbed it with both hands.

The Magnum bellowed.

Ortega's body slammed back. His arm was gone. From shoulder to fingertips, it was gone. Then it, too, returned and he was sorry. It seethed with pain.

Unable to remove the bear head, Ortega fell back against the rim of a fountain. Through the bear's eye holes he could see the house. He searched for the floor, for the room that he knew was hers. And he saw her standing at the window. Standing, watching. As he started to call out, she closed the shades.

Juan Carlos put the pistol's muzzle against the bear head and said, "Say goodbye." Then he fired.

28

The senator motored up to the library window. Two stories below him on the crazy paving apron the Nochenegra limousine had just parked. He watched as Juan Carlos and Luisa exited the Mercedes, then disappeared into the house under him.

Satisfactions in life, true satisfactions were so rare, he thought. He could count his on the fingers of one hand. As obsessed as he was with young, voluptuous women, none had to do with the conquest of same. Or with being elected senator. Such were trifling things, things impermanent. Women rarely stayed conquered. Elections came up every six years.

He was about to add one to his list tonight.

Behind him, Juan Carlos and Luisa were shown into the library by the manservant. The senator turned his chair. "Good evening to both of you," he said. "I'm so glad you could come."

"We always have time for you, Senator," Juan Carlos said. He looked quite elegant in his gray silk suit and cream paisley tie. Of course the sunglasses were a bit of a minus.

The senator drove his chair straight to Luisa. "Such a beautiful woman." He took her hand and kissed it wetly. He felt her shudder.

"You are too kind," Luisa said, smiling radiantly.

"Can I get you something to drink?" the legislator asked. Without waiting for a reply he motored to his bar. "I'm having a small whiskey. Juan Carlos?"

"Yes, that would be fine."

"Luisa, some wine?"

"Sparkling water, I think."

The senator already had three glasses set out on the silver tray. He poured the soda water first, then the whiskeys. "Here we are," he said, distributing the drinks. *"Salud."*

They all drank.

"Sit down, please," the senator said. "Sometimes I forget to say that because I'm always sitting."

The Nochenegras took places on the leather couch.

"I understand that you had a tragic accident in California," the senator said. "Your lieutenant Ortega, lost at sea."

"A terrible thing," Juan Carlos said. "He was so young. He had such promise."

Luisa said nothing.

"Is your drink all right?" the lawmaker asked.

"Oh, yes. Wonderful," she said, taking another sip.

"The reason I asked you here," the senator went on, "is because I feel that I've lived up to my part of the bargain, vis-à-vis your return to power in Mantuego. I did everything you asked. I even put my own career on the line."

"You have been a loyal friend to us," Juan Carlos admitted.

"What I'm trying to say is, our deal was that once you set foot on the island certain documents in your possession would automatically be turned over to me. That has not happened. I would like to know why."

Juan Carlos drained his glass and put it down on the couch arm. "First of all I want to assure you that I had every intention of fulfilling my part of the bargain when I made it. I am not a dishonest man. But you must see that the outcome in my country has changed things. Who could have predicted that my own generals would turn on me? That the weak-kneed Soarez would be able to turn three bullets in the chest into a mandate of the people for his reform government?''

"You're saying that you would have honored the deal only if you were successful in regaining control? You never mentioned that before now. Surely you can see that is unfair."

"Senator, what is fair about life? I should have a country to rule and instead I have nothing."

"You have a good deal of money."

"I do," he said, nodding. "And with your help I will soon have much, much more. I intend to make some investments that require international cooperation. I need federal authorities to be in the wrong places at the right times."

The senator laughed. "Oh, I'm sorry," he said. "But there was something in the tone of your voice...oh, dear..."

Juan Carlos glowered at him. "I expect you to help me as you have in the past."

"Or else?"

"I do not make threats against friends," the dictator said.

"So, may I take it that I am never to have the incriminating documents back? That I will have to be your errand boy for the rest of my life?"

"You take the dark side of everything," Nochenegra said. "Look at it as an opportunity to maintain our long-standing relationship."

"Frankly," the senator said, "I figured as much. That's why I have taken precautions."

Luisa's sprayed-on smile faltered.

"What precautions could you have possibly taken against me? There is nothing you can do. I have you like a little bug between my fingers. All I have to do is pinch and you are nothing but juice.''

"I am going to have another drink," the senator said. "Would either of you like one?"

Juan Carlos and Luisa declined.

While the senator poured more whiskey into his glass, he said, "You have underestimated me, Juan Carlos. A fatal mistake."

"I think we should leave, Juan Carlos," Luisa said.

"No, my dear, I want to hear this. I find it amusing. Please continue."

The senator drove his wheelchair back in front of them. "The first thing I did when you told me that an attorney here in Los Angeles had control of the documents was to have a talk with him. Actually I had several."

"But you couldn't buy him, could you? And you couldn't scare him, either, because he is more frightened of me."

"You're right. He wouldn't cooperate. But his partner in the firm was more eager to please."

"Liar! He did not have access..."

"He wasn't supposed to have access, but he got it. I didn't ask him how."

Juan Carlos folded his arms across his chest. "I don't believe you. If you had already gotten the material you wouldn't have asked me for it. You played your hand clumsily there, my friend."

"I asked you to give it to me because I wanted you to have a final chance to redeem yourself on your own."

"Juan Carlos," Luisa said, "I don't feel well. I think we should go home."

"Shut up. There are threats being made here. Final chance? What final chance?"

The senator sipped his drink. "I've had it with you, Nochenegra," he said. "I'll take no more blackmail. I'll never help you again."

"You are bluffing. I could destroy you with a phone call."

"No, you couldn't. The papers are over on my desk. The ones you entrusted to the hands of that lawyer. Go on, take a look at them."

Nochenegra tried to push up from the couch. His face paled and he slumped back. For a second he doubled over, locked in cramps. When he straightened up, beads of perspiration ran down his forehead. "What have you done?"

"I have killed you both," the legislator said. "Your drinks were poisoned."

"But you drank, too," Luisa said.

"The poison was in the bottom of the glasses, not in the beverages, Luisa. An old trick, but still potent. I'm sorry that you had to die, too. Such a waste. But there really was no other way to make sure this matter was finally laid to rest."

"Oh, Juan, I am so afraid," Luisa said, curling up into a fetal position on the sofa.

The senator sat not three feet away from Juan Carlos and Luisa and watched them die. They lost consciousness almost at once, and then their breathing slowed, grew erratic and finally stopped.

He waited another five minutes before he moved his chair forward, before he reached out to take Luisa's wrist. It was limp. And there was no pulse. He let her hand drop.

He then reached out and removed the dictator's mirrored sunglasses. The eyes behind them were wide open, frozen in astonishment. The senator flicked his fingernail against one eye, then the other. No reflex.

He motored over to the desk and picked up the phone. The number of the committee cleanup crew was written on the pad next to his hand. They would swing by in a few minutes, take out the chauffeur waiting downstairs, then pack all the bodies in the limo. Drive it over a cliff.

Nice and tidy.

29

Major Zed and El Ticón had been on the run for three days and three nights. Ever since the cadre of generals had fallen, and the Soarez factions had learned the truth about who had tried to kill him, the co-commanders of the PFM and their core group of guerrilla fighters had been pursued by government troops and civilian police. Pursued and harried as never before.

It was as if the pack of dogs could read their minds.

And nobody cared about their fate. The whole island had turned against them. Even poor farmers refused them shelter and food. For their refusals, the peons were hanged from their own rafters with wire garrotes.

Such lessons usually brought immediate results. Changes in attitude. But no more. When the farmers saw them coming, they just ran away.

The PFM had lost its power base.

Major Zed and El Ticón knew what they had to do. They had to disappear for a while to let the heat die down. To regroup. Then, when the government thought it had shaken them off for good, they would return.

That was why they were climbing into the highest mountain passes, into terrain so rugged and so steep that no one would dare follow. They had retreated to this secret base camp before. They were certain it was secure.

The co-commanders called for a rest stop after their column had reached the top of a long, narrow spine of rock, a buttress that connected to the side of a much larger mountain. They dropped like dead men into the deep shade. Overhead, the trees were so dense, their branches so intricately interlaced, that they made it perpetual evening below. They also cut off any hint of breeze. In the sweltering gloaming, the PFM fighters lay on their backs and tried to regain their strength.

In three days, they had lost one third of their number. To heat prostration, to ambush, to accident. As Major Zed looked at his soldiers, he could not help but think of the fable of the rats in the cane field. These men were being forged on the anvil of battle. The ones who survived would be unstoppable.

El Ticón passed him a canteen of water. He accepted it and drank deeply. "Soon we will be there," he said.

"It will be good to really rest," El Ticón said. "I could sleep for a week."

Major Zed nodded and wiped his mouth on the back of his hand. In the distance he heard the whup-whup-whup of a helicopter. He stopped breathing until it faded away.

El Ticón was watching his face. "You are nervous. That isn't like you."

"Things have been going so wrong for us. I am starting to expect disaster."

"Don't do that. What you imagine comes true."

Major Zed grinned. "Sometimes it does, sometimes it doesn't. For example, I have often imagined being the leader of the national assembly or the head of the executive branch."

"President Zed?"

"It has a ring..."

El Ticón shook his head. "We are a long way from the palace, comrade."

"And we have farther to go. We had better move along." Major Zed walked among his men, shaking them awake.

They crossed over to the larger mountain, then circled around its back. The canopy of jungle was even denser there, the trees taller, more fully branched. They came to the place they had been before. There was no marker. Markers could be found by the enemy. The terrain itself was the signpost. A massive boulder outcrop, a dome of bedrock sheeted with moss. Behind it was the narrowest, faintest of paths.

Single file they trekked around the boulder, then slowly and with care they followed the trail. They tried to disturb as little of the ground as possible. Another reason for the slow going was that with the path so poorly defined it could easily be lost.

They climbed up for a goodly distance, then took a twisted route down into a hidden gorge. It was not big—a hundred yards across—but it was completely insulated from above by the trees and below by the mountain. It had several springs.

Major Zed took his men straight to the water. They knelt on the water-smoothed bedrock and drank from stair-step pools the size of dinner plates.

The water was as sweet and cool as Zed had remembered it.

He stretched and looked around. One thing had changed. There were no birds. No birdsong. The place had a stony stillness to it, like a graveyard.

Major Zed saw something move out of the corner of his eye. He turned his head. It was gone. It was not a bird. It was large and close to the ground. There was only one animal that hunted in the high jungle.

He unslung his Kalashnikov and prodded El Ticón with his boot. The PFM co-commander looked up from his drink. When he saw the expression on his comrade's face, he knew. He whispered to the men kneeling next to him.

Then gunfire shattered the stillness. Bullets ricocheted off the smooth rock. Two PFM fighters cried out and fell, their legs kicking.

Zed sprayed a full-auto burst at the vague shapes filtering through the obscuring bush, moving down the slope toward them. "Pull back!" he shouted at his men.

Under fire, they retreated to the side of an outcrop.

"How many did we lose?" Zed asked El Ticón.

El Ticón held up three fingers.

The major peered around the rock and saw government troops in camou fatigues and warpaint. He thrust out his AK and savaged them with a sustained burst. Men flew right and left. He couldn't tell how many he had hit and how many had just jumped for cover.

"We have to move," he said, waving his men on.

As they tried to slip away, the rocks around them rang with slug impacts. Four guerrillas were momentarily stapled to the stone by 5.56 mm tumblers. They died without so much as a moan.

"Damn!" Zed said. They were trapped, pinned down. And the enemy was closing in.

"We might be able to make it down the streambed," El Ticón said. "If we can just reach the cover of those tree trunks..."

There was no time for discussion and debate.

Zed nodded and they took off, a ragged line that grew more ragged by the second as it soaked up autofire from two sides. The guerrillas crashed into the soft earth, their bodies transfixed by bullet tracks.

Only five men reached the streambed alive. The first five. Zed stormed down the channel, ducking under the low branches, keeping his weapon ready.

They heard shouts from above. The government troops were in pursuit.

Major Zed waded around a partially submerged boulder. As he rounded it, he saw the soldiers waiting for them.

Six men, one woman.

One of the men had white hair.

BARRABAS CAME OUT from cover firing. The M-16 in his fist stitched a line of death across the guerrilla leader's chest. The man known as Major Zed, his lungs slashed to ribbons, fell to his knees in the pool and then slid onto his side.

As Barrabas ran past him, he put two rounds into the center of his face.

The PFM guerrillas froze at the sound of gunfire so close, at the sound of booted feet splashing through the stream toward them. They couldn't climb the steep banks to get away. There was no going back, no going forward.

Caught, they stood and returned fire.

Barrabas and his mercenaries took them to pieces. Hayes, Hatton, Beck, Nanos, Starfoot and O'Toole—all of them cut loose at once. The PFM contingent was blown off its feet, sent staggering like drunks into the streamside trees, to hang there shuddering as slug after slug burned through their flesh.

It was over long before the government troops arrived from upstream.

Barrabas and the others checked the bodies for signs of life, and finding none, waded out of the stream and started back for the chopper that had flown them in.

Their job on Mantuego was finally done.

30

Walker Jessup stood under the street lamp, waiting. Behind him the Pacific Ocean crashed against the pilings of an old amusement pier. The pier still stood, but the amusements it had to offer were slim now. It was possible to fish from it—if you liked catching zoological marvels, mutant perch, cancerous tom cod, the aftermath of fifty years of unregulated chemical dumping. It was possible to spit from it—that was a safe pastime, assuming that you didn't happen to hit any of the derelicts and junkies who used its shadowy underreaches for their toilet and sea-view bar. He could see the lights of Santa Monica curving up the coast. He checked his watch. Some things were worth waiting for.

This was one of them.

Ten minutes later a van pulled up on the far side of the parking lot. Its headlights flicked off, and a minute later the side door slid back. A man in a wheelchair rolled onto the lift apparatus, lowered the chair to the asphalt, rolled off, then raised the lift again and shut the door.

The wheelchair's motor whined as it powered the chair and its occupant across the lot.

"This had better be important," the senator said.

"It is," Jessup said. "Come on, let's head this way while we talk." The fat man started off down the pier, forcing the lawmaker to follow or get left behind.

"On the phone," the senator said, "you sounded like you have a big problem with what went down in Mantuego."

"Yeah, I do."

"Things don't always work out the way they're planned. I don't need to tell you that."

"These things did. They worked out just as planned."

They passed a row of boarded-up arcades and rides. The Fun House. The Palm Reader. The waves hissed against the pilings beneath them.

"You intended for those guns to go to the PFM. Nochenegra had been supplying them for months, to make sure they kept the pressure on Soarez. You put my butt in the blender by not telling me what the score was. I think you did it on purpose. I think you never meant for me to come back from Mantuego."

"That's preposterous," the senator said. "We've worked together so many times over the years."

"You've worked with Barrabas, too. And you tried to get him killed on the same mission."

"I don't know what you're talking about."

"Deny, deny, deny, right? Well, that might cut it with an investigating committee of your peers, but you and I, we aren't peers."

The fat man stepped around behind the rolling chair.

"Hey! What are you doing back there? Stop!"

"Just making some adjustments," Jessup told him. "Don't worry, I read up on this model. I know exactly what I'm doing."

The joystick speed and direction control went dead in the lawmaker's hand.

"You've damn well broken it!" he shouted.

"No, I haven't; it's still moving along real good."

The chair motor was redlined, its steering locked on a straight-line course.

"Damn you, Jessup!" the old man said, trying to grab the wheels and slow down the chair. All he got for his trouble was wheel burn on his palms. He could do nothing to alter his course. "If this is some kind of sick joke..."

"No joke, Senator," the Texan said. "This is what's called payback."

"Stop this chair!"

"Sorry, this is as far as I can go with you," Jessup told him. "Think about me the rest of the way. You know I'll be thinking about you."

"Jessup!"

The senator craned his neck to look behind. The fat man had turned his back on him and was walking toward the parking lot.

"Jessup!"

It was no goddamned use. The lawmaker settled down in the chair. When he crashed into the end of the pier, he'd just have to crawl out of the chair and fix it.

That was the plan, at least, until he saw the tall figure standing against the railing at the end of the pier. "Hey, you!" he shouted. "Get over here and give me a hand. This chair is running wild."

The man stepped out of the deep shadow and the senator saw his hair.

White, as snow.

Dead white.

"Barrabas, this is all a mistake...."

The mercenary leader turned and took hold of the pier's railing. With a heave he lifted a six-foot-long section of it free. It had already been sawed through.

Then the senator got the picture. "Oh, no, no!" he cried, clawing at the strap that held him fast to the heavy chair. He was headed straight for the gap in the railing.

At the last second, when he could see the dark water just over the open end of the pier, he stopped fighting the belt; he resigned himself to what was about to happen.

He looked over at Barrabas, who stood there stone-faced, watching him fall.

At the splash, the mercenary leader turned away from the end of the pier. He walked to the parking lot without a backward glance.

Jessup was waiting for him under the streetlight.

As he stepped up, the fat man said, "Well, what do you think?"

"Well," Barrabas said, "I'd say that makes us even."

Out of the ruins of civilization emerges...

DEATHLANDS

The Deathlands saga—edge-of-the-seat adventure not to be missed!

		Quantity
PILGRIMAGE TO HELL became a harrowing journey high in the mountains.	$3.95	☐
RED HOLOCAUST brought the survivors to the freakish wasteland in Alaska.	$2.95	☐
NEUTRON SOLSTICE followed the group through the reeking swampland that was once the Mississippi Basin.	$2.95	☐
CRATER LAKE introduces the survivors to a crazed world more terrifying than their own.	$2.95	☐
HOMEWARD BOUND brings the journey full circle when Ryan Cawdor meets the remnants of his own family—brutal murderers.	$3.50	☐
PONY SOLDIERS introduces the survivors to a specter from the past—General Custer.	$3.95	☐

Total Amount $ _____
Plus 75¢ Postage   .75
Payment enclosed   _____

Please send a check or money order payable to Gold Eagle Books.

In the U.S.A.	In Canada
Gold Eagle Books	Gold Eagle Books
901 Fuhrmann Blvd.	P.O. Box 609
Box 1325	Fort Erie, Ontario
Buffalo, NY 14269-1325	L2A 5X3

GOLD EAGLE®

DL-A

Please Print

Name: _____

Address: _____

City: _____

State/Prov: _____

Zip/Postal Code: _____

DON PENDLETON's

MACK BOLAN.®

More SuperBolan bestseller action! Longer than the monthly series, SuperBolans feature Mack in more intricate, action-packed plots— more of a good thing

The Mission:
Attack and kill every Russian in North Vietnam
and get out ... alive.

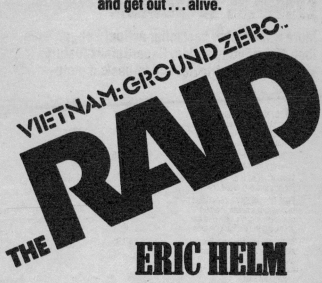

VIETNAM: GROUND ZERO..

THE RAID

ERIC HELM

When Washington is alerted to the existence of a Soviet-run training camp for the NVA, U.S. Special Forces Captain Mack Gerber is given a critical assignment—a task that may well commence the war's most dangerous mission of all.